PENGUIN

A Nurse's Story

Also by Donna Douglas

The Nightingale Girls

The Nightingale Sisters

The Nightingale Nurses

Nightingales On Call

A Nightingale Christmas Wish

Nightingales At War

Nightingales Under the Mistletoe

A Nightingale Christmas Carol

The Nightingale Christmas Show

A Nightingale Christmas Promise

Nightingale Wedding Bells

The Nightingale Daughters

Nurses on Call

A Nurse's Secret

DONNA DOUGLAS

PENGUIN BOOKS

PENGUIN BOOKS

UK | USA | Canada | Ireland | Australia
India | New Zealand | South Africa

Penguin Books is part of the Penguin Random House group of companies
whose addresses can be found at global.penguinrandomhouse.com

Penguin Random House UK
One Embassy Gardens, 8 Viaduct Gardens, London SW11 7BW

penguin.co.uk

Penguin
Random House
UK

First published 2025
001

Set in 10.4/15pt Palatino LT Pro
Typeset by Falcon Oast Graphic Art Ltd
Printed in Great Britain by Clays Ltd, Elcograf S.p.A.

The authorized representative in the EEA is Penguin Random House Ireland,
Morrison Chambers, 32 Nassau Street, Dublin D02 YH68

A CIP catalogue record for this book is available from the British Library

ISBN: 978–1–804–94374–8

To Ken
For all your love and support from
the first Nightingale Book to the last

PART ONE

October 1940

Chapter One

A bomber's moon, they called it.

It hung like a shining silver coin in the clear, cold October sky. Bright enough to guide the Luftwaffe all the way across the English Channel and up the snaking River Thames right to the doorsteps of the blacked-out East End of London.

And those German pilots had taken full advantage. For hours, wave after wave of Heinkel bombers had swept overhead, laying waste to the city. The drone of their engines mingled with the relentless retort of the anti-aircraft guns in Victoria Park as bombs and incendiaries rained down, leaving chaos and confusion in their wake. The fire brigade and rescue teams from the ARP struggled through the smoke-filled streets, fighting a losing battle against the voracious flames that consumed the rooftops of Bethnal Green.

And while hell was breaking loose outside, in a small, dimly lit basement at the Nightingale Hospital, a new life was coming into the world.

The young woman had been in labour for hours, engulfed in agony and exhaustion. She pleaded with the midwife to make it stop, but all she could do was mop her sweating brow with a damp cloth and whisper what words of comfort she could.

'It will all be over soon,' she promised. 'You're doing so well.'

No sooner had the words left her lips than another bomb came down, so close it made the bed rattle. The nurse flinched but the young woman was so consumed with the pain that she barely noticed. Neither did the older midwife at the end of the bed, who calmly carried on as if the building had not just rocked to its foundations like a tree in the wind.

'The baby's coming, but you're going to need to push harder,' she said briskly.

'I – I can't,' the young woman whimpered.

'Of course you can. And you must, if you want this child to be born.'

I don't. I don't want any of this. I just want it all to stop.

As if to punish her, another contraction hit her, the burning pain rolling slowly up, gathering strength until she felt as if it must be tearing her apart inside.

She cried out, but the older midwife snapped at her.

'Stop making such a fuss. You're not the first woman to give birth, you know. Now push!'

The younger nurse gave her hand an encouraging squeeze. She was about the same age as her, in her early twenties. Her face was kind beneath her starched cap, her eyes full of sympathy.

'Come on, love,' she urged softly. 'I know it's hard, but just a couple more pushes and it will all be over, I promise. Then you can have a nice rest.'

It already felt as if she had been pushing for an eternity, every contraction worse than the last. She had never imagined it would be like this. No one had prepared her for the pain. How could they? The nuns at the home might have delivered a lot of babies, but they had never been through it themselves. And her own mother, who might have been able to offer some words of advice, had abandoned her to her fate.

The only one who offered any comfort was the junior midwife. The young woman was so used to the contempt of the nuns at Our Lady of Eternal Piety, it came as a shock to be treated with kindness and sympathy.

'When you're ready, love.' The nurse squeezed her hand again. If she noticed the lack of a ring on her finger, her face gave nothing away.

She wasn't ready. She would never be ready for this. All she wanted was to be back at the home, reading her book or listening to the wireless with the other girls. She couldn't believe she'd been so desperate to escape the confines of the convent that she'd sneaked out into the night, with bombs raining down from dusk till dawn.

She'd thought she would be safe. It was too soon, the baby wasn't due for another month at least. But she had been too reckless.

She took a gulp of air, gritted her teeth and started to push.

'The head's coming,' the midwife said.

'Keep going, sweetheart,' the young nurse urged. 'You're doing really well.'

The girl tightened her fingers around the nurse's, her nails digging painfully into her skin, but the nurse held on steadfastly.

In a blur of pain, she thought she imagined one of the nuns standing in the shadows. Sister Benedicta, that sour-faced old crow in her long black habit, her rosary rattling at her belt.

But then she realised it was just an old piece of tarpaulin covering a filing cabinet that had been piled up against the whitewashed brick wall.

There were no windows in the room, nothing but the harsh glare of a bulb overhead that swung every time a bomb landed nearby. The room was stiflingly hot and rivulets of perspiration ran down her face, stinging her eyes.

As if her very surroundings could feel her pain, a cry of anguish suddenly ripped through the air. The young woman snapped her eyes open, her own agony instantly forgotten.

'What was that?'

'I'm not sure,' the nurse glanced towards the door. 'It sounds as if it's coming from next door—'

'Never mind that!' the older midwife snapped. 'Concentrate, Nurse, please!'

Another cry pierced the air.

'Should I go and see what's happening?' The young nurse started towards the door but the older woman stopped her.

'You're not going anywhere until this baby has been born.' She looked tense, her lips white in her taut face. 'Which it won't be unless you lend a hand!'

'Sorry.' The young nurse went to the other end of the bed, just as another contraction took hold. This was different from all the others, a feeling so immense and all-consuming that somehow instead of being lost in a haze of pain and confusion, the woman suddenly knew exactly what to do. Gripping the metal bedrail, she bore down and pushed with all her might.

The baby's first feeble cry filled the room just as the air raid siren wailed overhead, signalling the all-clear.

'Thank heavens that's over,' the midwife said, although the woman wasn't sure if she meant the birth or the air raid. She quickly clamped and cut the umbilical cord, then scooped up the newborn baby, wrapped it in a towel and placed it in the nurse's arms. 'Weigh and wash this little one, please, Nurse, while I deal with the placenta.'

The young woman lay back against the pillow, tears filling her eyes.

It was all over at last.

Chapter Two

The unearthly cries from next door started up again when the young nurse had gone.

'Who is it?' the young woman asked.

'Just another patient,' the midwife replied. 'Take no notice.'

She delivered the placenta and finished cleaning her up, then promptly left the room.

Shortly afterwards, a chirpy cockney VAD arrived. She kept up a stream of chatter as she made the bed and helped the young woman into a fresh nightgown.

'Boy or girl?' she asked.

'I don't know.'

'Oh! Didn't they tell you?'

The young woman shook her head, feeling suddenly foolish. She'd been so overwhelmed it hadn't occurred to her to ask.

'Still, as long as it's healthy, eh?' The VAD lowered her voice. 'Not like that poor woman next door.'

'What happened to her?'

'Stillbirth.' The VAD mouthed the word. 'Poor love's in a terrible state.'

Just then the door opened and the red-haired nurse appeared, holding a bundle in her arms.

A pink bundle.

'There's your answer,' the VAD turned to her, smiling. But the young woman had already averted her gaze to the tarpaulin-covered filing cabinet in the corner of the room.

'Why have you brought it back?' she whispered, her throat dry. 'I thought you were taking it to the nursery?'

'We haven't got a nursery since we closed down the maternity wing,' the young nurse said. 'Besides, this little one needs feeding.'

The nurse approached the bed, holding out the bundle towards her. The young woman shrank away in panic.

'No! I can't. Take it away, please!'

Over the nurse's shoulder, she could see the VAD gaping, open-mouthed.

The young midwife hesitated a moment, looking from the baby to her and back again, weighing up the situation.

'You'd best go,' she said to the VAD.

'But Miss Cox said I had to stay with her—'

'Yes, well I'm here now. And I'm sure you're needed upstairs in the Casualty Hall.'

The VAD shuffled off, looking mutinous. The nurse came to sit on the end of the bed.

'Right,' she said, her tone gentle. 'What's all this about?'

The young woman fixed her gaze on the bundle in the nurse's arms. Every fibre in her being ached to hold the baby, but she knew she mustn't.

'I can't keep it,' she blurted out. 'I've got no choice, really I haven't. I've got no money, nowhere to live. My family have disowned me.'

'So where are you staying?'

'The Convent of Our Lady of Eternal Piety.' Just saying the name made her shudder. 'Do you know it?'

'That old place on the other side of the park? Yes, I know it.' The young nurse looked grim.

The old gothic convent building was as stark and severe as the nuns who inhabited it. Its stone walls seemed to hold in the cold at this time of year, and the nuns refused to light a fire for the girls because 'sinners did not deserve comfort'.

They kept warm instead by carrying out a constant round of household chores, from preparing and serving meals to scrubbing floors and doing endless amounts of laundry. It was hard, back-breaking toil, especially for the girls who were heavily pregnant. But no one ever dared to complain.

Her mother and father could not even bring themselves to take her there. It was her sister who had gone with her, not meeting her eye as she dumped her suitcase on the steps.

'You've brought this on yourself,' were her parting words as she hurried back to the waiting taxi. As if just being there would somehow taint her.

'Oh, love, I'm so sorry.' The young midwife sighed, genuinely sympathetic. 'What about the father?'

'He's dead.'

Months later, it still hurt her to say the words. It didn't seem real. Her Jack, her brave pilot fiancé, shot down over the English Channel as his squadron flew to the rescue of the troops stranded on the beach at Dunkirk.

She stared at the pink bundle, stirring in the midwife's arms. If he'd lived, he would have rescued her too. With a wedding ring on her finger, she wouldn't have had to endure the scorn and the shame, the sideways looks at her swollen belly, the whispers that seemed to follow her wherever she went.

But here she was, alone with the tiny, living person that she and Jack had created.

Her baby.

'I can't keep her,' she said again, and this time her voice was heavy with regret.

'Well, that's your decision.' The midwife stood up and moved towards the door.

'Where are you going?' the young woman called after her.

'To make up a bottle for this little one. I'm sure we'll all hear about it otherwise.'

'Can I – can I hold it?'

The midwife hesitated. 'I'm not sure that's a good idea—'

'Please?' The young woman held out her arms. 'Just for a minute?'

Once again, the midwife hesitated. Then she returned to the side of the bed and gently placed the bundle in the young woman's arms.

'Be sure to support the head,' she said. 'I'll be back as quick as I can.'

She was so slight, the young woman hardly knew she was holding her. Tentatively she moved the pink blanket aside to gaze down on a perfect little face. The wrinkles already filling out, her skin turning pink. A pair of dark, unfocused eyes stared back at her.

Her baby.

'Hello,' she whispered. 'I'm your mummy.'

The eyes flickered and the little mouth pursed, as if she was trying to form words. A little starfish hand poked out of the blanket and she touched it, then laughed as the tiny fingers curled tightly around her own.

It was just a reflex, she told herself. But for a moment it really felt as if the baby knew what was to come and was holding on, afraid to let go.

This was wrong, she told herself. She shouldn't be doing this. If she was at the convent, the nuns would have whisked the baby away by now, never to be seen again. She had grown used to the sound of sobbing from behind closed doors, as mothers wept for their newborn babies.

But grateful as she was that she had been given the chance to spend a few precious moments with her baby, she also knew that she was setting herself up for even more heartache in the end.

'I'm sorry, I'm so sorry.'

A tear plopped from her cheek, soaking into the blanket, followed by another and another. And so she went on, weeping silently until they were both sound asleep.

Chapter Three

She woke up suddenly to a wailing sound, loud and unearthly, like a wounded animal.

Befuddled by sleep, she looked down, shocked to find the baby still in her arms. The infant slept peacefully.

Another heartbreaking cry filled the air. The young woman tensed, waiting for it to pass. But it went on and on in the darkness, the sobbing of a soul in torment.

The rough cement floor felt cool under her bare feet as she got out of bed and tiptoed across the room. She placed the baby carefully in the crib, then hurried out of the room.

The basement consisted of a low, brick-lined passageway with storerooms leading off on either side. From behind her came the muffled roar of a furnace, like a slumbering dragon. The flickering flames cast a dim, dancing light that faded into dense blackness at the far end of the passage.

The rough brickwork felt damp beneath her hands as she felt her way along towards the terrible keening sound.

One of the doors was ajar. She pushed it open and was confronted by a shocking sight. A white wraith, thin and wretched, her long hair plastered over her face, was kneeling on the brick floor. She was bent double, her arms wrapped around her body as she rocked back and forth.

The young woman wanted to run but she stood her

ground and watched as the ghostly figure uncurled itself slowly. As the head went back, the long hair parted to reveal the tear-ravaged face of a young woman. She was on her hands and knees beside a crib.

An empty crib.

Her agony seemed to fill the room, enveloping the young woman where she stood. She put her hands over her mouth to stop herself crying as she recalled what the VAD had told her.

'I'm sorry. I'm so, so sorry,' she said.

She knelt beside the woman, putting her arms around her thin, trembling shoulders. The woman barely seemed aware of her as she wailed out her agony and anger.

'It was supposed to be me,' she sobbed. 'I'm the one with the weak heart. I was the one who was supposed to die, not her.'

'Don't say that.'

She turned to look at her, her thin face ravaged with tears. 'Why?' she cried out. 'Why couldn't He let me keep her? I would have given her everything, loved her with all my heart—'

The young woman flinched from the raw grief in her face. It was as if the woman was being consumed by it, like fire.

'You'll have another baby, I'm sure.' It was a stupid thing to say, but she was desperate to say anything to stop the woman's pain.

'You don't understand. She was my last chance. My only chance. The doctors told me I wouldn't even be able to conceive, let alone—' She broke off. 'She was my little miracle.' She clung to the bars of the empty crib, her voice a hoarse whisper. 'I prayed to God I'd survive long enough to hold her. But then He took her instead . . .'

She pressed her face against the bars of the crib and cried, huge, gasping sobs that racked her slender body.

The young woman watched her, alarmed by the raw, animal emotion.

A mother's love.

She'd always thought of it as something gentle and tender, but this was powerful and shocking, a force that could move mountains.

Suddenly an impulse seized her, stronger than she had ever known.

'Take mine,' she said.

The woman lifted her face and stared at her. Looking at her more closely, she could tell she was a few years older than her – late twenties, or even thirty.

'I – I don't understand,' she faltered.

'I can't keep my baby. I want to, but I can't.' Her gaze dropped to her bare left hand.

'You want to give her away?'

It sounded so wrong, the way she said it.

Because it is *wrong*, a small voice whispered inside her head.

'You don't know me,' the woman said.

She was right, it was a stupid impulse. She didn't even know why she'd said it. Desperation, perhaps.

Or perhaps when she looked into the woman's eyes, she saw the love she could never offer her child.

'I know you'll look after her. You'll give her everything I can't.'

'I couldn't.' The woman shook her head. But even as she said the words, there was a spark of hope in her eyes. 'It wouldn't be right.'

'Please. I know I can't keep her and I'd feel happier if I knew she was going to someone who really wanted her, who'd love her.' She grasped the woman's hands impulsively. 'Just promise me you'd look after her?'

'I – I will.' The woman looked dazed. 'Of course I will, I promise. But what if you change your mind—'

'I won't,' the young woman cut her off. 'I can't.' She thought about the forlorn little bundle, wrapped up in her pink blanket. She did not deserve to be brought up in shame. 'She deserves better than me,' she said quietly.

I just hope one day she can forgive me, she thought.

As she went to leave, the woman called after her, 'Wait! I – I don't even know your name.'

She hesitated for a moment. 'It's Sadie,' she said. 'Sadie Evans.'

'I'm Margaret.'

They stared at each other, both of them knowing they would never meet again.

'Take care of my baby, Margaret,' she said. 'That's all I ask.'

Chapter Four

Back in the Casualty Hall, things were getting busier. There had been a direct hit on the Fox and Terrier pub, and the wooden benches in the waiting room were lined with dazed-looking people, their faces bruised and blackened, nursing injured limbs. Women from the Voluntary Aid Detachment passed among them, handing out blankets and hot water bottles and cups of tea.

Outside, the nurse could hear the distant clang of an ambulance pulling up at the doors of the Casualty Hall. The first of many this evening, no doubt. She could imagine the streets were already teeming with firemen and rescue workers from the ARP, stumbling through the smoke-filled darkness, putting out fires and rescuing people from the rubble.

All those poor people, wandering among the smoking ruins of what had once been their homes, desperately trying to salvage what they could.

As she emerged from the kitchen, she met Miss Cox, the midwife. She looked drawn, exhausted and much older than her forty years.

The nurse wasn't surprised. It had been a harrowing evening for all of them.

Seeing her, she suddenly remembered.

'Oh, my God!' she cried, clamping her hand over her mouth. 'Sadie Evans!'

Miss Cox looked up at her. 'What about her?'

'I forgot about her. I've left her with her baby.'

'What of it?'

Miss Cox listened carefully as the nurse explained what the young woman had told her.

'I see,' the senior midwife said, when she'd finished. 'And yet she asked you to leave the baby with her?'

'Yes, she did. I wasn't sure if I should, but she insisted. I only meant to leave her a few minutes, but then all those casualties arrived, and—' She glanced towards the door that led to the basement. 'I'd best go and make sure she's all right.'

'Finish what you're doing, Nurse. I'm sure she'll still be there when you're ready.'

Just then the insistent wail of the air raid siren filled the air.

'Here we go again,' Miss Cox sighed. 'Let's hope the roof doesn't fall on our heads.'

Little did she know how true her words would be.

Chapter Five

At first Margaret thought she must have been dreaming.

She opened her eyes and listened. Then, from somewhere in the darkness on the other side of the room, she heard the faint but unmistakable sounds of a baby's snuffled breathing.

So it wasn't a dream after all.

She couldn't keep the child. No matter how much she might want to, it was wrong. She would never be allowed to walk out with another woman's baby. Someone would stop her before she'd even reached the doors.

Either that, or the stranger would change her mind. She would track her down, take her baby away. Margaret could end up in prison for what she'd done.

And yet . . . She listened to the snuffling in the darkness. A stranger's baby. Could she really love it as her own?

And what about her husband? He'd never wanted her to go through with the pregnancy in the first place. How would he feel when she came home with another man's child?

You don't have to tell him.

Margaret held her breath, shocked at herself. Would she really lie to her husband? And how would she live with herself if she did?

This is your chance, an insistent voice whispered. *Your only chance to be a mother.*

She shook her head, as if she could dislodge the thought that was beginning to take root in her mind. That young woman – what was her name? Sadie. She wasn't in her right mind. She surely hadn't meant to give away her own baby. Margaret should take the child back to her now, tell her straight that it was wrong, that she should give the child up for adoption, do things the proper way . . .

Or you could pick up the baby and just walk out.

Once again, Margaret pushed the thought away. She sat up and pressed her hands together in prayer, as she always did when she was troubled.

'Please, Lord,' she whispered. 'Guide me in your wisdom. Show me what I should do . . .'

A splintering crash shook the walls. She sat bolt upright, listening to the sound of shouting and running footsteps coming from above her head.

She took in a quick, panicky breath and immediately began coughing as choking, bitter fumes hit her lungs. A moment later she realised the room was filled with thick, acrid smoke.

She swiftly got out of bed and blundered her way across the room to the cot. But before she reached it the door flew open and the dark shape of a fireman appeared, silhouetted against bright flame.

'What's going on?' she cried out.

'The basement's on fire. We need to get you out.'

'Wait a minute, my baby—'

She turned and grabbed the pink-blanketed bundle from the crib.

'Come on, love, we ain't got a second to lose.'

The man guided her out of the room and along the smoke-filled corridor. Flames crackled around them, and the heat was like a physical force, pushing them back with every step.

'What about Sadie Evans?' she asked, but the man didn't seem to hear her. He stumbled up the stairs, pushed open a door and shoved her through. Suddenly the air was clearer, filled with light and voices.

'Oh, thank God! There you are.'

The midwife appeared before her. Although she looked very different now, her smart uniform black with greasy smoke. Wisps of dark hair escaped from beneath her battered cap.

She grasped her, holding her at arm's length. 'Are you all right?' she asked.

'Yes. Yes, I think so.'

The baby stirred in her arms, starting to cry. The midwife stared at the child, then back at her.

'Where did you—'

'She gave her to me.' Margaret was instantly defensive. 'She wanted me to look after her.'

For a moment they stared at each other.

'The child belongs with its mother,' the midwife said quietly.

'But she can't keep her. She wanted me to look after her.'

Even as she said the words, she could feel her heart sinking, and all her hopes and dreams collapsing with it. The midwife was right. It was a foolish idea. She had to give her back.

'Where is Sadie?' Margaret asked, looking around. 'Has she been rescued?'

'Didn't the fireman bring her up with you?'

She shook her head. 'Oh God, you don't think she's still—'

Suddenly there was a fearful cracking and wheezing sound, as if the whole building around them was rousing itself into life. They all swung round in time to see flames licking from the doorway they had just emerged from, as the fire consumed the basement.

PART TWO

December 1958

Chapter Six

'Well done, Nurse Metcalfe. A very well-deserved award, I think.'

It was not Matron's rare smile or warm words that Amy registered as she handed her the medal. It was what she had called her.

Nurse Metcalfe.

She paused, enjoying the moment. She had only been a student for twelve weeks, which she knew was nothing compared to the years of experience in the row of stiff-looking sisters and tutors who lined the small stage behind Matron. But she was on her way. She had got through the three months of tough Preliminary Training, even though there had been so many times when she had feared she wouldn't make it.

She glanced at her friend Sonia, seated with the other girls in her set, clutching her own certificate of completion. She winked back at her. They had spent so many sleepless nights revising together, testing each other, swotting over their books and wondering how they would ever manage to cram everything into their heads.

Now Amy had not only passed, she had won the Florence Parker medal for the top student in her set. She had thought there must be a mistake when Matron first announced her name. Even seeing her name engraved on the gleaming gold disc in her hand, she could still scarcely believe it.

She looked to the audience and saw her mother and Auntie Eileen in the front row. Maggie Metcalfe was beaming with pride, while Auntie Eileen was dabbing away a tear with her grubby handkerchief.

There was no sign of her father, of course. Amy wasn't surprised, or even disappointed. If anything, she was glad he wasn't there. He would only be glaring at her over those half-moon spectacles of his, making her feel as if no matter what she did, she was still a disappointment to him.

The ceremony came to an end, and all the other girls in the set dispersed to meet their parents. Amy looked around for Sonia, but she had already slipped away with a couple of the other Jamaican girls. Amy felt a pang of sorrow for her friend, whose parents couldn't be there to see her collect her certificate.

'Well done, love. I'm so proud of you.' Her mother hugged her, and Amy tried not to notice how frail she seemed when her arms went around her. She had lost even more weight since she'd last seen her, and her best coat hung off her thin frame.

'Me too,' Auntie Eileen chimed in. Her robust figure and ruddy, smiling face were a stark contrast to Maggie Metcalfe's delicate pallor.

'Your father wanted to be here too, but some important parish business came up at the last minute.' Her mother could not meet her gaze as the lie spilled awkwardly from her lips.

'I don't mind, Mum. You're here and that's all that matters.'

She meant it, too. Her father had always been cold and distant towards her. Malcolm Metcalfe was more interested in his books and his theological studies than he was in his wife and daughter. Thankfully, her mother's love and devotion more than made up for her father's indifference.

'Are you joking? She wouldn't have missed it for the world. Would you, Mags?' Auntie Eileen grinned, nudging her friend. 'Just think! Our Amy, a proper nurse.' She smiled at her proudly. Even though she called herself Auntie, she was no relation, but she had been in Amy's life for as long as she could remember.

'Hardly,' Amy said. 'I've got another three years to get through first.'

'You'll do it, no trouble.'

'I hope so.' Amy looked down at her uniform, suddenly self-conscious in her blue pinstriped dress and starched cap, her sensible black shoes polished till they gleamed. When she'd first put it on she had felt like a child playing at dressing up. But as the weeks went by it had become part of her.

'And to think you were born in this very hospital,' Auntie Eileen went on. 'Right in the middle of the Blitz, wasn't it?'

'Don't remind me.' Her mother grimaced.

'Went into labour during an air raid, she did. Talk about bad timing! And there we were, stuck in an Anderson shelter. I thought I was going to have to deliver you myself!' Auntie Eileen grinned at Amy. 'But we braved the bombs to get you here instead. And didn't that miserable old midwife give us what for over it, eh? Reckoned we should have stayed at home and waited for her to come out. I told her, if you think you can deliver a baby in a bloody Anderson shelter, you're welcome to try!'

'I'm sure Amy doesn't want to hear that old story,' her mother said quietly.

'And what about Father?' Amy asked. 'Where was he while all this was going on?'

Her mother and Auntie Eileen sent each other a look Amy couldn't fathom.

'In that church of his, protecting his precious silver, I daresay,' Auntie Eileen said.

'It's all ancient history now, anyway,' her mother dismissed. 'This is Amy's day. Oh look, here comes Matron.'

'Stand by your beds!' Auntie Eileen chuckled, as Miss Groves approached them.

'Ah, Mrs Metcalfe. How nice to see you,' she greeted Amy's mother, who almost bobbed a curtsey in return. Miss Groves was an upright, angular woman with a formidable presence. Even Auntie Eileen was suddenly subdued.

'You must be very proud of your daughter?' Miss Groves said.

'I am, Matron.' Maggie beamed at her.

'She's done extremely well. We have very high hopes for her.'

Amy felt herself blushing to the roots of her red hair, but it was wonderful to see the pride glowing on her mother's face. It made all her hard work seem worthwhile. She had done all this for her, for her dear mother, to make her proud and repay her for all the love and devotion she had given her.

Matron moved on to speak to the next set of parents, and Auntie Eileen turned to her excitedly.

'Did you hear that?' she said. 'She's got high hopes for you. I reckon you'll be taking her job soon!'

'Steady on!' Amy laughed, shooting an embarrassed glance at Miss Groves' turned back. She only hoped the matron hadn't heard Auntie Eileen's excited comment. 'As I said, I've got to get through the next three years first. Anyway, she probably says that to everyone's parents.'

'I'm sure she wouldn't say it if she didn't mean it,' her mother said. She reached for Amy's hands. 'I'm so excited for you, love.'

She was smiling broadly, but Amy could see the hint of sadness in her mother's eyes. She held on to her hands, feeling the thin bones under her papery skin. She was in her mid-forties but looked at least ten years older, thanks to the illness that had plagued her for most of her life. Her face was tired and lined, and her hair, which she kept long and pinned up, had been grey for as long as Amy could remember.

'I don't have to stay in the nurses' home, you know,' she said. 'Some of the girls live out after the first year. I could come home—'

But her mother was already shaking her head.

'I won't hear of it,' she said.

'I should think not,' Auntie Eileen joined in. 'You don't want to miss out on all the fun, do you?'

'I don't mind. And someone needs to look after Mum—'

'Don't you worry about me,' her mother said. 'I'll be all right. I've got Eileen. And your father,' she added as an afterthought.

No one spoke. They all knew exactly what Malcolm Metcalfe was like.

'All the same—'Amy began, but her mother cut her off.

'Now you listen to me, Amy Metcalfe.' She wagged her finger at her. 'I don't want you worrying about me, all right? You're a young girl, you should be enjoying your life, not nursing your old mother. This is your future, and you need to embrace it.'

Amy was silent. She knew her mother was right, but she couldn't help feeling guilty. She wished she didn't have to leave her in that cold, loveless vicarage with only her father for company.

They stayed chatting a bit longer, until the other parents started to leave. Even then, Amy was reluctant to let her mother go until Sonia appeared and told her that the Home Sister wanted them to move their belongings into the main nurses' home.

'What are you waiting for?' her mother said with a smile. 'Go and be with your friends.'

Amy hugged her, breathing in her mother's soapy scent. 'I'll come home and visit soon,' she promised.

'My turn.' As Auntie Eileen pulled Amy into her bosom for a tight embrace, she said quietly, 'Listen to your mum, girl. She means what she says. She wants you to have a life of your own.'

'You will keep an eye on her, won't you?' Amy whispered back.

'Don't you worry about that.' When Auntie Eileen pulled away, there were tears glistening in the corners of her eyes. 'I've always looked after my little Maggie, and I always will.'

Chapter Seven

They talked about Amy all the way home.

It was a bright but bitterly cold day, and the trees of Victoria Park were starkly bare against the ice-blue sky. The biting wind stung Maggie's cheeks but she scarcely seemed to notice. She couldn't stop reliving the moment she had seen her daughter step on to that stage, so confident in her smart uniform, her head held high as she accepted her medal from the matron.

'She looked like a proper young woman, didn't she?' she said to Eileen. 'Seeing her up there made me realise she's not my little girl any more.'

'She'll always be your little girl,' Eileen reassured her, tucking her arm through Maggie's. 'You don't have to worry about that, love. But fancy her getting the prize for being top student!'

'I know! She doesn't get her brains from me, that's for sure.'

It was a rare unguarded comment and she glanced at her friend, anticipating her response.

'Now you listen to me, Maggie Metcalfe!' Eileen spun round to face her, her expression mock severe. 'I've told you before, stop putting yourself down. Just because you didn't finish your schooling, it don't mean you ain't clever.

You could have been anything you wanted to be, if you'd had the chance.'

'Stop it, you're making me blush!' Maggie looked away, embarrassed at the praise. Trust Eileen to stick up for her. She had been doing it since they were kids, growing up in the same tenement building in Bethnal Green. Maggie had been such a frail little thing since contracting scarlet fever, but big, tough Eileen Kelly had taken her under her wing. No one at school, or the garment factory where they worked after leaving, ever said a word against her when Eileen was around. They were as close as sisters, and she trusted Eileen more than anyone else in the world.

'Anyway,' Maggie went on, 'it's our Amy's turn to shine now, and I want her to make the most of it. I just hope she lets go of these silly ideas about coming home to look after me.'

'She cares about you, love. It's only natural.'

'Yes, but there's no need. I'm fine.'

'So you say.'

'I am,' Maggie insisted. 'It's been years since I had that last bout of rheumatic fever.'

'Yes, but you came down with pneumonia before Christmas,' Eileen reminded her. 'And anyway, I ain't talking about your health.'

They walked in silence for a moment, their arms still linked but a distance between them. Maggie prayed that her friend would not say any more. It had been such a wonderful day, and she didn't want anything to spoil it.

But she should have known better. Eileen was like a dog with a bone. Once she got her teeth into something, there was no letting go.

'Amy ain't the only one who's worried about you,' she said.

Maggie sighed. 'Not now, Eileen.'

'You've been saying that for twenty-five years.' Her friend sent her a sidelong glance. 'When are you going to leave him, Mags?'

'You know I can't.'

'Why not? I understand you've stayed together all this time for Amy's sake, but she's grown up now, she's got a life of her own. Anyway, she'd probably be as relieved as I would be if you—'

'Stop it, Eileen. It ain't that simple, and you know it.'

Without thinking, she slipped into her old cockney accent. She tried to be well spoken around her husband, but old habits died hard.

'I know you deserve better than the life he's led you all these years.'

'He ain't that bad.'

'Are you having a laugh?' Eileen twisted round to stare at her. 'I've seen it, don't forget. I know the way he treats you.'

'He's a good man, in his own way,' Maggie insisted staunchly. 'I've got a lot to be grateful for.'

'Is that what he's told you? I can just hear those words coming out of his sanctimonious gob.'

'Eileen!' Maggie looked around, even though the street was almost empty. Except for a policeman who stood on the corner, stamping his feet and blowing on his gloved hands to keep out the cold. 'You shouldn't talk like that. What if someone heard you?'

'I don't care if they do.'

'No, but I do.' Maggie glared at her friend. 'Malcolm is the local vicar, don't forget. He's got a position to uphold.'

'So he's always telling us.' Eileen lowered her voice. 'I wonder what his parishioners would say if they knew what he was really like?'

'Eileen, please. Don't spoil a lovely day.'

They walked the rest of the way in tense silence. Maggie knew she shouldn't have confided in her friend as much as she had. But she needed to talk to someone. And Eileen had always been good at keeping her secrets.

Agitation tightened her chest, and by the time they reached the top of Franklin Street she had to pause for a moment to catch her breath.

'Are you all right, love?' Eileen instantly forgot her bad mood as she peered at her in concern, one hand on her shoulder.

'I'm fine. Just a bit out of breath, that's all.'

'Have you seen the doctor recently?'

'I don't need to see the doctor. I'm fine.'

'Are you sure about that?' Eileen sent her a shrewd look. 'We've had to stop three times for you to get your breath back.'

'It's a steep hill!'

'Steep, my backside.'

'I'd like to see you run up it.'

They looked at each other and then they both laughed. They could never stay angry with each other for long.

They continued on their way, and said goodbye at the end of Church Road as usual.

'Take care of yourself, won't you?' Eileen enveloped Maggie in a fierce hug, drawing her into her warm bulk.

'And you. I'll see you soon.'

'Will you?' Eileen released her and held her at arm's length. 'When?'

'Soon.' Maggie's gaze slipped away. 'When I can get away.'

'You make sure you do or I'll be banging on that vicarage door!' Maggie's look of dismay must have betrayed her because Eileen laughed and said, 'I'm joking, Maggie. I know your old man don't like me.'

'It ain't that—'Maggie started to protest, but she saw her friend's shrewd look and gave up. Eileen knew as well as she did that Malcolm took a dim view of her friends and family. Especially Eileen, who he considered to be common and a troublemaker.

Thank God he never heard what she said about him, Maggie thought.

She went to leave, but Eileen held on to her. 'Now, are you sure you'll be all right?' she said, her face gentle with concern.

'I'll be fine. Now you get off, or your old man will think you've run off with the milkman!'

'He lives in hope, you mean!'

Maggie watched her friend as she trundled off back down the street. They might have grown up together, but their lives had taken such a different turn. Eileen was married to Derek, a burly docker. They lived in a cramped terraced house with their six kids. Their home overflowed with chaos, and laughter and love.

And then there was Maggie, rattling around in that big, empty vicarage.

St Luke's Church stood at the top of the hill, looking down on the surrounding shabby terraces. Maggie used to go there every week, first to Sunday School and then morning service with her mother.

On the way home, she would pause and gaze through the wrought-iron railings at the big gabled house on the other side of the churchyard. It looked like a palace after the poky tenement building where she, her two brothers and her mother lived.

She would never in a million years have imagined herself living there.

She still didn't feel as if she belonged there, even as she let herself in. Her footsteps creaked on the polished wooden floorboards and the familiar smell of damp and old books settled itself around her like a shroud as she paused to take off her shoes and change into the slippers she kept hidden away under the stairs.

She moved around the house cautiously, feeling like an intruder. She had lived in the house for nearly twenty-five years, but it had never felt like her home. It was full of dark old furniture and worn carpets.

The previous incumbents, Reverend Willis and his wife, had left the furnishings behind when they retired, and Malcolm saw no point in replacing them, even though Maggie hated them. She also detested the antique ornaments that crowded every surface, and the gloomy oil painted landscapes in their ornate gold frames. Malcolm thought they were wonderful, but all they did was collect dust.

When they'd first moved in, Maggie had been full of ideas for turning the old house into a nice, modern home. But Malcolm had rejected all her suggestions for changing the carpets and curtains or even replacing the old Victorian range in the kitchen with a new cooker.

When Maggie had tried to introduce a couple of cheery cushions and a few prints, they had been met with sullen disdain.

'Really, my dear, don't you think they're rather vulgar?' Malcolm had said.

Maggie had quickly taken them down, withering with shame at her own ignorance. It was all her fault for being common and not having refined tastes.

And as for having a television – Maggie did not dare even suggest it. Besides, Malcolm much preferred listening to the Home Service on the ancient wireless, just as he had all through the war.

But it wasn't just the fixtures and fittings. Maggie had tried her best to make it a home, but darkness and silence still lurked in the dusty corners of the old house. It might have been a vicarage, but it was not a place of warmth and love.

Or forgiveness.

'Malcolm? Are you home?' she called out tentatively. Silence closed in on her, punctuated by the ponderous tick of the long case clock in the hall. Maggie allowed herself to breathe out, relief flooding over her.

She went into the kitchen and put the kettle to boil on the range. The silence of the house seemed even more oppressive now that Amy was gone.

Maggie shook the thought away. She couldn't allow her daughter to know how much she missed her; it wouldn't be fair. She had her own life now.

She smiled at the thought. Amy was the light of her life, a blessing she kept close to her heart every day. Sometimes, when times were hard, it was only her love for her daughter that kept her going day after day.

She would do anything, endure anything, for Amy.

She opened the cupboard and took out the delicate bone china cup and saucer, teapot, milk jug and sugar bowl, then arranged them carefully on a tray. It seemed rather a lot of fuss for one cup of tea, but Malcolm liked things done properly.

As she waited for the kettle to boil, Maggie stood at the kitchen window, staring out over the garden. The fruit trees were bare in the hard, frosted ground, but in the spring they would be a riot of pink and white again. She remembered how Amy always loved to gather armfuls of the frothy blossom, throwing it up in the air then laughing as it drifted down around her like confetti, settling on her shoulders and the top of her head.

You should count yourself lucky, Margaret Bradshaw.

That's what her mother had told her when Malcolm Metcalfe had proposed. Joyce Bradshaw had always been an avid churchgoer, and she made sure her three children did the same. Every Sunday for as long as Maggie could remember, they had joined the congregation at St Luke's, always in the back pews because Joyce never considered herself good enough to sit at the front of the church with the grocers and the bank managers and their well turned-out wives.

So when the young curate had started courting Maggie and asked for her hand in marriage, it had been like a dream come true for her mother.

Maggie was not so sure. If she was honest, she'd had her doubts about Malcolm right from the start. She was only eighteen and he was ten years older. He was very cultured and well educated, and even though Maggie was quite bright, she struggled to understand when he talked about philosophy and art and theology. She often sensed his frustration and wondered what on earth he saw in her. As far as she was concerned, it was only a matter of time before their courtship fizzled out.

But then, to her utter astonishment, Malcolm proposed.

Her first instinct was to say no. Never in her wildest dreams could she picture herself being a vicar's wife. As far as Maggie was concerned, it seemed inevitable that she would find herself a dock worker like her friend Eileen. They had already planned the double wedding they would have.

But when she told her mother, Joyce Bradshaw was adamant.

'Of course you must marry him,' she'd declared. 'Why on earth would you say no? This is a wonderful chance for you to go up in the world, my girl. You should consider yourself lucky he even looked at you. Imagine, you a vicar's wife!'

Maggie couldn't imagine such a thing, not in a million years. That was the trouble. But she loved her mother and she didn't want to disappoint her. And perhaps it wouldn't be as bad as she thought, she'd reasoned. Malcolm Metcalfe was a man of God, he would love and take care of her.

How wrong she was about that.

The sudden knock on the front door broke the silence, making her jump. As Maggie swung round, her hand caught the bone china cup, sending it spinning off the tray and on to the floor, where it shattered into pieces on the quarry tiled floor.

She was still staring dumbly at the scattered fragments when there was a brisk tap on the back door. A moment later it swung open and a cheery voice called out,

'It's only me, Maggie. I called at the front door but you weren't—' The woman paused, taking in the scene. 'Oh dear! What's happened here?'

Maggie stared down at the shattered cup, dread settling like a cold stone in the pit of her stomach.

'It was part of a set,' was all she could say. Her voice sounded faint, even to her own ears.

'What a shame. Still, never mind. It was only a cup.' The woman peered closely at her. 'Are you all right, love? You look a bit faint.'

Maggie came back to the present. Nurse Riley was looking at her strangely, her head tilted to one side.

She had known Dora Riley for years, ever since they'd worked at Gold's Garments together, before Dora had started nursing. They were roughly the same age, and they'd grown up a few streets away from each other, near Victoria Park. Although Dora looked very different now, in her district nurse's uniform, her smart navy-blue raincoat tightly belted, her hat perched at a jaunty angle on her ginger curls.

Dora was like Eileen – tough and no-nonsense on the outside, but with a heart of pure gold. And, just like Eileen, she had a way of looking into your eyes and knowing exactly what was going on, even without being told.

Maggie glanced away quickly. 'I – I'll fetch a dustpan and brush,' she mumbled.

She could feel Dora Riley watching her as she hurriedly swept up the pieces and then wrapped them in newspaper. She went outside to put them in the dustbin, but at the last minute she changed her mind and hid them under a Japonica shrub close to the back door. She could bury them at the bottom of the bin later, and with any luck Malcolm wouldn't notice for a while.

She had pulled herself together by the time she returned to the kitchen, rubbing her cold hands together.

'I wasn't expecting you today?' she said.

'You're not on my list, but I thought I might as well drop in and make sure you're all right.' Dora had placed her large leather bag on a chair and was already taking off her raincoat.

'There's no need.' Maggie glanced nervously at the door. Malcolm could be home at any moment, and he wouldn't be too pleased at an unexpected visitor. Even his parishioners were discouraged from dropping in without an appointment.

'The doctor's asked me to keep an eye on you. That last bout of pneumonia left you very weak.'

Don't I know it, Maggie thought. She had been in bed for weeks, burning with fever and too feeble to crawl to the toilet.

'Yes, but I'm all right now. I ain't an invalid, and I wish everyone would stop treating me like one.'

'Let's just make sure, shall we?' Dora's smile was warm but determined. Maggie knew she would not leave the house until she had examined her at least.

With a sigh, she sat down at the kitchen table and began to unbutton her blouse.

'I called earlier, but your husband said you weren't in,' Dora Riley said as she rifled in her leather bag.

Maggie's hands stilled. 'You spoke to Malcolm?'

'He said you were at the hospital to see your daughter? Has she passed PTS?'

The mention of Amy made Maggie forget her apprehension. 'She got a medal,' she said. 'Top of her class.'

'What an achievement. You must be very proud of her?'

'I am,' Maggie said quietly.

'I bet your husband was disappointed he couldn't be there with you.'

Maggie's glow of pride disappeared. 'He's very busy,' she said automatically. 'With parish work.'

'I'm sure he is.' Dora's face was expressionless as she listened to Maggie's chest and took her pulse. 'So I suppose she'll be moving in to the main nurses' home now?'

Maggie nodded. 'She's looking forward to it.'

'My Winnie was the same. I'll have to ask her to keep an eye on your girl. It can be a bit daunting when you first start on the wards.'

'How's Winnie getting on?' Maggie asked.

'Oh, she's in her element,' Dora Riley beamed. 'She's on the children's ward now, and she loves it. She thinks the world of the ward sister. Such a nice woman, from what I hear.'

'Do you miss working at the hospital?'

Dora laughed. 'Oh no, I much prefer to be out and about on the district.' She paused, thinking about it. 'But I suppose I do miss some of the laughs we used to have on the wards.'

'I bet you got up to all sorts!'

'Well, we were kept under strict control in those days. But I do remember my friend Millie used to—'

Just then, Maggie heard the sound of a key in the front door. Dora was still chattering on, telling some story about her friend and a set of false teeth, but Maggie couldn't listen to her. She was rigid, her ears straining, trying to pick up clues.

And then a thought struck her. Oh God, had she remembered to put her shoes away? What if Malcolm fell over them? It had happened before and there had been hell to pay—

The kitchen door opened and there he was, a smile pinned to his face. He must have heard Dora's voice, Maggie thought.

'Oh, hello,' he greeted the district nurse. 'I didn't realise my wife had company?'

'I didn't know she was coming,' Maggie put in quickly.

'I told you earlier I'd drop in, see how she was getting on,' Dora said.

'And I told you Margaret was quite well and there was no need to come back.'

He sounded amiable enough. But Maggie, who was used to reading her husband's moods, could see the irritation beneath his practised smile.

Dora, thankfully, seemed oblivious to it.

'Well, I'm here now,' she said. 'Your wife was telling me about your daughter. You must be so proud of her.'

Malcolm Metcalfe's expression stiffened. 'She's done very well,' he said shortly. Then he looked at Maggie and said, 'I'm going to my study. I'll see you later.'

The door closed behind him.

'He's such a busy man,' Dora commented.

'Yes.' Maggie stared at the door. The ominous tone of his voice still haunted her. *I'll see you later.* 'Yes, he is.'

Chapter Eight

He didn't even ask about his wife.

The thought stayed with Dora as she made her way home after her shift was finished. She couldn't forget the look on Maggie Metcalfe's face when her husband walked in. The poor woman looked utterly terrified.

What was going on there? she wondered. Malcolm Metcalfe had been polite enough when she'd called earlier, but what kind of man stopped his sick wife from seeing the nurse? There was something about him that didn't ring true. Wives did not act as jumpy as Maggie for no reason.

And Dora had seen enough to know that the worst bullies were often the ones no one suspected. Her own stepfather had been one of them. To everyone else Alf Doyle had been a larger-than-life character, full of fun, the life and soul of the party. But behind closed doors, he had been a monster to Dora and her sister.

Was Malcolm Metcalfe the same? Surely not, she thought. He was a vicar, after all. A man of God. But still, she could not forget the picture of Maggie's terrified face as she stared down at that broken cup. The fear and dread in her eyes had been chilling to see.

Poor little Maggie. She had always been such a sweet girl. She'd stood out among the other workers at Gold's

Garments. She came from a religious family, so she wasn't used to all the cursing and swearing that went on in the sewing room. And her childhood illness had left her frail and delicate, so she looked as if she'd barely be able to lift a bobbin, let alone manage one of the heavy overlocking machines. But she'd worked as hard as any of the other girls, and her brilliant smile and cheeky sense of humour brightened everyone's day.

Until she'd met Malcolm Metcalfe.

Dora had already moved on to start her nursing training at the Nightingale Hospital when she heard from her mother that, at the age of eighteen, Maggie had got engaged to the curate at St Luke's.

'If you ask me, she did it to please her mother,' Rose Doyle had said. 'You know how religious Joyce Bradshaw is. She's always up at that church. I expect she's over the moon that her daughter's marrying a clergyman.'

Dora was sure Maggie probably had done it for her family, but not in the way her own mother seemed to think. Maggie's father had been killed in the Great War, and Mrs Bradshaw had struggled ever since to provide for her three children. Malcolm Metcalfe was much older than Maggie. The idea of marrying a decent man with a steady, settled income who could help with her mother's bills might have been very appealing to her.

Listen to yourself, Dora Riley! As if you know what goes on in anyone's mind. You want to start minding your own business instead of sticking your nose in where it ain't wanted!

She stopped herself, feeling ashamed. Being a district nurse meant she was invited into people's homes, into their lives. She had witnessed some very strange situations over the years, and she always did her best not to judge anyone if she could help it. As long as no one was getting hurt, it was none of her business.

But what if Maggie Metcalfe *was* getting hurt? That was the thought that had troubled her all the way home.

A welcoming fug of steam and delicious cooking aromas greeted Dora as she let herself in through the back door into the kitchen. The warmth enveloped her like a blanket after the brittle chill of the evening outside.

Her mother stood at the stove, stirring a pan on the hob.

'You didn't have to cook,' Dora said. 'I would have done it.'

'I thought I'd make a start, save you a job.'

'Yes, but—'

'Now, don't you start!' Rose Doyle turned around, pointing a metal fish slice at her. 'I've told you before, I don't want to be treated like an invalid.'

'You're the second person who's said that to me today.' Dora sank down at the kitchen table and pulled off her shoes.

'Then you should start taking notice.' Her mother turned back to the sausages she was frying. 'Anyway, you know I like to do something to earn my keep.'

Rose had defied all the doctors' expectations and made an impressive recovery from her stroke a couple of years earlier, but Dora still insisted on her living with them so she could keep an eye on her.

'You already do enough,' she said. 'Keeping this place tidy, and looking after Julie Rose.'

'When I'm allowed,' her mother muttered.

'What do you mean? Where is she?' Dora looked around.

'With her father.' Rose jerked her head towards the door that led to the hall.

'Nick's home?'

'He said he'd finished the job early, but if you ask me he just wanted to spend time with the baby. Here,' Rose picked up a cup of tea from the draining board and handed it to Dora. 'Take this to him, will you? He said he'd come and fetch it, so tell him not to blame me if it's stewed.'

As Dora crept up the hall, she heard a gruff, tuneless crooning coming from the living room. Peeping through the crack in the door, she saw her husband on the couch, cradling little Julie Rose in his powerful arms. His dark curly head was bent towards her as he sang to her softly.

Dora hesitated, not wanting to disturb the moment. She had never heard her husband singing a lullaby to his children before, certainly not to the twins or to Danny, their twelve-year-old. And yet here he was, gazing down at their baby girl as if she was the most precious thing he had ever seen in his life.

And to think she'd been too terrified to tell him when she first found out she was pregnant. She was desperately worried that Nick would think they were both too old to be parents again, but he had surprised her, just as he had throughout their marriage. At just over a year old, Julie Rose had her father twisted around her tiny finger.

Growing up on Griffin Street, Nick Riley had been the local tearaway, a snarling street dog of a kid who could send a man through a wall with his fists. There still weren't many who would mess with him now. But here, at home, he was the gentlest, kindest man Dora had ever known.

She suddenly thought about Malcolm Metcalfe again, and how she suspected he was the opposite of her husband.

'That tea will be cold if you stand there much longer.'

She looked up sharply, shaken out of her reverie by the sound of Nick's gruff voice.

'Oh, it's you,' she said, coming into the room and setting the cup down next to him. 'I thought it was Perry Como in here.'

Nick scowled at her, then turned back to Julie Rose.

'Mummy can talk, eh?' he said. 'She's no Connie Francis herself.'

He leaned forward, rubbing noses with his daughter, who squealed in delight. Seeing them together, Dora suddenly wondered if the Reverend Metcalfe had ever cooed over little Amy in the same way. She couldn't imagine it. Just as she couldn't imagine Nick ever missing the chance to celebrate his daughter's success.

Chapter Nine

'You'll love Miss Spencer. She's a real gem.'

Amy listened to Winnie Riley chattering away beside her, but she could hardly take in what she was saying. Her eyes ached with tiredness. She had been awake since before dawn, swotting by lamplight, polishing her shoes until they shone and practising over and over again with her cap so she could fold it without making the starched fabric grubby and soft. Even then, when she'd dressed this morning her hands were shaking so much she could scarcely fix the pins in place.

She found it hard to sleep at the nurses' home. She had shared a room with Sonia during their Preliminary Training, and she was still getting used to having a room to herself, and all the comings and goings. The student nurses had a strict ten o'clock curfew unless they had a late pass, but that didn't seem to stop anyone. Amy's room was at the end of the corridor close to the fire escape, and all night she'd heard muffled giggles and the sound of footsteps tiptoeing past her door.

She wished she had been assigned to a ward with one of her friends. Sonia had been put on Male Medical with Bridget Flanagan, and as they trudged to the hospital in the chilly December darkness, Amy could hear them excitedly discussing what might lie ahead of them.

At least she had Winnie with her. She could scarcely believe it when the tall, dark-haired second year had knocked on her door the previous night. There was a very strict hierarchy in place among nursing students, and seniors were not known to acknowledge the presence of probationers, let alone actually speak to them.

But Winnie didn't seem to let that bother her as she'd greeted Amy the previous night with a big smile on her face.

'Are you Amy? I'm Winnie Riley,' she'd said. 'My mum knows your mum, so she asked me to look after you. Not that you need looking after, I'm sure, but it can be a bit nerve-racking, your first time on the ward.'

Amy had met District Nurse Riley once or twice when she had come to tend to her mother. She was a very cheerful, down-to-earth woman, and Amy knew her mother looked forward to her visits. But physically, she could not see the similarity between mother and daughter. Dora Riley was a sturdily built woman with unruly red hair, green eyes and a broad, freckled face. Winnie was tall and dark haired, with bright blue eyes.

Perhaps she took after her father, Amy thought. She was glad she didn't have her own father's narrow face or pinched mouth.

The frosty path underneath their feet glittered in the lamplight. Amy pulled her navy-blue cloak tightly around her, grateful for the thick red lining that kept out the cold.

'They don't usually put pros on the children's ward,' Winnie chattered on beside her. 'They must think a lot of you.'

Amy was instantly nervous. 'I hope I'll do all right,' she said.

'You'll be fine, I'm sure. Matron would never have sent you there if she didn't think you'd cope. And like I said, Miss Spencer is a real sweetheart. Not like some ward sisters I could mention!' Winnie pulled a face. 'She loves the children and puts them before everything. As long as you do the same, you'll be all right.'

'Why don't they usually assign pros to the children's ward?' Amy asked. 'Is it very difficult?'

Winnie grinned. 'Have you ever tried taking a baby's blood pressure?' Amy shook her head. The only person's blood pressure she had ever taken was Bridget's, during class practice. And she'd been all fingers and thumbs doing that.

'It ain't easy, I can tell you! But it's not just that. We get all kinds of cases on the ward, including lots we might not have covered in training. And most of the children come and go so quickly, too. Sometimes we might get ten new admissions a day, which means the consultants and doctors are forever coming in and out, too. We get all sorts on the ward, from ENT to Cardiac. It can be a bit chaotic sometimes.'

Amy listened in wide-eyed silence as Winnie explained about the different sections of the ward, and who was nursed where. From what she had already gleaned from listening to the older students, most of the adult wards worked to a strict timetable, with the daily consultants' rounds carefully scheduled.

By contrast, the children's ward sounded like a madhouse. Amy really wasn't sure she would cope, whatever Matron seemed to think.

She was still wondering if it was too late to go to Miss

Groves to request a transfer when Winnie led the way up the stone steps to the main hospital building.

'The children's ward is on the top floor, at the back of the building,' she explained. 'And there's no point waiting for the lift,' she added over her shoulder as Amy approached it, her hand raised to press the button. 'It always takes ages, and sometimes it gets stuck. Honestly, you're better off using the stairs.'

Amy's carefully pinned cap was already sitting sideways on her head by the time she had huffed and puffed her way up the four flights of stairs to the top floor. By contrast, Winnie barely seemed out of breath.

'Don't worry, you'll get used to it,' she laughed. 'Come on, it's this way.'

She led the way down a long corridor painted in glossy beige. Even as they approached, Amy could hear children's excited voices and shrieks of laughter coming from the end of the passage. Winnie pushed open the double doors to reveal a scene of organised mayhem.

A couple of the night nurses were wearily clearing away the breakfast dishes, piling them on to a metal trolley and trying to keep order. But no one was paying any attention. Down the length of the ward, the children were sitting or kneeling up in their beds, craning their necks to look at the far end of the ward, where a ward sister in a dark blue uniform was sorting through an enormous cardboard box, pulling out strings of brightly coloured paper chains like a magician performing a trick. She was watched by a frowning staff nurse and a couple of giggling students.

By the doors, a couple of young porters in brown over-
alls loitered with step ladders, watching the scene.

'What's going on?' Winnie asked one of them.

'Her Ladyship's decided that now would be a good time
to put up the Christmas decorations,' one of the porters, a
skinny young man with greased-back hair and buck teeth,
replied. He sent Amy a sideways glance. 'Hello, I ain't seen
you before. New, are you?'

'Yes, she is, and you can keep your hands off her,' Winnie
replied. She grabbed Amy by the arm, steering her forward.
'Come on.'

As they approached the ward sister's desk, Amy heard
the staff nurse saying nervously,

'Are you sure it's a good idea to do this now, Miss
Spencer?'

'I promised the children we'd decorate the ward today,
Nurse Clackett,' the ward sister's voice was muffled, her
head buried in the box as she rummaged inside.

'Yes, but perhaps we could leave it until later? You know
Matron always does her rounds early on a Monday—'

'Good. She can lend a hand, can't she?' Miss Spencer
emerged from the box, holding a paper lantern in
each hand. She was in her forties, an energetic woman
with an open, smiling face and warm hazel eyes. 'Look at
them,' she said, nodding to the line of eager faces. 'They're
so excited, bless them. The Night Sister said they've been
awake since before dawn. They're already missing so much
of the fun of Christmas, why not make today special for
them?'

'Yes, I suppose so. But—'

'I'm glad you agree, Nurse Clackett. Now, why don't you busy yourself blowing up some balloons?'

As the staff nurse went off, the sister turned her attention to Winnie and Amy. 'Oh, hello. You must be the new student – Metcalfe, isn't it?'

'Yes, Sister.' Amy's tongue was so dry it stuck to the roof of her mouth and she could barely get the words out. She had not expected the ward sister to even acknowledge her existence, let alone remember her name.

'Welcome to Harris Ward. I'm afraid you've found us in rather a state of chaos, but I'm sure it will all be worth it when it's finished and the ward is decorated.'

'Can I help, Sister?' Amy asked.

'That's the spirit.' Miss Spencer smiled warmly. 'Here, why don't you find somewhere to put these?' She handed her the paper lanterns. 'And when you've finished, you can help put up the rest of these paper chains.' She looked around the ward absently. 'It's a shame we don't have a tree, isn't it? The children would have loved that, but unfortunately our funds wouldn't quite stretch to it.' She gave a bracing smile. 'Never mind, I'm sure we can cheer the place up with what we've got. But Nurse Clackett is right, we'd better get a move on before Matron appears.' She clapped her hands. 'Come on, everybody! All hands on deck!'

'I told you, didn't I?' Winnie nudged Amy as they hurried away. 'She's a real gem, ain't she?'

Chapter Ten

The children's ward was formed in an L shape, with the long side containing about a dozen beds arranged down either side of the room. Around the corner was a short corridor with two doors leading off it. Winnie had already explained that this was where the youngest babies were nursed. The door opposite led to a three-bed intensive care unit.

Amy peered in through the small pane of glass in the door, but she could see nothing inside the dimly lit room. Winnie had also explained that the children in the intensive care room had their own nurses, who were seldom seen on the main ward.

It seemed a shame that the very poorly children had to be so isolated and missed out on all the festive fun. And the nurses, too. Their work was so stressful, they would probably welcome a bit of Christmas cheer.

She looked down at the paper lantern in her hand, then up at the ceiling. If she strung it up from the light fitting, the children might be able to see it from inside the room.

She looked around for something to stand on. The porter with the greased quiff had a step ladder, but he was already halfway up it, stringing a paper garland across the middle of the ward. She glanced towards the intensive care ward.

Perhaps if she was very quiet she could just slip inside and take a chair without anyone noticing her?

But no sooner had her hand touched the doorknob than a voice rang out behind her.

'Where do you think you're going?'

Amy looked over her shoulder. A scowling dark-haired young man in a brown porter's overall stood behind her, hands planted on his hips. His black brows were knotted over angry grey eyes.

'I was just going to—'

'I hope you weren't planning to put that up in there?' He nodded curtly at the paper lantern in her hand.

Amy looked down at it, realisation dawning. 'Oh no, I was only going to borrow a chair—'

'There are some very poorly children in there,' he interrupted her again. 'Or didn't you learn anything about infection during your training?'

Amy prickled at his rudeness. 'As a matter of fact, I did,' she said. 'I probably know a lot more about it than you do.'

'And yet you still think it's all right to barge into an intensive care ward, looking for a chair!' the young man scoffed.

Amy glared at him. The worst of it was, she knew he was right. She should never have even thought about entering a ward like that without the sister's permission, and certainly not carrying a tatty paper lantern that had been in a dusty old box for months.

She felt tears pricking the backs of her eyes, and blinked them back furiously. Honestly, what kind of a nurse was she going to be if she couldn't remember a basic rule? She had been on the ward less than half an hour, and she'd already made a stupid mistake.

And to be told off by a porter, too. It was so humiliating. 'What's going on?'

As if things couldn't get any worse, here was Miss Spencer to witness her utter mortification.

'She was going into the intensive care ward to hang up Christmas decorations,' the porter answered for her before Amy had a chance to speak.

'I wasn't,' Amy said. 'I was going to hang it up outside. I thought it might be nice for the children. I was only going in there to fetch a chair,' she appealed to the ward sister. 'I'm sorry, Sister, I didn't think—'

'It's all right, Metcalfe,' Miss Spencer said. 'Actually, I think you're right. It would be lovely for the children to have something to look at.' She turned to the porter. 'Tom, why don't you go and fetch the step ladder? Then you can help her hang it up.'

'Yes, Sister.' The porter glared at Amy, then trudged off towards the main ward.

Miss Spencer smiled at Amy. 'It was very thoughtful of you, Metcalfe. That's what I like to see from my nurses on this ward.'

'Thank you, Sister.'

'Although I'd prefer it if you didn't disturb the patients in this room. Tom's right, some of them are very poorly and the nurses have their hands full looking after them.'

'Yes, Sister. I'm sorry.'

'There's no need to look so crestfallen, my dear. You're new, it's bound to take a while to get used to the way things are done around here.' Miss Spencer leaned in confidingly. 'We all make mistakes. Even me, as I'm sure Nurse Clackett will no doubt tell you!'

'I see you've upset Tom,' the young porter with the buck teeth commented when Amy returned to the ward a few minutes later.

'I'm sure I don't know what you're talking about,' she shrugged.

'I saw you having words earlier. Go on, what did you say to him?'

'I didn't say anything.'

She hadn't had the chance. Once he'd fetched the step ladder, Tom had practically snatched the paper lantern out of her hand.

'I don't need your help to hang it up,' he'd snarled.

'Suit yourself,' Amy had muttered, but he'd already stomped off.

'That doesn't surprise me,' the porter said. 'He's a moody swine at the best of times.'

'I can tell.'

Amy went to move past him, but the porter stepped sideways, blocking her path.

'Not like me,' he grinned, showing off his prominent teeth. 'I'm a real charmer.' He held out his hand. 'My name's Blakey, by the way. What's yours?'

'None of your business.'

Amy glanced around the ward, on the lookout for Miss Spencer. But she was busy unravelling a string of fairy lights and did not seem to be paying attention.

'Playing hard to get, eh?' Blakey tapped his nose. 'I know what you students are like. You think I ain't good enough for you because I'm only a porter. But that's where you're wrong, see. Because I'm destined for better things.'

'Oh yes?' Amy smiled, amused in spite of herself.

Blakey nodded. 'I'm a singer,' he said. 'I've got a manager and everything. He reckons I'm going to be the next Tommy Steele.'

'Is that right?'

'You wait and see. My manager says he's going to get me signed up with Decca Records. He reckons I've got what it takes to make it big.'

'Good for you.'

'You should come and watch me sing one night.'

The other porter, Tom, appeared from around the corner, the step ladder under his arm. His eyes met Amy's and he looked away, scowling.

'So what do you say?'

She turned back to Blakey. 'About what?'

'Will you come and watch me sing? Me and my skiffle group have got a regular booking on a Tuesday night in Soho—'

'I can't,' Amy lied. 'I go home to visit my mum on a Tuesday.'

'Some other time, then? We could go to the pictures—'

Amy shook her head. 'I'm sorry, I don't want to go out with you.'

'Oh, I see. Like that, is it?' Blakey looked crestfallen for a moment, then his confidence reasserted itself. 'No need to be sorry, sweetheart, it's your loss. You'll be kicking yourself when I'm a big star.'

'I s'pose I'll just have to take that chance, won't I?' Amy smiled.

'That new student's a stuck-up cow, ain't she?'

Tom looked down from the ladder he was perched on to see Blakey looking back up at him. He was holding the other end of the paper chain Tom was trying to pin on to the wall.

He made a non-committal grunt and went back to his work.

'D'you know, I just asked her to go to the pictures with me and she turned me down flat?'

He looked so comically affronted, Tom had to turn his head so his friend could not see him smile. Gordon Blake was a trier, he had to give him that. There wasn't a single student at the Nightingale Hospital he hadn't tried it on with. They probably had a poster with his unfortunate face on it hung up in the nurses' home, warning the girls to beware.

'Maybe she's already got a boyfriend?' he said.

Blakey considered it for a moment. 'Yeah,' he agreed. 'That's probably it. Anyway, I told her, she'll be sorry she passed up the chance while she had it. I bet she'll be interested when I'm rich and famous. But I'll have my pick of the girls then. I won't need to waste my time chasing stuck-up nurses!' His skinny chest puffed beneath his brown overall.

Tom shook his head, thinking about the porter's terrible singing. He and a few of the other porters had once traipsed all the way up to Soho to see him, and it had been a complete waste of a bus fare. He was shocking.

'Has your uncle got you that record deal yet?' he asked.

'My manager,' Blakey corrected him. 'He says he's working on it. It could be any day now.'

Tom finished pinning the paper chain in place and carefully stepped down the ladder. Blakey probably had as much chance of making it into the top ten as Tom did of starring in *Emergency Ward 10*, but he would never tell him so. They all had to have their dreams.

He certainly had his, although it had nothing to do with making a record or seeing his name up in lights.

But the difference between him and Blakey was that his dreams were definitely going to come true. All he had to do was wait a few more weeks, and he would have everything he ever wanted.

'She's pretty though, ain't she?' Blakey said.

'Who?'

'The stuck-up student, of course. Who did you think I meant, Nurse Clackett?'

Tom glanced over at Amy. 'Can't say I noticed,' he said.

Chapter Eleven

By the time the clock struck nine, the ward decorations were almost finished. Colourful paper chains were festooned the length of the walls and looped across the ceilings, gold and silver lanterns hung from the light fittings, and the children were sitting up in bed, happily drawing pictures of Santa and his elves which Liz Spencer had promised to put up on the walls to add to the decorations.

The smiling young nurses seemed to be having as much fun as the children. Even Staff Nurse Clackett had stopped looking anxiously at the clock. The last time Liz had passed her, she was sure she had heard her humming 'Jingle Bells' under her breath as she checked the ventilators.

Dear old Clackett, she thought fondly. The senior staff nurse drove her mad sometimes with her constant fussing, but after five years, they had got used to each other's funny little ways. More importantly, Liz trusted her. She knew Enid Clackett was a very good nurse, and even though they did have different ways of going about things, they both had the children's best interests at heart.

She left the others to finish putting up the decorations while she went to check on Billy Jeffries. He was nine years old and had been admitted two weeks earlier with appendicitis. He'd made a good recovery and was due to be discharged soon, but the previous night he'd been up complaining about stomach pains.

There didn't seem to be anything wrong with him this morning from what she could tell. He'd eaten all his breakfast without any complaint, and now he was sitting up and seemed very happy and lively as she approached his bed.

'Good morning, Billy. How are you feeling?' Liz asked him.

He looked up from the picture of a Christmas tree he had been studiously colouring in. He was a skinny little thing in his oversized blue striped pyjamas, his brown hair ruffled.

'All right, miss,' he replied in his cheery cockney accent.

'I'm pleased to hear it. I was told you weren't feeling very well in the night?'

His smile faltered. 'No,' he mumbled, his gaze dropping from hers. 'I had pains.'

'Can you show me where?'

'Sort of here. And here.' He vaguely rubbed his hand across his abdomen.

'I see. Well, I'd better check you over, hadn't I?'

As she reached for the thermometer, Billy said,

'Is it Christmas yet, miss?'

'Not for another three weeks, I'm afraid.' She smiled. 'Don't worry, you'll be home in plenty of time for Father Christmas to come down your chimney.'

With the thermometer clamped between his lips, he couldn't reply. Liz picked up his wrist and began counting his pulse, but she could see the thoughtful expression on his face.

As soon as she'd removed the thermometer from his mouth, he said,

'Couldn't I stay here?'

'Why on earth would you want to do that?'

'I dunno—'He looked around him. 'It's all done up so nicely. I thought it would be fun.'

'I'm sure you'd have a better time at home with your mum and dad, wouldn't you?'

'My dad's in prison,' Billy said matter-of-factly.

'Ah.' She paused, taken aback. But she did her best not to let it show. 'So there's just you and your mum?'

'And Uncle Wally.' His voice dropped. 'But he ain't really my uncle. My mum just makes me call him that.'

'I see.' Liz tried to remember. Billy's mother came in to see him every couple of days. But she couldn't recall ever meeting Uncle Wally.

Before she could say any more, a voice behind her said,

'Am I hearing this right? Who'd want to be in hospital over Christmas? Even I don't, and I work here.'

Liz turned to see the new paediatric consultant, Mr Bryant, standing behind her. Immediately her years of training kicked in and she jumped to her feet.

She still thought of him as new, even though he had been at the Nightingale for more than six months. He was in his forties, tall and wiry, with brown hair that receded slightly at the temples and an expressive face that never seemed to be far from breaking into a smile. Even when he was being serious, his brown eyes twinkled with amusement.

He had come from Australia, and his accent was still a novelty to the children as well as the nurses.

'I've come to check on this young man.' He turned to Billy Jeffries. 'I hear you've been having a bit of trouble, mate? A few aches and pains?' Billy nodded. 'Mind if I take a look?'

Liz watched him as he examined the boy. She wondered how Mr Bryant had heard that Billy Jeffries was unwell. She certainly hadn't had time to telephone him. She could only imagine that he must have asked the Night Sister for a report.

It was rare for consultants to do such a thing, and yet Liz wasn't at all surprised. Rob Bryant was very conscientious, and took a genuine interest in all his young patients.

He certainly wasn't like any other consultant Liz had worked with. The others would whisk in with their retinue of medical students and junior housemen, throw their weight about for a few minutes and then swiftly move on. And when they did grace the ward with their presence, they expected Liz and the other nurses to fawn over them as if they'd just descended from the heavens.

But Mr Bryant was far more down to earth. He expected no fanfares when he turned up. He didn't even look like a consultant, with his scuffed suede shoes and his white coat thrown over his shabby suit. He also made a point of listening to Liz, rather than treating her as little more than a glorified handmaiden.

Perhaps they did things differently in Australia, she thought. If so, it made a pleasant change.

'Your wound seems to have healed up nicely. No sign of infection that I can see.' Mr Bryant finished examining the boy's scar. 'What about his TPRs, Sister?'

'They're all perfectly normal, Doctor.'

'And he's been eating and drinking well?'

'Very well. And bowel and urine are normal too,' she added before the consultant asked the question.

'Well, this is a puzzle, young man.' Rob Bryant scratched his head. 'I'm afraid you might have proved too much of a puzzle for even my extensive medical knowledge.'

'Does that mean I can stay a bit longer?' Billy asked eagerly.

Liz and the consultant looked at each other.

'What do you reckon, Sister?' he asked.

Liz glanced at the boy's eager, freckled face. 'I suppose it's better to be safe than sorry,' she said.

'Will I still be here at Christmas?'

'I'm not sure about that. Hopefully we can get you better before then.'

They left one of the student nurses settling Billy back into bed and walked back to Liz's office.

'Did you notice how disappointed he looked at the idea of going home?' Rob Bryant commented.

'I think he's enjoying the company,' Liz said. 'Apparently he doesn't have any brothers or sisters, and he likes chatting with the other children. He got very excited when we put up the decorations this morning.'

'Oh, yes. The decorations.' Rob Bryant looked around him, his mouth twisting wryly. 'Very festive, I'm sure. But you seem to be missing something. Your tree?' he said, when Liz looked puzzled.

'Alas, we can't afford one.'

His brows rose. 'You have to buy your own?'

'The National Health Service was not created for the purpose of buying Christmas trees,' Liz recited the words

Matron had said to her when she'd posed the question. She just managed to stop herself imitating Miss Groves' clipped tones, but she could see from Rob Bryant's smile that he got the gist.

'Is that why you have a collection box by the door?'

Liz shook her head. 'That's for presents for the children. We're always looking for donations, if you can spare a shilling or two?'

'I'll see what I can do,' he smiled. 'Now, do you have any other patients I need to see before I go? The Night Sister mentioned a cleft palate—'

So he had been speaking to Miss Warren, Liz thought. She could just imagine the Night Sister's delight. Rob Bryant's arrival had set quite a few hearts fluttering among the nurses, including Kath Warren's.

She could see the attraction. Mr Bryant was warm and friendly, flirtatious without being forward. It was easy to be beguiled by the twinkle in his eyes, and even his scruffy appearance was endearing. It had certainly brought out the maternal side in her ward maid, Molly, who brought him homemade cake and offered to darn his socks.

'You can tell he don't have a wife to look after him properly,' Molly had said to Liz only the previous day.

'I really wouldn't know,' Liz had replied.

'Trust me, Sister. He ain't married.' Molly had given her a knowing look, as if it was supposed to mean something to her.

Liz was in the middle of explaining about the new case that had arrived the previous night when suddenly Staff Nurse Clackett started up with an alarming fit of coughing at the other end of the ward. Liz turned around to check she was all right, then realised what had set her off as she saw the hospital's Matron, Miss Groves, framed in the double doors.

Miss Groves radiated spiky disapproval, with her angular figure, pinched mouth and dark, beady little eyes that darted here and there, looking for trouble in every corner.

Liz's heart sank. It was all she could do to stand her ground as the matron swept down the ward towards her.

'Good morning, Miss Groves,' Rob Bryant greeted her with a smile.

'Good morning, Mr Bryant.' Miss Groves kept her narrowed gaze on Liz. 'I must say, Sister, I was surprised not to be greeted at the door?'

So that was why the old bat looked so riled, Liz thought. Like consultants, hospital matrons expected to be treated like visiting deities. It was customary for the ward sister and all the staff nurses to stop what they were doing to attend on Matron when she appeared to do her rounds.

The previous matron, Helen McKay, had never stood on such ceremony. Or at least she made sure she always did her rounds at the same time every day so they knew when to expect her. But Miss Groves clearly enjoyed keeping them all on their toes by appearing whenever she felt like it. Poor Miss Clackett was a nervous wreck about it. She constantly had one eye fixed on the door, waiting for Matron to appear. She had even organised an elaborate early warning system with the other wards, so they could telephone each other when she was on her way.

But it seemed as if the matron had even managed to catch her unawares this morning.

'I'm sorry, Matron,' Liz said, trying her best to sound sincere. 'I'll make sure it doesn't happen again.'

'It's entirely my fault,' Mr Bryant interjected. 'I'm afraid I distracted Miss Spencer.'

'Yes, I could tell.' Miss Groves looked around the ward at the paper chains looped from the light fittings. 'And that's not the only thing you've been distracted with, I see.'

'Do you like the decorations, Matron?' Rob Bryant asked. Liz shot him a warning look, which he ignored.

Miss Groves gazed around, and Liz could almost feel a frost settling around the ward wherever she looked.

'I can't say they're to my taste,' she sniffed. 'And I'm sure your nurses' time could have been put to better use, too.'

'I assure you, putting up a few paper chains did not affect the running of my ward,' Liz replied.

'If you say so, Sister.'

'Anyway, I promised the children I'd put them up,' Liz said. 'They would have been disappointed otherwise.'

'And is it so important to indulge their every whim? Surely that is a job for their parents, not you?' Miss Groves shook her head. 'You must remember, Sister, you are a nurse, not a doting mother.'

Her words cut deep, and for a moment Liz was too shocked to respond.

'I'll – er – leave you to it, shall I?' Mr Bryant must have sensed the building tension as he shifted uncomfortably beside her.

'Don't let us keep you, sir. I'm sure you must be very busy,' Matron replied.

Rob Bryant sent Liz a quick, embarrassed look, then he

was gone. He paused at the doors and rummaged in his pockets for a handful of coins, which he deposited in the collection box.

No sooner had he gone than Miss Groves turned on Liz.

'I must say, Sister, I am rather disappointed,' she snapped.

Liz suppressed a sigh. 'I'm sorry I wasn't there when you arrived, Matron. I was rather distracted—'

'Oh yes, Sister, I could see that.' Miss Groves stepped closer, and Liz got a whiff of the sickly lavender scent she wore. 'I could scarcely believe my eyes when I saw you, chatting and smiling with Mr Bryant just now. You seemed very familiar with him, I must say. A little too familiar for my liking, certainly.'

'Familiar?' Liz bristled. 'We were discussing a patient.'

'You looked as if you were flirting.'

'I hardly think a cleft palate counts as flirtation.'

'You must remember, Sister, you're in charge of this ward,' Matron went on, ignoring her. 'That means you're supposed to be setting a good example to the junior nurses and the students. If they see you making eyes at a consultant, they may feel it's appropriate to do the same.'

'Making eyes, Matron?' Liz could scarcely contain her anger.

She leaned in and once again, the sickening smell of lavender assailed Liz's nostrils. 'Please try to have some decorum in future, Sister.'

She moved on swiftly to begin her inspection before Liz could say another word. Which was just as well, since she was very likely to say something she might regret.

Chapter Twelve

'Flirting? Is that really what she said?'

'Can you believe it?'

Liz was still seething about Matron's comments when she returned home to the flat she shared with her best friend Jen that evening. She had been simmering quietly all day, even though no one would know it from her calm, professional manner.

But now, in the privacy of her own home, she could finally give vent to her feelings. And thankfully Jen was at home for once. She had been making a pot of tea when Liz walked in, but she'd taken one look at her face and immediately poured her a stiff gin and tonic.

'She acted as if she'd just caught us in a clinch in the sluice room,' Liz complained as she curled up on the sofa, sipping her drink.

'Now that really would have been a scandal!' Jen laughed. 'Although I wouldn't blame you. Rob Bryant is quite good-looking, in a dishevelled sort of way.'

'I can't say I've ever noticed.'

'Oh, come on, Lizzie! Even you must have a soft spot for him.'

'I like him,' Liz admitted. 'He's certainly a lot nicer

than most of the consultants. Apart from your boyfriend, of course,' she added, smiling at her friend.

'Ugh, don't call him that!' Jen blushed. 'Teenagers have boyfriends. I'm far too old for all that.'

It had been a source of great embarrassment to her since she had started going out with Johnny Davies, a cardiac consultant, the previous year. Anyone could see they were head over heels in love, but Jen refused to acknowledge the possibility, even to herself.

'Nonsense, you're in your prime,' Liz said.

'I'm forty and over the hill.'

'Well, I'm four years older than you so that must make me positively ancient!'

They both laughed. Jen could always bring a smile to Liz's face, no matter how down she felt.

The pair had been best friends since they met at the Nightingale. They had gone through their midwifery training together, and Jen still worked on the maternity ward while Liz had opted to go into children's nursing.

Nearly twenty years after they had first shared a room at the nurses' home, they were still living together, this time in a flat above a pawnbroker's on Roman Road. It wasn't the most salubrious place in the world, but the rent was cheap, the rooms were large and they had grown to love the place, for all its draughty windows and the faint whiff of mothballs and old, stale clothing that drifted up from the shop below sometimes.

'At my age I should be reconciling myself to respectable spinsterhood and concentrating on my career,' Jen said.

'Like me, you mean?' Liz smiled.

'I didn't mean that, and you know it. Besides, you could easily find a husband if you wanted.'

'You make it sound as if men are beating down my door!'

'You've never been short of admirers.'

'I've never found one I could bear for more than a week.'

'Perhaps you haven't given them a chance?'

'Or perhaps I'd rather just stay single?' Liz shook her head. 'I enjoy my work too much to give it up.'

'You'd rather look after other people's children than have any of your own?'

You must remember, Sister. You're a nurse, not a doting mother.

Matron's harsh remark came back to her, cutting her deeply. She couldn't brush it off because, if she was honest with herself, there was a grain of truth in it.

One of the reasons she'd chosen to work on the children's ward was because she loved them so much. And sometimes when she saw the way the children's faces lit up at the sight of their parents at visiting time, she felt a pang that no one would ever look at her like that.

But there was no point in pining for something that could never happen.

'It's a bit late for that now, isn't it?' she said ruefully. 'I shall just have to wait for you and Johnny to make me a godmother.'

'It's a bit late for me, too!' Jen's blush deepened. 'Anyway, Johnny and I have no plans to get married.'

'Don't you?'

Jen looked down at her drink again. 'Why would he want to marry me?'

'What are you talking about? He'd be lucky to have you.'

Jen always sold herself short. She was small and dark-haired, and looked far more youthful than her years. But it wasn't just her age. Jen was lively and light-hearted, and she deserved to find love and happiness.

And you don't?

She took a gulp of her drink to drown out the voice in her head.

'Anyway, I'm still furious with Matron,' she said. 'If you ask me, she just wanted to find something to pick on because she was annoyed about the Christmas decorations. It's plain that she doesn't like fun.'

'You're probably right.' Jen sighed. 'I miss Helen McKay, don't you?'

'Very much.' Liz could never imagine the previous matron being so mean and petty. Helen McKay had been firm but fair in all things. And she had truly cared about the nurses and the patients, too. She would have understood Liz wanting to make everything special for the children.

'I think it's because she was once a nun,' Jen said.

Liz looked up. 'Helen McKay was a nun?'

'No, silly!' Jen laughed. 'Miss Groves. That's where she did her nursing training, didn't you know? There was a place on the other side of the park. I think it was called Our Lady of – something or other.'

'Our Lady of Eternal Piety?'

'That's the one. There's a mother and baby home attached to the convent. I think she used to work there, after the war.'

'That makes sense.'

'Why?'

Liz looked down at the ice cubes clinking in her drink.

'I've heard stories about that place, and the way they used to treat those poor girls.'

'Like sinners, you mean?' Jen nodded, understanding. 'Yes, I can imagine Miss Groves fitting in very well there, don't you think? She'd rather enjoy snatching babies away from their mothers and telling them they were going straight to hell—'

Liz set down her drink. 'Right, it's my turn to cook. What shall we have to eat?'

'Nothing for me, thanks. I'm going out tonight.'

'Don't tell me. Johnny is wining and dining you again?' She smiled when she said it, but Jen looked anxious.

'You don't mind, do you? I know I haven't been around the flat as much as I used to be . . .'

'Don't be silly. Of course I don't mind.'

'You could always come with us?'

'Play gooseberry to you young lovers, you mean? No thanks!' Liz laughed. 'You go and have a good time. I'll be fine, honestly.'

She went into the kitchen and started to rummage through the fridge, pulling out ham and eggs and the makings of a salad. Jen watched from the doorway.

'What do you think of Rob?' she asked.

Liz frowned at the strange question. 'Why do you ask?'

'I was just curious.'

'He's very good at his job.' Liz examined the limp leaves of a lettuce. It was turning a bit brown at the edges, but it would do. 'And the children seem to love him. He goes out of his way to put them at their ease, which is more than most of the other consultants do.'

'Yes, but what do *you* think about him?'

'I don't think about him at all.' Then she saw the look on her friend's face, and realisation dawned. 'I'm not interested in him in that way, if that's what you mean,' she said.

And even if she was, after her brush with Matron that morning she was going to make sure she put a lot of distance between herself and Rob Bryant.

'Are you sure? He and Johnny are friends, I could get him to arrange something if you're interested—'

'I'm not,' Liz said firmly. 'I've already told you, Jen, I don't want a man.'

'I just want to see you happy,' Jen said.

'I am happy.'

'Are you?' Jen sent her a searching look. 'Are you really?'

'Yes, I am.' Liz turned away, back to her lettuce. 'Now go and meet your boyfriend before he thinks you've stood him up.'

Jen left, and suddenly the flat felt very large and empty.

Liz reflected on her friend's question. Was she happy? She had never really stopped to think about it. She was perfectly content. She had her work to keep her busy and she loved the children. She certainly felt fulfilled.

So yes, she was happy. As happy as she would allow herself to be, anyway.

But was there something missing? Of course there was. But it was too late for regrets now.

Chapter Thirteen

It was an icy December morning and still dark outside when Tom Weaver finished his grocery delivery round. He parked his bicycle in the yard behind the shop and stood for a moment, stamping his feet and blowing on his frozen hands to bring some life back into them.

It was nearly half past seven and his shift at the hospital started at eight o'clock. The Head Porter Mr Franklin would be peering out of the lodge window at him, tapping his watch. He'd already taken Tom to task about his time-keeping twice this month, and he wouldn't be let off with a warning again.

His Uncle Stan emerged from the back door, a box full of old cheese rinds and the mouldering remains of a ham in his arms. Tom caught the sour stench from halfway across the yard.

'There you are,' he greeted Tom with a grunt. 'You're late.'

'I know,' Tom muttered.

He watched as his uncle crossed the yard and tipped the contents of the box over the wall.

'What are you doing?'

'Getting rid of our rubbish, what does it look like?'

'But you can't throw it into the Patels' yard! It'll stink the place out.'

'They'll hardly notice,' his uncle dismissed, his lip curling. 'They live like pigs, anyway.'

'No, they don't.'

Mr and Mrs Patel owned the house next door, where they lived with their two daughters. Mr Patel was a bus conductor, and their eldest girl was a student nurse at the Nightingale.

They were quiet, decent people, but Uncle Stan and Aunt Lillian had taken against them because of the colour of their skin. His uncle never missed the chance to torment them.

'Here, give us a hand. I've got some more rubbish to throw over.' Uncle Stan went to go back inside, but Tom put out a hand to restrain him.

'Leave them alone,' he said.

Uncle Stan paused for a moment. He was a burly man, but most of his bulk was fat. Tom was younger and far stronger.

'I'll leave them alone when they go back to their own country,' he muttered, shrugging off Tom's restraining hand.

'What are you two arguing about now?' Aunt Lillian appeared in the doorway that led from the shop. She was as thickset as her husband but much shorter, like a little round ball.

'He thinks we should be nicer to our neighbours. Invite them round for tea.'

Aunt Lillian snorted. 'Catch me doing that!'

Tom ignored her, turning back to his uncle.

'And you can get someone else to do these deliveries every morning, too,' he said.

'Oh, I can, can I?' Uncle Stan set down the ham and

folded his arms. 'And why should I waste my money on delivery boys when you're here idle?'

Idle? Chance would be a fine thing, Tom thought. He never stopped working from the moment he woke up before dawn until he flopped exhausted into bed after midnight.

Unlike his useless cousin.

'Maybe Eric would like to do it?' he suggested.

Aunt Lillian looked shocked. 'You know very well Eric's got a bad chest.'

'That doesn't stop him going out all night, does it?'

He'd heard his cousin coming home in the early hours, clattering through the shop, not caring whether he woke the rest of the house. He was probably drunk again, Tom thought. He'd seen him often enough, hanging around on street corners with his Teddy boy mates, trying to start fights.

'He's young,' Aunt Lillian defended him. 'He's allowed to go out and have fun.'

'Anyway, Eric's already got a job,' Uncle Stan put in.

'So have I,' Tom reminded him.

'Yes, but Eric's doing an apprenticeship. He's going to be a fully qualified mechanic one day.'

If he lasts that long, Tom thought. Mr Braithwaite had only taken him on at the garage in the first place because he and Uncle Stan were in the freemasons together.

But he couldn't be bothered to stand there and argue with his aunt and uncle. They would never hear a word against their precious son, anyway.

He went to the old storeroom at the back of the shop that now served as his bedroom. He had shared a room with his cousin until Eric decided he wanted the place to himself, so Tom's few belongings were packed up and moved downstairs.

The room was cramped and reeked of damp, and the whitewashed brick walls were streaked with mould. The only light came from a tiny slit of a window high up on the wall above his metal camp bed. But Tom didn't really care. He was happy not to have to listen to his cousin snoring, or watch him fiddling with his brilliantined hair in the mirror for hours.

There was also a sink in one corner of the room with a single cold tap. Tom pulled off his jumper and shirt and washed quickly, gasping as the icy water hit his skin. He turned away, fumbling for the towel, then dried his face.

As he turned around, flicking wet hair from his eyes, he jumped to see a figure standing in the doorway, watching him.

'Val!' He snatched up his shirt, holding it against his bare chest.

'Sorry, I didn't mean to startle you.' His cousin Valerie's gaze shifted away to the cup of tea she was holding. 'I brought you this . . . I thought you might need warming up?'

'Thanks, that's very thoughtful of you.' He took the cup from her, still awkwardly clutching the shirt to his naked torso.

Valerie laughed. 'It's all right, you don't have to cover yourself up for my sake. We're family, remember? Anyway, I've lost count of the times I've seen our Eric in his jockey shorts!'

Tom laughed too, but he still turned away as he quickly pulled on his shirt. He and Valerie were almost the same age, and they'd grown up together since they were four years old. She was like a sister to him. In some ways she was closer to him than she was to her own older brother.

He glanced at her now as she lingered in the doorway. Poor Valerie, he couldn't help feeling sorry for her. She was even more put upon by her parents than he was. Unlike Eric, she'd done well in school and Tom knew she'd wanted to go to secretarial college to learn shorthand and typing. But Uncle Stan and Aunt Lillian had overruled her and insisted that she should help out at the shop instead.

Even her appearance seemed defeated. She was short and stocky like her parents, her light brown hair falling in curtains on either side of her plump face. Tom had never known her wear make-up, or dress in the latest fashions like the other girls her age. But she was good-natured, always smiling and cheerful with the customers who came into the shop. Only Tom knew how unhappy she was.

'I heard you talking to Mum and Dad just now,' she said. 'You're right, they should get Eric to help out more. It ain't fair that you have to get up at dawn and do the deliveries while my brother swans around doing nothing.'

'He ain't doing nothing,' Tom reminded her with a grin. 'He's got an apprenticeship, remember? He's going to be a fully qualified mechanic one day.'

'If he doesn't get arrested first! From what I can tell, my brother spends most of his time tinkering with his mates' stolen cars and motorbikes. Old Braithwaite is bound to get sick of him when the coppers start coming to his door.

Then he'll give him his marching orders, freemasons or no freemasons.' She looked pleased at the thought. 'You'll have the last laugh then, won't you? Especially when you take over this place.' She laughed. 'He might even come crawling to you for a job!'

'He won't get one.'

'Quite right, too. He'll have his hand in the till more than Dad!'

When you take over this place.

It was the thought that had kept Tom going all these years.

Once it had been his own parents behind the counter of the grocers' shop. It had been in the Weaver family for years. But Maurice and Peggy Weaver were killed by a doodlebug in 1944, when Tom was just four years old. He was left an orphan, and so it was decided that his mother's younger sister Lillian and her husband should bring him up with their own children. Stanley McBride had taken over the running of the shop too, on the understanding that it would all be handed back to Tom when he turned eighteen years old.

An agreement had been signed, but over the years his aunt and uncle had somehow managed to forget that the shop was Tom's birthright. He'd turned eighteen two months ago, but no one had mentioned handing the business over to him.

And even though he tried not to show it, Tom was worried.

'If you ask me, I reckon Uncle Stan will have some trick up his sleeve to do me out of my inheritance,' he said to Valerie.

'I don't think so,' Val said. 'Believe me, he's already tried. I overheard him and Mum talking about it the other day. Dad had been to see a solicitor and he seemed really worried. He told Mum we could all be out on our ears after Christmas!'

She was smiling when she said it, but Tom could see the apprehension in her grey eyes.

'You've got nothing to worry about,' he assured her. 'You'll always have a home here, Val, for as long as you want.'

'What about Mum and Dad? And Eric?'

Tom pulled a face. 'We'll have to see about that, won't we?'

He wasn't vindictive by nature. But Uncle Stan and Aunt Lillian had never shown him any kindness while he was growing up, so why should he show them any?

'Anyway, like I said, there's a long way to go until then,' he went on. 'I don't think Uncle Stan will give this place up without a fight.'

'Why don't you go and see Aunt Violet and see what she's got to say about it?' Val suggested. 'I'm sure she can set your mind at rest. You know she's always had a soft spot for you.'

Tom thought about it. His mother's eldest sister had always been his biggest supporter. She was under no illusions about her sister and brother-in-law, and the way they had treated Tom.

If anyone knew what was going on with his inheritance, she did.

Chapter Fourteen

Liz prided herself on being good with the parents of her patients. But Mr and Mrs Hedges were pushing her to the limits of her endurance.

She could understand why they were worried. Parents were rarely seen at their best in a hospital ward. They were in an unfamiliar, confusing environment, distraught and lacking in food or sleep, never knowing what the next day or even hour would bring. Their child was sick, often dangerously so, and they were powerless to do anything except put themselves and their precious baby at the mercy of strangers.

Liz knew all that, and she had done her best to reassure Mr and Mrs Hedges that their infant son's condition could be treated, even if his symptoms might seem alarming.

But that didn't stop little Colin's father raging at her.

'When is the doctor coming?' He paced around his son's cot. 'Why isn't he here yet?'

'Someone should be here soon,' Liz soothed.

'They should be here now! What if something happens to our son? Look at him. He could die!'

This set his wife off on another fit of noisy sobbing. Liz surreptitiously looked at her watch. She had summoned the junior registrar ten minutes ago, and she was beginning to share some of Mr Hedges' irritation.

'I assure you that is not going to happen,' she said.

'You don't know that, do you? You're only a nurse.'

He's just upset, Liz told herself. *Take no notice.* But she'd heard the words before, many times, and they always stung.

'I do have some experience—'

'Yes, but you're not a doctor, are you?' he cut her off rudely.

'No, she isn't. But you'll get more sense out of her than you would some junior houseman in a white coat.'

Liz looked up sharply. What was Rob Bryant doing here? He wasn't due to do his rounds for another hour at least.

Never mind, she thought. She was relieved to see any doctor who could satisfy Mr Hedges.

Although she wasn't sure he could, from the way the man looked him up and down, taking in his rumpled appearance. Rob Bryant was looking particularly dishevelled this morning. His shirt was creased and he appeared to have a scattering of pine needles on the shoulders of his jacket.

'Who the hell are you?' Mr Hedges demanded.

'My name's Rob, who the hell are you?' Rob Bryant replied amiably, although Liz could see the fixed edge to his smile.

'Mr Bryant is the consultant for this ward,' she put in quickly.

'Is he now?' Mr Hedges looked him up and down again.

'I take it this is your son?' Rob ignored him and went to look into the cot. 'What seems to be the trouble?'

'You're the doctor, you tell us!' Mr Hedges snapped.

Rob Bryant sent him a withering look. 'You're right, I am a doctor,' he said. 'But I'm not a psychic.'

'He keeps vomiting,' Mrs Hedges spoke up through her tears. 'He can't keep down a feed.'

'What about his bowel movements?'

The woman shook her head. 'Hardly any. Not for a few days, anyway.'

'And how long has this been happening?'

'Nearly a week.'

'But he doesn't seem to be in any pain?'

Mrs Hedges shook her head. 'But he cries because he's so hungry.' She appealed to Liz, her eyes wide and watery with tears. 'It's not right, is it? He wants to eat, but he can't. And he's losing weight.'

'No, it isn't right.' Mr Bryant looked thoughtfully down at the baby in the cot. Liz knew he was seeing the same as her – poor little Colin was listless, his cheeks sunken from dehydration. 'What do you think, Sister?'

'Why are you asking her?' Mr Hedges butted in.

Rob Bryant turned to look at him again. He was smiling, but Liz could see the chill in his eyes.

'Because Miss Spencer here has the benefit of having observed your son for longer than I have,' he said. 'And she's probably forgotten more about children's health than most doctors were ever taught. Including me, I suspect. So, if you wouldn't mind . . .' He left Mr Hedges gaping and turned back to Liz. 'What do you think, Sister?' he repeated his question.

Liz was almost left speechless by Rob Bryant's comment too. It was very rare that any doctor ever asked her opinion, let alone a consultant.

But she was aware of Mr Hedges watching her, so she

gathered herself quickly and replied, 'I would say pyloric stenosis, Doctor.'

'So would I. Although we must rule out any other obstruction.' He turned to Mrs Hedges. 'When did he have his last feed?'

'Just before we brought him in.'

Rob smiled ruefully at Liz. 'In that case we'd better take precautions,' he said.

They quickly moved to either side of the cot, and Liz watched as Rob Bryant leaned down and carefully palpated the baby's tummy.

Sure enough, a moment later Colin let forth with a spray of projectile vomit. Despite his precautions, it caught the toes of Mr Bryant's shoes.

Serves him right for wearing suede, Liz thought.

'I can't feel anything,' Rob Bryant declared after some careful examination. 'But you see the waves of muscle contracting here?' He turned to the parents, indicating the baby's sunken belly. 'As Miss Spencer rightly says, your son is suffering from what we call pyloric stenosis. That means food can't pass out of the lower end of his stomach, so he brings it up again.'

A worried look passed between Mr and Mr Hedges.

'Can it be treated?' Mr Hedges asked the question his terrified wife could not bring herself to utter.

'Yes, indeed. We can perform an operation called a pyloromyotomy, where we would cut away some of the thickened muscle to enable the opening to function better. Don't worry, it's a routine procedure,' he assured Mrs Hedges. 'Little Colin will be right as rain and feeding as normal afterwards.'

They left Mr and Mrs Hedges bidding a tearful goodbye to their baby and headed back to the main ward.

'Thank you for your help,' Liz said.

'All in a day's work,' Rob replied. 'I'm glad I happened to be passing.'

'Why were you here?' Liz asked, curious. 'You're not due on your rounds yet. Did you have another patient to see?'

'Actually, I came to see you.'

'Me?'

'I've brought you a Christmas present.'

'Oh.' Liz suddenly remembered Matron's stern warning a few days earlier.

You seemed very familiar with him. A little too familiar for my liking.

'Well, not you, exactly,' he added, as Liz looked dismayed. 'It's more for the children.'

They rounded the corner into the main ward, just as the double doors opened and Tom came in, staggering under the weight of an enormous Christmas tree.

'I hope you don't mind?' Rob Bryant said. 'I just thought the ward looked a bit bare without one.'

'It's wonderful,' Liz said. 'The children love it. Look!'

They were all sitting up in bed, chattering like little monkeys, excited by the new distraction. The junior nurses were grinning, too. Only Nurse Clackett looked worried as Tom dragged the tree up the middle of the ward.

'It's shedding everywhere,' she heard the staff nurse wail.

'That accounts for the pine needles,' Liz said. 'On your jacket,' she explained, as Rob Bryant looked blank.

Without thinking, she reached out to brush them from his shoulders.

Then she remembered Matron's warning about flirting, and quickly dropped her hand again.

Rob Bryant frowned.

'Are you all right, Sister?'

'Yes, I'm fine.' Liz pasted a brisk, professional smile on her face. She had become so self-conscious since her brush with Miss Groves, she now judged her every move. 'Thank you for the gift. It was very thoughtful of you.'

'It's my pleasure,' he said quietly. 'Call it a token of appreciation for everything you do for these children.'

Their eyes met. But a second later Mr Hedges came roaring round the corner from the baby ward, his face red with indignation.

'When is someone going to come and clean up this mess? Or does my son have to lay in his own vomit?' he demanded.

Liz smiled ruefully. 'It is nice to be appreciated,' she said.

Rob watched her walk away, cursing himself silently for the slip of his tongue. He'd seen the look of dismay that crossed her face when he'd said the tree was a present for her. He'd corrected himself straight away, but it was too late. Miss Spencer's manner had stayed the same, but he sensed the coolness beneath it. He'd pushed it too far, and she had withdrawn from him.

But for a moment he'd made her smile, and that was enough for him. It was almost worth getting up at the crack of dawn and bribing Blakey the porter to go up west with him to Covent Garden market to buy the biggest tree he could find. Although navigating their way back to Bethnal Green in Blakey's dad's milk float with the tree propped precariously on the back had been an adventure he did not wish to repeat.

At the far end of the ward Liz paused to speak to one of the junior staff nurses, half turning so he could see her profile. She was a very attractive woman, but it was more than just physical beauty. Her hazel eyes were so warm, and her mouth was always slightly uptilted, as if ready to smile. A stray lock of sandy hair had escaped her starched cap, and Rob watched as she pushed it back absently, her attention still fixed on the nurse.

He had admired her from the moment they had started working together. She was kind, friendly and they shared the same sense of humour. And she was clearly dedicated to her job, and the children in her care. But over the past couple of months his admiration had started to tilt towards a deeper appreciation, one he had not expected to feel when he'd come to England from Australia.

But isn't that why you came?

That was what had driven him to take the job at the Nightingale, to uproot his life – such as it was – and head to the other side of the world. He had wanted to escape the memories, to make a new start unburdened by the sadness that had dogged him back in Sydney.

But then he thought about Vanessa, and felt a pang of guilt. She was his past, good and bad. Was he wrong to run away from those memories, if it meant leaving her behind?

Chapter Fifteen

'What do you mean, you haven't got a boyfriend?'

Amy ignored Glenys' question at first. She was too intent on fishing nappies out of the laundry copper with a long wooden stick and trying not to splash herself with boiling water as she did so. It was hot, hard work and her back was already aching.

She had been on the ward for a week, and she had hardly seen the children at all. Most of her time had been spent in the sluice, cleaning bedpans and sterilising instruments, or here in the laundry, washing a seemingly endless supply of nappies.

At least it was warm in here, with the coppers bubbling away, belching out clouds of steam whenever their lids were opened. The sluice was always freezing, thanks to the chilly December wind that gusted through the narrow strip of glassless window.

And today she had some company. Glenys Matthews was a first-year student, and until Amy had arrived she had been the most junior on the ward. As such, she'd been given all the dirty jobs that none of the other nurses wanted to do.

Now it was Amy's turn to do them, and Glenys had been only too pleased to pass on her duties.

But today Miss Spencer had sent them both to the

laundry. Glenys was supposed to be rinsing and wringing out, but she didn't seem to be doing much of either. Instead she leaned on the mangle, chattering away.

Amy was surprised. Glenys had ignored her for the first week, being very conscious of her elevated position as her senior. She had, after all, been at the Nightingale for a full six months longer than Amy.

But finally boredom and a desire for gossip overcame her sense of her own importance.

And once she started talking, she couldn't seem to stop. So far, Amy had learned that Glenys came from a small village in Wales, but she had chosen to train at the Nightingale because of its reputation and because she wanted to get away from her family farm.

'Of course I miss the countryside, but at least in London I don't have my parents watching over me all the time,' she said to Amy in her lilting Welsh accent. 'I can really have some fun here.'

She seemed to be making the most of her freedom, too, from what Amy could tell. She had already found herself a boyfriend, a first-year medical student called Giles. They had met at a party in the students' lodgings. Apparently, he was 'very posh' and 'a real dish'.

After sharing her life story over the course of a couple of days, Glenys finally got around to asking Amy about herself. And she was deeply shocked when Amy confessed that she didn't have a boyfriend.

'How long did you say you've been here?' she wanted to know. The lenses of her spectacles had steamed up in the fug of the laundry, and she took them off to stare at Amy.

'I've been on the ward a week,' Amy replied, holding up a nappy to inspect it.

'I'm surprised you haven't found someone yet. I met Giles before I'd even passed PTS.' Glenys polished her spectacles on her apron and perched them back on the end of her turned up nose. 'I could probably find you someone,' she offered. 'Giles has lots of friends.'

'Thanks, but I don't really want a boyfriend.'

'What are you talking about?' Glenys looked incredulous. 'Everyone wants a boyfriend.'

'Not me.'

Amy hooked the last dripping nappy out of the copper and put it with the others in a bucket, which she carried over to Glenys, who paid no attention to it.

'What about when you go dancing? Or to parties?' she said.

'I don't really go to parties,' Amy replied.

'But everyone likes parties!'

Amy shrugged. Glenys glanced down at the bucket at her feet. 'Some of those nappies have still got stains on them,' she declared.

'Where?'

'Here, look. You'll have to give them another scrub with soap.'

She was right, Amy thought, despair washing over her. 'But that's going to take hours,' she sighed. And she'd already boiled them as much as she could. She doubted if another couple of hours in the copper would make much difference.

She was just filling the tub with hot water when Staff Nurse Clackett appeared.

'There you are,' she said briskly. 'Haven't you finished with those nappies yet?' Then, without waiting for an answer, she went on, 'Never mind, you'll have to leave them. You're both wanted on the ward.'

Glenys glanced at Amy. 'Both of us?'

'That's what I said, didn't I? We've had a new patient admitted, and he's just vomited all over his cot. You'll need to change the sheets.'

Amy's heart sank. She might have known it was too good to be true. What else would she be doing but clearing up yet more bodily effluent?

'And we've now got a Christmas tree to deal with, on top of everything else,' Nurse Clackett muttered. She couldn't have looked more put out if Santa Claus had filled her stocking with coal.

'A Christmas tree? Where did that come from?'

'Another one of Mr Bryant's brilliant ideas, it seems.' Nurse Clackett rolled her eyes. 'Never mind that it will take us all morning to decorate the thing. Well, don't just stand there,' she snapped. 'Get moving, both of you!'

Chapter Sixteen

They finished cleaning up little Colin Hedges and his cot and were heading back to finish the washing when Staff Nurse Clackett stopped them halfway down the ward.

'Where do you think you're going?' she asked.

They looked at each other. 'Back to the laundry, Nurse Clackett,' Amy spoke up.

Nurse Clackett tutted. 'You've taken far too long. Too busy gossiping, I'll be bound.' She looked from one to the other, her beady eyes coming to rest on Glenys. 'You can go and finish the laundry,' she instructed. 'And you,' she turned back to Amy. 'You can go and help with bed six. Billy Jeffries is being discharged today, so you'll need to make sure he's packed all his belongings and go downstairs with the porter when he brings the wheelchair for him. His parents are waiting with him.'

Amy glanced sidelong at Glenys. She didn't look too happy about it, but of course she didn't dare argue with a staff nurse. Especially not one as senior as Nurse Clackett.

Poor Glenys, she thought. She didn't envy her scrubbing all those nappies with Sunlight soap. She wasn't sure whether to feel guilty or elated at her lucky escape.

'And then when you've both finished, you can help do something with that,' Nurse Clackett jerked her head towards the towering but sadly bare Christmas tree now standing at the far end of the ward.

Billy Jeffries was already dressed, sitting on the edge of his bed. His mother was packing his case while a man stood over them, watching silently.

'Hello, Billy,' Amy greeted him brightly. 'I hear you're well enough to go home today. Isn't that good news?'

Billy hung his head and said nothing.

'The nurse is talking to you,' the man growled.

Billy looked up with big, sorrowful eyes. 'Yes,' he said in a small voice.

Amy frowned. She had only been on the ward a couple of times in the last week, but Billy Jeffries always seemed like a real character, laughing and joking with the other children and being cheeky to the nurses.

He was certainly nothing like the pale, withdrawn little boy before her now.

'I don't know why he's gone so quiet,' the man said. 'He's usually very good at talking back. Ain't that right, Ida?'

Billy's mother gave him a timid smile as she went on with the packing.

'He's a bit too fond of giving lip sometimes!' the man went on, with a forced laugh.

Amy looked at him, standing with his arms folded, his feet planted apart. He wasn't a big man, but he acted as if he owned the place.

'Your son's been no trouble,' she assured him.

'He ain't my dad.' Billy Jeffries spoke up.

'Billy!' His mother shot him a quick look.

'You're right, I ain't. Your dad's a wrong 'un.' The man glared at Billy.

'Wally's been looking after us while my husband is – away,' Mrs Jeffries explained in a quiet voice.

'As a kindness, you might say,' Wally added. 'His dad was a pal of mine, you might say. Until the bloody fool got himself banged up.'

Amy looked from the man to the boy in the bed. Billy Jeffries was sitting up, hugging his knees to his chest. His whole body seemed to be curling in on itself.

Just then Tom arrived, pushing an empty wheelchair. He stopped short when he saw Amy, then quickly looked away.

Amy suppressed a sigh. He'd been avoiding her for nearly a week now, jumping like a cat whenever their paths crossed. Surely he wasn't still annoyed about those daft Christmas decorations?

Whatever it was, he seemed intent on ignoring her as he turned to Billy and said,

'Taxi for Mr Jeffries.'

'He don't need that,' Wally stepped in. 'He can stand on his own two feet, surely?'

Tom sized him up slowly, his gaze travelling from Wally's face to his feet and back again. He was at least a head taller than the man, his shoulders broad under his brown coat.

'It's hospital policy,' he said. 'I don't make the rules.'

Wally looked as if he might argue, then thought better of it.

'Lot of fuss over nothing, if you ask me,' he muttered. He turned to Billy. 'I hope you ain't got too used to it, because it ain't happening once you get home.'

Billy turned to Amy. 'My belly still hurts,' he complained.

'Perhaps I should call Sister—' Amy started to say, but Wally cut her off.

'He's just doing it for attention.' He turned back to Billy. 'He'll be all right when he gets home.'

He reached out to ruffle Billy's hair but the boy flinched away instinctively.

'You'll be a good boy, won't you?' his mother said. She sounded desperate, almost pleading.

Amy glanced at Tom, wondering if he had noticed. But his expression gave nothing away.

'Come on,' he said. 'Your chariot awaits.'

They left the ward, Amy walking beside the wheelchair, and Billy's mother and Wally following behind. When they reached the lift, Tom turned to them and said,

'You'll have to use the stairs.'

Wally stepped forward, ready to argue again. 'Why can't we get the lift too?'

'It's for patients and staff only.'

Amy frowned. She'd certainly never heard of this rule. But once again, Tom's impassive face gave nothing away.

Wally opened his mouth to argue, then gave up.

'Come on, Ida,' he growled, taking the woman's arm. 'We've wasted enough time in this place as it is.'

They travelled down in awkward silence. Amy felt very aware of Tom standing beside her, their shoulders almost touching in the cramped confines of the lift. He stared straight ahead of him, barely acknowledging her presence.

This would not do, she decided. She couldn't go on like

this, it was too ridiculous. She had to ask him what she had done wrong.

But as she turned to speak, the lift suddenly stopped with a jolt that overbalanced her and toppled her into Tom.

For a brief moment Tom's arms went round her, steadying her. Then he released her so abruptly that for a moment she nearly lost her footing again.

'What happened?' Billy's voice quavered.

'The lift's stuck.' Amy fought to keep the panic out of her voice. 'Don't worry, I'm sure it will start working again in a minute.' She turned to Tom. 'What can we do? Should we call for help?'

'There's no point,' Tom said.

'But someone might hear us—' Amy lifted her hand to bang on the lift doors, but Tom grasped her wrist.

'There's no point because the lift ain't stuck,' he muttered.

'What? I don't understand—'

'I stopped it.' He turned her round to face him. 'Do as I tell you,' he hissed.

Amy looked at him, startled. 'What do you mean?'

'Just trust me, all right?'

Just then the lift lurched back into life and they were heading downwards again. The lift doors opened, and there were Billy's mother and her boyfriend, waiting for them.

'There you are!' Wally snorted, as Tom pushed the chair out of the lift. 'What took you so bloody long?'

'Sorry,' Tom said. 'Billy had a funny turn. We're going to have to take him back to the ward.'

He went to turn the wheelchair around, but Wally stepped into his path.

'You what? What's all this about?' He looked from one to the other. 'What sort of funny turn?'

They were all looking at Amy now. She caught Tom's gaze and saw the silent urging in his eyes.

'His abdominal pains seem to be getting worse,' she said.

'How can they get worse? He's had his appendix out. Or are you telling me the bloody thing's grown back?'

'We need to take him back to the ward,' she insisted. 'For tests.'

'And how long will that take? We've wasted enough time as it is.'

'It's better to be safe than sorry, Wally—' Mrs Jeffries started to say, but he turned on her.

'You can shut up and all!' he snarled.

Amy saw her flinch and realised with a pang that she had seen exactly the same look of dread on her mother's face whenever her father spoke sharply.

She looked down at Billy, trembling in his wheelchair, and suddenly she understood why Tom had done what he did.

They went back up to the ward in the lift. This time thankfully it went all the way to the fourth floor without lurching to a halt.

'Thank you for backing me up,' Tom said quietly.

'That's all right.' She kept her gaze fixed on the doors. 'But I'm not sure what Sister will have to say about it.'

'I'll talk to her. I'm sure she'll listen.'

The doors opened, and Tom pulled back the grille so Amy could push Billy's chair out. As she passed him, she whispered, 'What made you do it?'

Tom gritted his teeth.

'I can't stand bullies,' he muttered.

Amy watched him as he took the handles of the wheelchair from her and headed purposefully towards the double doors that led to the ward.

Perhaps they had something in common after all, she thought.

Chapter Seventeen

Liz Spencer sat behind the desk in her tiny office and listened carefully to what Tom had to say.

It must have taken a lot of courage for him to speak up, she thought. She could see the tips of his ears flaming red under his mop of dark hair, a sure sign he was nervous.

But he was a sensible lad, and bright with it. He took a real interest in what was going on around him, unlike many of the other porters.

And what he was telling her chimed with her own suspicions about Billy Jeffries.

'Thank you, Tom,' she said when he'd finished. 'You did the right thing to tell me. Leave it with me.'

'Yes, Sister.'

Liz stayed motionless behind her desk after Tom had gone, staring out of the window. Down below, the Clerk of Works and his men were at it again, digging up the foundations close to where the old Casualty Hall had once stood. There were rumours that it was going to be another outpatients department, although no one could be certain.

She'd been concerned about Billy Jeffries, ever since he'd kicked up such a fuss about going home. What kid wanted to stay in hospital at Christmas?

And there were other signs, too. His anxious little mouse

of a mother, with her bitten fingernails and downcast eyes. She'd never been able to meet Liz's gaze. Probably too used to looking the other way.

She heard the man's angry voice shouting as soon as she opened the door.

'What do you mean, you don't know? You work here, don't you? You must know why he's been brought back.'

Liz headed down the ward. Mrs Jeffries was standing beside poor little Billy, who was still in his wheelchair. They were both watching the man, who was berating a bewildered-looking Staff Nurse Clackett.

'Indeed I do not,' Nurse Clackett replied. 'As far as I was aware, Billy was discharged this morning.'

'Then what's going on?'

'Keep your voice down, please,' Liz said, as calmly as her temper would allow. 'You're upsetting the other children.'

'Oh, Sister, thank goodness!' Nurse Clackett looked relieved. 'There seems to have been a misunderstanding—'

'No misunderstanding,' Liz cut her off. 'We're keeping Billy here.'

She saw the flare of hope in the child's eyes. The man took a step forward, squaring up to her. 'How long for?' he demanded.

Until you're out of his life, Liz thought. 'Until we feel it's safe for him to go home,' she said.

His eyes narrowed. 'What's that supposed to mean?'

'I think you know.'

The man stared at her. He was slightly built, with a balding head and weak chin, but there was a cruel look in his pale eyes. He reminded her of the rats that swarmed in the sewers under their feet, cunning and vicious.

Liz squared her shoulders and looked straight back at him, tacitly daring him to take her on.

'I want a second opinion,' he said finally.

'You're welcome to take up the matter with Matron if you're not satisfied,' Liz replied. 'But I'm sure she'll agree with me.'

In truth, she was not sure of that at all. Helen McKay would have backed her up, but Miss Groves was not cut from the same cloth as the former matron.

But she would deal with that when the time came. For now, all she wanted was to keep Billy Jeffries safe.

'You've got no right to keep him here,' the man said.

'And you've got no right to take him,' Liz snapped back. 'You're not his father.'

'What's going on?'

Rob Bryant stood behind them for the second time that day. With everything else going on, Liz had forgotten it was almost time for his round. Thank God he wasn't the type to stand on ceremony or he would have been furious. As it was, he simply looked baffled at the sight of Billy Jeffries in his wheelchair.

'Hello, young man,' he greeted him cheerfully. 'I thought we'd seen the last of you. What are you still doing here?'

'I might ask you the same question.' The man turned on him. 'We want to take the boy home but she—' he jabbed an accusing finger in Liz's direction, 'reckons he's got to stay here.'

'Oh?' Rob Bryant turned to Liz, his expression curious.

'I examined him myself last night and he seemed fine then. Has something happened, Sister?'

They were all looking at her. Apart from Billy's mother, who kept her gaze rooted to the floor. Billy stared at her, his eyes wide with silent appeal.

She couldn't let him down. She wouldn't.

'Billy isn't ready to go home yet,' she asserted. 'In my opinion he should stay until after Christmas.'

'And why is that, Sister?' Rob Bryant looked genuinely puzzled.

'I have – cause for concern.' Liz stared back at him, willing him to understand the silent message she was trying to send him.

'Do you know what she's talking about, Doctor?' the man interrupted.

Rob looked back at her and for a moment Liz thought she'd got through to him, that he understood what she was trying to say. Then he said,

'I'm afraid I don't. As far as I can see there's no reason why Billy can't go home.'

Billy let out a hopeless little whimper that tore at Liz's heart.

'Well, I'm glad someone's talking sense at last!' The man went to seize the wheelchair but Liz stepped in.

'No!' She grabbed the handles from him. 'I can't let you take him. Anyone can see he's terrified of you.'

'Well, I like that!' The man looked outraged. 'As if I ain't looked after the boy like my own son. Tell her, Ida,' he turned to the woman at his side. 'Tell her what kind of a father I've been.'

Liz turned to her. 'Yes,' she said. 'Why don't you tell me?'

For the first time Billy's mother met her gaze, startled and guilty. A flush rose in her pale cheeks.

'I—'

'Think about it, Mrs Jeffries,' Liz urged. 'You want what's best for your son, don't you? You want him to be safe?'

'Miss Spencer—' Rob Bryant tried to interrupt, but Liz ignored him. All her attention was still fixed on Ida Jeffries.

'You're his mother,' she said. 'It's your job to protect him.'

There was a long silence.

'Wally's right,' Mrs Jeffries said quietly. 'We'll take him home.'

Liz could not bear to watch them go. She retreated to her office, but not before she heard the man say,

'How dare she? Dried up old spinster, sticking her nose in where it ain't wanted. What does she know about bringing up kids, eh?'

'Leave it, Wally,' Billy's mother pleaded. 'We've got the boy coming home, and that's all that matters.'

'All the same, I've a good mind to write a letter!'

Liz closed the door of her office and stood against it for a moment, fighting to control her breathing. Every time she closed her eyes, all she could see was Billy Jeffries' anxious little face, the look of reproach in his eyes.

She was at her desk, staring mindlessly at some paper-work, when Rob Bryant came in.

'Do you mind telling me what that was all about?' he asked.

Liz had been expecting him, and she had been trying to

106

calm herself. But one look at his face and all her composure vanished.

'How could you?' she snapped. 'How could you let them just take him?'

'He's their son.'

'Didn't you see his face? He's terrified of that man. So's his mother, by the look of her.' Although she could summon little sympathy for a woman who was too spineless to defend her own child.

'And what were we supposed to do about that?' Rob Bryant asked.

'We could have stopped them taking him!'

'How? We couldn't hold on to the boy forever. We had no medical grounds.'

'We could have tried. *You* could have tried.' She glared at him accusingly. 'You could have done something, instead of just smiling and waving them on their way.'

'I'm a doctor, Miss Spencer. My job – our job – is to look after sick children. That's all I can do.'

'So you don't care what happens to him once he leaves this hospital?'

He flinched. 'That's not fair.'

'I'll tell you what's unfair, shall I? A grown man bullying a small boy, making his life a misery.' She shook her head. 'I wonder you can sleep at night.'

That got to him, she could tell. Rob Bryant went very still, his face tense.

'I sleep at night, Miss Spencer, precisely because I make a point of maintaining a professional distance,' he said in a clipped voice.

Liz stared at him. Where was the man who'd brought in a Christmas tree because he cared as much as she did about the children?

'I thought you cared?'

'There's a fine line between caring for the children and becoming too emotionally involved.'

You're a nurse, not a doting mother.

'I'd rather be accused of caring too much than not enough,' she said.

'Is that what you think? That I don't care enough?'

Liz turned her cold gaze on him. 'We'll see how much you care when Billy Jeffries is brought into Casualty after he's been beaten black and blue, shall we? If it's not too late by then,' she added.

He froze, and she saw his dark eyes narrow as her words hit home.

'If you think I don't care then you don't know me at all,' he said quietly.

But she had already turned her back on him, dismissing him. 'I think we've said all there is to say to each other, don't you?'

'Miss Spencer—'

'Don't let me keep you, will you?'

For a while he didn't move and Liz held her body tense. Then the door closed behind him and finally she could let out the breath she had been holding.

Chapter Eighteen

Aunt Violet lived out to the south of London, in a peaceful rural village nestled among the hop fields of Kent.

It was a long journey by train out of the city, but Tom visited her as often as his days off would allow. It was a relief to escape London for a while, and he could feel himself relaxing as the factories and shops and crowded streets flashing past the train window gave way to oast houses and rolling green meadows.

Aunt Violet was waiting to greet him, as usual. Tom could see her tall, upright figure in the window of her cottage as he came down the lane that led from the village. He knew she would have been watching for the train as it passed by, and she would have timed precisely how long it would take him to walk from the railway halt. He also knew that when he knocked on the door of her cottage she would take her time to answer it, as if his arrival was of little consequence to her.

'There you are.' She didn't put out her arms to greet him, or kiss his cheek. Aunt Violet was mortified by outward displays of affection. 'Take off your coat and boots and close the door, you're letting all the cold air in.'

Inside, the cottage was warm and cosy. Downstairs consisted of a sitting room and a kitchen, with a narrow staircase leading up to a bedroom tucked into the eaves. The lavatory was in one of the outbuildings attached to the house, and a tin bath hung on the outside wall.

Tom often worried about how she coped with the lack of modern conveniences as she grew older, but Aunt Violet insisted she did very well for herself. Tom knew better than to argue with her.

The sitting room was small, but neat and orderly, with everything in its place. There were no knick-knacks or ornaments cluttering the place, except for the framed photographs on the mantelpiece. Most of them were of Tom over the years, from a baby with his parents, to various school photographs and then the most recent one, taken on his eighteenth birthday in October. Tom was in this very room, smiling self-consciously in front of a birthday cake Aunt Violet had baked for him.

Another cake now stood on the same cut-glass cake stand in the middle of the table. A simple Madeira this time, next to a plate of daintily prepared sandwiches.

'I thought you might be hungry,' Aunt Violet said. 'I know what young men are like.'

'Thank you,' Tom said. 'You didn't have to go to any trouble.'

'Oh, it was no trouble,' Aunt Violet shrugged. 'I just got a few things out of the larder.'

Tom eyed the sandwiches, cut into delicate triangles, their crusts carefully removed. The lingering smell of baking still hung in the air. She had probably spent all morning preparing for his arrival, not that she would ever admit it.

He watched her as she poured tea into fragile china cups.

Aunt Violet was in her late fifties, the eldest of the three sisters. Tom did not remember his mother, but he knew from the photographs on the mantelpiece that she had been similar in looks to Aunt Lillian, both of them plump with round faces.

Violet, by contrast, was tall and angular. Her greying hair was pulled back in a tight knot, emphasising the sharpness of her cheekbones. She appeared formidable, until you were close enough to see the tenderness in her grey eyes.

But she rarely allowed anyone that close.

Tom looked around the cottage. He often wondered what his life would have been like if he had gone to live with her and not Aunt Lillian after his parents died. Would he be living here, he wondered. Would there be tea and sandwiches and home-made cake waiting for him when he came home from work every evening, instead of endless chores? Would he sleep in a warm bed and not a draughty old storeroom?

But he knew it was no use to think that way. As Aunt Violet had explained so often, she had been in no position to take on a four-year-old orphan.

'How are things at the hospital?' Violet asked now. She was always very keen to hear about the goings-on at the Nightingale. Her rural retirement might be peaceful, but Tom suspected she sometimes found it rather dull.

He was happy to entertain her with the latest news. He told her all about the preparations for Christmas on the various wards, and how Blakey was driving them all mad rehearsing for the Christmas show.

'It's only a bit of entertainment to cheer up the patients,

but the way he's carrying on, anyone would think he was top of the bill at the Palladium!' he told his aunt.

Violet smiled. 'He still thinks he's going to be discovered, then?'

'I reckon he's secretly hoping Lew Grade will turn up and offer him his own television show.'

'Not much chance of that unless Mr Grade is suddenly struck down by a mystery illness just before Christmas.'

'Not much chance of that, full stop!'

'And are you taking part in this show?' Aunt Violet asked.

'Me? Get up on stage and make a fool of myself?' Tom laughed and shook his head. 'I leave all that to Blakey and the other boys.'

'What about the Christmas dance? You'll be going to that, surely?'

'I'm not really one for dancing. Besides, I've got no one to go with.'

'Isn't there someone you can ask?'

A picture of Amy Metcalfe came into his mind. Tom shut down the thought immediately.

'Blakey's already asked them all. They keep turning him down.'

'Yes, but you've got a lot more going for you than your friend Blakey.'

'Don't tell him that!' Tom joked, to hide his embarrassment.

'I'm serious,' his aunt persisted. 'You should find yourself a nice girl, Tom.'

Once again, he found himself thinking of Amy. He'd

really fumbled that, hadn't he? The first time he'd spoken to her he'd managed to snap her head off. He'd been so embarrassed he'd been avoiding her ever since.

But she'd backed him up a couple of days ago, over that business with Billy Jeffries. And since then she'd smiled at him whenever they came face to face on the ward.

Tom stared down into his cup. He could feel himself blushing. 'I wouldn't know what to say,' he mumbled. 'Eric's the one with the gift of the gab, not me.'

'Eric!' His aunt's mouth curled. 'I wonder that any self-respecting girl would go near him.'

Tom smiled, thinking of Shirley, Eric's latest conquest, with her tottering stilettoes, spiky black eyelashes and blonde bouffant hair. He wasn't sure Aunt Violet would approve.

'He takes after his father,' his aunt went on. 'They both think a lot of themselves for no reason.' She sighed. 'I sometimes wonder how Lillian ever ended up with him. But then again, my sister was always very easily led.'

'Uncle Stan's talking about buying Eric a motorbike,' Tom said.

'As if he didn't get into enough trouble!' Aunt Violet shook her head. 'They spoil that boy. Although God knows why, since as far as I can see he's done nothing to warrant it. But as I said, Lillian isn't known for her good sense.'

Tom was silent as he helped himself to another sandwich. He had come here with a purpose, but now he was here he found he couldn't bring himself to speak about it.

But Aunt Violet clearly knew him too well.

'Have you got something on your mind, my dear?' she asked as she refilled their teacups.

Tom looked up sharply. He was about to deny it, but once again his aunt got there first.

'You're thinking about the shop, aren't you?' she guessed. 'Your inheritance?'

Tom stared down at the sandwich in his hand, his appetite gone. 'That's not why I came to visit,' he started to say, but Aunt Violet cut him off.

'Yes, it is,' she smiled. 'And I can't say I'm surprised. You've turned eighteen. You're bound to be wondering what's going to happen. You'd be a fool if you weren't.' She set down the cup in front of him. 'I daresay your uncle hasn't mentioned it yet?'

Tom shook his head. 'I think he's hoping it will go away.'

'I suspected as much. But as I understand, the solicitor has written to him several times.'

'Val says he throws the letters on the fire. He says if he doesn't sign anything they'll be all right.'

'Then he's an even bigger fool than I thought,' Aunt Violet said crisply. 'He and my sister took on the shop after your parents died on the clear understanding that you would inherit it eventually. They were only ever supposed to be caretakers.'

'Yes, but—'

'That matter is already in the hands of the solicitor, Tom.' She looked at him over the rim of her teacup. 'I will speak to him again in the morning. But as far as I'm aware, if nothing has been signed by the first of January, then the business and the premises automatically become yours, regardless of whether your uncle signs them over or not.'

'Is that really true?' Tom stared at her.

'I believe so, my dear. But I will confirm it with the solicitor tomorrow morning, and I will make him aware of what your uncle is doing. Although I'm sure he already has the measure of him,' she said dryly. She looked up at Tom. 'I hope that sets your mind at rest?'

'Yes, it does. Thank you, Aunt.'

But Tom was still apprehensive. Aunt Violet might regard the matter as settled, but he did not think Uncle Stan would see it that way.

Violet stood at the window and watched Tom trudging back up the path towards the village to catch his train, his coat collar turned up against the sleet that had started to fall.

She wished he could have stayed for longer. She loved her little cottage and she did not regret moving to the village, but it meant she did not get to see the boy as often as she would have liked.

Not a boy – a young man now. Her sister Peggy would have been so proud of him. It was a tragedy that she and Maurice didn't get to see their adored son grow up, to witness the fine man he had become. They had been such a loving, devoted family; it was so sad they had so little time together.

Violet had done her best to keep her sister's memory alive for Tom, but she knew he barely remembered his parents. He'd been little more than a baby when that V2 rocket had whistled out of the sky, hitting the picture house where they were spending a rare night out together.

It shouldn't have been them, Violet thought. If anyone had to die, it should have been stupid, selfish Lillian and her greedy husband.

She stopped herself short, ashamed of the thought. She shouldn't wish ill on anyone, especially not her own flesh and blood. Lillian was still her sister, even if they weren't at all close.

She pressed her hand against the glass, feeling the cold against her palm. How she wished she had done things differently. She should have given the poor boy a home herself, instead of handing him over, but at the time she'd thought she had no choice. She was forty-four years old, an unmarried woman, working long hours. She was in no position to look after a child. In contrast, Stanley and Lillian had a family, two small children of their own. Violet was aware that they weren't perfect by any means, but they were there and they were willing to take the child on.

But now she knew she could have looked after him better than her wretched sister had. Tom never complained, but Violet knew he had been ill used over the years. Stanley in particular treated him as little more than cheap labour. Looking back on it, she was certain that Stanley had only agreed to look after Tom because he wanted to get his hands on the shop.

The shop.

Violet turned away from the window and pulled the curtains, shutting out the gathering dusk and the sleet that now pattered against the glass.

She might have assured Tom that everything was in hand regarding his inheritance, but she couldn't help sharing some of her nephew's misgivings. Tom was right to be wary. Stanley had made a lot of money out of the business, and not all of it legitimate, if Violet knew him. It was clear over the years he had come to think of it as his own personal goldmine.

She hoped there wouldn't be too much trouble when the time came. She did not want that for Tom. He'd already had too much unhappiness in his life.

Chapter Nineteen

What the hell am I doing here? Rob Bryant wondered.

It was the Monday morning before Christmas and he could not imagine a less festive place than the visiting room of Wormwood Scrubs. Someone had adorned the porridge-coloured walls with a few limp strands of tinsel, but rather than bringing Christmas cheer, they only served to make the place look even more depressing.

Matron would probably approve wholeheartedly, he thought with a grim smile.

The long room was divided into two by a glass partition that ran down its length. This was separated into a rather half-hearted attempt at cubicles, although the flimsy wooden barriers offered very little in the way of privacy. There was a line of chairs, which were now being quickly occupied by the women who had jostled into the room with Rob.

He studied them as they took their seats. Wives, mothers, daughters, sweethearts – Rob was the only man among them.

He wondered at their stories. Poor women, with their hunched shoulders and careworn faces. How many months or years had they been making this trip, trudging through those ominous gates, desperate to keep their memories alive and their families together? They would have kids at home, mouths to be fed and rents to be paid. How did they manage? It struck him that they endured just the same hell as their husbands and sons, even without the bars and the locked doors.

He took the seat to which the grim-faced warden directed him, still wondering what he was doing. What insane impulse had directed him here? He had never been to this grubby, depressed part of London before, and he sincerely wished he had never bothered.

He wondered if he should leave. This was none of his business. As he had made very clear to Liz Spencer, they should never get personally involved. Stay detached, that was his philosophy. It was the only way to stay sane in a profession where death, despair and heartache were woven into their daily lives.

But the memory of the ward sister's stricken face, and the reproach in her eyes as she had looked at him, still haunted him. He still thought she was wrong, but she had made him feel like the worst kind of man, and he could not forget that.

And why do you care so much what she thinks, Rob Bryant?

He told himself that she had a point this time. He had seen the look of fear in Billy Jeffries' eyes too, and it had unsettled him. But deep down he knew it was Miss Spencer's good opinion that had sent him here, to Wormwood Scrubs on a freezing morning in December.

Behind the glass partition a door opened, and the men began to file in. Rob did not have to see dreary prison uniforms to know they were incarcerated. Most of them looked hunched, defeated. Only a few swaggered in with their heads held defiantly high. At the sight of them the line of women beside Rob instantly straightened, pasting smiles on their tired faces as they prepared to greet their loved ones.

Rob watched as the men took their seats one by one. But the chair on the other side of the glass from him remained empty.

He's not coming, he thought. *I've come all this way, only to be stood up by a stranger.* He wasn't sure whether to be angry or relieved.

But then he saw him. A ferret-faced man with an unmistakable shock of brown hair. He watched as the man looked down the line and then turned to the warden. He saw his blank look as the guard directed him towards the only remaining empty chair, opposite Rob's.

He squared his shoulders, preparing himself.

'Hello, Mr Jeffries,' he said.

Frank Jeffries pulled out the chair with an ugly screech across the linoleum floor and slumped down into it.

'Who the hell are you?' he demanded rudely.

'My name is Bryant.'

The man's narrowed eyes scanned Rob up and down, taking in his appearance. 'Did my solicitor send you?'

'No,' he said. 'I'm a doctor, as a matter of fact.' Rob leaned forward. 'I'm here about your son.'

Mr Jeffries stopped dead and stared at him. 'My Billy? What about him? He's all right, ain't he?' The hard glint in his eyes vanished, replaced by uncertainty.

He cared, Rob realised. That was something, at least.

'He's been in hospital, but he's much better now.'

'In hospital?' Frank Jeffries shot to his feet. The warden moved forward, ready to restrain him, but Jeffries sat down again before the man could lay a hand on him.

'Didn't your wife tell you?'

His face darkened. 'She don't tell me anything,' he muttered. 'I ain't seen her in months. It's like she's forgotten all about me since I've been in here.' He looked down at his hands, picking at a callous on his thumb. 'I wouldn't be surprised if she'd taken up with another bloke, to be honest.'

'That's why I'm here, Mr Jeffries.' Rob sat back in his seat. 'I wonder if the name Wally Dodd means anything to you?'

Chapter Twenty

Four days before Christmas, Jennifer decided they should have a dinner party.

'We'll both be working over Christmas so this is our only chance to celebrate,' she said.

'It sounds like a lot of fuss, don't you think?' The last few days before Christmas were always very busy on the ward, and all Liz really wanted when she came off a long shift was a hot bath and an early night.

'Don't worry, you won't have to help with the cooking or anything,' Jen said. 'I've planned it all. All you have to do is dress up and dazzle our guests.'

'I can't make any promises about that.' Liz felt exhausted just thinking about it. 'Who were you thinking of inviting, anyway?'

'Just Sally and her husband and Tina, one of the other midwives. She's coming with her boyfriend. And Johnny, of course.' As always, she blushed when she said his name.

'Are you sure you want me there? I'll feel like a gooseberry among all those couples.'

'Oh, don't worry, Johnny can bring one of his friends to make up the numbers.'

Jen did not meet her eye when she said it, and Liz was immediately suspicious.

'Jennifer Teeson! I hope you're not setting me up again?'

'As if I would.' But her friend's guilty expression gave her away.

'Who is it?' Liz demanded.

'I'm not sure. Johnny just said it was one of the consultants.' Once again, Jen could not look at her.

'It's not Patrick Thwaite, is it? From Orthopaedics?' Liz groaned. 'He's such a bore. All he ever talks about is fishing.'

'He's a sweetie.'

'Fine. You can spend the evening listening to him explain the best way to land a trout.'

But it wasn't Patrick who turned up with Johnny on the evening of the dinner party.

Liz had barely spoken to Rob Bryant since Billy Jeffries was sent home. She was civil and professional when they were discussing a case, but any easy familiarity between them had gone.

'Surprise!' he joked feebly as he shrugged off his coat. He looked dishevelled, as usual, Liz noted. Did the man even own a tie? 'I bet you didn't expect to see me, did you?'

'No,' Liz said. 'I didn't.'

She glared at Jen, but her flatmate was too busy fussing over the coats to notice. Either that, or she was deliberately avoiding Liz's eye.

'I thought it might help break the ice, but I guess I was wrong?' Rob interrupted her thoughts. 'I could always leave, if you like?'

He gave her an appealing look which she assumed was supposed to melt her heart. It didn't work.

'It would ruin the numbers,' Liz said coldly. 'Jen would never forgive me.'

Not that she would forgive *her*, after being set up like this. Jen knew how she felt about Rob Bryant; she'd fumed over him enough times in the past few days.

'All the same, I'm sure you'd rather see anyone here but me.'

'Oh, I don't know. You could have been Patrick Thwaite.'

'You mean the orthopaedics guy? The one who only ever talks about fishing?'

'That's the one.'

'Christ, he's a bore.'

'Isn't he?'

They looked at each other. It was hard not to smile, in spite of herself.

'Well, I guess that's broken the ice?' Rob said.

Don't bank on it, Liz thought. She was still furious with him.

The other guests had not yet arrived. Jen and Johnny went off to attend to the cooking, leaving the pair of them alone in the sitting room. They sat opposite each other, nursing their drinks. Liz silently willed the doorbell to ring.

'You look very nice,' Rob said.

'Thanks.' Liz smoothed her skirt over her knees.

His gaze travelled admiringly over her simple wool dress. 'That colour suits you.'

'I wear navy blue every day.'

'And you always look good in it.'

Liz looked away, suddenly feeling self-conscious. Why did he have to keep looking at her like that?

'Jen's furious with me because she wanted me to dress up,' she said.

'Why would Jen take such an interest in what you wear?'

'She's trying to set me up.'

'Set you up?'

'She's always doing it. Ever since she found Johnny, she's on a mission to find me a man.'

'And that would be me?'

Embarrassment washed over Liz as she realised what she had let slip.

'Don't worry, I'm not interested,' she said.

'Who said I'm worried?'

His face was serious, but there was a glint in his brown eyes as he looked at her over the rim of his glass.

'I've missed you,' he said.

She stared at him, taken aback. 'I see you every day,' she said.

'Yes, but it's not the same, is it? You've been very distant recently.'

Liz looked away. 'That's hardly surprising, given the circumstances.'

'You're still angry with me about what happened to Billy Jeffries?'

She wasn't angry any more. As time went on and she'd calmed down, she'd realised that Rob Bryant was right. There was nothing they could have done. But that didn't stop her being worried about the child.

But before she had a chance to reply the doorbell rang and the other guests arrived.

Liz already knew Sally from their student days. She

had done her midwifery training at the same time as her and Jen, but no sooner had she completed the course than she married her boyfriend Alistair, who'd just been demobbed. They now had three children and lived on a farm in Hertfordshire. Sally and Jen had kept in touch, but Liz hadn't seen her in ages.

She hadn't missed anything, she decided. Sally had the smug, slightly superior air of a married woman who felt sorry for her single sisters.

Tina was a newly qualified midwife in her late twenties. She was part Italian, and a lively, dark-eyed brunette. Far too lively for her rather dull accountant boyfriend James, Liz thought. The poor young man seemed completely overwhelmed and sat staring at his shoes while Tina held forth at his side.

She seemed especially interested in Rob, Liz noticed. Even when they were all seated around the dinner table and they were next to each other, Tina monopolised him from his other side, chatting away about hospital gossip, and laughing loudly at the feeblest of his jokes.

Jen would be furious, Liz thought. But at least it meant she didn't have to make conversation with him. She was quite happy digging into the exotic chicken dish Jen had found in her Marguerite Patten recipe book.

She listened to the conversation flowing around her. Sally was holding forth about the local WI, and the cushion covers she had knitted for their recent Christmas Sale of Work.

'Although I daresay you'd find it all rather dull,' she said to Liz with a tight smile. 'With you being such a career girl.' She made it sound like an insult.

'Oh, I don't know. I rather enjoy knitting.'

'Do you?' Sally looked surprised.

'I find it helps pass the long, lonely hours of being single.'

Sally nodded sympathetically. Jen shot her a reproachful look. Rob started to laugh then pretended to choke on his food instead. Liz hadn't even thought he was listening, with Tina still rabbiting on beside him.

The party carried on. Sally's husband Alistair started telling a long-winded story about a sheep.

'But I suppose you'd know all about that, wouldn't you?' he said to Rob.

'Me? Why?'

'Well, you being from Australia. They have a lot of sheep there, don't they?'

'Not in the suburbs of Sydney, mate. I can't say I've ever come face to face with one.'

Alistair ignored him and carried on with his story. Rob turned to Liz.

'I need to apologise,' he said.

She stopped, her fork halfway to her mouth. 'What for?'

'Billy Jeffries.'

The mention of the little boy's name took away her appetite. She set down her fork.

'Then I must apologise too,' she said. 'I let myself get too involved. You're quite right, we have to maintain a professional distance.'

'That's just it.' Rob Bryant looked shamefaced. 'I didn't.'

'What do you mean?'

'I didn't keep my distance.' He paused, looking down at his plate. 'I went to see Billy's father in Wormwood Scrubs.'

'You went to prison?'

'Shh!' Rob glanced around the table, then turned back to her, shifting his shoulder so that only she could see his face.

'What happened?' Liz lowered her voice.

'I thought about what you said. I realised I couldn't stand the idea of Billy being left at the mercy of that vicious bully either.'

So much for not getting emotionally involved, Liz thought, hiding her smile.

'What was his father like?' she asked.

'He might be a villain but he loves his son,' Rob said. 'But he's not too fond of Wally Dodd, as it turns out. He wasn't happy at the idea of him taking advantage of his wife, and he was furious that he'd laid a hand on his boy.'

'But surely there's not much he can do about it?'

'You'd be surprised. I got the impression there are a few people on the outside who owe Frank Jeffries a favour.'

'I hope so.' Liz did not usually condone violence, but thinking about little Billy Jeffries' terrified face, she was prepared to make an exception.

'Thank you,' she said to Rob.

His brows rose. 'What for?'

'For giving Billy the best Christmas present he's ever likely to get. And me, too.'

Rob smiled. He looked as if he was about to speak, but just then Johnny rose to his feet and tinged on his glass with a spoon.

'If you wouldn't mind,' he called out. 'Jen and I have an announcement to make.'

Liz looked at her friend's shyly smiling face and already knew what he was going to say.

And she wasn't the only one, either.

'You're engaged!' Sally blurted out.

Johnny smiled ruefully. 'Well, I did have a speech prepared but it looks as if I won't be needing it now!' He looked down at Jen, sitting by his side. 'But yes, Jen has kindly agreed to become my wife.'

The next thing, everyone was on their feet, shaking hands with Johnny and fussing over Jen's ring. Sally in particular wanted to know all the details of their wedding plans.

'Steady on, we haven't given it much thought yet,' Johnny said, as Jen looked overwhelmed.

'But surely you must have some plans? After all, you must have been dreaming of this day for years!' Sally laughed lightly.

'Not everyone is fixated on finding a husband,' Liz muttered, seeing Jen's deep blush.

Sally turned on her scornfully. 'You mean to tell me you wouldn't say yes if someone asked you?'

'Not if it means knitting cushion covers for the WI,' she murmured. But thankfully Sally had gone back to admiring Jen's ring and didn't hear her. Only Rob Bryant's crooked grin told her he had appreciated the remark.

'Be honest, do you think I'm too old to be a blushing bride?' Jen asked when all the guests had gone home and she and Liz were washing up in the kitchen.

'Of course not. Don't be silly.'

'But it is rather ridiculous, isn't it? At my age?'

Liz threw down her tea towel. 'Jennifer! The way you're carrying on, anyone would think you didn't want to get married.'

'I do. Of course I do. It just feels rather silly, that's all, to be talking about white wedding dresses and so on when I'm forty.'

'You could always live in sin . . .'

Jen looked scandalised. 'Can you imagine?'

'I don't think Sally would allow it. She's even more determined to put a ring on your finger than Johnny is.'

'I'd forgotten how tiresome she could be.'

'I hadn't.' Liz picked up her tea towel and began drying dishes again. 'Anyway, I'm sure she won't seem tiresome when you're swapping jam recipes at the Women's Institute.'

'Stop it! I'm never going to end up like Sally Evans, and you know it.'

They worked together in companionable silence for a while. Then Jen sighed and said,

'This changes things for you too, doesn't it? Our living arrangements, I mean. Johnny and I will have to find a house together.'

'I hardly thought he was going to move in here!' Liz looked at her friend. 'For heaven's sake, Jen, cheer up! You're starting a whole new life with the man you love, and you look utterly miserable about it.'

'Yes, but I don't want to leave you in the lurch. Besides, I've enjoyed living here. We've had fun, haven't we?'

'Yes, we have. But all good things must come to an end.'

'What will you do when I'm gone?'

Liz thought for a moment. 'Get a cat and live a lonely spinster life, I suppose.'

'I'm being serious, Liz!'

'I don't know. Perhaps I'll find someone else to share this place.' Although she couldn't imagine rubbing along with anyone as well as she did with Jennifer.

Jen turned back to the sink and carried on washing up in silence. But Liz knew her friend well enough to realise she was working up to saying something.

Sure enough, a moment later, Jen said,

'You know, I think Rob Bryant likes you.'

And I like him, too. Liz was slightly horrified by the unexpected revelation.

'Perhaps I could ask him to be my new flatmate, in that case?' she said lightly.

A look of shock crossed Jen's face. 'You're joking, aren't you?'

'Of course I'm joking. Can you imagine the scandal? Me, living in sin with a man?' She laughed, imagining Matron's face.

'You could do a lot worse, you know,' Jen said, after a moment.

'I told you, I'm not interested. Besides, I hardly know him. For all we know, he might have a wife and children back in Australia.'

'He's a widower.'

Liz paused in the middle of drying a plate.

'His wife died of cancer a year ago. Apparently Rob gave up his career to nurse her until the end.'

'That's very sad.'

'Isn't it? Johnny says that's why he left Australia, to make a new start.'

Jen sent her a long, knowing look. Liz turned away to put the plate in the cupboard to avoid her friend's gaze.

'Then I hope he finds what he's looking for,' she said quietly.

Chapter Twenty-One

'Have you got a date for the Christmas dance yet?'

Amy looked up from the slice of bread she was buttering. It was seven o'clock in the morning and as usual, her first task was to help prepare and serve the children's breakfasts.

'I haven't had time to think about it,' she said.

'Honestly, Metcalfe, what am I going to do with you?' Glenys Matthews gave an exasperated sigh. 'You'd better get a move on or there'll be no one left!' She looked sideways at Amy. 'Someone must have asked you, surely?'

Amy said nothing as she stacked the slice of bread on to the plate and picked up another.

'They have, haven't they?' Glenys turned to her eagerly. 'I knew it! Go on, who was it?'

'One of the medical students.'

'Well, I guessed that, silly. Which one?'

She wasn't going to give up until she found out, Amy could tell. 'Brian Tanner,' she said reluctantly.

'Oh, him.' Glenys pulled a face. 'You want to watch that one. He's got a bad reputation among the girls – hands all over the place, if you know what I mean.'

'I turned him down, anyway.'

'You did the right thing.' Glenys paused for a moment,

then said, 'Giles has got a couple of friends who might take you. I could ask him, if you like?'

'Thanks, but there's no need.'

'It's no trouble, honestly. You don't want to be a wall-flower at the dance, do you?'

'Actually, I'm not sure I'll go.'

Glenys looked horrified. 'Why not? You're not on duty, are you?'

'No, but . . .' Amy hesitated. 'To be honest, I've never been to a dance before.'

'All the more reason why you should go, then,' Glenys urged. 'You'll be sorry to miss it, I promise you. It's the social event of the year!'

Amy smiled to herself. From what she could tell, the nursing students had a pretty good social life all year round. They always seemed to be going to parties and dances.

She didn't know how they found the energy. She was so exhausted after a long day on the ward, all she wanted to do was ease off her shoes and put up her aching feet.

And when she did have any time off, she went home.

Her mother had not been well in the weeks leading up to Christmas. She had caught flu, which had gone straight to her already weakened lungs. She always had a smile on her face when Amy came to visit, but anyone could see she was struggling.

'So who do you want to go to the dance with?' Glenys interrupted her thoughts.

'I told you, I—'

'Yes, but if you did go, who would you want to take you?'

'I can't think of anyone.'

Amy turned away, picking up the last slice of bread to be buttered.

'Liar!' Glenys giggled. 'I can see by your face you've got someone in mind.' She nudged her. 'Go on, who is it? Spill the beans.'

'I—'

Thankfully she was saved from answering when Winnie Riley came into the kitchen and demanded to know why the breakfast wasn't ready.

'Sister will have your guts for garters if the children are kept waiting,' she threatened. Then, turning to Amy, she added, 'She also wants a pot of tea brought to her office stat.'

On her way to Miss Spencer's office, Amy met Tom coming up the ward towards her, carrying a heavy toolbag. He gave her a quick, shy smile as they passed each other, and Amy couldn't resist looking back over her shoulder to watch his tall, dark-haired figure disappearing down the passageway that led to the sluice.

Balancing the tea tray in one hand, she knocked on Miss Spencer's door.

'Come in,' the ward sister called out.

'Your tea, Sister.' As Amy went to set the tray down on the desk, Miss Spencer said,

'Oh no, my dear, it's not for me. Take it down to Mrs Philips in Room Two.'

It took Amy a moment to understand who she meant. Ten-year-old Ruth Philips had been admitted the previous night. She was suffering from leukaemia and had been in and out of the hospital several times over the years, so the staff all knew her well.

She was now in the final stages of her illness, being specialled in a private room. Her distraught mother knew the end was nigh and refused to be parted from her. She had spent the night there, slumped in a chair beside her daughter.

It was most irregular for parents to sleep on the ward, and there had been much speculation among the nurses as to what Miss Spencer would make of it when she came on duty. But the ward sister had accepted the situation calmly, and even instructed a camp bed to be found for her.

'The poor woman has had a wretched night,' Miss Spencer told Amy now. 'I'm sure she'd be grateful for it. You might take her some breakfast too, although I daresay she won't feel like eating. In fact,' she said, rising to her feet, 'bring an extra cup, will you? I think I'll join her.'

'Yes, Sister.'

Glenys was not impressed when Amy returned to the kitchen and told her what was going on.

'So we're having overnight guests now, are we?' she sniffed. 'I'm sure Matron will have something to say about that!'

'I don't think Sister will care.'

Amy had come to realise that Miss Spencer put the welfare of the children before anything else. She went out of her way to make them feel happy and comfortable, and encouraged her nurses to do the same. She extended the same kindness and consideration to the parents, too.

'Put yourselves in their shoes,' she urged the nurses. 'Imagine how scared and worried they must be feeling.'

But she wasn't afraid to take the parents to task if she didn't think they were looking after their children properly, either. Amy had not forgotten how angry Miss Spencer had been when she'd confronted poor Billy Jeffries' mother.

'Why is she being allowed to stay? That's what I want to know,' Glenys said.

Amy stared at her in astonishment. 'Where else would a mother be but by the bedside of her dying child?'

Glenys did not reply. She was so wrapped up in herself she had no empathy for anyone else.

'I daresay Sister knows what she's doing,' Amy said as she went to the china cupboard and took out another cup and saucer.

'Well? Who is it?' Glenda said.

'What?'

'Your mystery man. The one you're hoping will ask you to the Christmas dance.'

'Oh, that.'

'Spill the beans, Metcalfe. I'm dying to know!'

'You don't give up, do you?' Amy set the cup and saucer on another tray, then turned to face her eager friend.

'All right,' she said. 'If you must know, it's Tom.'

'Tom who?' Glenys frowned. 'I don't think I know a student called Tom.' She paused, racking her brains. 'Or do you mean Tom Finlay, the junior doctor on Mr Thwaite's firm? He's rather dishy, I must admit. But I thought he was already going out with that third year—'

'I mean Tom Weaver. The porter?' Amy added, as Glenys looked blank.

The other girl stared at her for a moment, then she burst out laughing. 'You're surely not serious?'

'What's wrong with Tom?'

'Well – he's not a doctor, for a start!'

'So?'

'So . . .' Glenys' eyes were wide behind her spectacles. 'So why would you waste your time with someone who pushes a trolley? Honestly, don't you know the rules? Nurses only go out with doctors. That's the whole point of being here, don't you see?'

'And there I was, thinking we were training for a qualification,' Amy murmured.

'Well, yes, of course there's that. But you've got to think beyond that, haven't you? You need someone with prospects. Seriously, think about it. What does a nobody like Tom Weaver have to offer you?'

Now it was Amy's turn to laugh. 'It's only a Christmas dance we're talking about. I'm not planning to get engaged!'

'Yes, but you never know, do you?' Glenys was deadly serious. 'You want to start as you mean to go on, dearie. And you certainly don't want to be seen with a porter, or no one will ever take you seriously.' She patted Amy's hand. 'Are you sure I can't get Giles to find someone for you?' she said kindly.

'No thanks.' Amy drew her hand away, quietly furious. 'I'd best take this cup to Sister.'

As she headed for the door, Glenys said, 'There's no need to be so huffy about it, I'm only offering you some advice for your own good. I'd hate to see you ruin your chances of finding someone decent.'

'I'll bear that in mind,' Amy said through gritted teeth as she headed for the door.

'You do that. And set your sights a bit higher than a hospital porter!' Glenys called after her.

Set your sights a bit higher than a hospital porter.

Tom hadn't meant to eavesdrop. But he was just down the passage, fixing a blocked drain in the sluice, when he'd heard the voices carrying from the kitchen.

Even then, he hadn't really listened until he'd heard Glenys shriek his name, and the laughter that followed.

Mind your own business, he tried to tell himself. *Eavesdroppers never hear any good of themselves.* But then he'd heard Amy's voice, and before he knew it he was at the door, listening through a crack.

He only caught snatches of their conversation, but what he heard made his heart sink.

'Nurses only go out with doctors . . . What does a nobody like Tom Weaver have to offer you?'

Then he'd heard Amy laughing, and his heart sank even further.

Thank God he hadn't asked her to the dance. He'd been thinking about it for days, trying to sum up the courage.

Now he was glad fate hadn't presented him with the opportunity to ask her. He'd saved himself and Amy a lot of embarrassment.

Anyway, that Welsh nurse was right; nurses only dated doctors. It was an unspoken rule at the Nightingale. It had never bothered him before – how often had he laughed at Blakey's comical efforts to get the student nurses to notice him? – but now he found their attitude high-handed and snobbish.

But at least he knew where he stood now, he thought as he snatched up his spanner and went back to his work. He was just relieved he hadn't made a fool of himself.

He'd thought Amy was different, but it seemed as if she was just like all the others after all.

Chapter Twenty-Two

It was nearly closing time on Christmas Eve, and outside the Peabody Estate a bunch of drunken revellers were slurring their way through a chorus of 'O Come All Ye Faithful'.

In her flat up on the third floor, Ida Jeffries sat weeping in a darkened living room, a poker in her hand, and wondered how the hell she had managed to get herself in such a mess.

The electric meter had run out two hours earlier, and she had no more shillings. Wally had taken everything from her purse, along with the Christmas money she'd been squirrelling away in an old Sunlight Soap packet under the sink. God knows how he'd managed to find it. Wally seemed to have a nose for cash – he could sniff it out anywhere.

Now he'd been out at the pub all night and he was going to come home at any moment, and Ida didn't know what sort of mood he'd be in.

But for once she didn't care.

Him taking that Christmas money had been the last straw for her. She'd been putting a bit aside every week, just a few bob here and there whenever she could get away with it. She'd so wanted to make this year special for Billy. God knows the poor kid deserved it after everything he'd been through.

He still wasn't right after coming out of hospital. He was quiet and withdrawn, and nothing like the cheeky little boy he'd once been. And he'd barely touched any food, even though he used to be as hungry as a horse all the time.

Wally said she was making a fuss over nothing. But Ida had seen the look of reproach in her son's eyes that day they'd brought him home from hospital.

She'd let him down.

It was the same look she'd seen on that ward sister's face. She despised her, Ida could tell. She knew she hadn't done enough to protect her son, and the sister had practically said as much to her. She hadn't wanted to let Billy go home.

But she had no right to pass judgement, Ida thought with a sudden burst of anger. She might think she knew it all, standing there in her polished shoes and smart uniform, giving orders to those nurses. But she'd never been in Ida's shoes. She'd never known what it was like to be alone and scared. To feel so powerless you'd turn to anyone who offered to help . . .

She should never have got mixed up with him, she realised that now. Wally the Snake, they called him on the streets, and he'd certainly managed to slither his way into her life.

She'd been so desperate when Frank was first banged up. How would she and Billy survive without him, and no money coming in? Who would keep a roof over their heads, and food on the table?

Looking back on it, she could have managed. She might have got a job at Woolworth's, made ends meet somehow. But instead she'd panicked and taken the easy option.

Although it hadn't been easy in the end, for her or Billy.

At the time, Wally Dodd had seemed liked the answer to her prayers. He promised he would look after her and the boy. And with Frank doing a five-year stretch, she needed someone.

But Wally had not turned out to be a knight in shining armour. His charm had quickly worn off like the brass on a cheap lamp, revealing the ugly tarnish beneath.

The first time he'd hit her had been a shock. For all his faults, Frank had never laid a finger on her in all their years of marriage. Looking back on it, Ida knew she should have thrown Wally out, made a stand. But he'd made it seem as if it were somehow her fault, and Ida had let it go. He wouldn't do it again, she told herself.

But he had, over and over again, until it became almost expected.

And then he'd started on the boy. Poor little Billy. Wally didn't want him around, said he reminded him too much of Frank. He told Ida she wasn't a good mother, that she was too soft on him.

He was right about that, at least. She wasn't a good mother. If she was, she might have stood up for her son instead of allowing him to become a grown man's punching bag.

That last hiding Wally had given him the day before had nearly killed him. And all because he was in a bad mood. Someone owed him money, and they hadn't paid up. Wally was angry, and he'd taken out his rage on Billy.

The poor kid was black and blue, and Ida was afraid he'd cracked his ribs. But she was too scared to take him to hospital. She could still hear the sound of muffled sobbing coming from his room.

Now Wally had gone out drinking and he'd taken the Christmas money with him. There would be no food on the table for dinner, no presents waiting under the tree when her son woke up. She'd failed him in every way possible.

But she wasn't going to fail now. Things were going to be different. Her hands tightened on the poker. One way or another, Wally Dodd would not lay a finger on her son again.

She didn't know what would happen to her. There was every chance Wally would kill her, but she would make sure she took him with her. Even if she didn't die, she would end up in prison. But either way, they would both be out of her son's life.

And Billy would be better off without them.

Somewhere in the darkness, the mantel clock struck midnight. Ida leaned back in her chair, closed her eyes and prayed for a Christmas miracle.

Chapter Twenty-Three

As the distant bells of St John's chimed twelve, Wally Dodd stumbled out of the Blind Beggar pub and turned up Cambridge Heath Road. He'd been waiting all night for George Garrett, a lying scumbag of a pawnbroker who still owed him for a bag full of silverware he'd brought in the previous week. He'd already had to pay off the bloke who nicked it, and now George was refusing to hand over the money he'd got for the goods.

And Wally was not a patient man, as George was going to find out.

The night was cold and starless, with only a rind of moon half hidden by clouds. The perfect night to go robbing. Except Wally didn't go in for that sort of thing any more. He preferred keeping his hands clean, fencing stolen goods. Better to leave the thieving to mugs like Frank Jeffries.

He chuckled to himself, thinking of Frank. What a tough sod he'd been. They'd done a fair bit of business together, until Wally got a bit greedy and tried to skim off too much commission from Frank's ill-gotten gains. All fair as far as Wally was concerned, but Frank had given him a beating for it.

But he'd had the last laugh, hadn't he? Now Frank was locked away behind bars for a robbery gone wrong, thanks to Wally whispering in a police inspector's ear. Of course it wasn't done to grass on a mate, but Frank had to be paid back for that beating.

And while he was banged up, Wally the Snake had slithered his way into Frank's house and his old lady's bed.

He had no real interest in Ida. She wasn't his usual type, that was for sure. Too scrawny for one thing – he preferred his women with a bit more meat on them. And she was far too clingy, always crying and whining. He'd thought she might have some spirit, but the first time he'd clouted her she'd just taken it. There wasn't even any fun in it any more. It was like beating an old, sick dog that never fought back.

The kid had a bit more about him. He was a chip off the old block, all right. Every time Wally gave him a hiding, it was as if he was beating his old man. Although Ida would soon ruin him if she wasn't careful. The boy was getting far too soft. Wally would have to do something to toughen him up.

'All right, Wally?'

He was so lost in his own thoughts he didn't see the figure step from the shadowy doorway into his path. Wally stopped in his tracks, fear catching in his throat, until he recognised the man in front of him.

'George Garrett! Where the hell have you been? I've been waiting for you all bloody night.'

'Sorry about that.' The little pawnbroker examined his fingernails in the dim light from the streetlamp. 'I had to meet someone.'

'You were supposed to be meeting me.' Wally wasn't a big man, but he towered over George Garrett, and that gave him confidence. Never pick a fight with someone bigger than you, that was the secret. 'Have you got my money?'

'All in good time, Wally, all in good time.' George smiled up at him. 'As a matter of fact, I can go one better than that. I've got a present for you.'

'A present?'

There was something about the way George was grinning that sent a shard of ice down Wally's spine. He was suddenly aware of the darkness of the street, and how empty it was.

'What sort of present?'

No sooner had the words left his lips than another figure stepped out of the doorway. He was tall and thickset in his heavy coat, looming over them both.

'A present from Frank Jeffries,' said a gruff voice. 'Happy Christmas, Wally.'

The man's face was half covered by a scarf, but Wally saw his dark eyes and felt a sick jolt of recognition, at the same time as he caught the glint of a blade.

But by then it was already too late to run.

Chapter Twenty-Four

Even at Christmas, the vicarage still managed to seem oppressive.

Her mother had done her best to make it look festive, but even the tinsel-laden Christmas tree did nothing to lift the sombre atmosphere. The gloom seemed to press down on Amy as she sat flanked by her parents at the long, dark wood dining table, listening to her father intoning grace.

She found herself thinking of the bright cheer of the nurses' home. There always seemed to be something fun going on, with girls darting in and out of each other's rooms, and the sound of laughter and music from transistor radios drifting out on to the landings.

She stared down at her plate, feeling guilty. She knew how much her mother had looked forward to seeing her, and she could imagine how hard she had worked to put on a welcoming spread. The table groaned with roast turkey and all the trimmings, crispy roast potatoes and parsnips, carrots and brussels sprouts.

The effort had taken its toll on her. She looked frail and drained at the far end of the table. Even the dab of rouge on her cheeks could not hide her grey pallor. She picked at her food, turning it over as if even lifting her fork to her mouth was too much for her.

'Are you feeling unwell, Mum?' she asked.

'I'm fine, love. Just this wretched flu hanging on, that's all.' Maggie Metcalfe coughed, a delicate cough that quickly turned into a hacking fit.

'You should be in bed. Don't you think so, Father?'

Amy turned to Malcolm Metcalfe, still eating his dinner at the other end of the table, completely unconcerned.

'Not on Christmas Day,' her mother said. 'I want to make things nice.'

Amy looked at her father again, still in his black robes and dog collar. As if anything could be nice with his dark, forbidding presence looming over them.

'I hope you haven't been overdoing things on my account?' she said.

'I'm fine,' her mother dismissed. 'Anyway, let's not talk about me. I want to hear all about what you've been up to. How are you getting on?'

Amy told her all about the children's ward, the patients and the other nurses who worked there. She also told her about Miss Spencer, and how she worked so hard to make everything special for the children who had to spend Christmas in hospital.

'She's decorated the ward and put up a tree, and she's been collecting money to buy presents for them all,' she said. 'I think she's even planning for them to get a visit from Father Christmas this morning.'

'It all sounds very frivolous to me,' her father muttered.

'She sounds lovely,' her mother said.

'Oh, she is. She's put herself down to work on Christmas Day because she wanted as many of her nurses as possible to be able to have time off with their families.'

'Doesn't she have any family of her own?'

'I'm not sure.' Amy didn't know much about Miss Spencer's private life. The ward sister took a great interest in her nurses' welfare, but she gave away little about herself.

'She sounds lovely, anyway,' her mother said.

'Oh, she is. I'm so lucky I ended up on her ward.'

It could have been a lot worse, she thought. Her friend Sonia was having a terrible time on Male Medical, where the ward sister took them to task over the slightest thing. Only the day before, she'd had poor Sonia scrub the toilets three times because she'd missed a smudge on one of the taps.

They finished the meal and her mother got up to clear away the dishes.

'Let me help,' Amy offered.

'Oh no, love, you do enough fetching and carrying—'

No sooner had the words left her mother's lips than she stumbled. The plate she was carrying fell from her hands, crashing to the floor.

'Careful!' Amy's father snapped. 'That's an original Wedgwood.'

'Never mind that!' Amy rushed to help her mother, catching her just in time as her knees buckled under her. 'Are you all right, Mum?'

'I'm fine, honestly.' Maggie Metcalfe straightened up, brushing down her skirt. 'I just tripped, that's all. Silly me!' she smiled wanly.

'Why don't you go upstairs and rest?'

'What, and waste the chance of spending time with you?' Maggie Metcalfe shook her head. 'Anyway, we've got pudding yet.' She looked at the shattered remains of the plate on the floor. 'I'd better go and fetch a dustpan to clear up this mess.'

'I'll get it. You go up to bed.'

'But—'

'Mum, you're in no fit state. I'm putting you to bed, and that's the end of it.'

'She said she's fine!' Malcolm Metcalfe's voice rose, startling them both. Amy saw her mother flinch, as if she'd been struck.

'I'm putting you to bed,' she repeated.

Amy helped her mother up the stairs. Maggie Metcalfe felt as light and fragile as a bird as she leaned on her arm. She had stopped protesting, Amy noticed. It was as if all the energy had drained from her body.

'How long have you been feeling like this?' she asked, as she put her to bed and pulled the covers over her.

'A few days,' she said, her voice weak. But Amy noticed her sigh of relief as her head sank into the pillow. 'I told you, it's the flu.'

'What does the district nurse say?'

Her mother looked shamefaced. 'She hasn't been round,' she admitted. 'You know your father doesn't like strangers in the house. Anyway, he's quite right. It was a nuisance, her coming in and out every couple of days.'

'You need medical help, Mum. Let me call the doctor—'

'I don't want to trouble anyone on Christmas Day. Please, love,' she begged, 'don't make a fuss. I've had funny turns like this before, and they always pass.'

Amy looked down at her mother. Her face was as pale

as the pillow she rested on, but her expression was full of determination.

'Promise me you'll telephone the district nurse if you don't feel better by tomorrow,' she said.

'I will,' her mother said, but Amy could tell she didn't mean it. 'I've ruined everything, haven't I?' she reached for her hand. 'I'm so sorry, love. As if you don't do enough nursing people already!'

'I don't mind, honestly.'

'But I so wanted to make things nice for you.'

Amy squeezed her hand. 'You have, Mum.'

She sat with her mother for a few minutes, until Maggie drifted off to sleep. Then she went downstairs.

She found her father still at the dinner table, staring at the shattered remains of the plate on the floor.

'Someone needs to clear that up,' he said stonily.

It wouldn't hurt you to lift a finger, Amy thought.

'I'll fetch a dustpan,' she said.

He hadn't even asked how her mother was, she reflected, as she swept up the china from the floor a few minutes later.

'I'm worried about Mum,' she broke the silence. 'She's not getting any better, is she?' Her father said nothing. 'She says you won't allow the district nurse to come?'

'Oh, her.' Malcolm Metcalfe's mouth tightened. 'I don't want her in the house, poking into things that don't concern her.'

'All the same, I think you should call her. Mum doesn't seem well at all.'

'Your mother is never well, or hadn't you noticed?' Her father's voice was scathing. 'But of course, I forgot. A month of scrubbing bedpans has made you a medical expert, hasn't it?'

Amy ignored the jibe. 'You don't need to be a medical expert to see she's sick.'

'And we know whose fault that is, don't we?'

She stared at him, shocked. 'What do you mean?'

'Your mother did all this for you.' Her father gestured to the table, the remains of the lavish Christmas dinner still laid out in front of him. 'She should have been resting, but instead she worked herself to the bone trying to make Christmas special for her precious little girl.'

Her father's expression was bitter. The lamps had not been lit and the darkness cast shadows across his face. 'But just know this. If anything happens to your mother, it will be all your fault!'

Chapter Twenty-Five

It was Christmas morning, and Liz had been on the ward since well before dawn.

She made a point of arriving early so the night nurses could go home. Liz always said she wanted them to spend as much time as they could with their families. But really she loved being on the ward at Christmas time, seeing the children's little faces when they woke up. They were always so bright with excitement, wondering what the day might hold for them.

She started the day by serving the breakfast the night staff had already prepared. It wasn't a difficult task – they always tried to send as many children home as they possibly could before Christmas, so there were only a dozen or so left on the ward. The ward maid lent a hand, too. Molly was a crotchety old stick, but she was widowed and she had no family, and Liz suspected she enjoyed being on the ward as much as she did.

The day nurses came on duty just as Liz and Molly were clearing away the breakfast dishes. She'd allowed them to come in late, too. They worked so hard, they deserved an extra hour in bed. And if she knew young nurses, they'd probably sneaked out to celebrate the night before.

After the children had been washed and their hair

brushed, dressings changed and medications administered, Liz took the nurses into her office and gave them the gifts she had bought for each of them.

They had coffee and shared the chocolates brought in by grateful parents, which Liz had been carefully putting away in her cupboard for weeks, saving up for the big day. It was a lovely atmosphere, like a little party. She tried to make it all as special as she could for the poor hard-working nurses, knowing some of them were missing their families. One of them, Nurse Allen, was from Barbados and hadn't seen her parents in a long time, so Liz took extra care with her.

They had just finished their little celebration when Father Christmas arrived. She had been expecting the Head Porter, Mr Franklin, to do the job as usual, so she was surprised to recognise Rob Bryant's twinkling brown eyes above the cotton wool beard.

He made a far better Father Christmas than grumpy Mr Franklin, she had to admit. The children all roared with laughter when he pretended to forget where he'd put the presents, then shouted with glee when he finally upended the sack and all the brightly wrapped parcels tumbled out.

Mr Bryant seemed as excited as the children as he went from bed to bed, handing out gifts to each of them.

'I'm sorry,' he said to Liz afterwards. 'I seem to have made rather a mess of your nice tidy ward.'

They both looked ruefully at the drifts of ripped wrapping paper that surrounded each bed. A couple of the students were running around, trying to gather them up, but they seemed to be fighting a losing battle.

'The children are having a wonderful time, and that's

all that matters.' She turned to him. 'There's some coffee in my office, if you'd like?'

'Thank you. It's a long, cold ride back to the North Pole.'

They went to her office, where Molly had got a welcoming fire waiting for them.

'I was surprised to see you,' Liz said as she poured his coffee.

'I'm Father Christmas. Where else would I be on Christmas morning?'

Liz sighed. 'Be serious. I expected to see our esteemed Head Porter.'

'Mr Franklin is far too grand to demean himself. Anyway, I volunteered.'

'Why?'

'Same reason as you, I expect. I wanted to see the kids.'

Liz lifted her brows. 'What happened to professional detachment?'

He rolled his eyes. 'Not that again!'

'Sorry, I couldn't resist.'

'Anyway, who says I'm not being professional?'

'Says the man in a cotton wool beard and black wellington boots.'

He laughed. '*Touché*, Sister.'

His laughter sounded almost too intimate in the confines of her office. God only knew what Matron would make of it if she caught them. But Miss Groves was away visiting family on the south coast, leaving her assistant Miss Ellis in charge.

And if she knew the staunchly Catholic Freda Ellis, she was probably at Morning Mass.

And anyway, what did it matter, she told herself. She was doing nothing wrong, having coffee with a consultant on a Christmas morning. Even if Matron might not approve.

'Besides, I had nowhere else to be,' Rob Bryant went on. 'Christmas isn't the same when you don't have anyone to share it with.'

'I suppose all your family are back in Australia?'

He nodded. 'But my brothers and sisters are scattered all over the country, so it isn't as if we can get together.'

'Do you miss your home?' Liz asked.

'I miss the sunshine, especially at this time of year. We always used to spend Christmas Day on the beach.'

'You and your wife?'

She spoke without thinking, and only realised what she'd said when she caught Rob's sharp look.

'Jen told me,' she said.

'The good old hospital grapevine, eh?'

'I'm sorry. I didn't mean to be so personal—'

'It's all right.' He waved her apology away. 'It's no secret.'

His face was bland, but Liz could see the pain behind his eyes.

'Jen said you came to England for a new start?'

'Something like that.' His mouth twisted. 'The truth is, the continent just seemed too big without Vanessa. And I had this idea I could somehow leave all my grief behind.'

'But it doesn't work like that, does it?'

'Hardly.' His mouth twisted behind his fluffy white beard. 'Just another one of my stupid ideas, I suppose.'

'It's not stupid to want to escape your pain.'

'I suppose not.' He looked thoughtful for a moment. 'How about you? Do you have any family?'

She shook her head. 'Both my parents are long dead,' she said. 'I have a sister, but we're not at all close.'

She thought briefly about Julia. She couldn't remember the last time they had spoken. They had given up any pretence at a relationship a long time ago, and no longer even sent Christmas cards.

'Jen is the closest I have to a family,' she said.

'And the nurses.'

She frowned. 'What do you mean?'

'I've seen the way you are with them. You treat them like your daughters.'

Liz stared at him, too jarred to speak for a moment. Then she said,

'I suppose I do watch over them like a mother hen. But that's because I remember what it's like to be in their shoes. And some of them are so far from home, I feel responsible for them.'

'Hey, it's OK. You don't have to justify yourself to me.' Rob held up his hands. 'I think it's good that you're so caring. You're a nice lady, Miss Spencer.'

Liz looked away quickly, embarrassed by the compliment. Directly below her window was the site the Clerk of Works' men had spent the last two weeks digging. They had finally put down their spades for Christmas, leaving a gaping hole surrounded by makeshift fencing.

'You hardly know me,' she said lightly.

'I know what's in your heart.'

That's where you're wrong, she thought. He had only seen

one side of her, the caring and compassionate nurse who would do anything for the children in her care.

He did not understand who she really was, the dark hollow inside her that she tried so hard to fill.

Just then the door to her office flew open and Nurse Clackett appeared.

'Sorry to disturb you, Sister, but Casualty has just rung up to ask if we can take a patient with a fractured arm?'

'Of course.' Liz stood up, preparing herself. With many of the children sent home before Christmas, they had several empty beds. It would be the work of a moment to make one of them up and prepare for the new patient.

But then she saw the senior staff nurse's anxious face and her stomach clenched. Nurse Clackett was an experienced nurse. She would not be thinking to bother her unless there was something she needed to know.

'Was there something else, Clackett?'

The nurse took a deep breath. 'The patient, Sister. It's Billy Jeffries.'

Chapter Twenty-Six

'It ain't what you think,' Mrs Jeffries blurted out as soon as she saw Liz crossing the Casualty department towards her. She shot to her feet, looking utterly terrified.

Liz could hardly bring herself to look at her, she was so furious. She turned to Billy, slumped forlornly on a hard-backed chair, his skinny legs swinging.

'What happened, Billy?' she asked him.

'I can't say.' His gaze shifted away from her, towards the window. His clothes were dishevelled, his hands and face smeared with dirt, in contrast to the pristine white plaster cast on his right arm.

Rob Bryant squatted down in front of him. 'It's all right, mate,' he said. 'You can tell me.'

Billy shot his mother a nervous look, then shook his head. 'I don't want to get into trouble,' he said, his voice tremulous.

'You won't.' Liz knelt beside Rob, her face level with the boy's. 'Tell me,' she said softly. 'Did your Uncle Wally do this to you?'

'No, he didn't.' Mrs Jeffries jumped in quickly.

Liz glared at her. She could feel her anger rising, flaming her cheeks. 'Yes, well, you would say that, wouldn't you?' she snapped. 'You've been defending him for months—'

'He couldn't have done it because he's here. In the hospital.'

Liz and Rob glanced at each other.

'He was found in an alleyway in the early hours,' Mrs Jeffries said. 'Someone had roughed him up good and proper. He ain't conscious yet, and the doctors don't know if he ever will be. Good riddance to him,' she muttered under her breath. She looked at Liz, her drawn face filled with defiance. 'I was going to do it myself,' she said. 'I was going to tell him to go. And if he didn't, I had the poker ready to finish him off.' Her chin lifted. 'I didn't like the way you spoke to me, but it made me think. I thought taking up with Wally would be the best thing for Billy, that he would be a father to him, what with his dad being banged up. But I was wrong. And by the time I realised that, it was too late. I couldn't get away from him.' She looked at Billy, her eyes filling with tears. 'I didn't think I had the strength to fight him,' she said sadly. 'But when we came home from the hospital he gave Billy another beating and that was it for me. I thought I'd keep Billy safe, even if it killed me.'

She looked down at her hand, her bony fingers flexing as if she was picturing the poker in her grasp. 'But someone in a dark alley beat me to it,' she murmured. 'I dunno what it was about, but Wally had upset so many people I doubt if they'd ever catch who did it. I don't suppose it really matters.'

Liz looked at Rob again, and a look of understanding passed between them. She certainly wasn't going to say anything. The assault on Wally Dodd could stay a mystery forever as far as she was concerned.

She turned back to Billy. 'So what happened to your arm?' she asked again.

'I – I can't say.' He sent his mother a quick, furtive glance that spoke volumes.

Rob Bryant seemed to read it too.

'It's all right, mate,' he reassured Billy. 'You won't get into trouble. And neither will your mum, I promise.'

Billy was silent for a moment, his eyes fixed on his plaster-encased forearm. Then he quietly said, 'I fell off the coal merchants' roof.'

'Oh, Billy!' His mother seemed to understand before they did. 'What have I told you about stealing?'

'But we were cold, Ma!'

'We would have managed.' Colour rose in Mrs Jeffries' cheeks. 'That's no reason to go robbing.' She looked warily at Liz. 'I didn't know anything about it, I swear,' she said. 'He disappeared first thing this morning, before he'd even had his breakfast. Then the next thing I knew, he was limping home in tears, his clothes all torn and clutching at his arm.' She looked reproachfully at her boy. 'You could have broken your bloody neck, you silly little bugger!'

'I'm sorry,' Billy whispered. 'I only wanted to help.'

'I told you, we'll manage.' Mrs Jeffries looked at Liz. 'You won't tell the police, will you? He's a good lad really, he knows right from wrong.'

Liz looked at Rob. 'I won't say anything,' she said. 'I reckon that broken arm has taught him a lesson.'

'As long as he stays out of trouble in future,' Rob chimed in. He ruffled Billy's hair. 'You go to school and look after your mum, all right?'

'Yes, Mr Bryant.' Billy looked up at him hopefully. 'Does this mean I can stay in hospital for Christmas?'

'That's up to Sister.' Rob turned to her, his brown eyes mock-stern. 'Do you have room on the ward for this little rascal, Miss Spencer?'

Liz looked down at the boy's pleading face. 'I daresay we can find him a bed,' she said.

Billy gave her a toothy grin. His mother smiled too.

'You've made his day,' she sighed. 'He's been wanting to come back ever since the day he was discharged.' She gave a sad sigh. 'It says something, don't it, when a kid would rather be in a hospital than at home?'

A few days earlier, Liz would have agreed with her. But seeing Mrs Jeffries' contrite face, she understood how wretched the poor woman must have felt.

It wasn't just Billy who had suffered at Wally Dodd's hands, she realised. Beneath her threadbare coat, Ida Jeffries was barely skin and bone. Her face was gaunt and care-worn, her eyes haunted with pain. She looked as if she hadn't eaten a decent meal in weeks.

'Perhaps you'd like to join us for Christmas lunch, Mrs Jeffries?' she said.

Ida Jeffries stared at her, her jaw dropping. 'Me?'

'Go on, Ma!' Billy's little face lit up and Liz could see how much he loved his mother, in spite of everything. 'They have a lovely spread. Turkey and stuffing and roast potatoes and all the works!'

'It sounds a real treat.' Mrs Jeffries' eyes gleamed with hunger, but she was cautious as she turned back to Liz. 'Are you sure?' she said. 'I wouldn't want to be any trouble—'

'It's no trouble,' Liz assured her. 'We always have far too much food anyway.'

'In that case, I'd love to.' Her smile trembled. 'Thank you.'

But it wasn't just the food she was grateful for, Liz could tell. She was thanking her for giving her another chance to prove herself as a mother.

'And what about the Christmas show?' Billy interrupted the moment. 'I ain't missed that, have I?'

'Not at all,' Rob said. 'It's tonight.'

'Christmas show?' Mrs Jeffries looked from one to the other.

'Every Christmas, for one night only, the doctors and nurses put on a show for the patients,' Rob explained. 'It's a chance for us to show off our talents.'

'Make fools of themselves, you mean!' Liz put in.

'And are you in this show?' Mrs Jeffries asked Liz.

'Oh no,' she shook her head.

'I am,' Rob announced. 'I shall be treating everyone to my rendition of "Love Letters in the Sand".'

'Ooh, I love Pat Boone!' Mrs Jeffries said.

'You should come and watch it,' Billy said. Mrs Jeffries blushed.

'Well, I'm not sure about that—'

'You'd be most welcome,' Rob said. 'A bit of support might drown out the jeering medical students!'

Mrs Jeffries smiled, clearly overwhelmed by the kindness she'd been shown. Liz had the impression she was not used to it.

The porter took Billy up to the ward and Liz and Rob

went with him, Mrs Jeffries following on behind. As they headed for the lift, Billy's mother put her hand on Liz's arm, holding her back.

'Thank you,' she said. 'I won't let you down, I promise.'

'As long as you don't let Billy down, that's all that matters,' Liz replied.

Back on the ward, Liz left Billy with his mother and Nurse Clackett settling him into bed, and returned to her office. Rob followed her.

'It was a nice thing to do, inviting her to join you for Christmas lunch,' he said.

'Yes, well, you said yourself, I'm a nice lady.'

'You are indeed.'

She'd meant it as a jokey comment, but Rob looked at her searchingly and she glanced away quickly before his warm brown eyes could work their magic on her.

'Anyway, Christmas is a time for forgiveness, isn't it?' she went on lightly. 'Everyone deserves a second chance.'

They parted company at her office door.

'Will you be back to carve the Christmas turkey?' Liz asked him, as he took his leave.

'Of course. I wouldn't miss it.' He paused. 'And perhaps I'll see you later at the Christmas show?'

'I'm not sure—'She was already shaking her head. 'I'm usually too tired by the end of my shift—'

'Please. It would be nice to see a friendly face in the audience.'

'Billy and his mother will be there to cheer you on.'

'I meant your friendly face.'

They looked at each other for a moment. It hadn't

occurred to her until that moment, but Rob Bryant was still in his Father Christmas costume, his cotton wool beard dangling precariously from his chin.

She smiled. 'I'll see what I can do,' she said.

Chapter Twenty-Seven

As it turned out, Liz never got to the Christmas show, thanks to little Louise Watkins.

Three-month-old Louise had been admitted the previous night with a bad case of respiratory syncytial virus, or RSV. It could be very nasty, especially in babies, and poor little Louise had developed bronchiolitis because of it.

She had been put on a drip in the early hours and then in an oxygen tent in one of the private rooms, but it was clear she wasn't at all well. Shortly after Christmas lunch, Louise had stopped breathing and had to be intubated. She was now in the Intensive Care room, being watched over by one of the nurses. Liz knew the next forty-eight hours would be crucial in her little life.

Liz's heart was heavy, although she had done her best to put on a brave face for the other children, and for the baby's exhausted, terrified parents.

Mr and Mrs Watkins had taken up residence on two hard chairs in the hallway outside the Intensive Care room, their gazes fixed on the door. Liz made sure to keep her eye on them, sitting with them whenever she could spare the time, making sure they had something to eat and drink, and answering their questions.

She thought she might be intruding, but Mrs Watkins especially seemed grateful for her presence.

Then the evening came, and Mr Watkins had to go home. His elderly mother was looking after their three older children, and she wouldn't be able to cope on her own.

Liz agreed that Mrs Watkins could stay. She had a feeling the distraught mother wouldn't be moved even if she'd said no.

She'd tried to arrange for a camp bed to be put up in one of the side rooms, but Mrs Watkins insisted there was no need.

'This chair will do for me, Sister,' she'd said. 'I want to be near Louise. Besides, I doubt if I'll sleep a wink anyway.'

'As you wish,' Liz had said. But when she went to check on her as the day staff were preparing to leave, she found her slumped on the chair, her head lolling on her chest.

'Poor soul, she's completely exhausted,' the special nurse whispered. 'Should I wake her, Sister?'

Liz shook her head. 'Let her rest if she can. She needs to gather her strength.' She turned to the nurse. She looked almost as drained as Mrs Watkins. 'Why don't you get yourself off duty?' she said. 'I can look after little Louise until your replacement comes.'

'Are you sure, Sister? I don't mind staying on a bit longer.'

'Nonsense, you've worked very hard today. And besides, I hear you've got a starring role in the Christmas show.' She smiled.

'I don't know about that,' the girl mumbled. 'I only promised to play the piano for Mr Bryant.'

The mention of the consultant's name brought a smile to Liz's face. 'All the more reason you should go, then. Can't keep our consultant waiting, can you?'

The night staff came on duty shortly afterwards. The lights on the main ward were lowered, and Liz could hear their soft footsteps creeping past the door as she sat beside Louse Watkins' crib.

She looked at the baby's hand, like a little starfish, and fought the urge to reach in, to feel those tiny fingers tightening around hers.

She wasn't sure how long she sat there, lost in her thoughts. When the door behind her opened softly, she thought it was the night nurse returning from her supper to take over Louise's care.

Liz stretched out, shifting her stiff shoulders to release them.

'I'm happy to sit here for a while,' she whispered. 'But I wouldn't say no to a cup of tea.'

'Neither would I.'

She looked around sharply at the sound of Rob Bryant's voice. He stood in the doorway, looking remarkably dapper for once in an evening suit, although typically his bow tie was missing and the top buttons of his shirt were undone.

She looked at her watch. 'I thought you'd be at the show. Has it finished already?'

'Not yet. I left that young porter murdering an Elvis Presley song.'

'I'm sorry to have missed that.'

'Believe me, you're not.' He came to sit down beside her. 'Any change?'

'Not yet.'

'I suppose that's a good sign.'

'Let's hope so.' Liz sent him a sidelong look. There were lines of weariness fanning from the corners of his brown eyes, she noticed. 'I'm sorry I didn't see your performance. I'm sure you did Pat Boone justice.'

'Actually, I decided to give it a miss.' He rubbed his hand over his face. 'I decided I'd rather be here.'

He's worried about his patient, Liz told herself. But all the same, she was acutely aware of him sitting beside her, so close they were almost touching.

She quickly brought him up to speed on baby Louise's condition, not that there had been much change. Rob listened intently, asked some questions then checked her chart.

'I see Mum's still here?' he observed, nodding to the slumbering woman in the corner.

'I didn't have the heart to send her home,' Liz said. 'I daresay she wouldn't have gone anyway.'

'A mother's love, eh? I reckon it can withstand anything.'

'I think you're right,' Liz agreed quietly.

He took the seat beside her and they sat for a while, neither of them speaking, listening to the rush and hiss of the breathing machine.

'Did you always want to be a children's nurse?' Rob asked, breaking the silence.

She shook her head. 'I trained to be a midwife first. But then I realised I preferred working with children.'

'Why's that?'

'I suppose I thought nursing children would be more rewarding.'

'More rewarding than bringing a new life into the world?'

'To me, yes.'

Rob turned to look at her. 'Why do I think there's a story there?'

'A story?'

'A reason you gave up midwifery that you're not telling me?'

'Not at all. I simply made a decision to go in a different direction, that's all.'

Liz got up on the pretext of checking the flow of the drip. It was a lie, of course. But the truth was too complicated to explain, especially to a stranger.

Although looking at Rob Bryant, she had the feeling she could tell him anything. It was dangerous, how close she felt to him.

As if he knew what she was thinking, he suddenly said, 'I don't suppose – would you have dinner with me one night?'

'I'm sorry, I can't,' she blurted out the words so quickly, Rob stared at her in surprise.

'Are you sure you don't want to take a moment to think about it?' he said wryly.

Liz looked away, embarrassed. 'I don't like mixing my personal and my professional life,' she mumbled.

'Ah. I see.' He paused. 'I'm sorry, I hope I haven't embarrassed you by asking?'

'Not at all.'

'I'm glad. It's just you're the first woman I've asked out since my wife died, and I think I might be out of practice.'

He looked rueful. 'Thank you for not laughing in my face, at least.'

'I'd never do that.'

'No, I'm sure you wouldn't. Like I said, you're a nice lady, Miss Spencer.'

And you're a nice man, Mr Bryant.

Too nice, Liz thought. She was dismayed at how much she'd wanted to accept his invitation. It was only dinner, after all. What could be the harm in it?

But she could see herself wanting more. She could see herself falling for Rob Bryant, and she could not allow that to happen.

She didn't deserve the kind of happiness he might offer her.

The harsh, insistent jangling of a bell came out of the blue, startling them both. Liz looked out into the corridor.

'What? What the—?' Mrs Watkins woke up sharply, looking around her in a daze. Then she remembered where she was and immediately shot to her feet. 'My baby!'

'It's all right, Mrs Watkins.' Liz hastened to calm her. 'It's only the fire alarm. Nothing to worry about. We'll just need to evacuate the ward, that's all.'

In spite of her soothing words, her mind was already working frantically, wondering how she would manage to get the children to safety with only a couple of inexperienced juniors to help her.

Why did these things always seem to happen at night?

'I daresay it's a false alarm,' Rob Bryant said. 'Probably some drunken idiot's set it off by mistake. I'll go and see what's going on.'

But no sooner had he started along the corridor than they were caught in the sweeping flash of a torch beam, followed by a voice calling out,

'We need to clear the ward now. The Night Sister's on her way.'

Liz put her hands up to shield her eyes from the swooping torchlight. 'Tom?'

'Sister?' Tom Weaver called back. 'I beg your pardon, I didn't know you were still here.'

'What's going on, Tom?'

'I'm sorry, Sister.' The young porter sounded genuinely regretful. 'But someone reckons they've found a bomb!'

Chapter Twenty-Eight

'I hope this doesn't mean they'll cancel the dance?'

Amy stared at her. Only Glenys Matthews would be more concerned with her social life than the prospect of getting blown up.

'There's a bomb, Glenys,' she pointed out.

'Oh, it's only an old one. It probably wouldn't even explode, anyway.'

'All the same, they can't take chances.'

Amy had returned to the Nightingale that evening to find the place in a state of high excitement, with crowds outside the gates, cameras popping, reporters with notebooks and policemen trying to hold everyone back.

It had taken Amy a full fifteen minutes to convince the young constable that she lived there. It was only when the Head Porter Mr Franklin came out of his lodge to vouch for her that she was finally allowed inside.

It was Mr Franklin who explained how Blakey the porter had been coming back from the Christmas show, flushed with success from his performance and a couple of shandies, and had tripped and fallen through the fence into the hole the Clerk of Works had been digging. He'd twisted his ankle, but that was nothing compared to the shock of finding himself staring at the pointed end of what turned out to be a fifty-kilo high-explosive missile.

'Gave him a right shock it did,' he grinned. 'He couldn't get out of that hole fast enough!'

Amy had found the nurses' home deserted, guarded by yet more policemen. It had taken her a while to find the other students camped out in the orthopaedic outpatients department.

Her friend Sonia and the rest of her set were huddled in a corner. Glenys was with them, looking very dressed up in a pencil skirt and tight blouse.

'The whole hospital's had to be evacuated,' she told Amy. 'We were right in the middle of the Christmas show, too. Giles was doing his magic turn. He was so funny, everyone was falling about,' she said proudly.

'I can imagine.' Amy looked towards the windows, which had been covered with criss-crossed tape in case of an explosion. 'What do you think they're doing now?'

'Trying to make it safe, I suppose,' Sonia replied.

'Either that, or they're going to set it off and blow us all up.' Glenys took out her lipstick and began applying it, peering into her compact mirror. 'I don't care what the Home Sister says,' she declared. 'If I'm going to meet my maker then I'm going to look my best.'

Sonia smiled at Amy. 'I bet you wish you'd stayed at home now, don't you?'

Amy dropped her gaze, feeling guilty. No matter how uncomfortable she felt or what danger she might be in, she knew she would still rather be here than at the vicarage.

Another fifteen minutes passed. The others were talking amongst themselves, discussing the Christmas Day they'd spent on the ward. Glenys was giving everyone a full account of her boyfriend's performance at the Christmas show.

Only Sonia and Amy were silent, lost in their own thoughts. Sonia hugged her knees, and Amy could see she was trying to stop her teeth chattering with fear.

Poor Sonia, Amy thought. The last thing she probably expected when she got on that boat from Jamaica was that she would end up being blown up by a bomb left over from the war.

'How long before they let us back to the nurses' home, do you think?' Sonia whispered.

'I've no idea.'

'We could be here all night,' Glenys giggled. 'Imagine if we did. It would be like the time I went camping in the Mumbles with the Girls' Brigade.'

They all looked up at a sudden flurry of shouts and running footsteps from outside, then it fell silent again.

Amy thought about the patients who had been evacuated from the main building and were now sheltering in various outbuildings. If she was afraid, how must they be feeling?

'I feel sorry for those nurses on night duty,' Sonia said, echoing her thoughts.

'I know what you mean.'

There were usually only one or two looking after each ward at night, supervised by a Night Sister who took charge of the whole hospital. Bassett, the girl assigned to look after the children's ward, was a third-year student.

She and Sonia looked at each other, and Amy knew they were both thinking the same thing.

'Where do you think you're going?' Glenys looked up as they got to their feet.

'I'm going to see if I can help,' Amy said.

'How? What can you do?'

'I don't know, but perhaps we can lend a hand.' She looked at Glenys. 'Why don't you come with us?'

'Me, volunteer for extra duty? No thanks.' Glenys shook her head emphatically. 'And I don't know why you're bothering, either,' she said. 'You'll probably just be in the way,' she called after them, as Amy and Sonia picked their way over the students' slumped figures towards the door.

A policeman on guard at the doors to the main building told her that the children's ward had been moved down into the basement. While Sonia made her way to Male Medical, Amy skirted the far side of the building, keeping a careful distance from the bomb site, and followed a steep flight of stairs down to the rear entrance.

The children were in very good spirits. They were huddled together in a long row, swaddled in blankets. Some had managed to fall asleep, while others were chattering amongst themselves, excited by the unexpected turn of events. They treated it all as a great adventure, like Glenys and her camping trip.

There was only one baby in Intensive Care, and she had also been moved to the basement, along with her crib, drip stand, oxygen tent and other paraphernalia. Amy couldn't imagine what it must have taken to get everything down the steps. The mother sat beside the crib, watching over her daughter with fierce intent.

'Metcalfe?'

177

She turned to see Miss Spencer there, still in her ward sister's uniform. She instantly felt self-conscious in her civvies.

'What are you doing here?' Miss Spencer asked. 'You're not due on duty until tomorrow morning.'

'I came to see if I could help.'

Now she was here, she felt rather foolish. Glenys was right – what on earth did she think she could do? It was barely a month since she'd passed PTS. She hardly knew how to make a bed, let alone nurse anyone.

But Miss Spencer smiled warmly and said, 'Thank you, Nurse Metcalfe, that's very thoughtful. I'm sure we can make use of you.' She looked around. 'You might go and sit with Pamela Greaves for a while? Bassett has been trying to get her to sleep but she's rather unsettled.'

Pamela was curled into a tight ball, the covers pulled over her head. She appeared to be asleep, but as Amy drew closer she could hear muffled sobs coming from underneath the blanket.

'She's scared,' the boy next to her told Amy with a sneer. 'She thinks the hospital's going to fall on her head and she's going to be buried alive. Boom!'

I wonder where she got that idea, Amy thought, looking at his gleeful face. She leaned over the bundle of blankets.

'Pamela? It's all right, love, you can come out. You're not going to be buried alive, I promise. The men will make it safe soon, and then you can go back to your nice warm bed.'

'You don't know that,' the boy said. Gerald Patterson was ten years old and he had been in isolation, recovering from measles. He was clearly enjoying the chance to talk to someone again. 'My grandad's house fell on him in the war. The ARP took six hours to dig out his body—'

'That's enough of that!' Amy cut him off sharply. She leaned over Pamela and gently stroked the hump of her shoulder over the blanket. 'Shall I tell you a secret?'

'What?' Gerald asked, leaning forward eagerly.

'I was born here. In a basement just like this.'

'Why were you born in the cellar?' Gerald wanted to know. His face was sceptical.

'It was the middle of an air raid. There were bombs coming down everywhere, my mum said.'

'Was she frightened?'

'No, because she knew the nurses would take care of her, just like we're taking care of you now. It's our job to keep you safe.'

It took a while of stroking and soothing reassurances for Pamela's whimpers to subside. By the time Amy left her, she had poked her head from the blankets and was sleeping peacefully.

'Well done, Nurse Metcalfe,' Miss Spencer said, as Amy got to her feet. Her limbs were stiff and cramped from sitting still for too long.

'Is there anything else I can do, Sister?'

'I'm sure everyone would welcome a nice hot cup of tea.'

'Yes, Sister.' Amy tried to ignore her sinking heart. Did she really expect she would be saving lives?

As she walked away, Miss Spencer called after her,

'Were you really born in the basement?'

Amy looked back in surprise. She'd had no idea the ward sister had been listening.

'Yes, Sister.'

'And when was this?'

'Right in the middle of the Blitz, Sister. The twenty-fourth of October.'

'The twenty-fourth of October?' Miss Spencer repeated. 'Are you sure?'

I think I should know my own birthday! Amy was about to say, then checked herself quickly.

'Yes, Sister.'

Amy was just about to walk away when the ward sister suddenly blurted out,

'I was there.'

Amy looked over her shoulder. 'I beg your pardon, Sister?'

'I was at the hospital the night the Casualty Hall was hit. The night you were born.'

'Never!' Amy was astonished. 'Perhaps you remember my mother? Maggie? Margaret Metcalfe?'

Miss Spencer did not speak for a long time. 'No,' she said finally. 'No, it was a long time ago. And there was so much going on.'

'Yes, of course,' Amy said. 'I'll go and make that tea.'

But she was mystified as she walked away. She had seen the spark of recognition that flared in Miss Spencer's eyes when she'd mentioned her mother's name.

She glanced back over her shoulder. The ward sister was watching her, her stare so intense it made Amy feel uncomfortable.

What was going on? she wondered.

Chapter Twenty-Nine

'What do you mean, you ain't going?'

It was a dark, freezing Boxing Day morning, and Tom was in the yard fixing the broken chain on his bicycle. His fingers were so cold he could hardly feel them.

Val stood in the doorway, watching him.

'You said you wanted to go to this dance. You were looking forward to it.'

'I've changed my mind. Now could you shift out of the way? I can't see what I'm doing.'

Val stepped to one side and light spilled from the kitchen on to the frosty cobbles of the yard.

'But why?' she wanted to know.

'Why what?'

'Why don't you want to go to this dance?'

Tom stifled a sigh. How could he tell her? Every time he thought about Amy and Glenys and what he'd overheard, hot shame washed over him.

Why would you waste your time with someone who pushes a trolley? Set your sights a bit higher than a hospital porter.

He was embarrassed to think that he'd even considered asking Amy to this dance. Thank God he hadn't spoken up, or he would have been too mortified to show his face again.

'I hate dancing,' he mumbled. 'And anyway, no one's going to care if I'm there or not.'

Amy would have found a date by now. Probably some chinless wonder in a white coat. Good luck to her, he thought. It was none of his business anyway.

Don't you know the rules? Nurses only go out with doctors.

'I care,' Val said. 'I don't know what's happened to change your mind, Tom Weaver, but whatever it is I think you should go. You work so hard, you deserve to have a good time.'

Tom smiled. He knew he could rely on his cousin's loyalty. But the idea of walking into that dance filled him with dread.

'I'd feel like a fool, going on my own,' he said.

'Then I'll go with you.'

He looked up sharply. 'You?'

'Why not? I reckon we could both do with a night out. Why should Eric be the only one who has any fun?'

He shook his head. 'Honestly, Val, you'd hate it. It'll be full of snobby doctors and nurses.'

'Then we can have a laugh at their expense. Go on, Tom, it'll be fun.'

'No, Val. I don't want to go.'

He went back to fixing the bicycle, cursing as the chain slipped from his frozen fingers.

Val let out a sigh. 'Well, I know I'd jump at the chance of a night out. I never go anywhere.'

Tom looked up at her wistful face, outlined in the light from the kitchen. Poor Val, he rarely spared a thought for her. But no one ever did. She was always being ignored and overlooked. Even his uncle and aunt poured all their attention and affection into their good-for-nothing son. Val was as much of a misfit in the family as he was.

His pity must have shown in his expression, because Val's smile faltered.

'Unless you don't think I'm good enough?' she said.

'Don't be daft.' I'm the one who's not good enough, he thought.

What does a nobody like Tom Weaver have to offer you? You don't want to be seen with a porter, or no one will ever take you seriously.

'Take no notice of me, I'm just being silly,' Val said in a small voice. 'I mean, who'd want to be seen with someone like me? I'd only show you up—'

'I'd be proud to take you to the dance.'

He realised what he'd said when her eyes lit up.

'Would you?' she said. 'Do you mean it?'

He wanted to take the words back, but he couldn't do it to her.

'I don't suppose it will do any harm to have a night out.' Even as he said the words he was already regretting it.

'Oh, Tom! You've made my day.' Val ran out into the yard and threw her arms around his neck. 'Thank you, thank you!'

'Get off me, woman! You're strangling me!' Tom wrestled her off, laughing. At least he'd made his cousin happy, anyway. It was good to see a smile on poor, downtrodden Val's face for once.

Valerie stood in front of her wardrobe and surveyed its contents with a critical eye.

She had nothing to wear for a dance. Her clothes were all so drab and ordinary – all right for serving customers in the shop, but not for jiving the night away.

Her mouth twisted. As if she knew how to jive! She knew nothing about dancing, apart from what she'd seen on the television.

'Look at them! What do they think they look like, throwing themselves about like that? It ain't decent,' her father would grumble. But Val was fascinated by the dancers, with their whirling skirts and fast-moving feet. They seemed to belong to another world.

That was Eric's world, not hers. He was the one who went dancing and hung out at coffee bars up west, and had glamorous girlfriends.

Perhaps she should ask Shirley, his latest, for advice? She worked in a dress shop and she was always done up to the nines, her teased blonde curls done just right. She'd know exactly what to wear.

Val twisted a lock of dull brown hair around her finger. Shirley would never give her advice, she thought, and she would never dare to ask, anyway. Eric's girlfriend treated her with the same pitying contempt as her brother did.

But she needed to do something. She wanted to dress up, to wear something really special. Something that would turn heads.

Something that would finally make Tom Weaver notice her.

Excitement quivered inside her. After all these years of patiently waiting, he had finally asked her out.

You mean you pushed him into it, the voice inside her head taunted her. Val hated that voice; it was always sneering at her, telling her how worthless she was. She couldn't experience even the briefest flash of happiness without it chiming in, trying to put her down and make her miserable again.

But this time she was determined not to listen.

'He could have said no,' she argued out loud, then quickly looked around, hoping no one had heard her.

But it was Boxing Day, the shop was closed, and her parents were snoring in the next room.

Val turned back to the mirror. She wasn't much to look at, if she was honest. She was short and stocky, with a square jaw, heavy brows and straight brown hair that her mother cut for her with the kitchen scissors because really, what was the point in wasting money at a fancy hairdresser's? It wasn't as if Val was ever going to look like Elizabeth Taylor, was it?

No wonder Tom had never looked twice at her.

But she couldn't remember a time when she hadn't been in love with him. Right from the moment he'd first come to live with them, there had been something that drew her to him. He was so different from the rest of the family, with his mop of curly black hair and dark eyes. He wasn't a boisterous bully like her brother Eric. He was quiet and thoughtful, and he had real brains.

Eric couldn't stand him, but that was only because he was jealous. He couldn't beat Tom in a fight, and he certainly couldn't better him in an argument.

But Val adored him. Tom was the only one in the family who was kind to her. He took time to talk to her, he treated her as a friend. Val didn't have many friends of her own. Stuck behind the counter in the shop, she only ever spoke to customers, and most of them were grey, boring house-wives her mum's age. Most of the girls from school still lived nearby and were thick with each other, but they'd never had much time for Val when they were at school, so they certainly didn't bother to keep in touch now.

Tom was her only real friend in the world. But she didn't need anyone else.

Val had never had a boyfriend. Her dad and brother often teased her about it.

'Eighteen years old and still on the shelf?' they would laugh. 'You're going to end up an old maid if you're not careful.'

Her mother tried to help her, in her own way. She was always telling Val about slimming diets she'd read about in *Woman's Own*.

'You know, you wouldn't look too bad if you lost a bit of weight,' she would say, as if she was a fashion model her-self. 'You should try to make more of yourself.'

But Tom didn't mind what she looked like. He was the only one who never teased or criticised her. He liked her just the way she was.

And Val loved him for it.

Sometimes when she stood behind the counter serving customers, she fantasised about when Tom would take over the shop. He'd already told her that she would have a home there for as long as she wanted. That was as good as a mar-riage proposal in Val's mind.

He doesn't want to marry you. He was only being kind.

Val closed her eyes tightly, trying to shut out the carping voice inside her head.

He wouldn't have said it if he didn't mean it, would he? Tom wasn't the sort to say anything he didn't mean.

No, he definitely wanted her to stay.

They would get married and run the shop together. But they wouldn't bicker and argue like her own parents. Val would make him happy. Happier than either of them had ever been.

All she had to do was get him to notice her. He'd already asked her to the dance, and that was the first step.

She looked again at the drab rail of clothes in front of her. Perhaps she would pluck up the courage to ask Shirley for advice, after all.

Chapter Thirty

Maggie was drowning.

She could see light above her through the water, but no matter how much she struggled she couldn't swim upwards to break the surface. Her chest burned with the effort of not breathing as she flailed wildly with her hands. But something was holding her back, dragging her downwards, as if her feet were caught in weeds. She turned her head to look and saw her mother below her, gripping her ankles, pulling her downwards. She was smiling, trying to say something, but Maggie could only hear the muffled hum of the water in her ears.

And then a face appeared above her, blurry through the water. It was Malcolm. Maggie recognised the shape of his balding head, his mouth an ugly grimace.

His hands came down, plunging into the water. Relieved, Maggie tried to grasp them, but instead of pulling her out they fixed on her shoulders like claws, pushing her under the surface as her mother pulled at her feet, dragging her down and down.

And then suddenly she was awake, gulping for air, her chest still burning.

Maggie lay for a moment, her eyes wide open, trying to get her bearings. Where was she? She couldn't make out the room in the darkness, but she thought she might be at home in the room she shared with her brothers. Any moment now her mother was going to wake her up to get ready for work.

Her mother. She remembered those bony hands, clutching at her feet, that toothless mouth opening and closing.

What had she been saying?

You don't know how lucky you are, my girl.

And then she remembered. Breathing in, she caught the whiff of beeswax polish on old wood on the chilly air and realised she was in her bedroom at the vicarage.

It was very dark. Maggie couldn't tell if it was day or night. It always seemed to be so dark at this time of year.

In the bleak midwinter, as the choir always sang at Midnight Mass. Maggie preferred a more cheerful carol, like 'Hark the Herald Angels Sing', but Malcolm didn't approve.

Her mind seemed to be all over the place, her thoughts scattering like leaves on the wind. She couldn't seem to gather them together.

She went to sit up and immediately started coughing. That wretched cough wasn't getting any better. She would have to get some linctus from the chemist if it didn't go soon.

She coughed again, and felt a sharp, stabbing pain in her chest. It pulled her up short and frightened her. Where did that come from? Had her flu turned into pneumonia again?

Please God, no, she thought, clutching the sheet as the pain seized her again. She had almost died last winter; she wasn't sure she had the strength for another bout.

The pain began to ebb away, and Maggie felt herself relax. She was making a fuss over nothing, she told herself.

But then she remembered her promise to Amy, that she would seek help if she started to feel worse.

'Malcolm?' she called out for her husband, but there was no response. 'Malcolm, are you there?'

Perhaps he was asleep. It was too dark to see the clock and she wasn't sure how late it was.

Slowly she edged her way out of bed. Her feet touched the floor and she tried to stand up, but her legs buckled treacherously underneath her.

She stumbled across the room, as unsteady as a foal taking its first steps, and fumbled in the darkness for the doorknob.

There was a light on downstairs. She crossed the landing and looked over the banister rail to the square hall below.

'Malcolm?'

Her husband appeared from the sitting room. He was in his shirtsleeves, his thinning hair tousled.

'What do you want?' he called up. The impatience in his voice made her falter.

'I – I'm not feeling well,' she said. 'I have pains in my chest—'

'It's probably just indigestion. Go back to bed.'

Maggie was about to numbly submit to his better judgement as usual. Then she remembered her promise to Amy.

'I really think we should telephone the doctor,' she said.

'It's past midnight,' he said. 'Far too late to telephone anyone.'

'But—'

'You don't want to make a nuisance of yourself, do you?'

Maggie felt her resolve crumbling. The last thing she

ever wanted to do was make a nuisance of herself. She already took up far too much space in the world as it was.

'No,' she said quietly. 'No, I don't.'

'Go back to bed. This will all be forgotten in the morning.'

Maggie went back to her room and tried to sleep, but the pain only grew worse. Her ribs felt tight, stopping her breath. She started to panic, and that made the pain much worse.

'Malcolm!' she called out, but her voice came out as a breathless wheeze. He wouldn't be able to hear her.

Malcolm was right, she was being a nuisance. Who the hell did she think she was, demanding so much of everyone's attention, as if she were somehow important?

An image of Amy's lovely, smiling face drifted into her mind. She had made a promise to her daughter. She had to keep her promise.

Once again she crawled out of bed and staggered out to the landing.

'Malcolm!'

Still no reply. Maggie started down the stairs, clinging to the banister to prop herself upright. She could feel her legs buckling with each step.

All the while the pain and tightness in her chest grew worse. Her heart skipped and fluttered like a bird trapped inside the rigid cage of her ribs.

Halfway down the stairs, she sank down on the step to rest. She felt breathless and light-headed, but she did not dare call out. Malcolm would be angry if she disturbed him.

I don't know what you're moaning about, Margaret. You

should count yourself lucky. You've got a lovely home and a decent man. No marriage is perfect, you know.

Her mother's sharp words came back to her, as clear as the day she'd uttered them. Maggie should have known better than to try to confide in her. Malcolm Metcalfe could do no wrong in her mother's eyes.

Joyce Bradshaw might have thought differently if Maggie had told her everything about her son-in-law. But she was too ashamed to tell anyone the truth, especially not her God-fearing mother. She would probably have found a way to blame Maggie for her husband's shortcomings, in any case.

As if Maggie didn't already blame herself enough.

She rose slowly to her feet, every inch an effort. Her breath was coming in short, painful gasps now.

She had done everything she could to keep her marriage together. She had tried so hard to be the wife she thought her husband wanted her to be. How stupid and naïve she'd been! She should have realised she would never be enough for him.

She reached the foot of the stairs and clung to the newel post, afraid her legs might not hold her up.

The telephone was on the hallstand opposite. Only a few feet away, but it might as well have been a mile. If she could reach it, she could telephone for an ambulance. She could keep her promise to Amy.

'Malcolm!' Her voice was barely above a whisper now.

Despair enveloped her, closing over her head like the water in her dream. It was as if all the sorrow in her life was gathering like clouds, shutting out the light.

She pushed herself from the newel post and staggered a few steps across the hall, arms outstretched. She made a grab for the telephone receiver, lifted it from its cradle and briefly felt the weight of it in her hand, before overwhelming pain crushed her chest and it fell from her grasp.

Chapter Thirty-One

By the early hours of the morning the bomb had been made safe, much to everyone's relief.

And somehow during all the excitement, little Louise Watkins had turned a corner in fighting her infection. Her temperature, pulse and respiration had improved to the point where they could take out her breathing tube.

It took a while for Liz and the night nurses to settle the children back in their beds after all the excitement. Amy Metcalfe had come up to the ward to help them. Liz found herself watching the girl as she tucked Billy Jeffries into bed. She was not wearing her cap, and her red-gold hair flowed around her shoulders, framing her lightly freckled face.

She shook her head, as if she could somehow dislodge the thought that had stuck in her mind. It didn't make sense, she told herself. It was too extraordinary a coincidence to be real. She was just tired, that was all, and her mind was playing tricks on her.

It was too late to go back to her flat, so Liz snatched a few precious hours of sleep on the night block, the wing of the nurses' home where the staff stayed when they were on night duty.

She returned to the ward just before seven o'clock, just as

Staff Nurse Clackett and the other day nurses were coming on duty.

'I'm sure I hardly need to hear your report,' she smiled at the exhausted-looking night nurse. 'Why don't you go off duty? We can cope with the breakfasts.'

But no sooner had they begun than they were interrupted by the arrival of Mr Franklin the Head Porter. He was carrying an untidy bundle of what looked like rags in his arms.

'Good heavens! A baby!' Nurse Clackett realised what was happening before Liz's tired brain could take in that the bundle was stirring, a pitiful mewing sound coming from deep within the grubby towel the baby was wrapped in.

'One of the lads found him on the hospital steps this morning. Whoever left him must have sneaked in while all the kerfuffle with the bomb was going on.'

Liz stepped forward to take the infant from the Head Porter, cradling it in her arms. The baby was newborn, not more than a day or two old, judging by the mottled pink of his skin. A pair of dark, unfocused eyes stared back at her.

'Whoever it was took a chance, with all those police and firemen milling about,' Nurse Clackett observed. 'The mother could have easily been caught.'

'Perhaps she wanted to be.' Liz looked up at Mr Franklin. 'Was there a note?'

'There was, Sister. Tucked into the blankets.' Mr Franklin delved into his pocket and drew out a crumpled scrap of paper, which he handed to her. 'Not much of one, mind.'

He was right. Liz stared down at the single word scrawled on the torn paper.

Sorry.

'No name, no explanation,' Miss Clackett sniffed. 'She doesn't have a lot to say for herself, does she?'

Oh, I don't know. Looking at the word, Liz could almost feel the weight of sorrow and guilt behind it.

She stared at the note for a moment, lost in her thoughts.

'Sister?' Miss Clackett was watching her anxiously. 'Should we call the police, do you think? Or Matron?'

Her question was enough to pull Liz's weary brain back to the present. She quickly pocketed the note and turned to her senior staff nurse.

'Let's get a doctor to check him over first,' she said. 'Then we'll decide what to do next.'

Rob Bryant had had a sleepless night, thanks to the bomb. He could have returned to his flat but he'd stayed at the hospital, just in case he could make himself useful. The police were fairly sure that the missile wasn't dangerous, but Rob still wanted to be there to help with any potential casualties.

Once he was sure all was well, he'd decided to go home and snatch a few hours' sleep. He had nothing pressing in his schedule for the following day, and his routine work could easily be dealt with by one of the registrars.

Besides, he didn't really want to face Liz Spencer after what had happened the previous evening.

He'd taken a big step, asking her to have dinner with him, and she'd turned him down flat. He respected her decision, of course, and at least he knew where he stood now, but he still felt mortified every time he remembered the look of dismay on her face.

He'd been so sure she felt something for him, or he wouldn't have made such a bold move. Over the past few weeks they'd grown closer, their friendship deepening. Or so he'd thought.

And he still believed it. Not because he was one of those men who couldn't stand rejection, or believed he was God's gift to women. He was no Gregory Peck, he knew that. But there was something about the way Liz Spencer had looked at him, even as she was turning him down. A kind of regret, of longing. As if she couldn't allow herself to be attracted to him for some reason.

Or perhaps it's just your bruised ego talking, he thought wryly.

At any rate, he'd made up his mind to let the dust settle for a day or two at least, to give them both the chance to get over their embarrassment. But just as he was getting ready to go back to his flat, a call had come through about an abandoned baby that had been admitted to the children's ward.

Rob was surprised to find Liz Spencer there, sitting with the infant in her arms, giving him a bottle. She looked utterly exhausted, her hazel eyes ringed by purple shadows. Her freckled skin looked washed out and grey under the harsh overhead lights.

She looked up at him and once again Rob saw that look of dismay.

'I didn't expect to see you,' she blurted out.

'Likewise.' He turned his attention to the baby, determined to keep things professional between them. 'So who's this, then?'

'He was found abandoned on the steps this morning.' Liz looked down at the baby in her arms, holding him closer. 'I don't think he can be more than a day or two old.'

'He's certainly hungry.'

Liz smiled down at the baby. 'There's nothing wrong with his appetite. But I wanted to make sure he was all right. Heaven knows how long he was on those steps.'

'Of course. I'll take a look at him when you've finished feeding him, make sure all's well.'

They spoke formally, like strangers. Rob regretted the new-found awkwardness between them, especially since he knew he was the cause of it.

The baby certainly seemed to be none the worse for his ordeal. Liz Spencer was right, he was barely a day old. He was very small, just under six pounds, hungry and dehydrated, but otherwise in good health, considering what he had been through.

Miss Groves arrived on the ward as Rob was finishing his examination. He sensed Liz Spencer stiffen beside him at the sight of the matron striding towards them, although the smile on her face did not betray her feelings.

'Matron,' she greeted her. 'I thought you had time off?'

'I'm hardly going to abandon my post with an unexploded bomb and an abandoned baby at my hospital, am I?' Miss Groves glared at the infant in Liz's arms. 'This is the child, I presume?'

'We've called him Noel,' Liz smiled. 'Since it's Christmas.'

'Very fanciful,' Miss Groves sniffed. 'And what about the mother? No sign of her, I suppose?'

'She left a note, but it didn't give any clues.'

'I'm hardly surprised. If I know that sort of girl, she's probably run back to her boyfriend without a second thought.'

'We don't know that, Matron.' Liz Spencer's voice was even, but Rob could hear the effort beneath it.

Miss Groves shook her head. 'Believe me, Sister, I'm very familiar with that type,' she said, tight-lipped. 'This baby was a mistake, and the sooner she was free of it, the better.'

'Perhaps she didn't have a choice.'

Rob glanced at Liz. He was surprised that she seemed so understanding towards the baby's mother, when he'd seen her take other parents to task for what she perceived as neglect of their children.

'Of course she had a choice! There are places for unmarried mothers.'

'Like the Sisters of Eternal Piety, you mean?'

Miss Groves' head snapped up. 'Well, yes,' she said. 'She would have been taken care of there.'

'That's not what I've heard.'

'And what do you mean by that?'

'I mean if I was in this girl's position, I would probably rather give birth to my baby on the streets than have to endure the bullying and humiliation that goes on there.'

Matron's lips thinned. 'You do know I used to work there, Sister?'

'Yes, I do.' Liz Spencer looked unrepentant.

The two women glared at each other for a moment, and Rob could see the rage glimmering in Miss Groves' tight features. But Liz Spencer faced her down with a cold, implacable calm.

Miss Groves was the first to look away.

'The child must be handed over to the authorities as soon as possible,' she declared.

'Oh no,' Liz said. 'He's staying here.'

Rob saw the flare of anger in the matron's eyes.

'Nonsense,' Miss Groves dismissed. 'He needs to be placed in care. It isn't up to us to decide what happens to him.'

'And what if his mother comes back for him?'

Miss Groves smiled mockingly. 'I hardly think that's likely, Sister. And even if she does, she's already proved she isn't fit to look after a child.'

'Everyone deserves a second chance.'

Rob looked thoughtfully at Liz Spencer, holding the baby fiercely to her bosom, as if she would fight anyone who tried to take him from her.

'I think Miss Spencer is right,' he said. 'The baby should stay here.'

Matron turned her gaze on him, her beady eyes narrowing. 'And why is that, Mr Bryant? I thought you'd given him a clean bill of health?'

'I did. But it wouldn't do any harm to keep him under observation for a few days. Just to be on the safe side?'

For a moment he thought she might argue with him. But Miss Groves was one of the old school, trained never to contradict the word of a doctor. Normally, Rob found it frustrating that the senior nurses so seldom spoke up when they often knew better than he did, but for once he was thankful.

'Very well,' she said, then added, 'but if he's all right

by the end of the week then I shall call the authorities personally.'

'I'd expect nothing less, Matron.'

As they watched her walk away, Liz Spencer quietly said, 'She's right. You had no medical grounds to keep the baby here.'

'We don't know that.'

She turned to face him. 'You once told me that your job was to look after sick children. You said you didn't get personally involved.'

Yes, and I got that wrong, didn't I? He'd made the wrong decision with poor little Billy Jeffries, and he didn't mean to make the same mistake again.

He smiled. 'I guess it must be your bad influence,' he said.

'Thank you.'

He looked down at the baby in her arms and once again, an uncomfortable thought stirred within him.

'Do you really think she'll come back for him?' he asked.

Liz Spencer looked down at the baby in her arms.

'I would,' she said quietly.

Chapter Thirty-Two

'Have you seen what's just walked in?'

Much to Glenys' relief, once the bomb had been made safe, Matron had announced that the Christmas dance could go ahead on Boxing Day evening.

The nurses' dining hall had been transformed for one night into a makeshift dance hall, the chairs and tables pushed back against the wall and the lights turned down. A four-piece band played 'At the Hop' by Danny and the Juniors at one end of the hall, while at the other a buffet table had been set up. Lines of chairs marked out the dance floor, which was beginning to fill up as more and more couples drifted towards it.

Amy sat surrounded by the other student nurses, clutching a glass of lemonade and trying not to feel self-conscious in her green flowery dress. It felt very strange not to be in her uniform on hospital premises. She hardly recognised her own feet in her shiny black patent shoes instead of sensible brogues.

Beside her, Glenys was watching the door anxiously for Giles to arrive. The other girls were entertaining themselves, passing comment on the dancers.

But it was the couple who had just walked in that had grabbed their attention now.

'It's that porter – what's his name?'

'Tom, I think.'

'That's it. Tom something—'

'Weaver.' Amy stared at the doorway. She couldn't seem to drag her eyes away.

'Who on earth is he with?' one of the girls asked. 'I haven't seen her before, have you?'

'No, I think I would have noticed her!' another said, and the others sniggered in agreement.

'Look at the state of her,' one of them said. 'Where does she think she is?'

They all looked at the mystery girl. It was true, her outfit did little to flatter her short, dumpy figure. The puffed sleeves of her white blouse were far too tight and cut into her plump arms, and the scarlet satin circle skirt was stretched over her hefty hips. Her brown hair was teased into artful curls that seemed at odds with her square face. But she looked as proud as punch as she clung to Tom's arm.

'What was he thinking, bringing someone like that to the dance?' one of the nurses, a tall girl called Sarah, said.

'Perhaps that was the best he could do,' another suggested.

'Surely not? He's quite good-looking, isn't he? I'm sure he could have found someone decent.'

'Would you go with him if he asked you?'

Sarah shuddered. 'Of course not. I'd rather be a wallflower.'

Glenys sent Amy a knowing look, which she ignored.

'It might help if her outfit fitted properly,' a girl called

Mary commented. 'She looks as if she's going to burst out of that blouse, doesn't she?'

'Leave her alone,' Amy said, her eyes still fixed on the couple. It didn't feel right to criticise the poor girl, especially when she looked so proud and happy.

But all the same, she couldn't help feeling slightly hurt. She'd dropped enough hints to Tom about wanting to go to the dance, but he'd ignored them all. Then she'd heard on the grapevine from Blakey that he wasn't even planning to go to the dance. Amy had been disappointed, but at least it made sense of why he hadn't asked her.

And yet here he was.

He looked around and saw her. For a moment their eyes met and held across the dance floor.

'Here's Giles at last!' Glenys looked relieved as her boyfriend made his way through the crowd towards her. He was followed by a tall, dark-haired young medical student Amy had seen on the ward a couple of times.

'You remember Tony, don't you?' Giles introduced them. 'He was at a loose end so I thought he could join us.'

'What a coincidence,' Glenys exclaimed. 'My friend Amy doesn't have a date tonight either.'

She turned to her with a beaming smile. Amy looked from her to Giles' guilty face and realised immediately that she had been set up.

'Let's dance,' Glenys said, taking her boyfriend's arm.

'Can't we eat first?' Giles pleaded. 'I've been on duty all day and I'm starving.'

But Glenys was already steering him to the dance floor, leaving Amy and Tony alone.

'It looks as if you're stuck with me,' he said ruefully.

'Yes, it does.' Amy glared at Glenys' retreating back. She would have a few words to say to her when they were next on duty.

'I suppose we'd better make the best of it, eh?' He held out his hand to her. 'Would you like to dance?'

Amy looked past his shoulder to the dance floor, where Tom was already twirling his mystery girl.

'Why not?' she said.

Tom couldn't take his eyes off Amy and the medical student.

He shifted awkwardly in the middle of the dance floor as Valerie twirled and spun around him, but all his attention was fixed on the couple in the corner.

So she'd found herself a doctor, he thought bitterly. It hadn't taken her long, had it?

He knew the man. Anthony Walsh, his name was. Arrogant swine, forever snapping his fingers at the porters. And he fancied himself, too. From what Tom had heard, he'd already broken a few hearts among the nurses.

His charm was certainly working on Amy, Tom thought, as he watched her laughing in the student's arms. Served her right if it all ended in tears—

'Tom!'

He came back to the present to find Val standing in front of him, her hands planted on her hips.

'You're miles away,' she accused. 'If you're going to dance with me, you might pay me some attention.' She looked over her shoulder. 'Unless you'd rather be dancing with someone else?'

'Sorry.'

Tom dragged his gaze away from Amy and her partner, and back to his cousin.

Seeing her like this, with her hair teased and her face plastered in make-up, gave him a mild jolt, but nothing like the shock he'd felt when he first saw her back at the shop.

'Shirley helped me,' she'd said shyly. 'And she lent me her clothes. Do you like it?'

She'd seemed so anxious, he could hardly tell her the truth. Especially when his uncle and cousin laughed in her face.

'Jesus Christ, what do you look like?' Uncle Stan had guffawed.

'Are you off down the circus?' Eric joined in. 'I hear they're short of clowns.'

'Stop it, you two,' Aunt Lillian had said. 'She's tried her best. Even if she does look like a dog's dinner,' she'd added under her breath.

Tom saw Val's lip begin to tremble and her eyes fill with tears, and he stepped in quickly.

'I think you look very nice,' he'd said loyally.

'Then you must be as daft as she is,' Uncle Stan muttered. But at least it had cheered Val up.

'Thank you,' she'd said with a watery smile. 'I wanted to look nice for you. It ain't every day I get to go dancing.'

At the time Tom thought he was doing her a kindness. Now he wondered if he should have been honest with her. He could see some of the nurses looking over at them, sniggering behind their hands.

Snobs, all of them.

Seeing them filled Tom with righteous anger. Poor Val, she was trying so hard and tonight was really important to her.

He reached for her hands, pulling her towards him as the band struck up with Bill Haley's 'Rock Around the Clock'.

'There's no one I'd rather be dancing with than you,' he said.

Chapter Thirty-Three

Valerie stared at her face in the cloakroom mirror. Behind her the door opened and closed as other girls passed in and out. But Val did not take her eyes off her reflection.

She barely recognised herself. Her curls were turning limp in the heat, and her eyelids drooped from the unfamiliar weight of the mascara Shirley had applied to her lashes. But she still thought she looked like a million dollars.

Tom thought so, too. She could see it in the stunned way he had looked at her back at the shop.

Her father and brother had had to poke fun, of course. But Val had expected it. It would have killed them to say something nice.

There's no one I'd rather be dancing with than you.

That's what Tom had said. Val had heard him with her own ears. All those pretty nurses and he only wanted her.

She smiled at her reflection. He'd seen her with new eyes tonight, she was sure of it.

The door opened and a sandy-haired girl in a green dress walked in. Val felt a violent jolt. It was the girl Tom had been staring at all night.

The girl seemed to recognise her, too. She stopped in her tracks for a moment, then gave a hasty smile and hurried into a cubicle.

Val made sure she was still there a moment later when the girl emerged. She studied her out of the corner of her eyes as she went to the furthest basin and washed her hands.

She couldn't see why Tom was so fascinated by her. She was nothing special as far as Val could tell. She wasn't wearing make-up, nor had she done anything with her hair. She had a nice figure, Val conceded, but that green flowery dress was hardly knock-'em-dead. Not like her outfit.

She opened her bag and took out the lipstick Shirley had lent her. Shirley had made it look easy, applying it with a quick swipe and then pressing her lips together and finishing with a saucy pout. But somehow in Val's hand it felt clumsy. She sketched a quick slash of scarlet, but in her nervousness she missed the outline of her lips and smudged lipstick on her teeth.

'Here.'

She looked around. The girl in the green dress was standing beside her, holding out a white handkerchief.

'I've got my own, thanks.' Val rummaged in her bag, aware all the time of the girl watching her.

'You're with Tom, aren't you?' She had a nice voice, quite well-spoken. Not Tom's sort, she decided. He was better off sticking with his own kind.

'That's right.' Val lifted her chin. 'I'm Valerie. His girlfriend.'

'Oh!' Her green eyes widened. 'I didn't know he had a girlfriend.'

'No reason why you should, is there?'

'No,' the girl said quietly. 'I suppose not.'

Val fixed her with a baleful stare. She didn't stop staring

until the girl had left the cloakroom, closing the door behind her.

Then she turned back to the mirror and began savagely rubbing off the scarlet lipstick.

Tom was watching the couples on the dance floor as he waited for Val.

He hoped she wouldn't want to dance again. He'd already made a fool of himself enough for one evening.

Unlike Blakey, who was jiving enthusiastically with a ward maid, throwing his arms and legs around like a demented insect.

Tom smiled, and then he turned around and saw Amy. She was heading towards him, but when their eyes met she quickly veered off in the other direction.

He was still wondering about it when Val returned. There were black smudges under her eyes as if she'd been crying.

'I want to go home,' she said.

'Why? What's happened?'

'Nothing.' But her voice was choked. 'I – I just want to go, that's all.'

'Val?' He lifted her chin, tilting her face upwards. 'Have you been crying?'

'Take no notice, I'm just being silly.' She gave him a brave, watery smile. 'I should be used to people teasing by now, shouldn't I?'

Tom's defences prickled. 'Who's been teasing you?'

'It's nothing, honestly. I'm sure she didn't mean anything by it.'

'Who are you talking about?'

'That girl. The one in the green dress.' Val nodded past his shoulder to where Amy stood.

'You mean Amy? What did she say to you?'

'She didn't say anything. I just heard her whispering about me to her friend, that's all.' She looked at Tom, her eyes wide. 'You don't think I look like a clown, do you?'

'Of course not. Is that really what Amy said?'

Val nodded. 'I don't think I was meant to hear. I was in the toilet, so she didn't know I was there.'

'I'm going to speak to her—'

He turned away, but Val grabbed his arm. 'No, don't,' she pleaded. 'I don't want to make a fuss. I'd rather just go home, if you don't mind?'

Tom looked at his cousin. Poor Val looked so downcast. And he'd wanted this to be such a happy evening for her, too.

'I'll fetch our coats,' he said.

On the way out, he passed Amy by the door. She was standing with her friend Glenys and their boyfriends.

In spite of what he'd promised Val, he was too angry to let it go.

'I don't know why you had to be so nasty,' he hissed. 'Can't you just let the poor girl be?'

'Hang on a minute—' Tony started to say, but Tom had already walked away.

'What was all that about?' Glenys asked.

'I have no idea.' Amy stared after Tom, scarcely able to take in what had just happened.

'Ill-mannered swine,' Giles muttered. 'I've a good mind to report him.'

'I'm sure it was just a misunderstanding.'

'I'm not so sure,' Glenys said. 'If looks could kill!'

'Forget about him. Come and have a dance.'

Tony went to grab her hand, but Amy pulled away.

'I've had enough dancing for one night, thanks. I think I'll go home.'

'But it's still early! The party's only just getting started,' Tony protested.

'And I'm already too tired.' Amy stifled a yawn with the back of her hand. 'I didn't get much sleep last night, what with all the excitement over the bomb.'

She said her goodbyes and left. Tony followed her outside.

'Can I see you again?' he asked. 'Perhaps I could take you out one night—'

'I don't think so,' Amy cut him off. 'But thank you for a lovely evening.'

She walked away, leaving him speechless. From the look of surprise on his face, she didn't think Tony Walsh got turned down by many girls.

It was a cold, frosty night, and the waxing moon cast a silvery light as Amy made her way back to the nurses' home.

Her mind was all over the place, still trying to work out why Tom had spoken to her the way he had. She'd done nothing to deserve it, she was sure. If anyone should be upset, it was her. He hadn't even told her he had a girlfriend!

She climbed the stairs wearily to her room, already looking forward to an early night. But as she opened her door she was surprised to find a note pushed underneath it.

It was from the Home Sister, asking her to call in to her flat when she returned.

Amy was surprised. Miss Callaghan the Home Sister kept strict office hours and did not appreciate being disturbed in her private quarters. What could be so important that she would disturb her beauty sleep? Amy hurried back downstairs.

The Home Sister was still in her uniform when she answered the door, her face a picture of concern.

'Ah, Metcalfe. You'd better come into the office.' She plucked a jangling bunch of keys from her leather belt.

'What is it, Sister? What's wrong?'

Miss Callaghan hesitated for a moment, as if unsure whether to tell her. Then she said,

'I'm afraid I have some rather distressing news for you. It's about your mother . . .'

Chapter Thirty-Four

'I should have done something.'

Dora stood in the hospital corridor outside Maggie
Metcalfe's room. On the other side of the door, the poor
woman was fighting for her life. But from the carefully neutral looks of the nurses as they went in and out of the room,
Dora could tell it was a fight she was destined to lose.

'You mustn't blame yourself,' Eileen Kelly said. 'There
was nothing you could do.'

'She could have had treatment.'

'She's been dying for years, Dora. She knew that, and so
did the rest of us.'

'But she might have had a few more months,' Dora
insisted. 'Or at least I could have made her comfortable.'

She pressed her hand against the door, peering through
the small pane of glass. Amy sat by her mother's bedside,
her head bowed, holding her hand.

At least she was peaceful now, thanks to the morphine
she had been given. But Dora was haunted by the thought
of the terrible pain she must have been in.

She was still trying to fathom what had happened.
The first she'd heard was when the district nursing supervisor telephoned that evening to tell her Maggie had been
taken to hospital. Apparently her husband had found her

sprawled in the hall when he got up that morning. He had no idea why she had come downstairs, or so he said.

Dora had rushed to the hospital where she'd found Eileen Kelly waiting for her.

There was no sign of Malcolm Metcalfe.

'I shouldn't have taken no for an answer,' she said again. 'I should have forced her to let me help her, battered down her door if I had to—'

'Don't,' Eileen cut her off. 'If you want to be angry at anyone, it should be that old man of hers.'

'Where is he?'

Eileen shrugged. 'Your guess is as good as mine. He probably had "important parish business" to attend to.' Her mouth twisted mockingly over the words.

'What could be more important than being here, looking after his wife and daughter?'

Dora looked again at Amy, sitting at her mother's bedside. Her heart went out to the poor little mite. 'It ain't right that she's got to go through this alone. She needs her father with her.'

'Some father he's been!' Eileen snorted. 'She's better off without him if you ask me.'

She turned to Dora. 'Look, why don't you go and have a break?' she said. 'You look like you could do with one. I can keep an eye on Maggie.'

Dora read the unspoken message in the big woman's eyes. Eileen wanted some time to grieve in private.

'I'll go up to the children's ward and talk to the sister,' she said. 'I'm sure she's wondering what's happened to young Amy.'

It took her a while to locate the children's ward in the main building. It certainly wasn't in the same place it had been when she worked there. But then, very little about the building was the same. Everything had changed after the war, when the National Health Service took over.

There was a time when she could have found her way around the warren of passageways with her eyes closed. Now she had to stop every few minutes to consult the signposts, which seemed to send her in circles.

Finally, she found it. Like the rest of the building, it was nothing like the children's ward she'd known as a student. But for once, Dora could see an improvement.

The ward was a warm welcoming place, with children's pictures on the walls and a place for toys in the corner. It was just past eight o'clock in the evening, and the nurses were getting ready to hand over to the night shift. Dora wondered if the ward sister would still be there.

'Mum!' Her daughter Winnie came rushing towards her as she walked through the doors. 'What are you doing here? You can't just wander in and out, you'll get into trouble.'

'Keep your hair on, this ain't a social call. It's Miss Spencer I'm here to see. Is she here?'

'I'll fetch her—'

'Did I hear my name?'

And there she was. The ward sister, Miss Elizabeth Spencer. Medium height, attractive, with a freckled face and warm green eyes.

'Miss Spencer?'

'That's right.' The ward sister looked a little guarded,

Dora thought. Probably dismayed to see a district nurse on her ward. 'Can I help you?'

'It's about Amy Metcalfe. She's a pro on this ward.'

'Oh yes, of course. I heard that her mother had been taken ill. How is she?'

Dora lowered her gaze. 'Not well, I'm afraid.'

She didn't need to spell it out. She could see from her face that Miss Spencer understood her meaning.

'I'm sorry to hear that. Poor Nurse Metcalfe. How is she?'

'In bits, as you can imagine.'

'Of course.' Miss Spencer nodded thoughtfully. 'Is there anything I can do?'

'Amy will want to spend as much time as she can with her mother, if that's all right?'

'Of course. Tell her to take all the time she needs.'

'Thank you. I'm sure she'll appreciate it.' Dora paused again. 'I suppose I should speak to Matron, too—'

'Leave it with me. I'll deal with her.'

There was something about the firm way she said it that told Dora all she needed to know about Miss Spencer's relationship with the formidable matron.

'Thank you.'

As Dora turned to go, Miss Spencer said, 'Does Amy – Nurse Metcalfe – have anyone with her?'

'Her mother's best friend,' she said.

'And her father?'

Dora frowned. 'I daresay he'll turn up eventually.' She found it hard to keep the anger out of her voice.

'She shouldn't be alone at a time like this. I'll talk to the

Home Sister, see if we can arrange for her friends to keep her company. If you think that would help?'

'I reckon she'd like that.'

Winnie was right, Dora thought. Miss Spencer was a diamond, all right.

As she took her leave, the ward sister said, 'Mrs Riley?'

'Yes?'

'Give our regards to Amy, won't you? Tell her we're all thinking about her.'

'I will.'

Dora headed towards the doors. It wasn't until she was in the lift heading back down to the cardiac unit that she realised she hadn't told Miss Spencer who she was.

So how did she know her name?

Chapter Thirty-Five

The hospital at night seemed like the loneliest place in the world.

The hustle and bustle of the day had faded away, replaced by dimly lit wards, and the soft footsteps and whispered voices of the night staff.

Amy sat at her mother's bedside, listening to her ragged breathing. From time to time the door would open and the night nurse would creep in to check on her. At first she'd tried to insist Amy went home, but now she'd given up and ignored her presence completely as she silently checked Maggie Metcalfe's TPRs and filled in the chart at the bottom of her bed.

Aunt Eileen had stayed for as long as she could, and then Sonia and Mary from her set had dropped in when their duty finished and sat with her for a while. It was kind of them, but Amy barely noticed their company.

Her father had not come.

Amy had given up expecting him. At first she'd made excuses for him, just as her mother would have. Then she'd been disappointed, then angry. But as the hours passed, her emotions left her.

She would not waste her precious energy on a man who didn't deserve it.

Her mother's breathing halted and Amy leaned forward, touching her hand. Her skin felt papery under her fingers.

'Mum?'

Her mother's breathing steadied again, her chest rising and falling, and Amy let out a sigh of relief.

She knew that the end was coming. She could see it in the faces of the nurses as they came and went. The doctor had explained it all to Amy and Aunt Eileen, as if they didn't know. As if they hadn't been preparing for this moment for their whole lives.

But still Amy prayed it wouldn't happen.

'Just give me a few more days with her,' she begged silently. 'Give me the chance to tell her how much I love her.'

She was so tired. Like most of the other nurses, she had barely managed to sleep the previous night because of the bomb alert. The warmth of the room made her feel sluggish and weary, and she could feel her eyelids growing heavier. But she dared not close them. She would not leave her mother alone, not now.

She hadn't realised she'd drifted off to sleep, until she was woken by the sound of the door opening.

She shot awake and sat bolt upright. 'Father—'

'It's only me, Nurse Metcalfe.'

Miss Spencer stood in the doorway, still dressed in her uniform.

'It's all right, my dear, please don't get up.' The ward sister waved her hand as Amy automatically got to her feet. 'I just came to see how you were getting on.' Her gaze drifted to Amy's mother.

'It won't be long now,' Amy said. 'A few hours, the doctor said.'

'May I sit with you? I won't stay if you'd rather be alone.'

'No, please.' Amy moved her chair so that Miss Spencer could bring another one next to her.

'You look exhausted, my dear. Have you eaten?' Amy shook her head. 'You must be hungry. I can stay here with your mother if you want to go to the canteen?'

'I don't want to leave her.' She looked at the cup of tea going cold on the bedside table. It was the third she had not touched. 'I don't think I could eat, anyway.'

'I understand.' Miss Spencer's voice was gentle.

They sat in silence, but Amy didn't feel awkward. Liz Spencer's presence was so comforting without being intrusive. Amy thought about how often she must have sat like this with distraught parents on the children's ward.

'You mentioned your father?' the ward sister broke the silence. 'Were you expecting him?'

'Not any more.' She couldn't keep the bitterness out of her voice. 'He hasn't been to see her.'

'Ah.' Miss Spencer paused. 'Perhaps he can't bring himself to see her like this? Grief does make people behave in strange ways—'

Or perhaps he just doesn't care, Amy thought. But she said nothing.

The silence lengthened, broken only by the steady tick of the clock on the wall and the sound of the drip.

'Tell me about her,' Miss Spencer said.

Amy glanced across at her, surprised by the question. No one else had really known what to say. Her friends had tried to distract her with chatter and gossip, when that was the last thing she needed. And Aunt Eileen had been so distraught that Amy had ended up comforting her.

But there was no awkwardness with Miss Spencer. She was warm and kind and she talked naturally about her mother, not in the hushed, deathbed tones that Amy had come to dread.

'What do you want to know?' she asked.

'Anything you want to tell me. Where did she come from? What was she like?'

Amy thought about it for a moment. 'Her name was Margaret Bradshaw and she grew up in Bethnal Green,' she said. 'She worked as a seamstress until she got married. She told me she'd always wanted to work in an office, but she had to leave school when she was thirteen because her father died in the Great War and she had to support her mother and brothers. She always said she wasn't bright, but she was. She loved reading. *Jane Eyre* was her favourite book. And she liked flowers, especially chrysanthemums.' She smiled at the memory. 'And she was a good cook. The house always smelled of baking when I came home from school.'

'She sounds wonderful.'

'Oh, she was. It was hard for her, because she was sick so often. She'd had scarlet fever when she was a child, and that had left her with a weak heart.' Amy looked at the frail figure in the bed. 'But there was nothing weak about her heart as far as I could see. She was the kindest person I've ever met. Everyone loved her.'

Everyone except her own husband, she thought bitterly.

It hurt her to think how cruel and offhand Malcolm Metcalfe had been to her. Amy could barely remember him giving her a kind word.

'Was she a good mother?'

Amy pictured her mother's face, glowing with pride on the day Amy had passed PTS.

'She was the best mother anyone could have wanted,' she said.

'I'm glad.' Miss Spencer's voice was hushed.

'I just wish I'd done more to help her,' Amy said. She looked at her mother, her face as ashen as the pillow she rested on. 'I was so used to her being sick, I never really thought—' She paused. 'She just got on with things, you see. She never complained, or took the time to rest. And I just took it for granted that she'd be all right.'

If anything happens to your mother, it will be all your fault.

She thought about the Christmas dinner that her mother had served up with such pride. Was it that effort that had killed her? Amy couldn't be sure. She felt racked with guilt that her mother might have died because of her.

'What if I could have stopped it?' she blurted out.

'You mustn't think like that,' Miss Spencer took her hand. 'Your mother had been ill for years; this could have happened at any time.'

'But I'm supposed to be a nurse, aren't I? Why didn't I see how much she was struggling?'

'You did your best,' Miss Spencer said. 'You must never blame yourself, Amy. Look at me.' She cupped Amy's chin in her hands, turning her face towards her. Her hazel eyes were serious. 'If anything, you were the one who kept her alive this long. Your mother was very sick. But it was her love for you that gave her a reason to live. You were the light of her life.'

'That's what she used to say to me.' Amy smiled through her tears. '"You are my sunshine." That's what she always sang to me.'

'And that's what you were.' The ward sister's eyes glittered with tears. 'You were the best thing that could have happened to her, Amy. Please believe me when I tell you that.'

Amy nodded, taking in her words. Now she understood why the parents of the children on the ward were always so reassured after speaking to her. Miss Spencer was so warm and kind; listening to her made Amy feel safe. Her world might be collapsing around her, but at least she had Miss Spencer at her side, helping to hold her up.

They sat in silence, side by side. Amy felt weariness overcoming her again and fought to stay awake. The inside of her eyelids felt gritty and sore.

'Why don't you close your eyes?' Miss Spencer said softly. 'I'll watch over your mother.'

'No,' Amy said. 'I need to stay awake. Just in case—'

'I'll wake you if there's any change.' Her voice was lullingly soft. 'Your mother will still be here when you wake up, I promise you.'

'I'm all right, really.' But even as she said it, Amy could feel her body growing heavier, drifting towards sleep. Her head lolled and found something soft. Miss Spencer's shoulder. Amy wanted to sit up but she couldn't; her body felt too heavy. She breathed in, comforted by the clean starched smell of Miss Spencer's uniform. A moment later, she thought she felt an arm around her shoulders, pulling her close.

'You are my sunshine, my only sunshine . . .'

Someone was singing softly. Her mother.

'Mum?' she murmured.

But the voice just went on singing, lulling her to sleep.

Chapter Thirty-Six

Maggie Metcalfe died at twenty minutes to six in the morning of the twenty-seventh of December.

Tom knew the precise time because he was the one who was sent to remove her body to the mortuary.

There were still decorations festooning the corridor outside the private room. They seemed horribly incongruous, given what had happened. And even more so, considering the young girl who sat forlornly amid the brightly coloured paper chains.

Tom stopped at the sight of Amy Metcalfe sitting in the corridor ahead of him. No one had told him she would be here.

He tried to reverse the trolley silently out of sight, cursing under his breath at the squeaky front wheel. The sound made her look up and their eyes met.

'I'm sorry,' Tom mumbled. 'I – didn't know you'd be here. I'll come back later—'

'No, it's all right. I know you've got a job to do.' She stood up. 'I should be going back to the nurses' home anyway.' She looked down at herself. She was still wearing the green flowery dress she'd worn at the dance.

'Have you been here all this time?' Tom asked.

She nodded. 'I didn't want to leave her, in case—' She

broke off, swallowing hard. 'I wanted to be with her,' she said quietly.

'Of course.'

'Miss Spencer was here, too. She sat with me while I slept for a while.' She looked around, vaguely. 'She left a little while ago. I hope she manages to get some rest before she goes back on duty—'

'I'm sure she'll be fine.'

Better than you, at any rate, Tom thought. Poor Amy looked ashen, her eyes bruised from lack of sleep.

They were both silent for a moment, neither of them quite knowing what to do.

'I'm sorry,' Tom said again, knowing the words weren't enough.

'At least she didn't suffer, in the end. The nurses were so good, they kept her comfortable, made sure she wasn't in any pain—'

She broke off and suddenly she was sobbing, her hands over her face as if she could hold back her emotions.

'I'm sorry,' she said through her tears, 'I promised myself I wouldn't cry. I wanted to be strong for Mum . . .'

'Come here.' Before he knew what he was doing, Tom had taken her in his arms, pulling her close to him. They stood for a long time, alone in the empty, dimly lit corridor. It felt as if they were the only ones in the whole hospital.

'I know I shouldn't be upset,' Amy wept into his shoulder. 'I knew it was going to happen, and at least she's at peace now. I just – I don't know what I'm going to do without her.'

Tom said nothing, his arms tightening around her. He knew there was nothing he could say or do to take away her pain.

Finally she pulled away from him, drying her tears with her fingers.

'I'm sorry,' she said again, with a watery smile. 'I've made your overall all wet with my crying.'

'It'll dry.'

She reached up to pat the damp spot, then suddenly she seemed to realise what she was doing and stepped away, putting distance between them.

'I need to pull myself together,' she said, bracing herself. 'I'll go back to the nurses' home and get changed, then . . .' Her voice faded and a bewildered look came into her eyes. It was as if she'd forgotten how to be.

'I'll walk you back,' Tom offered.

'Really, there's no need.'

'I'm not letting you walk by yourself. Wait there a minute.'

He left her sitting in the corridor while he arranged for one of the other porters to collect Maggie Metcalfe.

Amy was still waiting when he returned. Tom was surprised, but she looked so lost, he realised she had no idea what to do.

'Here.' He took off his brown overall and draped it carefully around her shoulders. 'It's bitterly cold outside.'

'Is it?' Amy blinked at him. Bless her, she barely knew what day it was, let alone the time of year.

They walked back to the nurses' home in silence. Last night's rain had hardened into ice, making it slippery underfoot. Tom resisted the urge to put his arm around Amy to steady her.

They rounded the corner of the main hospital building and headed down the gravel path until the lights of the nurses' home came into view ahead of them.

'This is where I'll leave,' Tom said. 'You can make your own way from here.'

'Aren't you coming to the door?' Amy asked.

He shook his head. 'You don't want your friends seeing us, do you?' He fought to keep the bitterness out of his voice.

'Why not?' She looked genuinely puzzled.

Poor girl, Tom thought. *She really must be in a state.*

Chapter Thirty-Seven

Rob was disappointed not to see Liz on the ward when he called to do his rounds that morning.

Staff Nurse Clackett was there to greet him instead, standing at the door with a retinue of nurses, all beautifully turned out like a row of soldiers waiting for inspection. But Rob looked straight past them, his gaze searching for Liz.

'Is Miss Spencer not here?' He tried to sound casual but he could hear the disappointment in his own voice.

'Sister is indisposed and will be in later, Mr Bryant,' Nurse Clackett said. 'But if there's a particular case you wish to discuss with her, I'm sure I'll be able to—'

'Indisposed?' Rob cut her off. 'Is she ill?'

'Not as far as I'm aware,' the senior staff nurse replied, bristling a little at the interruption. 'She spent the night sitting with a young student who has just lost her mother.'

'Oh, I'm sorry to hear that. Which student was it?'

'Nurse Metcalfe, sir. She has been given some time off, and I understand Miss Spencer has returned home to rest—'

'Here I am.'

Liz Spencer appeared behind them, smoothing down her navy-blue uniform.

'Sister!' Miss Clackett looked put out at the sudden turn of events. 'We weren't expecting you until later?'

'Yes, well, I'm here now.'

The staff nurse peered at her closely. 'Are you sure you're well rested, Sister?'

'Very well rested, thank you.' Liz Spencer smiled, all brisk efficiency. But Rob could see the lines of strain around her eyes as she turned to face him. 'I'm sorry I wasn't here when you arrived, Mr Bryant. Are you ready to do your rounds?'

As they made their way down the ward to his first patient, Rob said, 'I understand you've had quite a night of it?'

'Nurse Clackett told you what happened?'

'Yes, she did. How is young Nurse Metcalfe?'

'Heartbroken, as you can imagine. I sent her home for a few days.'

'Quite right,' Rob nodded. 'She needs to be with her family at a time like this.'

'Yes,' Liz said. 'Yes, she does.'

There was something about the way she said it that made Rob turn to look at her.

'Are you sure you're all right, Miss Spencer?' he asked.

Liz looked back at him, and he caught a flash of something in her eyes, quickly masked.

'Of course,' she said. 'Why shouldn't I be?'

Chapter Thirty-Eight

'Over my dead body!'

Stanley McBride had been sitting at the kitchen table waiting for his breakfast when the postman brought the letter. He always looked forward to his wife's Saturday morning fry-up while Val minded the shop. But one look at his name typed on the thick brown envelope and he'd pushed the plate away, his appetite for bacon, eggs and fried bread forgotten.

Another solicitor's letter. He'd done a good job of ignoring them so far, stuffing them in the sideboard drawer so he didn't have to think about them. Somehow in the back of his mind he'd let himself believe that if he didn't reply, didn't sign the forms they kept sending, he could push the problem away.

Anyway, he'd reasoned, the first of January was a long time away. Something would come up before then, he was sure of it.

But this letter was not like the others. The others had been quietly cajoling, but this one was stern and official. It was full of fancy legal words, but Stan understood the meaning very clearly indeed.

On the first of January, one way or another he was going to lose his shop.

'How dare they?' he roared, slamming the letter down on the table so hard the cutlery rattled and his teacup jumped in its saucer.

'Calm down and eat your breakfast, Stan. You'll give yourself indigestion,' his wife said mildly, reaching for the teapot.

'How am I supposed to eat?' Stan stared at her. 'Are you stupid, woman? Don't you understand what's going on?'

'Oh, I understand all right.' Lillian McBride filled her cup. 'There's no need to shout.'

'I'll bloody well shout if I want to!' Stan picked up the letter, stared at the envelope then slapped it down again. 'It ain't right. Why should that little swine just come in and take everything I've worked for all these years?'

'What's going on?' Val appeared in the doorway, dressed in her overall. 'The customers can hear you downstairs.'

'I'll tell you what's going on!' Stan snatched up the letter again and waved it at her. 'I'm getting thrown out of my shop, that's what's going on!'

'But it ain't your shop, is it?' Val pointed out. 'It belongs to Tom.'

Stan stared at her fat, bland face. Sometimes he wondered if his daughter was a bit simple. But then other times he looked at her sly little eyes and thought she knew exactly what was going on.

'It's been my shop for the past fourteen years! There'd be nothing left if it weren't for me. I'm the one who's put in the hard work all these years. It should be my son who inherits this place, not him.'

'Tom's done his fair share,' Val said. 'He's done a sight

more than Eric, anyway. *He* doesn't care about this place. Where is he now? Still in bed, I s'pose?'

'He needs his rest,' Lillian defended him automatically.

'He's bone idle,' Val replied.

She wasn't wrong, Stan had to admit. Much as he loved his son, Eric drove him mad sometimes.

He'd hoped he might show a bit more interest in the shop, but all Eric cared about was motorbikes and making trouble. When he wasn't out getting into fights, he was sleeping it off.

'I don't know what you're looking so smug about,' he said to his daughter. 'You'll be out on your ear just like the rest of us.'

'Oh, I'll be all right.'

Stan narrowed his eyes at her. Val looked pleased with herself, as if she had some little secret she wasn't telling him. It made him wonder what she and Tom had been cooking up together. She'd certainly always been very thick with him. Perhaps she wasn't as daft as he'd thought?

As if she knew what he was thinking, Val said, 'You know, you might not be in this mess if you'd been a bit nicer to Tom.'

'Nice to him? I've put a roof over his head for the past fourteen years, ain't I?'

'But when you think about it, it was always his roof, wasn't it?'

Stan looked at his daughter's innocently smiling face and felt his rage boiling up inside. But before it could explode, his wife cut in.

'Go back to the shop, Val. I daresay there are customers waiting to be served.'

Val plodded off downstairs, and Lillian turned to him.

'Surely if you don't sign the forms they can't do anything?'

'Don't be stupid!' Stan turned his anger on her. 'They don't need my signature any more, it says so in the letter.'

He stared at the pages of incomprehensible jargon. He was not an educated man and he didn't understand most of it, but he knew an ultimatum when he saw one.

He had just been putting off the inevitable. The shop rightly belonged to Tom, and had done since the day he turned eighteen. But now the solicitor had run out of patience, and they would be forced to hand over the premises on the first of January.

It was the twenty-seventh now. Less than a week, and it would all be over.

'Tom doesn't deserve this place,' he said out loud. 'It's mine, whatever the law says about it.'

'Quite right,' his wife agreed. 'You've put everything into running this shop.'

Stan had consulted a solicitor himself, but they'd only confirmed what he already knew. Legally, he did not have a leg to stand on. And all because he'd signed some stupid piece of paper fourteen years earlier.

He wished now he hadn't been so rash. But at the time he'd been desperate to get his hands on the shop.

Tom's parents' deaths couldn't have come at a better time for Stan McBride.

He'd always fancied himself as a businessman. After being declared unfit for military service on medical grounds, he'd spent the war ducking and diving and getting involved in various schemes and deals. He'd dabbled in the black market, fenced some stolen goods. Some of his business ventures had worked out, but most had been less successful.

By the time Hitler sent his doodlebugs over London, Stan was barely scratching a living. He'd joined the ARP, and he liked to tell people it was him who had helped dig his poor sister-in-law and her husband out of the rubble of that cinema on the night they were killed. But in truth, he'd been looting the place at the time. It was a good night for him, since he'd managed to snatch the takings from behind the counter while the other ARP men were busy trying to rescue the victims.

But that aside, he'd been on his uppers when Maurice and Peggy were killed. Violet had asked them to take the child, but Stan was more interested in the shop. It was a little goldmine, and there was the opportunity for someone as enterprising as him to make a bit more on the side.

He'd known it wouldn't be forever; God knows, Violet had reminded him enough times. Stan had signed the forms the solicitor had put in front of him, desperate to get his hands on the place. Tom's eighteenth birthday seemed a long way off; anything could happen before then.

And for once he'd managed to make a go of it. Stan felt a sense of pride every morning when he unlocked the doors and pulled out the awning. He'd even had his name put up over the door. Violet hadn't liked that, but what could she do about it? Possession was nine-tenths of the law, as Stan was fond of saying.

But it turned out that wasn't true. Not according to this solicitor's letter, anyway.

Because now he had to hand it all over to Tom Weaver.

Perhaps Val was right, he thought. Perhaps he should have been a bit nicer to his nephew. But he'd honestly never believed that this day would come. Stan McBride prided himself on his ability to dodge his way out of any situation. Blimey, he'd even managed to get out of fighting for his country, thanks to feigned mental instability.

But there was no getting out of this.

The thought of Tom's self-righteous face sent his blood boiling. He couldn't stand it.

'I'll burn this place down before I let him get his hands on it,' he declared, gripping his knife so tightly his knuckles turned white. It was all he could do not to stab it into the table.

'It might not come to that,' his wife said mildly.

Stan stared at her. She was buttering a piece of toast as calm as anything.

'Haven't you listened to a word I've been saying? We're going to lose our home and our livelihood!'

'And I've just said it might not come to that. Can you pass the marmalade, please?'

He snatched up the jar and slammed it down in front of her. 'What are you talking about?'

Lillian McBride gave a careless little shrug. 'Let's just say I've still got a card to play. And if I play it right we might not have to move out.'

'What card? What are you talking about?'

'You'll have to wait and find out, won't you?' Lillian pushed his plate back in front of him. 'Now eat your breakfast before it gets cold.'

Chapter Thirty-Nine

Violet was not surprised to see her sister.

As far as she could recall, Lillian McBride had not once paid her a visit since she'd moved down to Kent. And yet somehow as the year drew to an end, she'd had a feeling that was about to change.

She watched from the window as her sister marched down the path towards her cottage. She looked ready to do battle, her shoulders straight under her tightly buttoned coat, handbag tucked over her arm and face set in a pugnacious expression.

Violet wondered if Stan had sent her. It would be just typical of that crawling little coward to send his wife to plead for him. She had no idea what her sister had ever seen in him, although over the years she had watched Lillian becoming every bit as sneaky and conniving as her husband.

But she managed to keep her distaste to herself as she opened the door.

'Lillian,' she greeted her sister. 'What a pleasant surprise.'

'This isn't a social call,' Lillian snapped, marching past her without waiting to be invited.

'So I see,' Violet said tightly as she closed the door behind her. She followed her sister into the parlour. 'In that case, I don't suppose you'll want a cup of tea?'

'Of course I want tea!' Lillian took off her coat and thrust it at her. 'Do you think I'd come all this way and you not offer me anything to drink?' She looked at Violet scathingly. 'You've forgotten your manners.'

And you never had any, Violet thought as she went off to the kitchen to put the kettle on.

When she returned to the parlour with the tray, Lillian was standing at the mantelpiece, examining one of the Staffordshire figurines. She'd upturned it and was peering at the maker's mark on the bottom.

Wondering what it's worth, Violet thought. She'd only been gone five minutes and Lillian had probably put a value on everything in the room.

'Pretty, isn't it?' she said, putting the tray down with a clatter. Lillian jumped, the figurine nearly falling from her hands.

'You gave me a start,' she said accusingly.

'Sorry.' Violet glanced at Lillian's capacious handbag and wondered if her sister had slipped anything inside. She wouldn't have put anything past her.

She hated to admit it, but she sometimes felt ashamed of her sister. She had always been the odd one out, even when they were children. Violet was much closer to her middle sister Peggy, but Lillian was the youngest and had never been like them.

'So what's brought you all this way?' she asked as she poured the tea. *As if I didn't know*, she added silently.

'It's about the shop.'

'What about it?'

'You know very well what!' Lillian was instantly impatient. 'All this nonsense about us having to give it up. You've got to tell that solicitor to stop sending his nasty threatening letters. We've had enough of it.'

'He'll stop sending letters when you hand it over.'

Lillian huffed. 'Stan won't give it up, you know. And I don't see why he should.'

Violet stifled a sigh. She'd known it would come to this. Stan had been so keen to get his hands on the place, he couldn't sign the papers fast enough. The fool had probably never read any of them. Or if he had, he'd probably imagined he'd be able to wriggle out of whatever agreement he'd made.

He had no sense of honour, of what was right and wrong. And his wife was just as bad.

'It was in Peggy and Maurice's will. Your husband agreed to it . . .'

'But it's not fair!' Lillian whined. 'Stan's worked so hard to build up that business. It's a little goldmine.'

'And I've no doubt Stanley's made the most of it.'

Her sister's chin lifted defensively. 'And what's that supposed to mean?'

'I mean I daresay he's skimmed off a decent profit for himself. He's probably got quite a bit put by, hasn't he?'

'Are you accusing my Stan of being a thief?'

Her sister's outrage was so comical, Violet almost laughed. The whole world knew Stan McBride was a crook.

'Why don't we look over the books and find out?' she said.

They stared at each other for a moment. Lillian's lips were pressed together in a thin line, but she did not try to defend her husband any more, Violet noticed.

'I'm sorry, Lillian, but there is a legal agreement in place,' she said. 'The shop was left to Tom in his parents' will.'

'Yes, but that's not quite right, is it?'

Violet looked up sharply. 'What do you mean?'

'There's something you're not telling anyone, isn't there?'

An icy trickle ran down her spine. 'I don't know what you're talking about.'

'Oh, I think you do.' Lillian smiled. 'I'm not daft, Violet, even though you and Peggy always thought I was. I keep my eyes and ears open, you see. I notice things, things no one else might notice. I know you and Peggy had your little secrets.'

Violet stirred her tea, forcing herself to stay calm.

Lillian didn't know. She *couldn't* know. Surely if she had, she would have used it to her advantage by now?

'I don't want to cause any trouble,' Lillian was saying now, sounding innocent. 'Far be it from me to stir things up. Let bygones be bygones, that's what I say.'

'Then what do you want?' Violet asked in a low voice.

'I just want what's rightfully ours, that's all.' She looked up at Violet. 'And I want you to talk to that solicitor and tell him to stop sending those letters.'

'There's nothing I can do—'

'Oh, I think there is. And if you don't talk to him, then I will. I'm sure he'll see everything from my point of view once I've explained everything to him.'

'And what about Tom?' Violet asked.

'Oh, I don't know. He's your concern, not mine,' Lillian shrugged. 'Although I suppose he'll want to know what's going on,' she went on slowly, her face thoughtful. 'Perhaps I should explain everything to him, too? That would really set the cat among the pigeons, wouldn't it?'

Violet fought to keep her expression neutral, but her face must have given her away.

'You wouldn't like that, would you?' Lillian smirked. 'What's the matter? Are you worried your precious little nephew wouldn't think so highly of you if he found out what you'd done? I can't say I'm surprised. I wouldn't be happy if I found out what you'd been keeping from me. And you always were so fond of him,' she sighed.

She set down her cup. 'Don't worry, I won't say anything – yet. But secrets don't stay buried forever, Violet. Remember that.'

Chapter Forty

The funeral was held at St Luke's church, the day before New Year's Eve.

Dora went to pay her respects. She sat in the back pew, huddled in her best black coat, which was still no match for the chill inside the draughty church.

Malcolm Metcalfe conducted his wife's service in a flat voice, devoid of emotion. He might have been burying a stranger, from the perfunctory way he delivered the prayers.

Perhaps it was the only way he could keep his grief in check, Dora thought. But looking at Malcolm's expressionless face, she wondered if he was feeling anything at all.

But she mustn't judge, she told herself. Her work on the district had taught her that death affected different people in different ways. Some people fell apart immediately, others carried on for days or weeks before the shock hit them. Some were relieved, especially if their loved one had suffered for a long time. Some mourned, while others rejoiced for a life well lived. And some – especially the very elderly – simply gave up and died themselves.

She hoped her Nick might shed a few more tears than Malcolm Metcalfe when it was her time to go.

What am I saying? she thought. Nick would tear down

walls in his rage and grief. He certainly wouldn't be fit to stand up there in a pulpit, dry-eyed and stern.

By contrast, Maggie's best friend Eileen Kelly was crying her eyes out in the front row, her arms around Amy Metcalfe. While Eileen's big shoulders heaved, Amy sat very still, her eyes fixed on her father.

The poor girl, Dora thought. She hoped Malcolm Metcalfe showed a bit more warmth towards his daughter than he did to his wife. God knows, Amy looked as if she could do with some comfort. She seemed utterly lost. Eileen was doing her best to comfort her, but Dora could tell she only wanted her mum.

If only I could have done something.

The thought had been haunting her, ever since she was called to the hospital. The nursing supervisor had tried to reassure her that there was nothing she could have done, but Dora still blamed herself. She knew how ill poor Maggie was, she should have insisted on seeing her. She certainly shouldn't have let Malcolm Metcalfe keep her away.

She stared at him as he stood up there in the pulpit, intoning a prayer. Talk about holier than thou! It really made her wonder what had gone on behind the closed doors of that vicarage.

The door at the back of the church creaked open, and Dora looked around to see a woman slipping into the rear pew just across the aisle from her. It was Elizabeth Spencer, the ward sister.

Dora caught her eye and nodded. Miss Spencer flashed her a quick, nervous smile and then reached for her prayer book.

Dora watched her. The ward sister seemed ill at ease as she fumbled through the book, trying to find the right place. She wore a black coat over her navy-blue uniform, and she'd taken off her cap to reveal red-gold hair pinned at the nape of her neck. She had the kind of smooth, strawberry-blonde hair Dora had always envied, nothing like her own frizzy ginger curls.

There was something familiar about her, but Dora could not quite recall where she'd seen her before.

Elizabeth Spencer.

She tried the name out in her mind, attempting to jog her memory, but nothing came to her.

The service was brief, with no eulogy and only one very doleful hymn. Even the mourners looked confused as they were ushered out of the church.

Is that it? their faces seemed to say. It hardly seemed like a fitting send-off for someone as well loved as Maggie Metcalfe had been.

Dora caught up with Miss Spencer outside the church. It had started to rain and she had paused by the lych gate to open her umbrella.

'Miss Spencer?'

The nurse turned, and Dora thought she caught a fleeting look of panic on her face before she smiled.

'Hello again, Mrs Riley.'

'I didn't know you were going to be here?'

'I thought I'd pay my respects. And I wanted to make sure Amy was all right.'

'That's very thoughtful of you.'

They both looked over to where Amy stood outside the

church, Eileen Kelly's protective arm still around her slim shoulders. Her father was nowhere to be seen.

'How is she, do you think?' Miss Spencer asked.

'Still in shock, poor lamb. She was so close to her mum.'

'You know the family well?'

'Maggie and I worked together before I trained as a nurse.'

'I see.' Miss Spencer paused. 'Well, do give Amy my best wishes, won't you? Tell her we're all thinking of her.'

As she turned to walk away, Dora said,

'Aren't you going back to the house?'

Miss Spencer shook her head. 'I don't think it would be appropriate. I don't know the family very well, and I'm expected back at the Nightingale. I left my senior staff nurse holding the fort.'

'I'm going the same way as you. I'll walk with you.'

'Aren't you staying? I thought you knew the family.'

'I knew Maggie. I can't say I know him very well at all.' Dora glared at Malcolm Metcalfe, who had just emerged from the church. The less time she spent in his company, the better.

Maggie had never said anything, but Dora suspected he was not a good husband to her. She had never seen a bruise, and she doubted if Malcolm had ever raised his hand to his wife. But there were more ways to inflict cruelty on someone than with a beating. Just the fact that he would not allow his wife to have the treatment that might have prolonged her life told Dora everything she needed to know about him.

'Very well, we'll walk together.' Miss Spencer looked less than enthusiastic about the idea, Dora noticed.

They skirted the park in silence. Dora could never pass this part of Bethnal Green without thinking of Griffin Street, the cramped little terrace where she had grown up. It was long gone now, flattened by the Luftwaffe. Black and white prefabs had been put up where the street once stood, each with its own patch of garden.

'You don't seem very keen on Amy's father?' Miss Spencer observed.

'As I said, I don't know him. But I don't believe he's the pious man he makes out.'

They walked in silence for a while. Then Miss Spencer asked, 'Do you think he mistreats Amy?'

Dora thought about it. 'Let's just say I'm glad she's not living under his roof any more.'

'I see.'

They continued on. The rain fell steadily from the bleached grey sky, dripping off the bare branches of the trees.

'I have to ask,' Dora said. 'Have we met before?'

Miss Spencer looked startled. 'What makes you think that?'

'You just seem familiar, that's all. And the other day, when I came to the ward, you knew my name.'

'Of course, you're Winnie Riley's mother.' She said it as if it was the simplest thing in the world.

'Yes, but how did you know that? We don't look alike.' No one would ever imagine ginger-haired Dora and her tall, dark, willowy daughter were related. If she hadn't given birth to her and her twin brother Walter, she scarcely would have believed it herself.

'No, but Winnie often talks about her mother being a district nurse. So when I saw the two of you talking, I put two and two together.' She smiled. 'And you might not look alike, but you have a very similar manner.'

'That's true,' Dora conceded. Winnie definitely had her stubborn streak!

And yet . . .

'I'm sure we must have met before,' Dora insisted. 'Did you train at the Nightingale?'

'No, I trained at the City Hospital. I only came to the Nightingale to do midwifery.' They reached the corner and Miss Spencer stopped short. 'Well, this is where I leave you,' she said. Was it Dora's imagination, or did she sound relieved? 'It was nice meeting you again, Mrs Doyle.'

'Please, call me Dora.'

Miss Spencer smiled. 'And you must call me Liz.'

Liz. Liz Spencer.

It still didn't sound right.

She watched the ward sister walking away. She didn't care what Miss Spencer said about it, she was certain they had met before.

If only she could remember where . . .

Chapter Forty-One

'I'm so sorry for your loss, my dear.'

It was the hundredth time Amy had heard those words that day. She wanted to scream and howl, but all she could do was smile and proffer a plate of sandwiches.

They were at the vicarage after the funeral. A select number of people had been invited to pay their respects.

'She was such a kind person,' the woman went on. 'She'd do anything for anyone. I'm sure your father will miss her terribly.' She turned to look across the room. 'Look at him, poor man. Putting a brave face on.'

Amy followed the woman's gaze to where her father stood on the other side of the room, talking to the church-warden's wife. She'd laid her hand on his arm and Malcolm Metcalfe stared down on it with a fastidious expression.

It was all he could do not to shrink away, Amy thought. Her father hated to be touched.

But of course he wouldn't pull away because he knew that was not what was expected of him. Her father always did what was expected. It was the only reason they were here now, having this tea in the vicarage.

'How is he bearing up?' the woman asked Amy, full of concern.

'Well—'

'He was so brave, carrying out the service,' the woman rushed on, not waiting for an answer. She was in her sixties, with stiffly permed white hair and overly large false teeth. 'I don't know how he did it, I really don't.' She sighed. 'He was so devoted to his wife, poor man.'

Then why didn't he try to save her? Why didn't he come to the hospital when she was dying?

She had tried to speak to her father many times over the past few days, but every time she was met by a blank wall of silence, and any hope she might have had that this would bring them closer together had proved futile. Malcolm Metcalfe had seemed to go out of his way to avoid her since she'd returned to the vicarage. He'd spent most of his time locked in his study, or he'd found some reason to stay at the church until long after Amy had gone to bed. He certainly hadn't offered her any love or comfort.

Amy had started to wish she hadn't come home at all. She would have been better off at the nurses' home. At least she would have been among friends there. The vicarage had never felt like her home, and now without her mother's presence it seemed even more cold and oppressive.

She was about to open her mouth to tell the woman exactly how devoted her father had been when Auntie Eileen suddenly appeared at her side.

'There you are,' she said. 'You're supposed to be handing out those sandwiches, remember?'

Amy stared down at the tray in her hand. She'd forgotten she was holding it.

'Excuse us, won't you?' Without waiting for an answer,

Auntie Eileen grasped Amy firmly by the elbow and steered her away from the woman.

'Here, give me those.' She took the tray away from her and set it down on a table. 'You looked as if you were going to tip the lot over that woman's head!'

'I nearly did.' Amy shot the woman a look of dislike. 'She kept going on about my "poor father" and how heartbroken he must be.'

'Ah.'

'Heartbroken! He hasn't shed a single tear since Mum died.'

'You don't know that, love,' Eileen reasoned, but even she didn't sound convinced.

'You saw him during the funeral service. He looked bored. He didn't even bother to give Mum a eulogy.'

That had hurt her deeply, that her father couldn't even summon a few warm words for his own wife. Her mother deserved better than that.

'Perhaps he was worried he might not be able to get through it?'

'More like he didn't care.' Amy looked at her. 'Come on, Auntie Eileen. You know him better than that.'

Eileen sighed. 'You're right,' she said. 'But I do think you should try and make peace with him. You've barely spoken to him since your mum died.'

'I can't.' Amy shook her head. 'I can't forgive him for not being there.'

Not just for her mother, but for herself. She had been so alone and frightened in those few final hours, and she'd desperately needed someone to comfort her. But as it was, she'd had more comfort from Miss Spencer than she'd had from her own father.

'I know, love. But it's what your mother would have wanted.'

She was right, Amy thought. All Maggie Metcalfe had ever wanted was a happy home and a family. She wouldn't have wanted to see Amy estranged from her father.

'He's a complicated man,' she'd once told Amy. 'And it's hard to make other people happy when you're so unhappy yourself.'

And yet she'd managed it. Her mother always put on a cheerful face, but Amy knew she didn't have an easy life with Malcolm Metcalfe.

Finally, when all the tea had been drunk and the sandwiches eaten, the guests began to go home.

Finally, it was over. Auntie Eileen was the last to leave.

'Now, don't forget I'm always here if you need me,' she sniffed back her tears as she took her leave on the doorstep. 'I know your mum would have wanted me to keep an eye on you.'

'Thank you.'

'I mean it, love.' Auntie Eileen grasped her hands. 'Promise me you'll let me know if you ever need anything?'

'I will, Auntie Eileen. I promise.'

'Bless you.' Eileen Kelly reached out to stroke Amy's cheek lovingly. Her own face was blotchy and ravaged by tears. 'You were the light of your mum's life, you know. I think sometimes if it hadn't been for you—'

She broke off, tears spilling down her cheeks.

'Anyway, I mustn't keep on,' she said, dashing them

away with the back of her hand. 'As I said, you know where to find me if you need anything.' She lowered her voice. 'Look after yourself, love.'

She shot a quick glance over Amy's shoulder, and then she was gone.

Amy closed the door and leaned against it with a sigh. She had been looking forward to the guests going home, but now the vicarage seemed hollow and full of shadows. Amy felt a pang as she realised she would never again walk in and call out for her mother, then hear her cheery voice in response.

Her shoes squeaked loudly on the polished parquet. She knew her mother had never liked the house, although she'd done her best to hide it. Now she understood why. The oppressive atmosphere seemed to weigh down on Amy's shoulders, making her feel heavy.

The chenille-topped dining table was littered with the remains of the tea. Amy began to clear everything away, knowing how much her father detested mess.

There was no sign of him in the house. His study door was closed as usual, and she wondered if he'd retreated there. She remembered how many evenings she and her mother had spent alone while he was locked away, preparing a sermon or working on parish business. Not that either of them minded; Amy always preferred it when it was just the two of them. They could talk and laugh without Malcolm Metcalfe's disapproving presence looming over them.

She was in the kitchen washing up the dishes at the sink when he finally appeared again.

Amy felt the warning prickle on the back of her neck before she turned around and saw him standing in the doorway watching her, a stony expression on his face.

'I've nearly finished clearing this lot up,' she said, her voice light as she turned back to the dishes. 'Then I can make you something to eat, if you like?'

'I'm not hungry. And you can leave those.' He nodded to the dishes stacked on the draining board.

Amy frowned. 'But you don't like things left lying around.'

'I've engaged a housekeeper. She's starting in the morning. They can wait until then.'

'A housekeeper?'

'I'll need someone to keep this place in order now your mother's gone. Which reminds me, I've packed up everything you left behind in your room. You can take it all with you when you go.'

Amy stared at him, scarcely able to believe what she was hearing.

'You – you're throwing me out?'

'As I said, the housekeeper will be here in the morning. She'll need that room.'

'Can't she sleep in one of the other bedrooms?'

'That's the room I've chosen for her.' He stared back at Amy, as if it was the simplest thing in the world.

'But where will I sleep?'

'You don't live here any more.'

'But this is my home!'

'I don't want you here.'

'But why? What have I done?'

This wasn't happening. It couldn't be. She stared at her father's impassive face, searching for clues.

Amy stared at him, hardly able to take in what he was saying. This was utter madness. But her father was no madman. He had the cold, implacable look of someone who knew exactly what they were saying.

This is the day of my mother's funeral. The thought came into her mind. *We only buried her a few hours ago.*

'You can't do this,' she said. 'What would Mum say?'

'Your mother is gone,' he said flatly. 'And I want you to go too. You're no longer welcome in this house.'

He turned on his heel and started to walk away. Amy followed him to the kitchen door.

'Why are you doing this?' she called after him. 'You've got to give me a reason. You can't just throw out your own daughter—'

The slam of his study door reverberated through the house, drowning out her words.

Chapter Forty-Two

It took Amy a while to drag her suitcases through the rain to the narrow terraced street where the Kellys lived.

Eileen Kelly looked surprised when she answered the door.

'Hello love, I didn't expect to see you. Is everything all—' Her gaze dropped to the suitcases at Amy's feet. 'What's happened?'

'Father's thrown me out.'

'He what?'

'He says I'm not welcome there any more. That it's not my home.'

Suddenly the tears she had been holding in since she'd left the vicarage began to flow, mingling with the rain that dripped from her hair.

Auntie Eileen stared at her for a moment.

'You'd better come in,' she said.

The Kellys' house was one of the few old dockers' cottages that had survived the war. There was a tiny parlour at the front and a passageway leading to a kitchen and scullery. It was humble, but warm and welcoming after the chilly atmosphere of the vicarage.

'Derek's on nights and the kids are out, so we've got the place to ourselves,' Auntie Eileen said as she led the way down the passage. 'Here, let's get your coat off. You poor thing, you're soaked to the skin. Now go through to the kitchen, it's warmer in there. I'll hang this up to dry, shall I?'

Amy sat down at the Formica-topped kitchen table and watched as Auntie Eileen bustled around, setting up the clothes horse in front of the gas fire and draping her coat over it.

'Here we are.' She set a cup of tea down on the table in front of Amy. 'Can I get you something to eat? I've got some pie left over from Derek's tea—'

'No, thank you. I'm not hungry.'

Eileen sat down opposite her, a cup in front of her. 'Right,' she said. 'What's all this about, then?'

She listened carefully, her face creasing with gentle concern as Amy told her what had happened at the vicarage.

'And that was all he said, was it?' she said, when Amy had finished. 'Nothing else?'

Amy frowned. 'What else could he say?'

Auntie Eileen didn't reply as she spooned sugar into her cup and stirred it.

'Perhaps he spoke without thinking?' she said at last. 'People can say all sorts of things when they're upset—'

'He wasn't upset,' Amy said. 'And you know my father, he never does anything without thinking.' She shook her head. 'No, this was calculated. As if he'd been waiting to say it for a long time. But why choose the day of Mum's funeral? It would break her heart if she knew.'

'Perhaps that's why he did it?'

'What do you mean?'

257

Auntie Eileen looked down at the spoon she was twirling in her cup. Then she took a deep breath and looked Amy in the eye.

'I've not said anything before out of respect for your mother. But the truth is, your father is a very cruel man. He was unkind to your mother for years, but she learned to put up with it. God knows why, but she did. I think she stopped caring about herself in the end. But there was someone she cared about very much.'

'Me,' Amy said dully.

'You were the only thing that kept her going. And your father knew it. She's safe now, out of his reach. But I wonder if he was trying to hurt her by hurting you?'

Amy thought about it. It was one way of explaining her father's behaviour.

Auntie Eileen was right; he had always been cruel to her mother. He went out of his way to hurt her every chance he took. And poor, gentle Maggie had taken it.

'Why did he hate her so much?' she asked.

'I don't know the answer to that, love,' Auntie Eileen sighed. 'If you ask me, he didn't really want to marry her.'

'Then why did he?'

'Because he thought it would be good for his career, I suppose. Your father's an ambitious man, he probably thought he had a better chance of getting his own parish if he was married. But he had no interest in having a wife, especially not your mother. He despised her. Thought she was beneath him.'

Her words came as a shock to Amy, even though she knew they were true. How many times had she seen her father belittle her mother? He mocked her poor background and lack of education, dismissed her tastes as 'vulgar'. He took pleasure in humiliating her, in front of people and in private. In the end her mother had rarely expressed an opinion of her own.

'She should have left him,' she said.

Auntie Eileen laughed. 'If I had a penny for every time I'd told her that, I'd be a rich woman! But your mother believed in those vows she took. For better or for worse, God help her. She tried to make the best of her marriage in any way she could. And then you came along, and she knew she could never leave.'

'So it was my fault?'

'No!' Auntie Eileen reached across the table for her hand. 'Like I said, you were the light of her life, her little miracle. She didn't think she'd be able to have you, you see, on account of her weak heart. From the moment she held you in her arms, you were her whole world.' She smiled fondly at the memory. 'She poured every bit of love she had into you. But of course, your father didn't like that. He might not have cared for your mother, but he was bitterly jealous of you.'

Amy remembered her father's cold fury whenever he found them laughing together. He'd always resented their closeness.

But it didn't have to be that way. If only he hadn't set himself apart from them, they could have been a real family.

'It might have been better for her if I hadn't been born,' she said.

'You must never think that.' Eileen's plump hand

squeezed hers. 'You don't know what your mother went through to have you. You were her whole world and she would have gone to the ends of the earth for you. She would have made a deal with the devil himself, I reckon.'

There was something about the way she said it that made Amy suddenly wary.

'You would tell me, wouldn't you? If there was anything I should know?'

'There's nothing you should know, I promise.' Eileen slowly withdrew her hand from hers. 'Now drink your tea, it'll warm you up.'

Eileen put Amy to sleep in her own bed. She had wanted to go back to the nurses' home, but the poor love was too exhausted to move. Derek was on nights, so Eileen decided she would share with her youngest, Betty.

She tucked Amy in and stood for a moment, watching her. It was a relief that she was finally asleep. She wasn't sure how much longer she could go on lying to the poor girl's face.

Eileen went downstairs to the parlour and helped herself to a nip of brandy. She was glad her old man wasn't there to see it. She didn't know what Derek would have made of her drinking, but she needed something to steady her nerves.

Damn Malcolm Metcalfe! She might have known the cruel swine would pull a trick like that. And after everything Maggie had put up with, too.

She would have made a deal with the devil himself, I reckon.

And she had, hadn't she? Eileen remembered her friend

sitting at her kitchen table, in the very same spot Amy had sat tonight, breaking her heart.

Poor, foolish Maggie, always looking for love and always being let down.

Eileen should never have allowed her to marry Malcolm Metcalfe. Some friend she was! If she'd known then how it would all turn out, she would have stood up and stopped that wedding before Maggie had had the chance to make the biggest mistake of her life.

No, not the biggest. She'd made another decision a few years later that had changed the course of her life.

And they had all been living a lie ever since.

Eileen took a gulp of her drink and stared up at the ceiling, where Amy slept.

She thought about the letter Maggie had given her, weeks before she'd died.

'I want you to give this to Amy,' she'd said. 'When I'm gone.'

At the time, Eileen hadn't wanted to take it, hadn't even wanted to think about it. 'Don't talk rot,' she'd said. 'You'll outlive us all.'

'You know that ain't true.' Maggie had pressed the letter into her hand. 'Take it, please. And promise me you'll give it to her. When the time comes.'

Eileen had taken the envelope reluctantly. 'What does it say, anyway?'

'Everything.'

Eileen looked up sharply at her friend. 'Maggie, no!'

'She needs to know, Eileen.'

'Then I'll tell her.'

261

Maggie shook her head. 'She needs to hear it from me. God knows, I never wanted to lie to her. I've kept too many secrets.'

Eileen took another steadying gulp of her drink. Her friend was in a place now where the truth could not hurt her any more. But it could hurt Amy.

'Forgive me, Maggie,' she whispered. 'I can't do it.'

Chapter Forty-Three

Amy returned to the ward on New Year's Eve.

The other nurses greeted her warmly, and even Staff Nurse Clackett managed a cordial, 'Hello, Nurse Metcalfe. It's nice to see you back.'

Miss Spencer was not on the ward that day. She was attending a wedding, Glenys told her. Amy felt relieved. The last time they'd met she'd fallen asleep in Miss Spencer's arms at her mother's bedside. She'd also come to the funeral, although Amy had scarcely been aware of her at the time.

She wasn't sure how she would face her again. It felt as if the ward sister had seen her at her most vulnerable. But then she reminded herself that Miss Spencer was used to seeing people at their worst, and she would probably think nothing of it. Amy was just being silly.

Staff Nurse Clacket put her on bedmaking duties with Glenys.

'No sluice today?' Amy said, as they piled fresh linens from the cupboard on to the trolley.

'Another pro transferred from Female Surgical, so she's doing all the dirty work,' Glenys informed her gleefully. 'Just think, you're not the most junior any more. You can start throwing your weight about like the rest of us!'

As they changed the beds, Glenys caught her up on all

the ward gossip Amy had missed. After her mother's death and all the horrible business with her father, it was a nice distraction to listen to Glenys telling her who was going out with who, and how two second years had ended up fighting over a medical student at the dance.

'They're barely speaking now,' she said. 'I'd steer clear of the common room if I were you. You could cut the atmosphere with a knife.'

She was also thrilled to tell Amy that Tony was still interested in her.

'Who?'

'Tony. Tony Walsh? Giles' friend?'

'Oh, him.'

'He told Giles to let you know he's forgiven you for abandoning him at the dance.'

'I did not abandon him!'

'You walked off and left him in the middle of the dance floor.'

'I was tired. I wanted to go home.'

'Yes, well, he's forgiven you, anyway,' Glenys said. 'And I have to say you're lucky, because he's quite a catch. I know at least three other girls who've got their eye on him. But he wants you to go with him to the New Year's Eve party tonight.'

'No thanks.'

Glenys stared at her. 'What do you mean?'

'I mean I don't want to go to a party.' *And certainly not with Tony Walsh,* she added silently.

'But you can't stay at home. Think how miserable you'll be.'

Amy stared at her. It was less than a week since she'd lost her mother. Did Glenys seriously expect her to go dancing?

But she had a point, she thought. If she was stuck in the nurses' home, she would only start to think about her mother, or her father. It was very hard to stop herself being consumed with misery, even when she was occupied. If she was alone with her thoughts, she wasn't sure what would happen.

Glenys was still nagging her about it when they finished the bed round. Amy was tempted to agree to go to the party just to shut her up, but thankfully Staff Nurse Clackett ended the discussion by telling Amy to go down to theatre to collect a post-operative patient.

It was quite a responsibility to bring a patient back from theatre. Amy had to accompany the trolley back to the ward, then help to settle the patient and sit with them until they came round from the anaesthetic.

But her pride and self-confidence evaporated when she saw Tom Weaver waiting with the trolley in the corridor.

For a moment they stared at each other, and Amy was immediately transported back to that terrible day when her mother had died and she'd fallen sobbing into Tom's arms.

It had all been so surreal, like a dream, she wasn't sure it had even happened. But then she saw Tom's face, and the blush creeping up from the collar of his brown overall, and she realised that it had.

Neither of them spoke. Amy stared at a noticeboard on the shiny beige wall and wished the ground would open up and swallow her.

They were still carefully ignoring each other when the

theatre sister appeared and told them they would have to wait a bit longer for the patient.

The silence between them stretched for a few more minutes. Then Tom said,

'How are you?'

Amy immediately thought about her father. She hadn't heard from him since he'd thrown her out of the house, and she still had no idea what was going on.

'I'm a lot better now I'm back at work.' She sent him a shy sideways glance. 'Thank you, by the way,' she said.

'What for?'

'You were very kind to me – the night my mother died.'

He shrugged it off, embarrassed. The silence went on a while longer.

'What did you mean when you said I wouldn't want my friends seeing us?'

He looked at her. 'What?'

'When you walked me back to the nurses' home. You said you wouldn't take me to the door because I wouldn't want my friends to see us.'

He turned away, shoving his hands into his pockets.

'You should know the answer to that one,' he mumbled. 'Nurses don't like to be seen with porters.'

'Who says?'

'Your friend Glenys, for one. You were talking about it in the sluice, and I heard her telling you that nurses only go out with doctors.'

'You obviously weren't listening very carefully, otherwise you would have heard me telling her that I wanted you to ask me to the dance.'

Tom looked up sharply. 'Did you?'

'Yes, I did. Although I didn't know you had a girlfriend at the time.'

'What girlfriend?'

'That girl you brought to the dance.'

'You mean Val? She's not my girlfriend, she's my cousin.'

Amy frowned. 'But she told me—' She broke off. Surely Val had told her that, otherwise where would she have got the idea?

But so much had happened since then, she couldn't recall.

'You must have got the wrong end of the stick,' Tom said. 'Val would never have said something like that.'

'So it's not true?'

'No!'

Just then, the doors to theatre opened and the sister appeared.

'You can come and collect your patient now,' she said.

The patient was a seven-year-old boy who'd just had his appendix removed. Amy held back the lift doors and stepped aside so that Tom could push the trolley inside.

Her thoughts were racing. She hardly dared say what was on her mind. But she wasn't sure if she would ever get another chance.

The lift juddered to a halt and Tom lurched sideways.

'What the – don't tell me this thing's stuck?'

He went to press the button but Amy said,

'I did it.'

'You did? But how did you—'

'Blakey told me how to do it. You're not the only one who knows how to stop a lift, you know.'

'So I see.'

She turned to him. It was now or never.

'I don't suppose you want to go to a New Year's Eve party with me tonight?' She spoke fast, her words tumbling over each other in a rush to get out. 'I mean, I don't really want to go, and I daresay you won't either, since there'll be a load of nurses and medical students there. But I wanted to go out with you, and I know you'll never ask me, so—'

'No,' said Tom.

'Oh.' She stared at him, taken aback.

'You're right, I can't imagine anything worse than having a bunch of medical students looking down their noses at me. I get enough of that during the day, thank you very much. But I'd like to go out with you too,' he went on. 'So how about we go to the pictures tonight instead?'

'Oh yes,' she said. 'I'd like that.'

He leaned towards her, and for a moment Amy felt certain he was going to kiss her. Until he reached behind her head and pressed the lift button.

'Come on,' he said. 'We'd best get this kid back to the ward before he wakes up and wonders what on earth is going on!'

Chapter Forty-Four

A lifetime of prayer and devotion might have earned Sister Catherine Rosina of Our Lady of Eternal Piety a place in heaven, but it hadn't done her knees any good at all.

It was all the poor old dear could do not to howl in pain during their weekly sessions as Dora massaged her arthritic joints. Dora wouldn't have blamed her if she had, but the elderly nun had too much pride and self-control to give in to such weakness. Only the occasional hiss escaped her tightly pressed lips, her knuckles white as she gripped the arms of the chair.

They were in Mother Superior's modestly furnished sitting room. It was light and airy, and flooded with a rare burst of winter sunshine. The weather had finally turned on the last day of the year, as if determined to end on a high note.

In the distance, a piano played, and from time to time the sound of girlish voices would rise and fall as they passed the door. Not nuns, but the fallen young women of the mother and baby home attached to the convent.

Although they didn't sound much like fallen women to Dora. They reminded her of her daughter Winnie, or the students she'd lived with at the nurses' home. Just ordinary young girls who'd been unlucky, or reckless, or ill-used.

Sister Catherine Rosina drew in a short, sharp intake of breath.

'Sorry,' Dora said. 'Did that hurt?'

'It's quite all right, my dear,' the elderly nun replied stoically. 'If Our Lord could suffer for our sins, then I'm sure I can put up with a bit of pain.'

'I suppose if you put it like that,' Dora said.

Finally the treatment was over.

'Thank you,' the old lady said as she rolled up her thick lisle stockings over her knees. 'I feel much better.'

'I'm glad,' Dora said, packing up her bag. 'I'll be back next week.'

'I'm looking forward to it.'

Dora wasn't sure if she was joking or not. Sister Catherine Rosina was a merry soul with twinkling eyes and a comfortably plump figure under her black habit.

On her way out she met the Mother Superior. She was in her fifties, but her serene, unlined face was ageless, framed by a white headdress. She regarded Dora with clear blue eyes.

'All finished, Nurse Riley?'

'Yes, Mother Superior. Thank you for letting us use your private quarters.'

'Not at all.'

As Dora turned to leave, the Mother Superior called after her, 'I wonder if I might ask a favour?'

'What's that?'

'You're a midwife, are you not?'

'I'm not fully qualified, but I have done some midwifery as part of my district nurse training. Why?'

The Mother Superior looked towards the ceiling. 'One of our girls has gone into labour and she seems to be having some difficulty. I wonder if you could help?'

'You'd be better off calling an ambulance, surely?'

'Sister Benedicta won't hear of it. She insists she can manage, but I thought perhaps you might offer some assistance?' Her pained look spoke volumes. 'I'm afraid she's rather traditional and prefers not to involve outsiders in the convent's business.'

She's not going to appreciate me butting in, then, is she? But the Mother Superior looked so worried, Dora sighed and said,

'All right, I'll see what I can do.'

She did not need the Mother Superior's directions to the delivery room. As Dora reached the top of the stairs, she could already hear the tell-tale yelling of a woman in labour coming from the other end of the corridor.

'Oh, be quiet,' she heard an older woman snap. 'You're making far too much fuss.'

The delivery room was overheated and basically furnished, with just a bed in the centre of the room and a chair in one corner and a cupboard in the other where the instruments were kept. There was also a sink with an Ascot heater above it and a bar of red carbolic soap.

Sister Benedicta looked up sharply when Dora walked in. She must have been at least seventy years old, wizened and bent over with a face as creased as a walnut. The apron she wore over her black habit was stained with blood.

'Who are you?' she demanded.

'I'm Nurse Riley. The Mother Superior sent me.'

'What did you say? Speak up, I can't hear you.' The old woman cupped a hand around her ear.

'I said the Mother Superior sent me.' Dora smiled at the girl on the bed. She looked very young, and very frightened. Tears ran down her sweating face.

Sister Benedicta looked put out. 'I don't know why she did that. I told her I could manage.'

'Yes, well, now I'm here I might as well help.' Dora dumped her bag down on the chair and shrugged off her coat, then went to the basin to wash her hands.

'There isn't much you can do. The baby is dead.'

The soap slipped from her hands. Dora flashed another look at the girl on the bed. She was sobbing, her face contorted with grief and pain.

'What's happened?'

'The cord has prolapsed. I checked it, and there's no pulse.' She looked at the sobbing girl, her face impassive. 'I've already told her the child will be stillborn.'

Dora was shocked by the old woman's bluntness, but she fought for control as she reached for the towel. 'Let's have a look, shall we?'

As Sister Benedicta had said, there was a loop of cord protruding. As Dora went to grasp it, the girl let out an angry, terrified roar through gritted teeth.

'That's it, love,' she encouraged. 'Just breathe through it. It will pass in a minute.'

The girl clutched the bedclothes, her chin to her chest as she struggled to control the pain. Then, slowly, the hectic colour faded from her cheeks and she flopped back against the pillows.

Dora waited until the contraction had fully subsided and then grasped the cord again.

'I can feel a pulse,' she said.

'What? Nonsense,' the elderly nun dismissed.

'Here, feel it for yourself.'

Sister Benedicta checked the cord. Dora watched as her expression changed from impatience to disbelief.

'Well, I never,' she muttered.

'Perhaps you felt it during a contraction?' Dora suggested tactfully. 'That can sometimes shut off the blood flow to the—'

'I know what I'm doing, thank you! I don't need a lecture from a district nurse.' The old woman prodded the girl on her thigh. 'Turn over on to your front. Quickly, girl! You want this baby to be born, don't you?'

'Curled up like this, with your knees to your elbows,' Dora guided her more gently. 'That's it. Now we're going to try to push the cord back in. Take another deep breath, there's a good girl . . .'

They had to pause while another contraction took hold. But within a few minutes the prolapsed cord was back in place and the delivery could proceed.

'I can manage now, thank you,' Sister Benedicta tried to dismiss her, but Dora wasn't going anywhere. Not after the nun had made such a fundamental and potentially tragic mistake.

'I think I'll stay, just in case,' she said.

She pulled the chair to the side of the bed and sat there, holding the girl's hand.

'What's your name, love?'

'Beryl, miss.'

'Keep going, Beryl.' She wiped a damp lock of hair from the girl's face. 'It won't be long now. You're doing really well.'

'But I'm tired!'

'I know, love.'

Poor kid, she was barely more than a child herself. Dora wondered about her story, but she knew better than to ask.

Another contraction took hold and Beryl gripped Dora's hand, her nails biting into the flesh.

'I want my mum!' Beryl screamed.

'Your mother doesn't want you,' Sister Benedicta snapped back. 'That's why you're here. Now push!'

'Come on, love,' Dora urged softly. 'I know it's hard, but just a couple more pushes and it will all be over, I promise. Then you can have a nice rest.'

The words felt familiar to her, as if she'd said them before. But she'd only assisted on a handful of births since she started district nursing.

Beryl let out a hopeless wail and gripped her hand again, bringing her back to the present.

'I can't do it! It hurts!'

'In pain thou shalt bring forth children,' Sister Benedicta quoted. 'It's God's will. Now stop making such a fuss.'

'There speaks someone who's never given birth,' Dora murmured. Her comment seemed to make Beryl smile, at least.

'I don't know why she's quoting the Bible, when she's such a wicked old cow,' she said through clenched teeth.

'Shh! She'll hear you.'

'She's as deaf as a post. A bomb could drop and she wouldn't hear.'

A bomb could drop . . .

Moments later, a bouncing baby girl came into the world, announcing her arrival with a roar of outrage.

'Well, we can all tell where she gets her lungs from,' Sister Benedicta commented, as she cut the cord and scooped the child into a pink blanket.

'Can I hold her?' Beryl asked, putting out her arms.

'Certainly not.' Sister Benedicta looked affronted.

'But I want to see her!'

'Surely it wouldn't hurt?' Dora said.

Sister Benedicta shook her head. 'It's for her own good,' she told Dora. 'Since she is not going to keep the child, it's better that she doesn't get too attached.'

'But I only want one cuddle,' Beryl wept, as the door closed. 'Just one cuddle, to remember her by.'

'I'm so sorry, love.' Dora put her arms around the girl, comforting her as she sobbed. But all she could think about was the baby in the pink blanket.

A bomb could drop . . .

Suddenly the memory came back to her, as clear as if it had happened yesterday. How could she not have seen it before?

Mother Superior emerged from her office as Dora came down the stairs half an hour later.

'Thank you so much for your help, Nurse Riley,' she said. 'I understand you were invaluable.'

'I'm not sure Sister Benedicta would agree.'

'As a matter of fact, it was Sister Benedicta who told

me.' The Mother Superior smiled ruefully. 'She means well, although she is rather set in her ways. I'd like to find someone to assist her, but suitable novices are so hard to find. Girls simply aren't interested in a vocation any more . . .'

But Dora was too distracted to listen. 'Mother Superior, do you believe in life after death?' she asked.

'I'd be seriously questioning my own vocation if I didn't,' the Mother Superior smiled. 'What makes you ask such a question, Nurse Riley?'

Dora looked back up the stairs. 'Because I think I might have met a woman who came back from the dead,' she said.

Chapter Forty-Five

It was a bright Friday afternoon, the last day of 1958, when Jennifer Teeson married Johnny Davies at Caxton Hall register office in Westminster.

It was quite the fashionable place for weddings, according to Johnny. The former Prime Minister Anthony Eden had got married there, apparently, as had Elizabeth Taylor. Although not to each other, as Johnny laughingly pointed out.

'Let's hope our marriage lasts a bit longer than Miss Taylor's,' Jen said grimly.

They certainly didn't draw the same crowds as a movie star. There were no press photographers, or crowds of well-wishers blocking the street. Just a handful of guests and a bride in an apricot silk dress and matching jacket.

'I refuse to wear a long white frock,' Jen had said. 'I would feel too absurd. Besides,' she added, ever practical, 'I can wear this again.'

But at least Liz had persuaded her to carry a discreet posy of flowers. Chrysanthemums, she'd chosen, in rich shades of crimson and burnt orange. Seeing them made Liz think about poor Maggie Metcalfe.

As if she had thought about anything else for the past week.

Jen had wanted her to be her bridesmaid, but Liz thought she was far too old.

'Aren't bridesmaids always little girls in frilly dresses?' she asked.

But she couldn't be Matron of Honour either because she wasn't married, as Sally was at pains to point out. Finally, they settled on a compromise. Liz would stand at Jen's side as long as no one referred to her as a bridesmaid. She wore a deep red dress for the occasion that flattered her sandy hair and warm, freckled colouring, with a borrowed fur stole around her shoulders to keep out the cold. It was a bright, sunny day and the sky was a particularly beautiful shade of ice blue, but it was still too crisp and chilly for anyone's comfort.

Especially Rob Bryant. He looked almost respectable for once, Liz thought. At least he was wearing a tie, although his suede shoes were still scuffed. He huddled in an overcoat, grumbling about brutal British winters, and how much he missed Christmas in Australia, where the sun shone and the warm water of the Coral Sea lapped the beach.

'It sounds idyllic,' Jen's friend Tina sighed. She had come to the wedding without her boyfriend James because he was at work and couldn't get the time off. Not that Tina seemed too upset about it, since she took the opportunity to flirt outrageously with Rob.

Liz was dismayed at how jealous she felt, watching them together. *You had your chance*, she reminded herself.

She'd been concerned about how Rob would be towards her after she'd turned him down, but she need not have worried. He was as friendly and cordial as ever on the ward. He certainly hadn't shown any sign of resentment or bitterness.

It was a refreshing change, Liz thought. Most men's egos couldn't take a rejection.

After the wedding, they all went for tea at the Ritz. It was as opulent as Liz had imagined, with delicate gold chairs covered in yellow brocade, white linen-topped tables and gleaming silver teapots. A pianist played softly in the background, the tinkling melody mingling with the muted chink of cups and hushed conversation.

Waitresses in black dresses and spotless white aprons passed among them, bearing cake stands piled high with delicate sandwiches, pastries and cakes.

'I bet you don't get this in Australia?' Tina teased. She'd made sure to position herself at Rob's side. Liz took the seat across the table from them.

'You mean sandwiches?' Rob replied dryly. 'You'd be surprised. We don't all live on roasted kangaroo, you know.'

'Oh, you!' Tina laughed, as if he'd made the funniest quip in the world.

Liz toyed with the cucumber sandwich on the plate in front of her and said nothing.

'Are you all right?'

She looked up. Rob was watching her intently from across the table. Liz forced a smile.

'I'm fine,' she said. 'Just a bit preoccupied, that's all.'

'Are you thinking about the baby?'

She looked up at him, shocked. 'What?'

'Little Noel? They found his mother, didn't they?'

'Oh yes. Yes, they did.'

'What's this?' Tina, keen not to be kept out of the conversation, immediately jumped in. 'What are you two talking about?'

Liz could sense Rob's reluctance as he turned to face his companion.

'We had a baby abandoned on the steps of the hospital a week ago,' he said. 'The police have been searching for his mother ever since, and they finally found her yesterday.'

'I hope they locked her up?'

'Why?' Liz asked.

'She deserves it. She left her baby to die.'

'She left him at a hospital,' Rob pointed out quietly.

'Yes, but she didn't really care what happened to him, did she?'

'I daresay she didn't know what she was doing. She was sixteen years old, barely more than a child herself,' Liz said.

'She was old enough to have a baby.'

'Hardly. She was too naïve to understand what was happening to her. Apparently she didn't even know she was pregnant until one of the older women at the factory noticed her swollen belly.'

'A likely story!' Tina snorted.

Liz stared down into her bone china cup, fighting to control her rising anger. Now was not the time or the place. 'Don't you believe it?'

'Look, I've dealt with a lot of these unmarried mothers, and I know what they're like. They'd tell you anything to get some sympathy.'

Liz glanced at Rob. His expression was unreadable, but the muscle working in his jaw gave him away.

'I don't think—' he began, but Tina cut him off.

'They certainly don't get any sympathy from me,' she went on. 'As far as I'm concerned, they're all thoroughly disreputable young women. How do you think they get themselves into such a mess?'

'Doesn't it take two?' Rob said.

Tina shrugged. 'Men will always try to get away with what they can. It's up to the girl to protect her morals and say no,' she said primly.

Liz stared at her, fighting the urge to slap her pretty, self-satisfied little face.

'So you don't believe anyone can make a mistake?' she said.

'Is that what this one told you? That the poor little thing made a mistake?' Tina's mouth twisted mockingly.

Liz flashed a glance at Rob, saw the imperceptible shake of his head. But it was too late, rage was already scorching through her veins.

'She couldn't tell us anything,' she said, struggling to keep her voice steady. 'We only know what the police found out. After they dragged her body out of the Thames last night.' She lifted her gaze to meet Tina's, grimly satisfied by the look of shock she saw there. 'So I suppose it must have been a mistake, don't you think? One she obviously couldn't live with.'

After tea, Liz and Jen caught a cab back to the flat so Jen could pick up her trousseau and get changed into her going-away outfit. Johnny was going to be picking her up later so they could catch the evening flight to Paris for their honeymoon.

'It seems strange, doesn't it?' Jen mused, as Liz tidied her hair for her. 'This is the last time we'll be together in this flat.'

'I know,' Liz sighed. 'It won't be the same without you.'

'We've had some good times, haven't we?'

They were both silent for a moment, lost in their own thoughts.

'Anyway, we should look forwards, not back,' Liz said bracingly. 'You've got an exciting future ahead of you, Mrs Davies.'

Jen grimaced. 'I don't think I'll ever get used to changing my name. Perhaps I should have asked Johnny to change his?'

Just then the doorbell rang.

'Speak of the devil,' Liz said. 'Now, have you got everything?'

The pair of them hauled Jen's suitcases down the stairs, where Johnny was waiting.

He surveyed Jen's luggage with dismay. 'Is that what you're taking? We're only going to Paris for a week, darling, we're not emigrating!'

'Oh, stop it. We're going to the capital of *haute couture*. I need to dress up, don't I?'

She turned back to Liz, tears in her eyes. 'Well, I suppose this is goodbye—'

'It's *au revoir*,' Liz corrected her, trying to ignore the lump in her own throat. They hugged quickly and the next thing she knew they were in the cab and she was waving them off.

Liz closed the front door and headed back up the stairs to the flat. It already seemed lonely and empty without Jen.

She pulled out a bottle of gin from the sideboard and poured herself a generous measure, smiling to herself as she remembered how she and Jen would often have a glass to commiserate after a long, difficult day.

'Look forwards, not back,' she reminded herself aloud. But it was very difficult to do when everything seemed to be dragging her into the past.

She thought about her argument with Tina earlier. Thankfully, their conversation had not been overheard by the rest of the table so it hadn't spoilt Jen and Johnny's celebration.

She should have ignored her, Liz thought. But Tina's ignorant comments had got under her skin, especially so soon after they'd found out about little Noel's poor mother.

Annie Ward, her name was. Liz recalled the photograph the policeman had shown her. She was just a child, her eyes huge in her pale, innocent face. How terrified she must have been, giving birth on her own in a dark alley on Christmas Day while the rest of her family gathered at her parents' little terraced house for a party.

And then, hours later, driven by guilt and pain and fear, she'd climbed over the parapet of London Bridge and plunged into the cold, dark waters of the Thames.

Liz's heart welled with pity for her. She must have felt so alone and afraid. Liz wished she could have protected her, put her arms around her and told her that everything would be all right, that one day life would be worth living.

But it wouldn't have been the truth. Because her guilt and the terrible feeling of loss would have followed her for the rest of her life.

The doorbell rang, interrupting her thoughts.

It must be Jen, Liz thought. She'd probably forgotten something vital from her trousseau. She could imagine Johnny's frustration as she insisted on the cab turning round so she could go back for it.

The doorbell rang again, and she hurried downstairs to answer the door.

'I'm coming.' She was smiling as she opened the door. 'What did you—'

But then she saw the figure standing on the doorstep and the words died in her throat.

'Hello, Sadie,' said Dora Riley.

Chapter Forty-Six

'It is you, isn't it?'

Dora didn't have to ask the question. It was written all over Liz Spencer's face as she stood framed in the doorway.

She stared at Dora for a moment, then took a step back.

'You'd better come in,' she sighed.

Miss Spencer led the way up a steep flight of stairs to a flat. The sitting room was tastefully decorated, with sleekly modern teak furniture, a couch and two spindly armchairs.

A bottle of gin stood on the coffee table, a glass beside it.

'Would you like one?' Liz Spencer offered. Dora shook her head.

'No, ta. I ain't much of a drinker.'

Liz sat down in one of the spindly armchairs, then gestured for Dora to take the other.

'Why have you come?' she asked.

Dora paused. 'To be honest, I don't really know,' she admitted. 'Curiosity, I s'pose. I just wanted to know if I was right.'

'Well, now you know.'

She leaned back and crossed her legs. She seemed almost resigned, Dora thought. As if she had been waiting for this day for a long time.

Dora looked at her and wondered how she had missed

it for so long. She remembered envying that glorious strawberry-blonde hair.

'I wondered how long it would take you to realise who I was,' Liz said.

'I didn't at first. I suppose the name threw me.'

'Oh, yes. Sadie Evans.' Liz smiled. 'It was the name my sister gave to the nuns at the mother and baby home. My mother didn't want anyone associating me with the family, you see.' She lifted her gaze to meet Dora's. 'But I knew it was you the minute I saw you.'

'That's why you called me by my name?'

Liz Spencer nodded. 'I've never forgotten how nice you were to me that night. How you held my hand and told me I'd get through it.' She smiled sadly. 'It was the first time anyone had shown me kindness in months.'

'You were petrified, poor love. I really felt for you. We were about the same age, and I'd not long had twin babies myself. I had a husband and a family to help me, so I couldn't imagine going through it by myself.'

Liz picked up her glass and took a gulp. 'I thought I was going to die that night.'

'I thought you were dead.'

Liz looked up at her sharply. 'Me?'

'I left you in that basement with your baby. I didn't mean to leave you for so long, but then I was called away. The local pub had been bombed and there were a lot of people who needed treatment, and I was so busy I forgot about you. The next thing I knew, a bomb had dropped on the basement.'

She looked at Liz. 'The firemen managed to get some

patients out, but there was no sign of you. We all assumed you'd both perished.'

She shuddered at the memory.

'I'd already gone before the bomb came down,' Liz said.

'You discharged yourself?'

'I walked out. There was so much chaos, no one even noticed me leaving.'

'And you took your baby with you?'

Liz lowered her gaze. 'No,' she said quietly.

'What?' Dora stared at her. 'What do you mean? Surely you didn't leave your child behind?'

'It's not how it sounds,' Liz Spencer's words tumbled out in a rush. 'The minute I held my baby, I never wanted to let go. But I knew I couldn't – it was hopeless. I didn't know what to do. Then I heard crying coming from the next room. Someone breaking their heart, I'd never heard anything like it.'

Dora tried to think. She'd had no memory of it until Liz Spencer said those words. Now she vaguely recalled an unearthly wail, like a wounded animal, reverberating through the brick wall.

'I went to see what was going on and there was this woman, crying by an empty crib,' Liz said. 'You can't imagine how heartbreaking it was to see someone like that—'

I can, Dora thought. She'd seen so much heartbreak in her years of nursing.

She tried to think back to that fateful night, to a woman who'd lost her baby. Who was it? She didn't recall seeing her, but perhaps Miss Cox or one of the other midwives had attended to her. Everything had been happening so fast that night, with bombs raining down and chaos everywhere. No wonder the memory escaped her.

'You gave your baby away to a stranger?'

Dora's horror must have shown on her face because Liz Spencer grew defensive.

'I was going to have to do that anyway, don't you see?' she said. 'At least this way I knew who would be caring for her. And as soon as I saw this woman I knew she would love my baby. She had this kind of fierceness about her, you see. Like she would protect her, move mountains for her.' She looked down at her drink sadly. 'I could never give her that.'

'It sounds as if you already did.'

Liz looked up at her sharply. 'What do you mean?'

'You gave up your baby to someone who could give it a better life. I can't imagine what it must have taken to do that.'

'I've never seen it that way.' Liz's gaze dropped again. 'I've hated myself ever since for what I did. The minute I walked out of that hospital I regretted it. I tried to go back but by then the bomb had dropped and they wouldn't let me in. Then I read in the paper the next day that a mother and baby had perished, and I knew—' She choked back a sob. 'I've blamed myself ever since. I kept thinking, if only I'd taken my baby with me, if only . . .'

'I'm so sorry. It must be hard to live with that kind of guilt.'

'It was.' She looked up at Dora, her hazel eyes shining. 'And then I found her.'

'What?'

'I found my baby.'

'But I don't understand—'

Dora stared at her. Liz Spencer's freckled face had lit up, her eyes shining with joy.

'I think I will have that gin after all,' she said.

She sipped her drink and tried her best to hold on to the thread of what Miss Spencer was saying. But her story veered all over the place, and it was difficult to follow.

'I had no idea when I first met her . . . Born at the Nightingale on that very same night. That's when I started to think . . . but I still wasn't sure. It might have been a coincidence . . . But then her mother died, and I knew it had to be her.'

'Had to be who? Slow down, you're hardly making any sense!'

Liz Spencer took a deep breath, but her voice trembled with excitement.

'The woman at the hospital, the one I gave my baby to look after? Her name was Margaret.'

'Margaret?' Slowly it began to dawn on her. 'You mean to tell me—'

'Amy Metcalfe is the baby I gave away all those years ago.'

Suddenly she was talking again, the words tumbling out.

'She was exactly as Amy described her. She told me she had a weak heart and never thought she could have children. Margaret Metcalfe died of heart failure, didn't she?'

Dora didn't reply. She couldn't begin to find the words.

But Liz Spencer didn't seem to notice her silence. It was as if someone had turned on a tap and now all her thoughts were gushing out.

'It's a miracle, isn't it? But should I tell her? I know it would be an awful shock for her, especially so soon after losing her mother. I suppose I should wait. Or perhaps I shouldn't say anything? But I don't think I can do that. I don't want to put a foot wrong, not after all this time. Amy's always thought of Margaret as her mother, I know that. But I can't just let this go—'

'Don't say anything.'

Liz looked at her, slightly crestfallen. 'Well, obviously not right away. But don't you think she has the right to know—'

'Amy Metcalfe isn't your child. She can't be.'

Liz froze. 'What are you talking about? Why not?'

Dora took a gulp of her gin. She could already feel it making her head spin.

'Because you gave birth to a baby boy,' she said.

Chapter Forty-Seven

Liz stared at her, her expression caught between shock and disbelief.

'What are you talking about? It was a baby girl. *My* baby girl.'

'I should know, I helped to deliver the baby. I'm telling you it was a boy.'

'But you wrapped her in a pink blanket!' Liz Spencer insisted.

'It was the only one I had to hand. It was the middle of an air raid, remember? The place was in chaos.'

She was lucky to have found a blanket to wrap the baby in, as she recalled. But if she'd known that such a simple act would cause so much confusion and heartache eighteen years later, she might have taken more care. 'I left you with him, Liz. You held him. Surely you must have seen—?'

'I – I didn't. I just saw the pink blanket and I thought – I assumed—' Dora could see the doubt creeping into her mind. 'A boy,' she murmured. Then she shook her head as if to dislodge the thought from her mind. 'But it can't be. It's Amy, I know it is. I can feel it.'

'I'm sorry, but Amy isn't your daughter. Maggie Metcalfe is her mother.'

'No! Her baby died. I talked to her—'

'You couldn't have. Maggie gave birth before I came on duty. I didn't even know it had happened until one of the other midwives mentioned it later.'

'No!'

'It's true,' Dora insisted. 'I didn't see Maggie myself until the morning after the air raid, when I went up to visit her on the ward.'

'That's not true! I heard her crying out. You heard her, too.'

'I heard someone crying out, but it wasn't Maggie.'

'Then who was it?'

'I don't know. Truly, I don't.'

Liz stared at her, her face hostile. 'I don't believe you,' she said flatly. 'I know she was a friend of yours. You're only saying all this to protect her—'

'I'm saying it because I don't want you upsetting Amy!' Dora snapped back. 'She's already been through far too much heartache, she doesn't need you putting ideas in her head.'

'But she's my daughter. She must be . . .'

There was less conviction behind her words this time. Dora could feel her crumbling.

'It's got to be her. It's got to be. I've already lost my baby once, I can't lose her again.'

'I'm sorry, love,' she said. 'Truly I am.'

Liz stared at her, and slowly her face crumpled. 'I can't bear it,' she sobbed. 'I've spent eighteen years wondering what happened, feeling guilty about what I did. Then I met Amy and I thought I'd been given a second chance. And now . . .' She buried her face in her hands.

Dora patted her shoulder. She wished she could find the words to help her, but they wouldn't come.

'But if I didn't give my baby to Margaret Metcalfe, then who did I give him to?'

'I don't know, love. I wish I did.'

She tried to think about that night. The sweltering heat of the basement, the unearthly cries coming from beyond the damp brick wall. If she didn't know better, she would have almost thought it was a ghost they were hearing.

A ghost who had taken Liz's baby and then disappeared into the night.

But if it was a ghost, then they weren't the only ones who had heard it.

She looked at Liz. 'I think I know who might be able to help,' she said slowly.

Chapter Forty-Eight

Tom looked at himself in the mirror and was surprised to find his usual scowl replaced by a smile.

For once, things seemed to be going his way. Tomorrow morning was the first day of January, and the day he finally inherited his parents' shop. There would be no more fetching and carrying, no more answering to his uncle and aunt, watching as they enjoyed his birthright.

Not that they showed any signs of moving. There were no bags packed, no one had even mentioned it. When Tom had asked where they might live after they left the shop, Aunt Lillian had replied with an enigmatic,

'We'll have to wait and see, won't we? Nothing's been decided yet.'

'You can't stay here,' Tom had said.

'Like I said, we'll have to wait and see.'

In spite of Aunt Violet's assurances, Tom still found it worrying. He'd known Uncle Stan would try to pull some sort of stunt, but he had no idea what he might be planning.

But he was putting his concerns aside for now because he had his date with Amy to think about. The thought of seeing her was enough to put the smile back on his face.

He couldn't get over her asking him out! He was glad,

because he would probably never have plucked up the courage otherwise.

He grinned, thinking of how she'd stopped that lift. Fancy her asking Blakey how to do it. He should never have told her, of course – it was an old porter's trick, and everyone had been sworn to secrecy – but he was glad he had.

'What are you smiling about?'

There was Val, reflected in the mirror behind him. She stood in the doorway, watching him. She was still dressed in her shop overall, her brown hair pinned back off her square face.

'Nothing,' he said.

'You've been grinning like the Cheshire Cat ever since you got in. Go on, you can tell me.'

'If you must know, I'm going out.'

'Well, I didn't think you'd got dolled up like that to do the ironing!' She looked him up and down, taking in his smart trousers and best shirt. 'And is that cologne you're wearing?'

'I nicked some of Eric's Old Spice,' Tom admitted sheepishly.

'You've gone to a lot of effort, I must say,' Val said.

'Yes, well, it's New Year's Eve.'

'Don't remind me.' Val came into the room and flopped down heavily on Tom's camp bed. 'I reckon I must be the only one in the world not going to a party tonight. I thought we'd be stuck at home together. I was going to make us something nice to eat.'

'Sorry, Val.'

Tom turned away from her, back to the mirror to fasten his tie.

'Can I come out with you?' Val's face brightened.

Tom shook his head. ''Fraid not, love. I've got a date,' he said shyly.

He'd expected her to tease him but Val sat bolt upright. 'Who with?'

'Amy.'

'Not that girl from the dance?' Her face dropped.

'That's the one.'

'I'm surprised you're having anything to do with her, after the horrible way she spoke to me,' Val said sulkily.

Tom turned to face her, still fiddling with his tie. 'Are you sure that's what she said?'

'Are you calling me a liar?'

Her flare of temper surprised him. 'No, of course not. I just thought you might have misunderstood?'

'I know what she said.' Val glared down at her hands. She was grinding her teeth, her jaw working back and forth, as she always did when she was agitated. 'I don't like her. And I don't think she's right for you, either. She's a snobby cow.'

'I think you'd like her if you got to know her—'

'I don't want to get to know her!' Val's voice rose, her cheeks flushing.

'Val!'

'You said you only wanted to be with me.'

Tom stared at her. 'What are you talking about?'

'That night at the dance. You said there was no one else you'd rather be dancing with. You said it, Tom!'

'Yes, but I didn't mean it like that.'

She was on her feet now, facing him. Tom saw the look in her eyes and realisation dawned.

'Did you tell Amy you were my girlfriend?' he asked gently.

'No!'

'But she said—'

'Then she's a liar!' Her face was mottled with hurt and fury. 'Don't you see? She's trying to stir up trouble, trying to come between you and me.'

'Oh, Val.' Tom took a step towards her but she flinched away. 'I'm sorry,' he said. 'I didn't realise . . .'

He should have known. How could he not see what was in front of him? He'd always thought of Val as a sister; he'd had no idea she had other feelings for him.

She was crying now, her face buried in her hands. Tom went to comfort her. But the moment his arms went round her Val lunged at him, her mouth pressed wetly to his in a fierce, clumsy kiss.

He pushed her away. 'What the—?'

'I love you, Tom. I've always loved you. Just give me a chance.'

The next thing, she was fumbling with the buttons of her overall. Tom watched her, appalled.

'What are you doing?'

'I can give you what you want. You don't need her. She'll never love you the way I do.' Her breath was coming in short gasps as she struggled out of her overall to reveal a grubby slip, the thin straps digging into her pudgy bare flesh.

'Val, please—'

'You want me, Tom. I know you do. We can be together, just like we always said we would be.'

She made another lunge for him. Tom's hands touched her cold, goose-pimpled flesh and he recoiled, pushing her away.

'Stop it,' he shouted. 'I don't want you, Val. Do you understand me? I don't want you!'

She fell back on the bed and stared up at him with bewildered grey eyes. 'But you promised. You said you'd look after me—'

He turned away from her abruptly. 'I think you'd better go,' he said.

He heard the camp bed creaking as Val rose slowly. He could see her out of the corner of his eye, gathering up her overall.

She looked so defeated, her shoulders rounded, that for a moment he felt a pang of pity for her. Poor Val, if he'd had any idea she felt this way about him . . .

'I'm sorry,' he said.

She looked up at him, her doleful eyes meeting his in the mirror.

'So am I,' she murmured.

Chapter Forty-Nine

The church clock had just struck midnight.

Out in the street, Val could hear the sound of revellers spilling out on to the streets, laughing and singing and shouting greetings to each other.

There was no one to hug her, or to wish her a happy new year. Her parents were out at a party at the Freemasons' lodge, and God knows where Eric was, but they wouldn't be seeing him until the morning.

And as for Tom . . .

Val's hand shook as she topped up her glass with her father's sherry. He would have something to say about it when he got home, but she didn't care. She was determined to numb the pain somehow.

She didn't want to think about what Tom was doing, but she couldn't stop torturing herself, like probing a sore tooth with her tongue.

She thought about him and Amy, kissing on the stroke of midnight. Would he kiss her? Of course he would. Even strangers kissed each other on New Year's Eve. She could almost picture the shy, slightly embarrassed smile they would give each other as they moved in for the kiss, their arms going around each other . . .

Then Val remembered the look of revulsion on Tom's

face when she'd kissed him, the way he'd recoiled from her touch. She was filled with shame.

Of course he didn't want her. She had seen herself through Tom's eyes in that moment and realised what she truly was.

A clown.

She was never going to be one of those pert, pretty girls, the ones who got everything they wanted. Life would never be that easy for her because she was plain, ugly. And all the make-up and fashionable clothes in the world were never going to change that.

She took another gulp of her sherry, grimacing at the taste. Did people really enjoy drinking? Eric certainly did. But it seemed to be doing the trick, making her head swim, loosening her thoughts.

Except one, that went round and round in her mind.

She'd ruined everything.

It would never be the same after this. There would be no more laughter between them, no more easy familiarity. Tom would never smile at her or crack a joke.

The memory might fade in time. They might even laugh about it, when they were older and both married with kids of their own.

Do you remember that time when . . .

But he would never trust her. There would always be a wariness between them. And Val couldn't bear that.

Her hand shook, splashing sherry down herself, and Val made a half-hearted attempt to dab away the stain. God, how she hated herself. The dingy nylon slip clung to her pudgy rolls of flesh. No wonder Tom had recoiled from her.

He could have his pick of girls, so why would he ever look at a disgusting nobody like her?

She set down her glass on the coffee table. The room was warm, with damp washing gently steaming on the clothes horse in front of the fire. Val had promised her mother she would keep an eye on them.

She would have to go to bed soon. The room was beginning to spin, and her eyelids felt heavy. Was this what being drunk was like? It was quite a nice feeling, once you got used to it.

Better than having to think, anyway.

Chapter Fifty

Tom walked home from his night out on cloud nine. Midnight had come and gone but the streets were still thronged with people, merry from drink, weaving their way home. Tom found himself joining in with their laughter and wishing them well.

Was this what being in love felt like?

He barely remembered the film they'd watched. All he was aware of was Amy beside him, the light perfume of her hair, the way she tucked herself into the crook of his arm, sharing a bag of sweets, as if it was the most natural thing in the world.

A regular Rudolf Valentino, you are, he mocked himself. *Tickets in the cheap seats and a bag of humbugs between you. You certainly know how to show a girl a good time, don't you?*

But Amy had seemed to enjoy it, and she'd agreed to go out with him again, so perhaps he hadn't done so badly . . .

'Show me the way to go home, I'm tired and I want to go to bed . . .' A man was singing on the steps to the pub, ignoring the indignant shouts of the landlord from the window above.

'I wish you bloody well *would* go home!' he shouted.

The man sang louder, his voice rising above the insistent

sound. The landlord mouthed a curse Tom could not hear and slammed the window shut.

He suddenly thought about Val, and his heart sank.

He'd nearly forgotten all about her in his happiness. Now he would have to face her.

He was sorry he'd been so sharp with her. She didn't deserve that, poor girl. He wished he could have been kinder to her, but when she'd lunged at him, he'd panicked and pushed her away.

He liked Val, but not in that way. He'd had no idea she felt like that about him. It had completely taken him by surprise. He wondered if he'd ever given her any sign, or if she'd made the whole thing up in her head.

He was going to sort it out with her, he decided. He didn't want to have bad blood between them. He was going to make peace with her, explain as kindly as he could how he felt.

He tried to push the image of her face from his mind as she loomed towards him, the clammy, suffocating feel of her lips on his . . .

The shop was in darkness as he turned the corner. Aunt Lillian and Uncle Stan would still be out at their party, he thought. Hopefully Val would be in bed and he wouldn't have to face her until the morning.

The acrid smell of smoke reached him as soon as he opened the door. Confused, Tom fumbled for the light switch and flicked it on.

'Val?' he called out. There was no reply.

He opened the door that led to the passageway and immediately fell back as a thick, choking blanket of smoke poured through the door, engulfing him in blackness. Tom covered his mouth with his arm while scrabbling for the light switch with the other, but he could not find it.

From above his head came the ominous crackle of flames.

'Val!' He called out again, coughing as the hot smoke filled his lungs. 'Val, where are you?'

For a moment there was nothing. Tom made his way along the passageway, his hand out in front of him, groping in the blackness. Stumbling into the telephone table, he cursed and fell headlong.

There was a whimper from the sitting room above him. Tom stiffened to listen.

'Val?' he called out again.

Silence. And then a feeble voice called out,

'Tom?'

He scrambled to his feet, tripping over the telephone cord. He should stop and call 999, he thought.

He groped in the darkness for the telephone, but he couldn't find it. He must have knocked it on to the floor when he'd stumbled.

'Tom?' The voice above him grew fainter.

'I'm coming, Val.'

He gave up looking for the phone and took a few steps forward, into the thick wall of smoke. His eyes stung and his chest felt tight, making it hard to breathe.

His free hand found the newel post at the bottom of the banisters and he grasped it like a lifeline. As he slowly climbed, his feet finding each step, he could feel the heat growing more intense, scorching his lungs. Sweat pooled under his shirt, but he forced himself onward and upward, towards the living room.

It took him a moment to find the door, groping around in the bitter, choking fog until he found the doorknob. Tom grasped it and cried out in pain as the hot metal burnt through his skin, but he forced himself to turn it and threw open the door.

It was as if he'd opened the door to hell itself.

Flames rolled across the ceiling and down the walls, creating a fiery canopy above his head. The smoke was even thicker in here, a dense, acrid blackness everywhere Tom turned, lit with an eerie glow from the flames.

'Val?'

Something crackled in the gloom as it succumbed to the flames. But his cousin was silent.

Every nerve and sinew in Tom's body told him to get out of the room. His skin was slick with sweat, his eyes and throat burning. He could feel himself growing weaker as he fought to draw in each heated breath.

But he pushed on urgently, stumbling in the gloom, his hands outstretched in front of him, searching for Val.

His shins struck something solid and he pitched forward, losing his balance.

He'd found the couch.

As he struggled back to his feet, Tom's hand brushed against a shape stretched out on the couch. It was larger, more solid than cushions, encased in quilted nylon.

It was Val, wrapped in her old housecoat and stretched out on the couch.

'Val!' Tom's voice was little more than a helpless croak as he tried to rouse her, his hand shaking her shoulder. His cousin's body shifted but she did not wake up.

Another ominous crack overhead, as the flames devoured the ceiling above him. The whole thing could come down at any moment.

In the distance he heard the jangle of bells. Someone must have noticed the smoke from the street and called the fire brigade.

With his last ounce of strength, Tom struggled to his feet and hoisted Val off the couch and over his shoulder. His knees buckled under her weight, his lungs on fire. He didn't even know if she was alive or dead, but he had to do something.

The jangle of bells grew louder, coming to a halt outside. Tom staggered through the gloom towards what he thought was the open doorway.

Downstairs, a door burst open, followed by the sound of heavy boots.

'Hello?' a voice shouted out. 'Anyone in here?'

'We're up here!' Tom tried to cry out, but no sound emerged from his smoke-clogged throat. He took another faltering step, his hands outstretched, but he could not feel the door.

He stared around in the blackness, disorientated. He had no idea how to get out of the room. The smoke seemed to fill his brain now, rendering him unable to think clearly.

He sank to the floor, giving way to despair. The canopy of flames seemed to be bearing down on him now, tongues of flame taunting him.

Heavy boots were coming up the stairs now, but they were too late.

'I'm sorry, Val,' he whispered as the breath left his body.

Chapter Fifty-One

After the bright sunshine of the previous day, the first day of January came as a disappointment. Rain drizzled half-heartedly from the dull grey sky as Liz and Dora Riley stood in a churchyard waiting for Miss Cox.

They had called at her home, but her elderly neighbour had told them that she had gone to church.

'That's where you'll find her,' the old man said, as his equally grizzled terrier yapped around their ankles. 'She always goes to church on a Sunday morning. Never misses.'

The churchyard was filled with crumbling, lopsided gravestones, their inscriptions too worn and covered in thick moss to make out. Liz couldn't seem to stop shivering. She was wearing her thickest coat, but somehow the dampness still managed to seep into her bones.

Dora Riley barely seemed to notice as she peered out from underneath her umbrella, her gazed fixed on the doors to the church.

'Won't be long now,' she said. 'You'll soon have your answer.'

That's what I'm afraid of, Liz thought. It wasn't just the cold and damp that were making her shiver.

They had come down on the train to see Miss Cox. But now they were here, Liz felt a pit of dread in her stomach.

She had thought she wanted answers, but now she was afraid of what the elderly midwife might have to tell her.

'Here they come.'

Liz looked up. The doors to the church were open and the congregation were spilling out. They emerged slowly, putting up umbrellas and turning up coat collars. The vicar stood at the doors to bid them goodbye. He was young and fresh-faced in his spotless white surplice.

She was suddenly reminded of Malcolm Metcalfe, standing up in the pulpit, intoning in that dry, flat voice of his.

Was he really Amy's father? It scarcely seemed possible to Liz. Up until yesterday, she'd firmly believed he wasn't. But since talking to Dora Riley, everything had shifted and now she had no idea what was real and what wasn't.

She had a son.

She'd lain awake all night, trying to take it in. In the back of her mind, she still couldn't be sure that Dora Riley was telling her the truth.

That was why she'd agreed to meet Miss Cox.

'That's her.'

She didn't need Dora to tell her that. Even after eighteen years, Liz would have known Miss Cox anywhere.

Her dark hair had turned iron-grey, but she had the same sharp-featured face and imperious expression. Her frame was rigid and upright in her sober dark coat as she stopped to exchange pleasantries with the vicar.

Liz felt a sudden, jarring sensation. Seeing the elderly midwife, she was immediately transported back to that night.

'We don't have to do this, you know.' Her apprehension

must have shown on her face, because Dora was looking at her searchingly. 'We can just go home, if that's what you want?'

Liz shook her head. 'No,' she said firmly. 'We're here now. We might as well talk to her.'

The old woman picked her way down the gravel path, her head down against the rain. She didn't notice them until Dora stepped into her path and said,

'Miss Cox?'

She looked up, and Liz wondered if she'd imagined her quick look of dismay.

'My name's Dora Riley. I don't know if you remember me? We worked together—'

'Of course I remember you.' Miss Cox smiled. 'Goodness, it's been a long time, Nurse Riley.'

'Nearly eighteen years.'

'Really? Has it been that long? I suppose it must have been. I've rather lost track of time since I retired.' She looked at Dora. 'You gave up nursing after the war, didn't you?'

'For a while. But I went back into district nursing a few years ago.'

'I'm sure that type of work must suit you,' Miss Cox nodded. 'You always liked talking to people. You were very good at putting them at their ease, as I recall.'

Dora blushed at the compliment. Liz cleared her throat.

'I'm Elizabeth Spencer,' she cut in.

'I'm pleased to meet you, Miss Spencer.' Miss Cox looked from one to the other. 'So have you come all this way to see me? I assume this wasn't a chance meeting?'

Dora shook her head. 'I got your address from the

League of Nurses. We were hoping you might be able to help us?' She glanced at Liz.

'I see. Well, I'll certainly try, if I can.' Miss Cox turned up her coat collar. 'Why don't you come back to the house? It's far too cold and damp to talk here.'

They walked the short distance down the lane to Miss Cox's little whitewashed house. Liz listened as she and Dora made small talk about the village and her retirement. Miss Cox talked about her garden and how she'd learned to play bridge, then she asked some questions about Dora's family.

All the while, Liz's mind was churning impatiently. It was all she could do not to blurt out her questions right there, on the street.

They reached the house, and Miss Cox led them around the path to the back door.

'Wipe your feet on the mat,' she instructed. 'I don't want any mud on the floor.'

The kitchen was small and cosy, with a pine table in the centre of the room. Miss Cox hung up their coats but she didn't offer them tea. Clearly she didn't want them to be too comfortable.

She sat down at the kitchen table and gestured for them to do the same, even though Liz could glimpse a comfortable sitting room through the half-open door.

'So what can I do for you?' Miss Cox asked.

'We want to ask you about the Blitz,' Dora said.

'What about it?'

'The twenty-fourth of October. The night the bomb dropped on the basement. Do you remember it?'

'Of course I remember. How could I forget?'

Liz looked towards the half-open door. The sitting room looked cosy and inviting, with a comfortable moquette three-piece suite, and photographs on the mantelpiece.

'It was the night that poor girl was killed,' Miss Cox said.

'That was me,' Liz said.

Miss Cox whipped her head round to stare at her. 'I don't understand—'

'I was Sadie Evans. The girl who died.'

Miss Cox looked from Liz to Dora and back again. Shock drained the colour from her face. 'You escaped?'

'I left the hospital before the bomb came down.'

'We wanted to look for you,' Miss Cox murmured. 'But then the basement gave way, and the ARP men said no one could have survived—'

She glanced at Dora, who nodded. 'That's what I remember, too,' she said. 'It was chaos, wasn't it? All those people running around—'

'There was someone else in the basement that night,' Liz interrupted her. 'A stillbirth.'

Was it her imagination, or did Miss Cox's face grow a little paler? 'What about it?'

'You remember her?' Dora said.

'Of course I remember her.' Her voice was clipped, tense.

Dora and Liz looked at each other.

'Do you remember her name?' Liz asked.

'No. No, I don't.'

'Did you see her that night? After the bomb dropped?'

Miss Cox was silent for a moment.

'I – I think so,' she said slowly. 'I seem to recall the

311

fireman bringing her upstairs. I went to see if she was all right. She seemed very shaken, but of course we all were—'

'Did she have a baby with her?'

Miss Cox turned her head slowly to stare at Liz. 'A baby?'

'My baby.'

The elderly woman's frown deepened. 'But I don't understand. Why would she have your baby—'

'Did she have the baby or not?' Liz cut her off bluntly. 'You surely must have noticed?'

'Liz!' Dora sounded reproachful.

'I'm sorry,' Liz muttered. 'I just want to know what happened, that's all.'

'I'm sorry, too,' Miss Cox said feebly. 'I wish I could help you. I'm doing my best to remember what happened. But as I said, it was chaos that night—'

It was hopeless, Liz thought. Too much time had passed, and Miss Cox's memory clearly wasn't as sharp as it might have been.

They were wasting their time. The midwife was never going to tell her what she needed to know. She could feel her hopes slipping away, giving way to despair . . .

Then something caught her eye, through the half-open door to the sitting room.

'Where are you going?' Miss Cox looked up sharply as Liz got to her feet. 'You can't go in there, you'll tread mud on my good rugs—'

But Liz had already made her way into the room to study the photographs on the mantelpiece, and especially the silver-framed one of a strapping young man with dark hair.

'Who's this?' Liz held up a photograph.

'My nephew.'

Miss Cox stood in the doorway, her hands clasped in front of her. Her knuckles were white, Liz noticed.

'He's a handsome lad,' Dora said, taking the photograph from Liz and studying it. 'What's his name?'

'Tom,' Liz answered, her gaze still fixed on the young man's face. 'Tom Weaver.'

Chapter Fifty-Two

Violet Cox watched in agonising slow motion as Dora Riley took the photo from Miss Spencer's hands and examined it closely.

She had always dreaded this day happening, but at the same time she'd always known in her heart that it would come.

Secrets don't stay buried forever, Violet. Remember that.

'How do you know him?' Nurse Riley asked.

'He's a porter at the Nightingale,' Miss Spencer said. 'Isn't that right, Miss Cox?'

'Yes, he is.'

Violet fought the urge to rush in and snatch the picture from Dora Riley's hands. She had to stay calm. It was the only way to protect her secret.

But Miss Spencer was already looking through the other photographs on the mantelpiece, and Violet knew it would only be a matter of time before she found what she was searching for.

'Who's this?'

Sure enough, she'd plucked out another silver-framed image of a smiling woman in a flowery summer dress, a plump baby perched on her knee.

For a moment Violet thought about lying, then realised it would be no use.

'It's my sister Peggy.'

'Peggy?' Liz Spencer echoed. 'That's short for—'

'For Margaret,' Nurse Riley finished for her.

Violet looked back through the doorway to her kitchen. She wished she could turn back the clock to when she'd first seen them, waiting outside the church. She would have hidden herself away until they'd gone.

Or perhaps she should turn the clock right back eighteen years, to the moment she'd seen Peggy emerge from that basement, carrying that baby in her arms? She should undo the great wrong she had done, that split-second decision that had changed so many lives forever.

But seeing her sister's face, so full of joy and hope, she knew she could never do that.

'She was admitted to the Nightingale that night in labour,' she said. 'One of the other midwives had already gone out to her but she was in distress, so they sent for an ambulance to bring her in.'

She'd known nothing about it at the time, as she was already helping a young woman with no wedding ring to give birth.

Peggy had been crying out for her, the midwife told her afterwards. Even now, Violet felt guilty thinking about it. If only she'd known her sister was in labour in the next room, she would have gone straight to be with her.

'There was nothing that could have been done for her,' Violet said. 'Peggy's baby was already dead when she arrived at the hospital.'

Violet remembered how she'd held her as she sobbed in her arms afterwards. The midwife had already taken the baby away. In all her years as a nurse, Violet had never felt so helpless.

'It was her last chance, and she knew it,' she whispered. 'She had already suffered a number of miscarriages, and her health was too poor to risk another pregnancy.'

And then a miracle had happened . . .

'So you did see her with the baby that night?' Dora said.

Violet nodded. 'She told me you'd given her the child,' she said to Liz. 'I said it was wrong, that the baby should be with his mother. But then the basement collapsed. We thought you were dead,' she insisted.

Liz Spencer did not seem to be listening. She had picked up another photograph of Tom from the mantelpiece and was examining it closely.

'He looks like Jack,' she said. 'I wonder I've never noticed the resemblance before.' She turned to Violet. 'I'm right, aren't I? He's my son?'

Violet moved forward and snatched the photograph from her hands.

'He knows nothing about this,' she said. *He mustn't know*, a voice inside her head added. 'As far as he's concerned, his parents died when he was four years old.'

Liz Spencer looked shocked. 'She's dead?'

'They were killed in an air raid.'

'What happened to Tom?'

'He went to live with our youngest sister and her family.'

'Did they look after him?'

Violet thought about Lillian and Stan. It was another decision she'd made that she would have to live with.

'As well as they were able,' she said.

'Why didn't you take care of him yourself?'

'The same reason as you. It wasn't possible.'

They stared at each other for a long time in silence. Violet waited for Liz to speak, but what could she say? She had given her baby to a stranger, after all. She had no right to stand in judgement on anyone.

As if she knew what Violet was thinking, Liz dropped her gaze in shame.

'Why didn't you tell someone what had happened?' Dora broke the silence.

'Why?' Violet turned on her.

'You should have reported it to someone.'

'What good would it have done? The baby had been left without a mother either way. He would probably have ended up being sent to a children's home, or adopted by strangers. At least this way I knew he was going to a good home, to someone who would love him.' She turned to Liz. 'Someone his mother had already chosen to look after him.'

'Hardly chosen!' Dora scoffed. 'It was an act of madness, she wasn't in her right mind—'

'And did she?' Liz interrupted, her urgent gaze fixed on Violet. 'Did she love him?'

'Oh, yes,' Violet said quietly. 'She adored him. She and her husband both did.'

Liz nodded. 'I knew she would,' she said quietly. 'I could see it in her eyes.'

'Peggy was a good mother,' Violet said. 'And she never stopped being grateful to you for the chance you gave her.'

'And no one ever knew?' Dora Riley said.

Violet thought briefly about her conversation with Lillian, how she had turned up with her sly little threats and insinuations. She had no idea how her sister had found out. Listening at doors and reading other people's letters, probably. She had always been sneaky like that.

Or perhaps it was just a sister's intuition?

'No one knew,' she said. 'I considered telling him after his parents died. But he was so young, and he was already heartbroken after what had happened. It hardly seemed like the right time. But then, the right time never seemed to come,' she shook her head sadly. 'And as he got older, it only grew harder to tell him the truth. I was hoping I might never have to.'

She looked from one woman to the other.

'He'll have to know now,' Dora Riley said.

'I can't see what's to be gained by telling him. The poor boy's already been through so much—'

'But she's his mother!'

'She gave up any right to that name when she gave him away.'

'Now hang on a minute—' Dora Riley started to protest, but Violet Cox spoke over her.

'How dare you come here and try to claim that boy?' she said to Liz. 'What kind of a mother hands her newborn baby to a stranger and then runs off into the night?'

'A desperate one,' Liz Spencer replied in a low voice. 'And believe me, not a day has gone by since then when

I haven't regretted doing what I did. I thought my baby died that night. I've tortured myself ever since, wishing I hadn't walked out of that hospital. If I'd known that bomb was going to drop, I would have stayed and died with him, because believe me, my life hasn't been worth living since that night.'

Violet stared at her. Her heart went out to the poor girl, who had clearly spent the rest of her life trying to atone for what she had done. Punishing herself.

But then she thought about her sister, and Tom. She had to protect him, to do what was best for him – and Peggy.

'I'm sorry,' she said. 'Truly I am. But I really think it's too late. Even if you did tell Tom, I can't imagine he would accept you as his mother after all this time.'

Liz stared at her, and Violet saw the brightness in her hazel eyes dim, as if a switch had flicked off inside her brain.

'You don't know that—' Dora Riley started to say, but Liz interrupted her.

'She's right,' she said in a dull voice. 'I'm not Tom's mother and I never will be.'

Chapter Fifty-Three

They were both quiet as they travelled back on the train. Dora looked at Liz, her head resting on the window, watching pensively as the countryside rolled past. She could not imagine what the poor woman must be thinking.

Dora had never imagined everything would unfold the way it had. When she'd suggested going to visit Miss Cox, she'd never expected such a revelation.

'You don't have to do as she says,' she said, breaking the silence. 'I still think he has a right to know you're his mother—'

'But I'm not, am I? As far as he's concerned, his mother died when he was four years old.' Liz Spencer's voice was heavy with sadness.

'Yes, but—'

'I don't want to turn his life upside down. From what Miss Cox says, he's already been through enough heartache in his life.'

Spoken like a true mother, Dora thought. She remembered a Bible story from her Sunday school days, about a king who had to decide which of two women was the true mother of a baby. Unable to get to the truth, he'd suggested cutting the child in half, at which point one of the women had immediately given up and handed the baby to the other. Her act of self-sacrifice had shown the king who the true mother was.

The judgement of Solomon, that was it.

'But what about *your* heartache?' she asked.

Liz gave her a sad smile. 'I'm used to it, Mrs Riley.'

'Call me Dora.'

'And you can call me Liz.'

They both fell silent again. Outside the window, the rolling green fields were starting to give way to streets and houses as they approached London.

'What's Tom like?' Dora asked.

Liz shifted her gaze from the scenery and thought for a moment.

'He's not like the other porters,' she said. 'He's quiet, and very hard-working. And he's bright, too. He notices things, sometimes even before I do. There was one time, just before Christmas—'

Dora listened as Liz told the story of a small boy who was being bullied by his mother's boyfriend, and how Tom had spotted what was happening and tried to do something to help him.

She spoke warmly, Dora noticed. She heard the note of pride in Liz's voice. She was talking about him as a mother would.

'Is that the reason you became a nurse?' Dora asked, after a while. 'Because you wanted to be around children?'

'And because of you,' Liz smiled.

'Me?'

'You were there when I needed you. You were the only

one who showed me any kindness. I've never forgotten that.'

Dora felt herself blushing. 'I was only doing my job.'

'No, you were special. I decided I wanted to do the same for other girls in my position.'

'But you gave up being a midwife?'

'I realised it wasn't for me.' Liz looked rueful. 'It was so hard for me. Every time I had to hand a newborn baby over to its mother, it felt as if I was giving away my child all over again.'

She looked at Dora. 'What about you?' she asked. 'What made you give up hospital nursing?'

Dora shrugged. 'I just felt as if I wanted to help out in the community a bit more,' she said. 'Patients come and go in hospital and you never find out how they're getting on. But now I can really get to know people, get involved in their lives.'

She thought about poor Maggie Metcalfe. If only she'd got more involved in her life, perhaps she'd still be alive now.

'Matron would probably say I let myself get too involved in my patients' lives!' Liz said ruefully. 'She says I care too much about the children on the ward.'

'How can you care too much when it comes to kids?' Dora was outraged.

'That's what Miss Groves thinks.'

'Then Miss Groves sounds like an old battle-axe!'

Liz smiled but said nothing.

'You know, you'd make a good district nurse,' Dora said thoughtfully.

'Oh, I don't know about that.'

'I mean it,' Dora said. 'If you ever get tired of hospital life, come and see me.'

Liz smiled again. 'I'll think about it,' she said.

It was supposed to be her day off, but Liz couldn't resist heading back to the Nightingale rather than going home. She told herself she needed to check on a few patients on the ward, but the truth was the flat seemed unbearably quiet and lonely with Jen gone.

Besides, she needed to distract herself from the torrent of thoughts raging through her head.

Tom Weaver was her son.

Everything she had imagined had been turned upside down. The picture of the little girl she'd cherished in her mind for the last eighteen years was gone, replaced by a strapping young man with dark curls and laughing eyes who was very real indeed.

And to think they'd been working together for the past three years! She could still remember him as a fifteen-year-old boy, pushing a trolley down the corridor with the strength of a grown man, his head turned shyly down. She had always had a soft spot for him; he was bright and sensitive, unlike the other porters. He took a real interest in the patients, he cared about them. Was it too fanciful to imagine he'd got that from her? He certainly inherited his father's dark good looks.

How had she not recognised Jack in him before? Probably because up until that morning she'd had no idea that her child had been a boy. She had always been looking for a girl, searching strangers' faces, always wondering if perhaps her long-lost daughter was behind a shop counter, or sitting behind her at the cinema.

And she'd really thought she'd found her in Amy Metcalfe. They looked so alike, and the fact that she'd been born in the very same place on the same day had been too much of a coincidence to ignore.

And that her mother's name was Margaret, too . . .

Liz shook her head in wonder. Thank God she hadn't said anything. The poor girl was already feeling lost enough, without her adding to her heartache.

But should she say anything to Tom? She'd thought she'd made up her mind on the journey home. She'd meant it when she told Dora that she didn't want to upset him, but didn't he deserve to know the truth? And how could she go on working alongside him, knowing what she knew?

She was so lost in thought, she barely noticed as she walked in through the high, wrought-iron gates to the hospital, and found herself staring at the Porters' Lodge. She usually went past it without thinking, but now she found her footsteps slowing as she approached.

A dark-haired figure leaned against the wall of the lodge, dressed in a brown overall, head bowed, smoking a cigarette. Liz's heart leapt, thinking it might be Tom. But as she drew nearer, she recognised Blakey's lank, greasy locks.

'Good evening, Blakey,' she greeted him.

He straightened when he saw her, throwing away his cigarette and taking his hands out of his pockets.

'Evening, Sister.' His voice sounded hoarse. Drawing

closer to the pool of lamplight where he stood, Liz could see that his eyes were red-rimmed.

'Are you all right, my dear?' she asked.

Blakey drew his sleeve across his face, wiping away what she knew had been tears. 'I—'

But before he could reply, the door to the lodge was flung open and Mr Franklin the Head Porter appeared.

'I thought I heard voices,' he said. He jerked his head towards Blakey. 'Get inside, lad. I've made a nice brew.'

Blakey headed past Liz and into the Porters' Lodge. She watched him go, astonished. Since when did Mr Franklin start making tea for his juniors?

'Can I help you, Sister?'

The Head Porter was looking at her with a polite smile of enquiry. Liz ignored the question, her gaze still fixed on the door where Blakey had disappeared.

'Is he all right?' she asked.

Mr Franklin looked sombre. 'He's just had a bit of bad news, miss. We all have. It's hit us hard, you might say.'

A warning prickle began to crawl up Liz's spine.

'What is it? What's happened?'

'It's young Tom Weaver, I don't know if you know him—'

Her blood ran cold. 'What about him?'

Mr Franklin shook his head. 'There's been an accident, Sister. A fire at his family's shop last night. Tom was trapped, and—'

But Liz didn't stop to hear the rest. She was already running towards the hospital building.

Chapter Fifty-Four

Miss Judd, the sister in charge of the Male Medical ward, was surprised to see her. She was a small, wiry woman in her thirties with black hair drawn tightly off her face and a reputation for being difficult. She was the scourge of young students, who dreaded being assigned to her ward.

'Miss Spencer.' She looked Liz up and down, taking in her lack of uniform. 'What are you doing here?'

'I'm looking for a patient of yours – Tom Weaver?' She fought to keep her voice steady, even though her heart was pounding.

'The porter?' Miss Judd's dark brows lifted. 'What do you want with him?'

'I'm a friend of the family.'

'Really?' The ward sister's brows rose even further, almost disappearing under the edge of her starched cap.

'Where is he? Can I see him?' Liz looked around the ward.

'He's being specialled in Room Three.'

'How is he?'

'He's not doing very well, I'm afraid. He hasn't regained consciousness since he was brought in.'

Liz barely took in what the ward sister was saying to her. Every word cut her like a knife.

'Smoke inhalation . . . Damage to the trachea . . . Blood tests showing high levels of carbon monoxide . . .'

'Has the doctor seen him recently?' Liz interrupted her.

'He did a blood test about an hour ago. We've been giving him oxygen and CO_2 since he arrived, and we're hoping it will make a difference to his levels.'

But her sombre face told a different story.

'I'd like to sit with him,' Liz said.

'Well, I'm not sure about that—'

'I'd like to sit with him.' She repeated her statement, more firmly this time.

Something in Liz's manner must have warned the sister not to argue. 'I suppose you could stay until the doctor comes,' she agreed grudgingly. 'We're rather busy at the moment and we haven't been able to arrange a special for him yet. So I suppose you could make yourself useful.'

She looked Liz up and down again, frowning at her lack of uniform. 'There are aprons in the linen cupboard,' she said.

Liz already knew what to expect, but it still came as a shock to see Tom lying in the bed, a breathing tube down his throat. The room was silent but for the steady hiss of the oxygen tank.

She automatically went to check the levels and then read his notes. He was being treated for shock with saline and a hypodermic injection of Coramine. Miss Judd had already mentioned his last blood test had revealed high levels of carbon monoxide, but it shook Liz to see how high the levels were.

She looked down at him, his dark hair pushed back

from his pale face, chest labouring. She knew how carbon monoxide worked on the body. It choked the blood vessels, preventing them from carrying life-giving oxygen.

He was slowly but surely being poisoned. She was losing him again, before she'd even really found him.

Liz sank down in the chair beside the bed and reached for his hand, then stopped herself. The skin on his hands and forearms was covered in compresses.

I can't even touch him, she thought.

She had watched many anxious parents at their children's bedside, more than she could possibly count. She'd sat with many of them too, holding their hands, listening to their prayers, trying to offer what comfort she could.

But it wasn't until now that she truly understood the anguish they were going through. The raw yearning of a parent who tried to make bargains with the Almighty, who would give absolutely anything they had to be able to change places with their child, to go through their agony instead.

Take me, she begged. *Do anything you want, send me straight to Hell if you like. But please God, spare him.*

The doctor arrived just as tea was being served. Liz could hear the clatter of cups and dishes coming from the ward.

Miss Judd would not be pleased, she thought. The last thing a ward sister wanted was a doctor on the ward when she was trying to get on with her duties. Especially as she usually had to abandon whatever she was doing to accompany him so she could hang on to his every word.

Dr Harper was a houseman on the Senior Physician's staff. Liz didn't have much to do with him on the children's ward, but she had known him since he was a nervous student.

He hadn't grown much in confidence over the past five years, she thought. He walked into the room, his head buried in his notes. When he looked up and saw Liz sitting there, he immediately started to blush.

'Miss Spencer! What are you doing here?'

'I—'

'She says she's a friend of the family,' Miss Judd said. She sounded very sceptical. 'Although why she's here and the boy's own family isn't is a mystery to me,' she added under her breath.

'Have you got the results of the blood test?' Liz asked, ignoring her.

'Yes. Yes, I – er – have them here somewhere . . .'

He shuffled the papers in his hands. Liz clenched her fists at her sides to stop herself snatching them from his hands.

'Here they are. Let's see—' Dr Harper paused for a moment, his eyes flicking down the column of figures. Liz held her breath. 'Ah.'

'What?'

The young doctor looked up, his expression regretful. 'I'm afraid the carbon monoxide levels haven't come down at all.'

Liz looked at the oxygen tank, still hissing softly. None of it was getting into Tom's blood.

She had been afraid of this. It had been one of the many frightening pictures that had been going through her head.

'What about a blood transfusion?' she asked.

Dr Harper frowned. 'Well, yes, that might be possible,' he agreed. 'Except—'

'What?'

'He has a very unusual blood type. B negative. That means he can only receive blood that's type O negative or B negative, and I very much doubt if we'd be able to find a suitable donor at short notice.'

'Perhaps his family could help?' Miss Judd said. 'He has an aunt listed as his next of kin. I'll telephone—'

'I'm B negative.'

They both looked at Liz.

'Are you sure?' Dr Harper said. 'It is very rare—'

'I do know my own blood type, Doctor,' Liz cut him off.

'Well, I never.' Dr Harper ran his hand through his hair. 'Isn't that the most extraordinary coincidence, Sister?'

Miss Judd looked at Tom, then back at Liz. 'Uncanny, Doctor,' she agreed.

Chapter Fifty-Five

After the transfusion, Liz was sent to a private room on the Female Medical ward to rest and recover.

Ellen Potter, the ward sister, could not have been less like Miss Judd. She was in her late twenties, a real blonde bombshell, with a figure like Marilyn Monroe and a fondness for laughter and gossip.

'I can't believe what you did,' she said to Liz. 'I mean, we all like Tom, but to offer to give him your blood . . .' She shook her head in wonder.

'How is he?' Liz asked. 'Do you know?'

'I'm sorry, love, I don't. I suppose time will tell, won't it?'

Time will tell. It wasn't the answer she'd wanted to hear. Liz looked at the clock. It was almost half past eight in the evening, two hours after the transfusion had taken place. Surely they should have news by now?

Unless it was bad news and no one had the heart to tell her.

'Did you hear what happened?' Ellen Potter interrupted her thoughts. 'He was a real hero, by all accounts, rushing into that shop to save his cousin.'

Liz stared at her. 'Who told you that?'

'His cousin's on the ward. She's suffering from smoke

inhalation, but she didn't sustain nearly as much damage as Tom, which is a miracle. She could have died, from what I gather.'

'What happened?' Liz asked.

'It was a clothes horse that caught light, apparently. Valerie – the cousin – reckons she fell asleep in front of the fire. The rest of the family were out when it happened, but Tom came home and found the place ablaze. The fire brigade were trying to put it out, but when he heard his cousin was trapped in there he just rushed in to rescue her. He should get a medal, I reckon.'

Stupid, stupid boy. Liz was caught between pride and anger.

'And his cousin survived?'

'Oh yes, she's recovering nicely. Although she feels utterly wretched about what happened. She won't stop crying, poor thing.'

Liz tried to summon some sympathy for the girl, but her heart felt as hard and cold as a stone in her chest.

'And you're sure there's no news about Tom?' she asked.

Miss Potter shook her head. 'Not as far as I know. Look, why don't you try to get some rest?' she suggested.

'I can't. I need to see how he's getting on.'

Liz tried to swing her legs off the bed but Ellen Potter pushed her back firmly against the pillows.

'You're not going anywhere tonight,' she said.

'But I'm fine—'

'You're recovering,' Ellen said. 'Now do as you're told and try to sleep. Do you want me to get the doctor to prescribe you something before I go off duty?'

Liz sullenly refused her offer. She did the same when the Night Sister came round an hour later.

'Have you heard anything about Tom Weaver?' Liz asked.

'Don't worry about him. Get some rest.'

'I wish people would stop telling me to do that!' Liz snapped, then regretted it when she saw the reproachful look on Kath Warren's face.

'I'm sorry,' she said. 'I'm just worried about Tom, that's all.'

'I haven't been down to Male Medical yet,' Kath replied. 'But I'll be sure to find out and let you know.'

'Thank you.'

'As long as you agree to try to sleep. I promise I'll wake you when I have news,' she said, as Liz opened her mouth to argue.

Liz tried to do as she was told, but sleep evaded her. She had once again refused the sister's offer of a sleeping pill, determined to stay awake until she returned. But time seemed to drag as she lay there, staring up into the darkness, her thoughts racing.

What if the transfusion hadn't worked, and Tom was dead? No one would think to tell her. They would be on the telephone to Violet Cox, or his other aunt.

She flung back the covers and stood up, then immediately regretted it as her head started to swim.

She sat down again, taking a deep breath to collect herself. Then she stood up again, just as the door opened.

'I'm getting up,' Liz sighed into the darkness. 'I can't rest and I don't want a sleeping pill. No one will tell me what's happening, so I'm going to go and find out for myself.'

'And they say doctors make the worst patients,' a man's voice drawled in the darkness.

Liz looked up. In the dim light from the hall, she could just about make out Rob Bryant's dim shape standing in the doorway.

'What are you doing here?'

'The Night Sister told me there was a particularly troublesome patient on Female Medical,' Rob said.

Liz reached across and switched on the lamp, flooding the room with light. Rob stood before her in his white coat, looking tired and drawn. He must be one of the physicians on call that night.

'I came to check on you,' he said.

'I'm fine,' Liz dismissed.

'Are you sure?' He reached out to look at her more closely, but Liz jerked away from his touch.

'Never mind me,' she said. 'Have you heard what happened to Tom Weaver?'

'He's the talk of the hospital. As are you,' he added. 'You're quite the hero, Miss Spencer.'

She ignored the comment. 'How is he? Have you heard?'

'He's starting to respond to the treatment.'

'Oh, thank God!' She sobbed with relief. 'So he's going to be all right?'

'We won't know for sure until he regains consciousness.' He regarded her thoughtfully. 'Why do you care so much?'

The question brought her back to her senses, her guard back up. 'I'm concerned, that's all.'

'Concerned enough to drop everything and rush here

on your day off to sit at his bedside? Concerned enough to give blood for him?'

She didn't like the way he was looking at her, as if he could somehow see into her soul.

'You know me,' she joked feebly. 'I always get too emotionally involved.'

'Especially when it comes to your own flesh and blood.'

Chapter Fifty-Six

Liz stared at him. His words hung in the air between them. She wanted to deny it, but there was something about his steady brown gaze that told her there was no point in denying the truth any more.

'How did you know?' she said quietly, then added, 'Was it because I gave him my blood?'

'The fact that you were able to seemed nothing short of a miracle,' he said. 'But it wasn't just that. I've seen you with the children on the ward. The love you give them is almost – maternal.'

You must remember, Sister, you are a nurse, not a doting mother.

Matron's words came back to her. Miss Groves could not have known how much they would hurt her.

'And then the way you defended Noel's mother,' Rob went on. 'I expected you to feel angry towards her for neglecting her son, but instead you felt sorry for her.'

'You'd have to have a heart of stone not to feel compassion for the poor girl.'

'Yes, I suppose so. But with you I could tell it was personal. As if you knew what it was like to be in her shoes, to have to give up your baby.' He sat down on the edge of the bed, so close he could touch her if he reached out. 'Is that what you had to do, Liz? Give him up?'

It was the first time he'd called her by her first name. Feeling him so near to her, hearing her name on his lips, his voice so full of gentle understanding, suddenly seemed too intimate to bear. She didn't deserve his compassion.

'For crying out loud, Liz!' He sighed in exasperation. 'Don't shut me out, please. I'm your friend. You can trust me.'

Liz looked back at him. She *could* trust him, she realised. She wasn't sure why, but there was something in that steady brown gaze that told her he really cared.

Don't shut me out, please.

She'd been shutting people out for so long, refusing to allow them too close, that she'd forgotten what it was like to do anything else. She'd spent her whole life keeping a secret, guarding her good name.

'It's not as simple as that,' she said.

'So tell me.'

'It's a long story.'

He reached for her hand, his fingers warm as they curled around hers.

'I'm not going anywhere,' he said.

He listened so attentively as she explained what had happened, what she'd done. She kept her eyes fixed on the bedclothes, painfully aware of his unwavering gaze that never left her face.

She didn't dare look up, worried about what she might see in his eyes. She was so ashamed of what she'd done, she couldn't imagine him not hating her for it. He was such a kind man, how could he not condemn her?

But when she finally dared to look up, all she saw in his face was compassion and understanding.

They talked all night. As Liz gradually unburdened herself, she could feel herself becoming lighter, as if the weight of her guilt and sadness had been lifted from her. She had never opened up to anyone the way she did to Rob. She only hoped he wouldn't hate her for it.

But even if he did, she still felt better having told her story to someone.

As the first light of dawn began to creep through the crack in the drawn curtains, they were still talking. Outside the door, the sounds grew more distinct, as the whispering voices and creeping footsteps of the night nurses gave way to the normal morning activities of the day staff.

Ellen Potter came in to check on her, and was clearly surprised to find Rob Bryant at her bedside.

'Oh! Is everything all right?' She looked from one to the other, obviously dismayed to find a consultant in attendance on one of her patients.

'Everything is fine, Sister,' Rob reassured her.

'How is Tom Weaver doing?' Liz asked the first question that came into her mind.

'I don't know. I'm more concerned with how you're getting on, since you're my patient.'

Ellen grasped Liz's wrist to take her pulse, her puzzled gaze still on Rob Bryant. Liz could understand why she was so confused. It certainly wasn't usual for a consultant to visit a patient unannounced, especially when she wasn't even supposed to be under his care.

She could see the ward sister's mind working feverishly as she took Liz's TPRs, trying to add it all up.

'Everything seems normal,' she declared at last, putting the thermometer away.

'Does that mean I can go?'

'I see no reason why not. The doctor will have to see you first, although—' Her gaze shifted to Rob. 'You seem to have your own physician on call.'

There was no mistaking her speculative look. But Liz had more pressing things on her mind.

'Can you find out about Tom?' she asked, as Ellen left the room.

'I'll send one of my nurses over to Male Medical,' Ellen promised. And then, with a final curious glance over her shoulder, she was gone.

Liz kept her eyes fixed on the door. 'You do realise we'll be the talk of the hospital by lunchtime?' she said.

'I don't care.'

She looked back at him. 'So you don't hate me, then?'

'Hate you?' He looked genuinely puzzled. 'Why on earth should I hate you?'

'Because I'm not the woman you thought I was.'

He reached for her hand. 'Nothing you've told me could make me think any the less of you, Liz. The opposite, if anything. After everything you've been through, I admire you even more. You're strong, compassionate—'

'Stop.' She pulled her hand from his grasp, embarrassed. 'I don't deserve it.'

He sent her a long, shrewd look. 'That's the problem, isn't it?' he said. 'You don't feel you deserve anything.

Not forgiveness, or compassion – or love?'

She was silent, taking in his words. He was right, she knew. That was probably why she'd avoided relationships for so long. She'd told herself that it was because of her career, but if she was truthful with herself then she didn't feel as if she should be happy after what she'd done.

She had been punishing herself for years, she realised.

'I suppose I can't believe anyone would love me,' she said sadly.

'I do.'

Liz stared at him, shocked at his confession. Had he really just uttered those words?

Rob looked as surprised as she did. 'Sorry,' he said. 'I probably shouldn't have just blurted it out like that. It's hardly the time or the place, is it?' He looked around ruefully. 'But I do. I started falling for you from the minute I arrived. Despite your efforts to keep me at arm's length!'

Before Liz could reply, the door opened and one of the staff nurses walked in. Even though Liz and Rob had been sitting apart, she still blushed, feeling as if she had been caught in the act of something.

'Miss Potter sent me to tell you that Tom Weaver has regained consciousness,' the nurse said.

'Oh, thank God!' Liz looked at Rob and saw her own happy relief mirrored in his smiling face. It was all she could do not to throw herself into his arms.

Instead, she pulled herself together and said, 'Thank you for letting me know, Nurse.'

The nurse left the room, giving them the same curious look that Ellen Potter had.

'We're definitely going to be the talk of the hospital now,' Rob said ruefully.

But Liz was too preoccupied to care. Even Rob's startling confession of a few moments earlier had completely gone from her mind.

'He's awake,' she said. She felt as if she'd been given her own life back.

'Thanks to you,' Rob smiled. 'I bet you can't wait to see him?'

Liz shrank back, shaking her head. 'I can't.'

'Don't you want to see your son?'

'More than anything in the world. But I don't think it would be a good idea to – let myself get too close.'

Rob looked shocked as her words sank in. 'You mean you're not going to tell him?'

'How can I? It wouldn't be right, especially not after everything he's been through . . .' Her voice trailed off.

'Are you sure you're not just scared?'

She looked at him sharply. Once again, Rob had seen right through her. How was it that he understood her so well?

Because he loves you, whispered a voice inside her head.

And she loved him too, she realised with sudden, blinding clarity.

'Of course I'm scared,' she admitted. 'How could he ever forgive me? What if he turned against me?'

'He won't.'

'But what if he does?' It was better to stay in ignorance than to face rejection from him.

'There's only one way to find out.'

Liz shook her head. 'I wouldn't know how to tell him.'

'Perhaps I can help?'

Liz turned to see Violet Cox standing in the doorway.

'Miss Cox! What are you doing here?'

It was a stupid question, and the old lady's pinched expression told her as much.

'Where else would I be? I would have come sooner, but my sister only saw fit to tell me what had happened last night.' She looked quietly furious. 'I caught the first train up from Kent this morning, praying I wouldn't be too late. How is he?'

'He's just woken up.' Liz looked at Rob. He knew who Violet Cox was because Liz had told him all about her meeting with the elderly midwife, but it was hard to tell what he was thinking from his unreadable expression.

'Thank God.' Violet Cox closed her eyes briefly. She looked tired and drained, and even older than when Liz had first met her. 'And I understand he has you to thank for saving his life?'

Liz looked down at her hands. 'I only did what—'

'What any mother would?' Violet Cox finished for her.

Liz winced at the jibe. But when she looked up, she could see the old lady's eyes were filled with gentle understanding.

Rob cleared his throat. 'I was just telling Liz I thought she should go and see Tom.'

'So I heard.' Miss Cox looked at him, her spine straightening. Any deference she'd once had for doctors had clearly gone years ago.

'Don't worry, I wasn't going to say anything to him,' Liz put in quickly.

'I think you should.'

Liz stared at her. 'But I thought—'

'I know what I said, my dear. And afterwards I realised that I'd been too harsh. I was only trying to protect Tom, just as I always have. But now I realise that it would be a mistake to keep the truth from him.' She tilted her head and regarded Liz consideringly. 'All these years I've kept my sister's secret because I thought it was best for Tom. You were dead, there was nothing to be gained by telling him the truth. But when you appeared, I realised that you might be his chance of happiness, and I could never deny him that. Peggy adored Tom, and I know she would have wanted him to know a mother's love, even if she couldn't give it herself.'

'Thank you.' Liz felt weak with gratitude. Miss Cox's approval meant the world to her. She knew she would never have said a word without it.

'All I ask is that you give me the chance to speak to him first?' Violet Cox pleaded. 'This situation is largely of my making, and I feel I should try to explain, if I can?'

Liz nodded. 'Of course,' she said.

Chapter Fifty-Seven

Tom was still drowsy from the morphine they'd given him. His head was thumping and his throat felt as if he'd swallowed razor blades. His blistered skin stung beneath the tannic compresses that swathed his hands and arms.

He was still trying to piece together what had happened over the past few hours. He had no recollection of anything from the moment he'd rushed blindly into that burning shop. The first thing he knew was when he woke up in a hospital bed with Aunt Violet at his bedside, telling him he'd almost died.

'How's Val?' he whispered.

'She's quite well,' Aunt Violet said. 'They're keeping her in for a couple of days, but they reckon she'll recover.'

'I'm glad.' He winced as he croaked out the words. The pain relief was wearing off, and even taking a breath hurt him.

'Here.' Aunt Violet reached for the glass of water beside his bed and held it to his lips. 'Sip it carefully.'

'Thanks.' He lifted his head to take a sip, then sank back against the pillows. Aunt Violet leaned over and wiped his mouth tenderly with her lavender-scented handkerchief.

She looked strangely out of place in the hospital, dressed in her old-fashioned coat buttoned up to the neck, her hat perched on her head.

'It was good of you to come,' he croaked.

'You nearly died. I think that warrants a visit, don't you?' Aunt Violet smiled.

'Did I?'

'We were all very worried about you. You might not be here if the doctor hadn't given you a blood transfusion. It saved your life.'

Her voice trembled as she said the words. Aunt Violet rarely showed any emotion, and Tom could tell she was trying to keep her feelings in check as she spoke.

'You have a very rare blood type,' she went on. 'They had to find a family member to be a suitable donor.'

Tom looked at her. 'Is that why you're here? Did you give me your blood?'

'No,' she said, her gaze lowering. 'No, it wasn't me.'

'Who, then? Not Auntie Lillian?'

Aunt Violet shook her head. 'She wouldn't have been able to do it.'

Another thought struck him. 'It wasn't Eric, was it? Surely not? He's never done anything for anyone in his life.'

'Tom—'

'I think I'd rather die than have his blood running through my veins.' He chuckled. 'Here, what if I suddenly start wearing crepe-soled shoes and—'

'Thomas, will you listen to me?' Aunt Violet's face was so serious, it wiped the grin from Tom's face. 'It was Miss Spencer.'

'Miss Spencer? But how—' He frowned. 'I thought you said it had to be a family member?'

Aunt Violet looked away, and for the first time ever Tom saw a lack of certainty in her face.

'I have something to tell you,' she said. 'Something I should have told you a long time ago. And I want you to listen carefully, and try not to judge any of us until you've heard what I have to say.'

A warning prickle crept up his spine. 'What have you got to tell me?'

She took a deep breath and reached for his hand.

'It all started the night you were born . . .'

'They've been in there for a long time,' Liz said.

She kept her eyes fixed on the door to Tom's room, willing it to open. Her shoulders ached with tension.

'I expect they've got a lot to talk about.' Rob, by contrast, seemed relaxed, almost nonchalant as he sat beside her.

It felt as if they'd been there forever, lingering in the corridor outside the Male Medical ward. Miss Judd was certainly put out that they were there. She kept coming to the door to frown at them through the glass.

Liz had told Rob he didn't have to stay, but he'd insisted.

'I'm not letting you go through this by yourself,' he'd said.

'I'm fine, honestly. And you've got patients to see—'

'Liz, I want to stay. You're not pushing me away again.'

Liz smiled, grateful for his calm, untroubled presence.

She stood up and paced the corridor again, her arms wrapped around herself. She was so full of nervous energy she couldn't keep still.

'What if he hates me?' she said.

'Why should he hate you?'

Liz stopped pacing and stared at him. 'Have you forgotten I abandoned him?' she said.

'You didn't exactly abandon him.'

'I handed him over to a stranger. What else would you call it?' She shuddered now to think of her recklessness. 'Anything could have happened to him.'

'You did what you thought was best at the time.'

'No, I didn't. I was selfish. I had no idea what was going to happen to him, and I didn't even care.'

'You did care,' Rob said. 'You haven't stopped caring ever since. You said yourself, that moment changed your whole life.'

He was right, she thought. It had changed her life. But it had changed Tom's, too.

'I just don't want him to hate me,' she said quietly.

'Oh, Liz.'

Rob stood up and came to her. When he put his hands on her arms she didn't flinch or pull away.

'He'll forgive you,' he said quietly. 'But you've got to forgive yourself first.'

The door to Tom's room opened and Miss Cox appeared. She looked weary and nothing like the brisk, upright woman Liz had first met in the churchyard. Was it really only the day before? It seemed like an eternity.

'How is he?' Rob asked.

'He's recovering well, I think. He's still on morphine for the shock and the pain, but his blood test results are much better, and—'

'What did he say when you told him about me?' Liz interrupted, unable to bear it any longer.

Miss Cox turned to her. 'He's still trying to take it all in,' she said. 'As you can imagine, this has all come as a shock to him.'

'But he's willing to talk to me?'

'Oh, yes.' The old woman gave her the smallest of smiles.

Liz looked at Rob, nerves suddenly assailing her. 'Perhaps I should leave it for a while?' she said. 'Until he's feeling better—'

'I don't think you should leave it any longer, Miss Spencer. It's been eighteen years, after all.'

'She's right,' Rob said. 'There's no time like the present.'

Miss Cox reached out and patted her hand. 'Don't look so worried, my dear,' she said. 'Thomas is an intelligent boy. I'm sure he'll give you a chance.'

Liz looked at Rob, standing beside her. 'I hope so,' she said.

Chapter Fifty-Eight

It must be the medication playing with his mind, Tom thought. Or perhaps he wasn't awake at all? Perhaps he was still unconscious, and the morphine was causing some strange, unfathomable dream?

It couldn't be real, that was for sure. This surely couldn't be Miss Spencer, the unflappable ward sister, sitting here by his bedside, tears running down her face, telling him she was his mother.

And yet just a few moments before, Aunt Violet had been here, sitting in this very same spot, telling him the same thing.

Except she wasn't his aunt now, was she? She wasn't his flesh and blood at all. Everything he'd grown up knowing was no longer true.

And his mother and father, whom he'd loved and idolised for so long, were not his parents. His mother had stolen him, sneaked off with him like a thief in the night.

She was desperate, she wasn't thinking straight, otherwise she would never have done what she did . . .

Aunt Violet's words came back to him. But was she talking about Miss Spencer or his mother?

'You gave me away,' he said flatly, still trying to take it in.

'Yes,' Miss Spencer said. She raised her gaze to meet

his. 'I don't expect you to understand, or to forgive me,' she said. 'Believe me, I find it hard to forgive myself, even after all these years.'

But Tom did understand. He thought about all the young girls he'd seen admitted to the hospital. Sad, desperate girls who'd been abandoned by their families, by the men who'd sworn they loved them, that they would stand by them.

How many young girls had he taken down to the mortuary after a botched backstreet abortion? At least Miss Spencer had not gone down that awful path.

'What about my father?' he asked.

Pain flashed in Miss Spencer's eyes, and for a moment she seemed to find it hard to speak.

'His name was Jack,' she said at last. 'He was a pilot in the RAF.'

'Did he know about me?'

She nodded. 'We were going to be married.'

'What happened to him?' But he already knew the answer to his question. It was written all over Miss Spencer's distraught face.

'He was killed at Dunkirk.'

Tom paused, taking it in. 'So we might have been a family?'

'Yes,' she said. 'We would.' There was a faraway look in her eyes. 'You look just like him, you know. You have his dark hair.'

Her hand moved, as if she was going to brush his hair from his eyes, then she seemed to think better of it and settled it back in her lap.

'What happened to you then?' Tom asked.

'I had to tell my parents. They were horrified, of course. My father was a bank manager, and my mother was worried about what it might do to his reputation, having an illegitimate grandchild.'

'So they didn't help you?'

'My mother arranged for me to go to an unmarried mothers' home in London, as far away as possible from where we lived. She was determined to avoid a scandal. So she left me at the mercy of the Sisters of Eternal Piety.' Her mouth tightened at the memory.

'So you were going to give me away?'–

'I had no choice.' Her hazel eyes pleaded for understanding. 'I'd had to give up my job, so I had no money. And my mother had made it very clear that I wouldn't be welcome under her roof with a baby.'

'Did you go home after . . .' He let the words trail off.

Miss Spencer shook her head. 'I never saw her again. After I lost you, when I thought you were dead, I couldn't face her. I was too angry. I blamed her, you see. If all this hadn't happened, if she'd helped me, you might have still been alive.' She lowered her gaze to her hands in her lap. 'But I know it was wrong. It was my fault you were dead, no one else's. I made my choice to leave you behind that night.'

Now it was Tom who fought to resist the urge to put out his hand and touch her, to reassure her.

'But I tried to come back,' Miss Spencer said. 'I wandered the streets, with bombs and incendiaries raining down around me. I didn't want to take shelter, I didn't care if I died. I wanted to die, I think. Then I realised I couldn't do it, I couldn't leave you behind. I ran all the way back to the

351

hospital, but by then the place was in flames, with police at the gates. They told me the Casualty department had been hit. And then I read in the paper that a mother and baby had perished, and I knew it must be you.' She hung her head. 'I would have come to look for you if I'd thought you were alive. I would have spent my whole life searching—'

Tom believed her. He could see the desperation in her eyes.

'You did the right thing,' he said.

She looked at him blankly, as if she did not quite understand what he was telling her.

'You knew my mother would look after me, give me everything you couldn't.'

'Yes,' she said quietly. 'Yes, I did.'

'Even if you'd come back to the hospital that night, even if you'd taken me with you, you couldn't have looked after me. You couldn't have given me the stable home that my parents did.'

Miss Spencer closed her eyes briefly. 'You're right,' she admitted quietly. 'I suppose I've always known that, deep down. I just wish things had been different, that's all.'

So do I, Tom thought.

He pictured his father, the brave, handsome pilot shot down at Dunkirk. He thought about the life he might have led, had Jack lived. How different might it have been for him, with two loving parents, away from the cruelty of Uncle Stan and Aunt Lillian?

But it was futile to regret the past, to think about what might have been. All they had now was the future.

Chapter Fifty-Nine

The following day, Tom was allowed to get out of bed. And the first thing he did was visit his cousin.

Val was on the Female Medical ward. As it was visiting time, her mother and father were with her, sitting side by side. It did not seem to be a cheerful visit, judging by the glum look on Val's face.

'Tom!' She looked shocked to see him as he approached her bed. 'What are you doing here?'

'I came to see you – what do you think?'

'They told me you nearly died!'

'As you can see, I'm alive and well.' He forced a grin, even though he was still in pain. He looked at his aunt and uncle. Uncle Stan was staring at his shoes while Aunt Lillian fiddled in her handbag, clearly too embarrassed to look at him.

'How are you getting on?' he asked Val.

'All right.' She looked down at her hands, still encased in dressings.

'The doctor said she's doing very well,' Aunt Lillian said, still not quite able to meet his gaze.

'I'm glad to hear it.'

'Can't say the same about the shop,' Uncle Stan muttered. 'The whole place is damaged. It'll cost a fortune to rebuild.'

'I'm sure the insurance will cover it,' Tom said.

'And in the meantime we've got nowhere to live.' Uncle Stan glared at Tom accusingly, as if it were somehow his fault.

'Stan, please!' Aunt Lillian hissed. 'That's the least of our worries. Val's safe, and that's all that matters.'

Uncle Stan said nothing, but his silence spoke volumes.

'And we've got you to thank for that,' Aunt Lillian went on, glancing at Tom for the first time. 'You saved her life.'

'I only did what anyone else would do.' Tom looked at Val. Their eyes met for a moment, then her gaze slid away.

'Can you go, please?' she said to her parents. 'I'd like to talk to Tom alone.'

'What? No!' Uncle Stan's flabby jowls wobbled in outrage. 'We're not leaving for him.'

'Come on, Stan, let's go.' Aunt Lillian was already on her feet, gathering up her things. 'We can come back tomorrow.'

'Why can't he—'

'Stan!' Aunt Lillian cut him off. 'Will you do as you're told for once?'

She shot another quick, embarrassed look at Tom and then she was off, shoving her husband ahead of her.

'You didn't have to send them away,' Tom said.

'I couldn't wait for them to go. All Dad talks about is the wretched shop. I think he's more upset about that than he is about me.'

I wouldn't be surprised, Tom thought.

'I thought it might have been him who set the place on fire,' he admitted slowly. 'You know, to stop me getting my hands on it?'

Val shook her head. 'No, it was all my fault,' she said sadly. 'And I don't think Dad will ever forgive me for it.'

Tom sat down in the chair Aunt Lillian had vacated. 'What happened that night, Val?'

She hesitated for a moment, then said, 'It was a stupid accident. There were some clothes drying in front of the fire and I fell asleep on the couch. I didn't know anything else about it until I heard you calling my name. I woke up and the room was full of smoke.' She looked up at him, her eyes huge in her round face. 'I might not have woken up at all if you hadn't arrived when you did.'

'I heard the firemen found an empty sherry bottle on the floor beside you?'

Val's face reddened. 'I did have a drink,' she admitted. 'I was angry and upset and I wanted to calm myself down.'

'You were upset about me?'

Val said nothing, but her flaming cheeks gave her away. She looked as if she was about to cry.

'Val, I—'

'I'm sorry, I—'

They both started speaking at once, then stopped abruptly.

'You go first,' Val mumbled.

'No, you.'

She took a deep breath. 'I'm sorry about what happened that night. Honestly, I can't bear to think about the way I behaved—' She buried her face in her bandaged hands. 'What must you think of me?'

'It's all right,' Tom said.

'I got it all wrong,' she said, her voice muffled. 'You've

355

always been so good to me, not like everyone else. I – I just got the wrong idea, that's all. I really thought you loved me—'

'I do love you,' Tom said. He reached for her hand, gently lowering it from her face. 'But not in that way. You're like my sister, Val.'

'Not like Amy?' There was a trace of bitterness in her voice. 'You love her, don't you?'

Tom stared at her, taken aback by the question.

'I hardly know her.'

'But you're falling for her?'

'I – I don't know.'

'I'm sorry.' Val started to cry again. 'I'm doing it again, ain't I? Getting all jealous when it's none of my business. I don't know why you even bothered saving my life, when I'm such a horrible cow!'

'You ain't horrible, Val. I saved your life because I care about you.'

'I don't know why. I ain't worth caring about.'

'Don't say that.'

'It's true though, ain't it? Look at me. I'm no oil painting, as Mum's always pointing out. I don't know why anyone would look at me. I'm just a plain, fat, boring kid with nothing to say for herself!' Tears rolled down her cheeks.

'Now, you listen to me!' Tom said. 'Why would I have risked my life for you if you weren't worth saving?'

'I – I dunno.'

'I'll tell you, shall I? I saved you because you're one of the sweetest, kindest, funniest girls I know. I told you, you're my sister.'

'Except I ain't, am I? We ain't even related.'

Tom stared at her in shock. 'Who told you that?'

'Mum did. She said you ain't even family any more.'

'Did she now?' Tom simmered with silent anger. He had only just found out himself, and he and Miss Spencer had made the decision to keep it between them for the time being.

He only hoped his aunt hadn't spread it any further. He didn't want to think what might happen if any of the staff got wind of the gossip.

'She said now you've got your mother you won't want to know us any more.' Val was looking at him, her eyes shining with tears.

Tom smiled at her, putting his worries firmly aside. 'Don't think you can get rid of me that easily,' he said. 'You're my family, Val. And you always will be, whatever happens.'

Chapter Sixty

Liz should have known it would be impossible to keep a secret at the Nightingale. Within a day of her first heart-to-heart with Tom, she was summoned to Miss Groves' book-lined office.

'Is it true?' Matron demanded. She sat behind her imposing polished walnut desk, upright and angular, her beady gaze fixed on Liz. In front of her was a flawless blotter, with a row of fountain pens lined up precisely to one side. A leather-bound diary lay open at today's date.

The room smelt of leather and old books, overlaid with Miss Groves' sickly sweet lavender scent.

'Is what true?' Liz asked innocently.

Miss Groves looked irritated. 'This rumour I'm hearing about you and Tom Weaver. Is it true he's your son?'

'Where did you hear that?'

She already knew the answer to that one. Tom had told her that his aunt had told his cousin. Any word breathed on the Female Medical ward inevitably got back to Ellen Potter, who was a delightful woman and great fun, but a terrible gossip.

Liz took a steadying breath. 'Yes,' she said. 'It's true.'

'I see.' Was that disappointment in Miss Groves' eyes? Perhaps she'd expected more of a fight before Liz confessed.

'Why didn't you speak to me about it?'

'Because I didn't think it was any of your business.'

Miss Groves' face twitched. 'But I'm in charge of this hospital!'

'I know that, Matron. But this happened nearly twenty years ago. Before I ever became a nurse.'

'Nevertheless, it still speaks of a lack of judgement and moral tone,' Miss Groves said gravely.

'Moral tone?' Liz echoed coldly.

'I do not see how you can expect to continue as a ward sister at this hospital when your past is so – questionable.'

'For heaven's sake! I had a baby out of wedlock, I didn't sell my body to sailors down at the docks!'

Miss Groves bristled with shock. 'You see?' she said, tight-lipped. 'This is exactly the kind of attitude that sets a bad example among the younger nurses.' She adjusted the blotter, squaring it with the edge of the desk. 'I think you ought to know I shall be speaking to the Management Committee—'

'There's no need for that.'

'Oh, I think there's every need.'

'There's no need because I resign.'

'Oh.' Miss Groves' face fell a fraction. It was definitely disappointment Liz could see this time. 'Oh well, I see.' She fidgeted with the row of pens, picking one up and then putting it down again.

'I would offer to work out my notice, but I'm sure you won't want me setting a bad example with my lack of moral tone?'

'Yes, of course.'

'Will that be all, Matron?'

'Yes, that will be all.'

Miss Groves' frustrated expression was the last thing Liz saw as she rose to her feet and left the office.

She was still smiling about it when she met Rob for dinner that evening.

'You should have seen the look on her face,' she laughed. 'She had been so looking forward to giving me the sack – she was utterly furious when I walked out!'

Rob didn't seem to find it so amusing.

'How dare she try to get rid of you over something that happened years ago?' he fumed. 'You should fight it.'

'That's what Nurse Clackett said.'

Liz was surprised when her senior staff nurse had telephoned her earlier that day. She'd half expected her to agree with Matron as she was rather set in her ways. But Enid Clackett was also a decent, loyal woman, and she'd been outraged on Liz's behalf.

'Pardon me for saying so, Sister, but that's ridiculous,' she'd said. 'And I'd be happy to tell Matron the same thing if you decided to fight the matter. So would the other nurses, I'm sure.'

Liz had been so touched, she had barely known what to say.

'That's very kind of you, Nurse Clackett, but I don't think it would do any good. And I'd hate to land anyone else in trouble.'

'Well, I for one will be very sorry to see you go,' Miss Clackett said. 'I've learned a great deal from you, Sister.'

'Have you?' Liz was surprised. Clackett always seemed

rather put out by her lack of timekeeping and her habit of making up rules as she went along.

'Indeed. And the children will miss you, too. They've been asking after you for days.'

'I'll miss them.' Liz's heart was heavy with regret that she wouldn't be able to say goodbye to the children. Although perhaps it was easier that way. She couldn't bear the idea of turning her back on their little faces.

'It won't be the same without you.' The nurse's voice had sounded choked with emotion. 'I just don't have your knack with them, you see.'

'I'm sure you'll do very well, Nurse Clackett. Just listen to your heart.'

'I've a good mind to talk to the Management Committee myself,' Rob said now, as he helped himself to another glass of wine.

'Please don't,' Liz begged. 'Between you and me, I think Miss Groves has been trying to get rid of me for years. Even if I managed to stay, I'm sure it would only be a matter of time before she found some other excuse.'

'Then she's a fool,' Rob said. He leaned over and refilled her glass. 'So what will you do now?'

'I have something in mind.'

'Sounds intriguing.'

'I don't want to say too much yet. But I hope it will work out.'

'So do I.' He smiled across the table at her. The candle-light on the table cast a golden light across his face, making him look even more handsome.

It was the second time they'd had dinner in this Italian

restaurant. Rob worried that she wouldn't think him adventurous enough, but Liz loved the intimate setting, with its low lighting and quiet music, and the rich scent of delicious food in the air.

They changed the subject, and Liz told him how she'd asked Tom to come and stay at her flat.

'The shop's in ruins so he can't go back there,' she explained. 'The rest of the family have moved in with his uncle's family, but Tom knows he wouldn't be welcome there.'

'Poor kid,' Rob said. 'But aren't you afraid you might be rushing things a little? You and Tom have barely got to know each other.'

'I know, but what else can I do? He doesn't have a roof over his head. Besides, this will give us a chance to get to know each other, don't you think? It might turn out to be a blessing in disguise.'

'I hope you're right.' Rob sipped his wine thoughtfully.

'I'll admit everything is happening very fast at the moment,' Liz sighed. 'Tom, and my job, and—'

'And us?' Rob finished for her.

'Well, yes.'

A couple of weeks ago she could never have imagined herself having dinner with him, but now she couldn't imagine herself being without him. She had been in desperate need of his quiet, loving support as she'd navigated through the past few days.

But at the same time, she wondered if she was being fair to him, leaning on him so much when they still hardly knew each other.

'I was thinking,' Rob said, his eyes still fixed on his wine. 'Perhaps you'd prefer it if we held off for a while?'

Panic clutched at her. *Here it comes*, she thought. *This is all too much for him and he wants to escape.*

'What do you mean?' she said lightly. 'Are you trying to get rid of me already?'

'Not at all. It's you I'm concerned about. You're being pulled in so many different directions at the moment.'

'I'm sorry I can't give you the attention you deserve.'

'It's all right, Liz. I'm a big boy, I can take it.' He reached for her hand. 'I just wanted you to know I'll be here waiting when you're ready.'

'Will you?' She was surprised at how much she cared, how much he meant to her. 'You will wait for me, won't you?'

He leaned across the table and kissed her. A long, lingering kiss that told her everything she needed to know.

'Believe me, you're worth waiting for,' he murmured.

Chapter Sixty-One

A few days later, Tom had recovered enough to be discharged from hospital and move into Miss Spencer's flat.

Except she's not Miss Spencer any more, is she? She's your mother.

He pushed the thought from his mind. He couldn't think of her as anything else, no matter how hard he tried.

The flat above the pawnbroker's was smart and tastefully decorated, but Miss Spencer had seemed anxious as she'd shown him into his room.

'I'm sorry about the flowery wallpaper,' she'd said. 'This used to be my flatmate Jen's room. I'm afraid it might not be to your taste—'

'It's fine.' Tom hadn't wanted to tell her about the damp little storeroom where he used to sleep, with its bare bulb hanging down and mice scuttling behind the skirting boards.

He didn't feel ready to tell her about himself yet. And the last thing he wanted was for her to feel sorry for him.

'Are you sure? Of course, you're welcome to redecorate once you've settled in. I'm sure the landlord won't mind.'

Once you've settled in. How long did she think he was going to stay? Tom had assumed it would only be a temporary arrangement, but Miss Spencer had clearly decided that this was to be his home.

He watched her from the couch now as she fussed around him, plumping his cushions and bringing him tea and sandwiches. He wasn't used to being waited on, and certainly not by her.

It felt very wrong.

Miss Spencer certainly didn't seem like herself. Tom was used to her being capable and confident, taking charge of the ward and issuing orders. But now she seemed vulnerable and unsure of herself around him.

He'd expected Miss Spencer to go back to the hospital, but she insisted on staying with him.

'I'm sure they can manage without me,' she said.

Amy called round that afternoon and Tom was relieved to see her friendly face. He was beginning to feel rather awkward with only Miss Spencer for company.

His mother seemed just as pleased to see her.

'Sit down, my dear,' Miss Spencer said. 'Would you like a cup of tea, or some coffee?'

'Yes, please, Sis— Miss Spencer. Tea would be very nice.'

Amy sat down on the couch beside Tom, tucking her skirt nervously under her.

'I'll go and put the kettle on while you two have a chat,' Miss Spencer said. 'I'm sure Tom will be glad of your company. He's very bored, although he's far too polite to say so!'

Miss Spencer smiled fondly at him and then she left.

'It feels strange, having Sister making tea for me and not the other way round,' Amy whispered, when she'd gone.

'I know what you mean,' Tom said.

'How are you getting on? Are you settling in all right?'

'I'm fine.' How many times did he hear himself saying that?

'Have you heard from your family?'

'They're not my family, are they?' Tom snapped, then regretted it when he saw the hurt look on Amy's face. 'Sorry,' he said. 'I didn't mean to bite your head off.'

'It's all right. It must be hard for you, I'm sure.'

'I saw Val just before I came out of hospital.'

'How was she?'

'Devastated, as you'd expect. It doesn't help that Uncle Stan blames her for burning his shop down.'

'Isn't it your shop now?'

Tom shook his head. 'I think he's planning to talk to his solicitor about that. He thinks that since I'm not Maurice Weaver's son, I shouldn't be entitled to inherit his property.'

Amy frowned. 'He didn't waste any time, did he?'

'That's Uncle Stan for you.'

Tom was surprised at how little he cared any more. Perhaps Uncle Stan was right. The shop no longer felt like his, anyway.

Nothing felt as if it belonged to him.

Miss Spencer came in with the tea things on a tray, and set them down on the coffee table.

'Now, is there anything else I can get you?' she asked.

'No, thank you.'

'Would you like a biscuit, or a slice of cake?'

'No.'

'Are you sure? You hardly ate anything at lunch—'

'I said I'm fine!' Tom cut her off abruptly.

'Oh.' Miss Spencer looked startled. 'Well, in that case, I'll leave you to it.'

She shot a quick look at Amy, and then she was gone.

'That wasn't very nice,' Amy hissed, when they were alone.

'I can't help it. She keeps fussing over me, and it's driving me mad.'

'She's only trying to look after you.'

'I know.' Miss Spencer had been so kind to him, and he felt churlish that he couldn't bring himself to return her affection. 'It just feels strange, that's all.'

'Is it because you feel disloyal to your mother? To Peggy, I mean?'

Tom shook his head. 'I don't really remember her, to be honest. My only memories are what other people told me.'

'Then why don't you like it?'

'I don't know. I suppose it's because it's never happened to me before. I don't know how to be.'

'Neither does Miss Spencer.'

He stared at Amy. It had never occurred to him before she said it. No wonder Miss Spencer was so skittish and unsure around him. She was trying to work out how to navigate their new relationship as much as he was.

'I wish I still had a mother to fuss over me,' Amy said wistfully.

'Oh God, I'm sorry.' Tom was instantly contrite. 'Here I am, moaning about having a nice home and someone who cares about me, while you're—'

'It's all right,' Amy shrugged. 'I had a mother for eighteen years, don't forget. You're just getting used to yours.'

'Have you heard from your father?'

She shook her head. 'Not a word. I tried to call round, but his new housekeeper said he didn't want to see me. I was thinking of writing to him.' She smiled sadly. 'Anyway, I've got Auntie Eileen. She's asked me to go round for tea later. Said she had something important to tell me.'

'What's that, I wonder?'

'I'll find out, won't I?' she said. She glanced back towards the door. 'I wish you could try to be a bit nicer to poor Miss Spencer. She's been through such a lot.'

Haven't we all? Tom thought. 'It might be easier when she goes back to work.'

Amy stared at him. 'Haven't you heard?'

'Heard what?'

'Miss Spencer's been dismissed.'

'No!' Now it was Tom's turn to stare. 'Why?'

'Apparently Miss Groves decided she was not morally fit to be in charge of the children's ward any more.'

'Because of me?'

'I suppose so.'

Tom looked at the door. Miss Spencer was humming in the kitchen, blissfully unaware she was being discussed. 'Why didn't she tell me?'

'You'll have to ask her that, won't you?'

Amy left shortly afterwards and Tom went looking for Miss Spencer. He found her in the kitchen, chopping vegetables.

'I thought we'd have shepherd's pie for dinner. You do like shepherd's pie, don't you? I never thought to ask. I could always make something else if—'

'Why didn't you tell me you'd been dismissed?'

She laid down the knife and turned to face him. 'I suppose Amy told you?'

'I wish I'd heard it from you.'

'I know. I'm sorry. It just didn't seem fair to burden you with my problems.'

'But we're supposed to be family!' He said it without thinking. Liz gave him a watery smile.

'Is that what we are? Because we seem more like strangers.'

Tom's gaze slid from hers, towards the black and white tiled kitchen floor.

'I'm sorry I haven't appreciated your help more,' he said. 'I want you to know I'm grateful for everything you've done for me, letting me stay and everything—'

'I don't expect you to be grateful.'

'Then what do you expect?'

Their eyes met and held across the room for a moment. This time she was the one who looked away.

'I'm sorry,' she murmured. 'I know the last few days haven't been easy for either of us. And I'm aware that I've probably been a bit too much for you at times—'

'And I haven't been enough for you,' Tom said.

'I suppose it's difficult,' Miss Spencer said. 'You've only been my son for a few days. But I've been your mother for eighteen years.' She raised her eyes to look at him. 'I completely understand if you need to take things more slowly.'

Tom remembered Amy's words.

I wish I still had a mother to fuss over me.

'I think I just need more practice,' he said.

Miss Spencer had a lot of love to give. He just had to learn to accept it.

'I'm sorry you lost your job because of me,' he said quietly.

'I didn't lose it because of you. I lost it because of what I did.'

'Yes, but if you'd kept it a secret—'

Miss Spencer shook her head. 'Oh no,' she said. 'I've lived a lie for too long. You're my son, not some shameful secret I have to hide from the world.' She smiled at him. 'I might not have brought you up, but I'm proud of you. And I want the whole world to know that I'm your mother. Whatever Miss Groves thinks about it!'

Chapter Sixty-Two

'For heaven's sake, Auntie Eileen, spit it out. You're making me nervous!'

Amy sat at the table, watching Auntie Eileen going back and forth across the kitchen.

She'd asked Amy to visit, but now she seemed as jumpy as a cat. One minute she was at the sink filling a kettle, the next she was rummaging in the larder. She couldn't seem to stand still for more than a few seconds.

If Amy didn't know better, she would have sworn Eileen was avoiding her.

'Why don't you sit down?' Amy said gently. 'You said you had something to say to me?'

'I have.' Auntie Eileen folded a tea towel and set it on the edge of the draining board. 'But now you're here I don't really know where to start.' She picked up the tea towel and folded it again. 'I've been thinking about it all day and I still don't know if I'm doing the right thing. But I made a promise to your mother, and—'

'You made a promise to Mum? What sort of promise?' She thought for a moment. 'Has this got anything to do with Father?'

Auntie Eileen looked at her sharply. 'What makes you say that? Has he spoken to you?'

'I haven't seen him since the funeral. I've called round a couple of times, but his new housekeeper says he doesn't want to see me. Why do you ask?'

Auntie Eileen sat down opposite her. 'Your mother left a letter for you,' she said.

'A letter? Where is it? Why haven't you given it to me?'

'Because I wasn't sure if you should see it. I'm still not sure, truth be told. But your mother wanted to tell you, and I suppose I'd best abide by her wishes . . .'

'Tell me what?' Amy was leaning forward in her seat, every fibre in her body straining with tension.

Auntie Eileen pulled a grubby envelope out of her apron pocket and set it down on the table between them. Amy recognised her mother's carefully curled handwriting straight away.

'See for yourself,' Auntie Eileen said.

Dearest Amy

This is a very difficult letter for me to write. As you know, I'm not very good with words. But there's something I need to tell you, something I've been keeping from you.

Auntie Eileen silently set down a glass of brandy in front of Amy then sat down opposite her again.

If you're reading this then it means I'm gone. I'm so sorry, love. I tried so hard to stay with you. You were the only reason I kept going as long as I did. I only wish I could have stayed with you longer, but I count myself lucky I was able to see you grow into such a beautiful, confident young woman. You've made me so proud.

Anyway, I'm writing this letter because I've always taught you to be honest, and yet I haven't been honest with you.

You don't know how often I've wanted to tell you, but I was too afraid. I didn't know what you'd think of me, and I didn't want you to hate me. Believe me, I've hated myself enough.

Listen to me. I'm avoiding it now, trying not to say the words. But I'm worried if I don't tell you then you'll find out in some other way, and I don't think I could bear that. Malcolm might tell you, and I can't trust him not to hurt you.

So here goes.

Malcolm Metcalfe is not your father.

The words swam in front of her eyes. Amy looked at the brandy; even though she hadn't drunk a drop, she felt as if she was drunk.

I hope you can keep reading and allow me to explain. You can judge me later for what I've done, but hear me out first.

Our marriage was always difficult. Your Auntie Eileen always said I shouldn't have married him, and she was right. Perhaps he shouldn't have married me, either. But we did, and I swear to you I tried my hardest to make the marriage work.

I knew Malcolm wasn't the most loving of men, but I didn't realise how cold he truly was until it was too late.

But I still tried. I blamed myself. I thought it must be my fault he didn't like me as a husband should. I thought if only I tried harder, changed myself, did my best to be everything he wanted me to be, he might love me. But nothing I did was good enough.

I was so lonely and unhappy. You have to understand that. It's no excuse, but that was why I did what I did next.

I met Andy when I was volunteering with the WVS. We'd set up a mobile canteen at the docks, and he was one of the merchant seamen who'd stop for a cup of tea and a chat.

I called him Andy but his real name was Anders, and he was Norwegian. You know me, I've never been further than Margate, so I was fascinated to hear all about his travels, and the places he'd been. He spoke very good English, and he even taught me a few Norwegian words, although I've forgotten them now.

But I haven't forgotten Andy. How could I? He was my first love.

I didn't mean it to happen. But he was so kind and gentle, I'd never met a man like him. You look like him, by the way. You've got his height, and his red hair. I wish I had a photograph of him that I could show you, but perhaps it's better that I haven't. You might not want to see it anyway. Perhaps you're already disgusted with both of us for what we did.

But we couldn't help it. I felt so foolish and so guilty. Malcolm was no kind of husband, but he didn't deserve that.

Andy wanted me to run away with him, back to Norway. Of course I said no, but he kept on at me. He said

*he loved me, that he couldn't live without me. He wanted
to take me away, off to a new life across the sea, where there
were mountains and lakes and pine forests and the air was
as clean and crisp as could be.*

Amy looked up from the letter. It all seemed so far-fetched, like a novel. Was this really her mother? Maggie Metcalfe was such a timid little mouse, she couldn't imagine her in the arms of a burly Norwegian sailor.

She took a gulp of the brandy, and returned to the letter.

*He gave me a week to make up my mind, while he was away
crossing the North Sea. But I never gave him my answer
because he never came back.*

*Would I have gone? I honestly don't know. I still
believed in my vows, even though Malcolm made it clear
he had no love for me.*

*I'm sure you can guess what happened next. I found
out I was pregnant. I was shocked, naïve little thing that
I was. But I was excited, too. I truly didn't think I'd ever
have a baby. Malcolm had made it very clear that he
didn't want children, and we weren't close in that way.
I don't want to embarrass you with too many details,
but Malcolm made it clear he wasn't interested in me,
and we'd never been intimate. We even slept in separate
rooms.*

*I had to tell him what had happened, and believe me
when I tell you it was one of the hardest things I've ever
had to do. I thought he'd be hurt, but he wasn't. He was
furious, accused me of humiliating him. I said I'd leave, but*

he told me to stay. He said he'd bring you up as his child,
that no one need ever know the great sin I'd committed.

Except he knew. And he punished me for it every day
for the rest of my life. Not a day went by when I wasn't
made to suffer one way or another.

Perhaps I deserved it. Perhaps I should have left. But I
stayed because of you. I didn't want you to face the shame
of coming from a broken home. I thought he might forgive
you, that he might be kinder to you, at least. But he wasn't,
was he? He punished you just as much as he punished me.

He promised he'd never tell you, but I'm afraid that
when I'm gone he won't keep his promise. I'm worried he
might make you hate me.

I probably deserve that too. I don't know. Maybe just
reading this letter will make you hate me as much as he did.

But just know that I loved you. Everything I've ever
done has been for you. You're the joy I never thought I'd
find, and I'll be grateful for that forever.

If I regret anything, it's that I didn't have longer to
spend with you.

Your loving mother x

Auntie Eileen watched her fold up the letter and slip it back into the envelope.

'So now you know,' she said.

'Do you want to read it?' Amy offered it to her.

'No, ta. I know what's in it.' Eileen took a nervous sip of her brandy. 'You mustn't blame her, you know. You don't know how cruel that man was to her.'

'I don't blame her.' Amy looked down at the envelope

in her hands. She didn't know quite how to feel, if she was honest. 'So my father is dead?'

Eileen nodded. 'They found his vessel at the bottom of the North Sea after the war. There were no survivors.'

'Did you ever meet him?'

'Yes, I did. I worked on the mobile canteen with your mum. He was a nice lad. Anyone could see they were head over heels with each other. I reckon he would have looked after her.'

'Do you think she would have gone with him?'

'She would if I'd had anything to do with it. She deserved better. You both did.'

Eileen put down her glass. 'So what are you going to do now?' she asked.

Amy put the letter in her pocket.

'I'm going to talk to Malcolm Metcalfe,' she said.

Chapter Sixty-Three

The last place Tom wanted to be was in court.

'It will be all right.' Amy squeezed his hand as they sat side by side in the corridor outside the court room, waiting for the case to be heard. 'The judge will see your uncle is just trying to make trouble for you.'

'I just wish it hadn't come to this.' Tom ran his finger around the inside of his starched shirt collar. It was so stiff, it felt as if it was choking him. 'Perhaps I should just hand the shop over to him and have done with it?'

'But that isn't what your parents wanted – sorry, I mean . . .'Amy amended awkwardly, then lapsed into confused silence.

'It's all right. I still think of them as my parents too.'

Which was why he was intent on winning this case. Uncle Stan was so determined to overturn the terms of their will, he had hired a solicitor and taken it to court.

Tom didn't care about the shop himself. There were too many bad memories attached to it as far as he was concerned. But he owed it to the memory of Maurice and Peggy Weaver to fight for their last wishes to be carried out.

Most of all, he wanted some good to come out of all the bad that had happened.

'I'm sure they're looking down on you, wishing you well,' Amy whispered.

'I hope so,' Tom smiled. He liked to think they would approve of what he was doing. 'Thanks for coming with me, by the way. I'm sure it can't be much fun for you, being stuck in a court room.'

'You wanted me to be here,' Amy replied simply.

You're falling for her. Val's words came back to him, but this time he didn't try to deny them. Val was right.

Or perhaps he already had fallen for her.

He moved in to kiss her, then stopped short.

'What's wrong?' Amy asked.

'This wretched shirt!' he complained, pulling at the rigid collar again. 'It's so stiff, it keeps digging into my neck. How do people in offices wear them all day?'

'Nurses have to wear them all day too,' Amy reminded him. 'We put Vaseline around our necks to stop them chafing.'

'I wish you'd told me!'

'Here, let me help you.' As Amy moved in to loosen his collar, Tom put his arms around her, pulling her towards him.

'Tom, don't!' Amy ducked away, giggling.

'Go on. Give me a kiss for luck.'

'What are you doing, Tom?'

He looked over his shoulder to see Aunt Violet striding down the corridor towards them and jumped to his feet to greet her.

'Sorry, Aunt Violet. I didn't see you there.'

'Obviously.' She sent Amy a withering glance.

Tom noticed how she stiffened when he put his arms around her. It saddened him that some of their easy familiarity had gone since the truth had come out. He wished she could understand that she was still his favourite auntie as far as he was concerned.

'I hope you're ready for this?' Aunt Violet herself looked more than ready for battle, her old-fashioned coat buttoned up to the neck, her umbrella in her hand like a weapon.

'As ready as I'll ever be,' Tom said, with a nervous glance at Amy.

'I must warn you, Stanley will probably try every trick to get his hands on that inheritance. You should be prepared for anything.'

'All I can do is tell the truth,' Tom said.

'Yes, well, let's hope he does the same,' Aunt Violet said, her lips tightening.

Inside the courtroom, Uncle Stan had put on quite a show. His wife and children were gathered around him, all done up in their Sunday best. Even Eric's suit was freshly pressed, although his smart appearance was ruined by his outlandish crepe-soled shoes and towering quiff.

As Tom entered the courtroom Val looked up and gave him a nervous smile, which turned into a scowl when she saw Amy behind him.

Aunt Violet led the way to a row of seats on the opposite side of the court, behind where their solicitor, Mr Jarvis, sat with his clerk, a stack of papers in front of him.

Mr Peck, Uncle Stan's solicitor, sat on the other side, with an almost identical bespectacled clerk and a similar stack of papers.

The judge, a portly, balding man, sat above them both, looking down at them all.

'Shall we proceed?' he said gravely.

Mr Peck began. He explained in ponderous tones that the will was being contested because certain facts had come to light that proved Thomas Weaver was not entitled to the estate in question.

'What facts?' the judge asked.

'The fact that Thomas Weaver was not the son of Maurice and Margaret Weaver.'

The judge peered down at Tom. 'Then who is he?'

'He was born illegitimately, and stolen by Margaret Weaver.'

The judge's bushy brows shot up. 'Stolen?'

'That ain't true,' Tom protested. 'My mother gave me to her.'

The judge glowered at Tom. 'Please be silent until you are asked to speak.' He turned back to Uncle Stan's solicitor. 'Proceed, Mr Peck.'

'The adoption was not legal, Your Honour,' Mr Peck said.

'Indeed?' The judge's brows rose even further. 'And how to do you know all this, Mr Peck?'

'The truth came to light after Mr Weaver's birth mother came forward to claim him. My client's sister-in-law, Violet Cox, colluded in the deception,' Mr Peck added, glaring across the courtroom at Aunt Violet.

'Am I to understand that Mr and Mrs Weaver were aware Thomas was not their son?' the judge asked.

'Of course,' Mr Peck replied, slightly uncertain.

'And they were aware of this when they made their will in his favour?'

'Well yes, but—'

'Then surely there is no contentious probate here?'

'Your Honour—' the solicitor began, but the judge held up his hand.

'As you well know, Mr Peck, we live in a free country. Mr and Mrs Weaver were fully entitled to leave their estate to whoever they chose, not just their nearest blood relative. Why, they could have left it to the milkman or the coalman, or indeed your client, and they would have been perfectly within their rights.'

Across the courtroom, Tom could see Uncle Stan shifting in his seat, growing more and more frustrated.

'As I've said, I see no contentious probate here,' the judge went on.

'But Your Honour—'

'Mr Peck, please. I've heard all you have to say and—'

'What about the insurance?' Uncle Stan blurted out.

The judge eyed him narrowly. 'Who is this person?'

Mr Peck rose hurriedly to his feet. 'Your Honour, this is my client, Stanley McBride.'

'And what is he talking about?'

'The insurance policy on the shop was in my name,' Uncle Stan interrupted, before his solicitor had a chance to speak. 'I should be the one to get the money.'

A hush fell. The two lawyers looked at each other across the courtroom. Neither of them seemed to know what was going on.

'Well, this is most irregular, I must say.' The judge sat back in his seat. 'Would someone care to clarify the situation for me?'

Mr Peck turned to consult Uncle Stanley. While they were having a murmured conversation, Tom looked across and caught Val's eye. She smiled helplessly back at him.

Finally, Mr Peck was ready to address the court again.

'It seems, Your Honour, that the property was due to pass to Thomas Weaver on the first of January, when he would legally benefit from the insurance policy. However, the fire technically began on the thirty-first of December, while my client Mr McBride was still in possession of the property. Therefore he remains the beneficiary of the insurance policy.'

'I should get it all,' Uncle Stan confirmed, with a gleam in his eyes.

'So it all depends when this fire broke out?' the judge said. He turned to Tom. 'What do you say to that, Mr Weaver? You were there when it happened. You of all people should know the timing of it all.'

Tom glanced across the courtroom. Uncle Stan and Aunt Lillian were glaring at him, tense with expectation. Val was watching him intently too. She seemed to be silently willing him to say something – but what?

All I can do is tell the truth.

'Uncle Stan's right,' he said. 'The fire must have started just before midnight.'

From the other side of the courtroom, Uncle Stan let out a whoop of triumph. Val's shoulders slumped in defeat.

Tom couldn't bring himself to look at his aunt, sitting next to him. He could already sense her disappointment.

'You do realise what you're saying, young man?' the judge said to Tom. 'This means you will own the shop under the terms of Mr and Mrs Weaver's will, but you won't be able to rebuild it because all the insurance money will go to Mr McBride.'

'I do understand that, sir. Your Honour,' Tom amended. 'But I can't lie about it, no matter how much I might want to.'

'Indeed.' The judge stared at him for a long time. Tom couldn't be certain if it was with admiration or pity.

And then a voice piped up from the other side of the courtroom.

'What if it wasn't an accident?'

Everyone turned to look at Val. She was on her feet, clutching the rail in front of her. Her bandages were gone, revealing fresh burn scars.

The judge let out a sigh. He seemed to have accepted that normal court procedure was not going to be followed in this case. 'And who are you?'

'I'm Valerie McBride, Your Honour.' Val's cheeks were bright red. She looked as if she was going to be sick.

Mr Jarvis got to his feet. 'Miss McBride was also present at the shop on the night it burned down,' he said.

'I'm the one who set it alight,' Val said.

Gasps echoed around the courtroom. Tom stared at Val but she wouldn't meet his eye. She looked straight ahead, her chin lifted in defiance.

'My dad told me to do it,' she said.

Uncle Stan jumped to his feet. 'You lying little cow!'

'You did. You said you'd burn the place down before you handed it over to Tom.'

'Yes, but I didn't tell you to set light to the place, did I?'

'Sit down, Mr McBride,' the judge ordered. Uncle Stan

hesitated for a moment, then sank reluctantly back into his seat.

'Well, I must say this case is proving to have more layers than an onion,' the judge went on. 'Just when you think it's one thing, it turns out to be another. Now we find ourselves faced with a case of deliberate arson.' He turned to Uncle Stan. 'Well, Mr McBride? Did you say those words?'

'I might have,' he admitted reluctantly, then added, 'but I didn't mean it. I say all sorts when I'm angry.'

'I didn't know that, did I?' Val's voice wavered on the edge of tears. 'I thought it was what you wanted.'

'If this is indeed the case, I very much doubt there will be any insurance money to be paid,' the judge said.

Tom looked at his uncle. Stan McBride was slumped in his seat, looking poleaxed.

'Well, if no one else has anything to say . . . ?' The judge looked warily around the courtroom, and then concluded the case. The executor would continue to administer the estate, and Tom would inherit his shop.

'Much good it will do him, I'm afraid, given the unfortunate circumstances,' the judge muttered in a sympathetic undertone.

Uncle Stan was waiting for him outside the courtroom.

'I hope you're satisfied?' he snarled. 'You heard what the judge said. That shop ain't worth anything. Not if you ain't got a penny to rebuild it.'

'I won't need a penny,' Tom said. 'I've already found someone else to do it.'

'Eh?' Uncle Stan looked confused. 'What are you talking about?'

'Your neighbour, Mr Patel? It turns out his brother is coming over from India with his family and he wants to buy the shop. They're happy to do the repairs once I've sold it to them.'

'The Patels!' Uncle Stan's florid face darkened with fury. 'You'd sell it to them?'

'At least they won't have to put up with anyone throwing their mouldy rubbish over the fence once they own the place.'

'Maurice and Peggy would be ashamed of you,' Aunt Lillian said. 'They must be turning in their graves at what you're doing.'

'They'd be more ashamed of you,' Tom said. 'Your husband ain't fit to have his name over that door, and you know it.'

Stan and Lillian stormed off. As Tom watched them go, a voice behind him said,

'Was it something you said?'

He swung round. Val was standing behind him, smiling shyly.

'More like something *you* said.' Tom shook his head, bemused. 'What happened, Val? Why did you set the place alight? You could have got us both killed—'

'Don't be daft.' She winked at him. 'You might not be able to tell a lie, but I can.'

'You mean you made it all up?'

'Not all of it. Dad did say he'd rather burn the place down. And I didn't want him to get his hands on the insurance money.'

He stared at her in astonishment. 'I never knew you were so devious.'

'Yes, well, I learned it from my mum and dad, didn't I?' She glanced down the corridor towards them. 'Although I don't suppose they'll ever forgive me for it.'

'I don't suppose they will.'

She shrugged. 'I'll get away with it somehow. If I can lie my way into trouble I'm sure I can lie my way out of it. And it will teach Mum and Dad not to underestimate me.'

'I don't think anyone will ever make that mistake again.'

Amy emerged from the courtroom.

'Hello, Val,' she said.

Val sent her a sour look. 'Look after him,' she muttered. And then she was gone, heading down the corridor after her parents.

Chapter Sixty-Four

Amy made sure she was sitting in the middle of the front pew for evensong.

She had been to the vicarage but once again Mrs Finch the housekeeper had made it clear that her father did not want to see her.

So Amy decided to meet him in the only place where he couldn't turn her away.

She wasn't sure why she needed to see him, but since reading her mother's letter she had started to view him in a different light. It didn't excuse the way he had treated her mother, but he had not abandoned her, and he taken on another man's child. Why had he done it? Was it because somewhere deep down he really had loved her? Or was it so he could spend the rest of their marriage punishing her? She wanted to talk to him, to understand why he had done what he did.

She knew she was probably being a fool, but like her mother she couldn't quite bring herself to give up on him. She felt she owed him the chance to explain.

Malcolm Metcalfe did his best to ignore her as he conducted the service, but Amy could see he was rattled by her presence. His bespectacled gaze kept flicking to her, almost as if he wasn't sure what she might do. He missed out two lines of the Lord's Prayer, announced the wrong hymn number, and when he mounted the steps to the pulpit to deliver his sermon he dropped his notes, scattering them all across the stone-flagged floor.

All the while Amy kept her cool gaze on him. He didn't feel like her father any more. She wondered if he ever had.

Afterwards, she waited in the church while he exchanged pleasantries with the parishioners at the door. A couple of people stopped to greet her, too. They asked how she was and expressed regret at her dear mother's passing. They assured her that the Reverend was bearing up very well, under the circumstances.

I'm sure he is, Amy thought.

Finally they were alone.

Malcolm Metcalfe swept down the aisle towards her, his robes flapping.

'What do you want?' he demanded, then added, 'You'd better be quick, the churchwarden will be back in five minutes to lock up.'

'I thought you'd be pleased to see me?' Amy said. 'You always insisted I come to church at least twice every Sunday.'

'I don't have time for your tiresome humour.' Malcolm thumped his prayer book down on the altar. 'Just say whatever it is you have to say and then go.'

'I called at the house but Mrs Finch wouldn't let me in. She's a charming woman, isn't she?' She thought of the woman's bony, unsmiling face. 'I think she quite enjoyed turning me away.'

'She has her instructions,' Malcolm said shortly. He

turned away from her to unfasten his robe. 'I don't know why you'd bother to call, since I made it quite clear you weren't welcome.'

'I wanted to speak to you.'

'What about?'

'I know,' she said.

'What do you know?'

'That you're not my father.'

He went very still.

'My mother wrote me a letter. Auntie Eileen gave it to me.'

'I see.' Amy tried to read the expression in his eyes. But all she saw was indifference. 'Well, if that's all you came to say—'

'Why did you do it?' Amy said as he turned away from her.

'What?'

'Why did you take my mother back? She was pregnant with another man's child.'

That shocked him, she could tell. He froze, his hands still on the buttons of his robe.

'Is it because you loved her?'

Amy willed him silently to say what she wanted to hear. She desperately wanted to believe that her father had loved her mother, that he'd tried to make their marriage work until the bitterness and resentment became too much for him.

Even if he'd told her he'd acted out of Christian charity she would have understood.

She didn't want to imagine that he'd set out to punish

her and cause her pain, because that would make him the monster she feared he was.

'Love?' he spat the word back at her, his mouth twisting. 'You really think I could love her after something like that?' He shook his head. 'I did it because I would have looked like a fool otherwise! I couldn't have the whole parish talking about me, pointing their fingers, gossiping.'

'But you tried to forgive her—'

'Your whore of a mother humiliated me. How could I forgive her for that?'

Amy stared at him, realisation dawning. Her mother hadn't hurt him, she'd hurt his pride. He didn't care about her falling in love with another man, or about saving their marriage.

'You – you wanted to punish her? That's why you wanted her to stay . . .'

'You think I wanted to bring up a sailor's bastard as my own?' he snapped.

'You should have let her go.'

'How could I? There would have been questions asked, the bishop would have to be involved. As a divorced man I would not be considered for another, better parish. I would end up rotting in this loathsome place for the rest of my life . . .' He looked around the church, contempt on his face. 'Your mother served a purpose.'

'Is that why you married her? Because she served a purpose?'

'The previous incumbent made it clear to me when I was a curate that it would serve my future prospects better if I were married.'

'So your marriage was a means to an end?'

'If that's the way you want to put it. Oh, don't look at me like that!' he sneered. 'Your mother did very well out of it. Where would she have been if she hadn't married me? Living with some filthy drunken docker in a damp little terrace like her guttersnipe friend Eileen, no doubt. You might say marrying her was an act of Christian charity!' He laughed at his own joke.

She might have been happy, Amy thought. She pictured Eileen's little cottage, always so full of love and laughter.

'What do you know about Christian charity?' she said. 'You're so full of hatred and spite, there's no room in your heart for anything else.'

'I think we've said all we have to say to each other.' He turned away, dismissing her.

As he walked away, Amy said, 'You hated my mother and you hate me. I bet you're glad she's dead, aren't you?'

He stopped and turned slowly. 'You expect me to mourn her, after she made a fool of me? To be honest, she lived far too long anyway. I expected that weak heart of hers to kill her years ago. But she went on and on and on.' He sighed. 'I blame you for that.'

'Me?'

'You gave her something to live for.'

'And you made her want to die.'

They stared at each other up the length of the aisle.

'My mother was too good for you,' Amy said.

Malcolm Metcalfe laughed, the sound echoing up into the rafters of the empty church. 'Your mother was a simpleton.'

'She might not have had your education, but she was kind and loving.'

'As I said, she was a means to an end. Although she barely even served that purpose.' He looked bored. 'I could have moved on to a better parish if she hadn't dug her heels in and refused to move.'

'This was her home. She loved this place.'

'I suppose that's where she belonged, in a filthy hovel.'

'You've never liked it, have you?'

He laughed again. 'Do you really think I wanted to spend the last twenty years in a stinking cesspit like this?'

As he turned away, Amy said, 'I think you've forgotten something.'

He sighed heavily. 'What?'

'You've forgotten what time the churchwarden comes to lock up.'

She glanced over her shoulder to where Mr Campbell the churchwarden and head of the Parochial Church Council stood in the shadows.

'I hope you heard all that, Mr Campbell?' she said.

'Every word,' he said.

PART THREE

October 1959

Chapter Sixty-Five

'I feel so ridiculous,' Jen said.

'You're not ridiculous at all,' Liz replied. 'You're blooming.'

'You know what they call women like me, don't you? Geriatric pregnancies.' Jen shook her head. 'I'm far too old to have a baby.'

'And yet here you are.'

Liz smiled down at the infant in Jen's arms. Master Hugo Jonathan Davies had come wailing into the world just after midnight, after an almost textbook labour lasting just under five hours. He was pink-cheeked with a shock of dark hair and weighed in at a very respectable eight pounds two ounces.

After being sure she was far too old to have a boyfriend and far too old to get married, Jennifer could now add motherhood to her list of things she should not be doing at her age.

'Of course, I shall probably be a laughing stock at the mother and baby clinic,' Jen predicted. 'And everyone will think I'm his grandmother when I take him to school.'

But she was beaming with pride as she said it. She hadn't stopped smiling since Liz had arrived to visit her at the hospital.

Liz had come bearing flowers, only to find that Jen's room already resembled a florist's shop.

'I take it those are from Johnny?' she said, examining the most lavish bouquet of red roses.

'Your daddy's been very extravagant, hasn't he?' Jen stroked her baby's round cheek. 'He's so pleased with himself, I think I could have asked for a Rolls-Royce and he'd have bought one.' She touched the baby's feet and laughed in delight. 'Oh, look! He's ticklish.'

Liz smiled wistfully, remembering her delight when she'd stroked her own baby's tiny feet. That fleeting moment when she'd held him in her arms and felt like a mother.

'You should have one.'

Jen's voice broke into her thoughts. Liz laughed.

'You want me to have a baby?'

'Why not? I don't see why I should be the only laughing stock in the playground. Go on, we can be geriatric mothers together.'

'I'm already a mother, remember?'

'Oh God!' The colour drained from her friend's face. 'Liz, I'm so sorry. How thoughtless of me.' She covered her eyes with her hand. 'Here I am, droning on about babies and the joys of motherhood, completely forgetting what you missed out on.' She looked up at her, her face full of anguish. 'Can you forgive me?'

'There's nothing to forgive,' Liz assured her. 'But I'm afraid you're going to have to go through motherhood alone, my dear. One child is quite enough for me.'

She was enjoying spending time getting to know Tom, making up for the years they'd lost. It was a slow, tentative process, but they were gradually growing closer.

'And what does your husband say about it, I wonder?' Jen looked mischievous.

'My husband knows better than to argue with me.'

My husband. She and Rob had been married a while now, but the word still felt strange when she said it out loud.

'I'm sure he does. He dotes on you. And Tom, of course,' Jen added.

'Yes, he does.'

That was what had clinched it for her, seeing how well the two of them got on. In fact it was Tom who had persuaded Liz to accept Rob's proposal.

'He's desperate to marry you, Mum. For heaven's sake, put the poor man out of his misery. Anyway, it's about time you gave me a father,' he'd added teasingly.

It was the first time he'd called her Mum. He'd said it so casually that Liz wondered if it had been a slip of the tongue.

'Talking of which,' Liz checked her watch. 'I'll have to go. I'm meeting them both in an hour.'

'Oh, yes? Special occasion, is it?'

'A very special occasion.' Liz smiled at the baby in her friend's arms. 'Little Hugo isn't the only one celebrating their birthday today.'

'Happy birthday!'

Amy beamed around at her friends. She had been putting on her uniform that morning when Sonia knocked on her door. At first she'd thought her friend wanted to borrow a safety pin or a clip for her hair. But Sonia had grabbed her hand and led her excitedly downstairs to the kitchen, where the other girls were waiting for her.

There was no time for breakfast as they were all going on duty, but they'd prepared a piece of toast with a candle in it. There were also presents and cards arranged around her plate.

'But you're going to have to open them stat,' Sonia warned. 'We're due on duty in twenty minutes!'

Amy hurried through them, oohing and aahing at the scented soaps and the Bobby Darin LP and the very practical Epsom bath salts, which she knew would be very welcome at the end of a long day. She opened all the cards and laughed at the funny messages the girls had written inside.

There was no card from her father. Amy checked her pigeonhole as she left the nurses' home that morning. She didn't know why she'd expected one, since she hadn't heard from him for several months.

She didn't even know where Malcolm Metcalfe was living since he'd retired from St Luke's.

Not retired, exactly. He'd clung on for as long as he could, but with the Parochial Church Council and the bishop both against him, he hadn't had much choice. Either he had to go quietly, or he would be pushed out.

And Malcolm Metcalfe's pride would not allow for him to be dismissed.

St Luke's now had a new, much younger vicar. Amy had seen him when she passed the high gates of the vicarage one day. He was in the garden, playing ball with his children. They all looked so happy, it made her smile to see them.

That big garden deserved to be played in. And perhaps their laughter would help lift the gloom of the old house.

Glenys was waiting for her when she arrived on Female Surgical. They'd only recently been assigned back on the same ward after a few months apart, and Glenys was keen to catch Amy up on all the gossip.

Unfortunately, she and Giles had gone their separate ways, so Glenys no longer talked about him. But now she had her eye on a young anaesthetist, so at least she'd stopped crying.

She was very pleased that Amy had a boyfriend at last. And since Tom was now studying at technical college and no longer a porter, he was finally deemed acceptable.

'Are you seeing him later?' she asked, as they did the breakfast round together.

Amy nodded. 'We're having supper together.'

'Very romantic.'

'Hardly. His mother's joining us.'

'I'm not sure I'd like my boyfriend to bring his mother on a date.'

'It's not exactly a date. Anyway, I like Liz.'

'Liz, eh?' Glenys nudged her. 'Fancy you being on first name terms with a ward sister!'

'I can't keep calling her Mrs Bryant, can I?' Amy said. 'Anyway, she's not a ward sister any more.'

She was now working as a district nurse alongside Winnie Riley's mother, which seemed to suit her down to the ground. Amy had never seen her so happy.

Although, of course, that might also have had something to do with her new husband. She and Rob Bryant had married in the summer, but even though the wedding had been some months earlier, the couple still behaved like newlyweds.

'Just imagine, she might be your mother-in-law one day!' Glenys giggled.

'Steady on!' Amy felt herself blushing. 'There's no pleasing you, is there? First you nagged me to find a boyfriend, now you're trying to rush me down the aisle!'

'Would you like to marry him?'

'I don't know, do I? Anyway, I've got my training to think about first. It'll be another two years before I'm qualified.'

Glenys pulled a face, as if this was of no importance. Not as important as securing a medical man for a husband, anyway.

'I reckon you could have a worse mother-in-law than Liz Spencer,' she said, over the hiss of the tea urn.

'Maybe.'

Amy was thoughtful as she handed out the cups of tea. No one could ever replace her own mother, of course. But Glenys was right. She could do a lot worse than Liz Spencer.

'Happy birthday!'

Val placed the cake down in front of Tom, then stepped back.

'I hope you like it,' she said nervously.

He smiled. 'It looks good.'

'Not sure what it tastes like, though. Mum always said I was very heavy handed when it came to baking. And I slipped a bit there with the icing, just there—'

'Val!' Tom cut her off, exasperated. 'What have I told you? You've got to stop apologising.'

'Sorry.' Then she realised what she'd said and giggled. 'Oops, there I go again!'

She looked pretty when she laughed, Tom thought. She'd started paying more attention to herself recently. She'd had her hair cut by a real hairdresser, in carefully styled waves that softened the angles of her face. And her lipstick was a nice rosy pink that lit up her face.

'What are you staring at?' Val grinned.

'I was just thinking how nice you looked.'

'Oh, stop!' Val looked bashful. Tom noticed how she hid her hands in the folds of her skirt so he wouldn't see the puckered skin. He had the same scars on his own hands, healing slowly but still visible after all this time.

'Mum and Dad send their regards,' Val said. 'They would have been here, but they had to go and visit Eric.'

Tom didn't bother to ask how his cousin was getting on. As far as he was concerned, Eric had got what was coming to him. He'd finally gone too far when he'd stolen a motorbike from Mr Braithwaite's garage, gone for a joyride and ended up crashing into the back of a police car.

Only Eric could be that stupid, Tom thought.

Not that Uncle Stan and Aunt Lillian thought he'd done anything wrong. As far as they were concerned, Eric was just a high-spirited lad letting off steam. Unfortunately, the judge did not agree and he'd ended up with three months in Wormwood Scrubs.

Tom picked a piece of icing off the cake and licked it from his fingers. 'I'm sure Uncle Stan and Aunt Lillian are heartbroken they can't celebrate my birthday with me,' he said dryly.

Val didn't even try to argue with him. She knew as well as he did that there was still a lot of bad blood between them, even though she did her best to keep the peace.

Tom had never regretted his decision not to rebuild the shop. As far as he was concerned, it held too many unhappy memories. And the money had been put to much better use for Val's secretarial course and the down payment on a little flat for her. He used the rest to get a place for himself and to pay for an engineering course at technical school.

They both deserved a second chance, in his opinion.

After much begging from Val, he also gave some money to his aunt and uncle. Not that they were grateful for it. But he refused to give a penny to Eric.

'Are you going to be celebrating later?' Val asked as she fetched a knife from the drawer to cut the cake.

'Mum's gone to visit a friend, but we're going out to supper later.'

Mum. It was strange how easily the word came to him these days. He could remember the day it had first slipped out, and how embarrassed he'd been. His mother had not remarked on it, but Tom had seen her smile as she turned away from him.

'You're welcome to join us,' he said to Val.

'Oh no, I wouldn't want to intrude.'

'You wouldn't be intruding at all. Aunt Violet will be there.'

'Will Amy be there too?'

He noticed the edge to her voice. There was still a trace of jealousy, but it was getting better.

'Yes, she will. It's her birthday too.'

'Wish her well from me, won't you?'

'Why don't you come and tell her yourself?'

'I can't. Sorry.'

Tom sighed. 'I wish you'd make an effort to get to know her. I'm sure you'd like her if—'

'This is nothing to do with her.' She paused. 'If you must know, I can't come because I already have a date.'

So that explained the haircut, Tom thought. He was relieved it wasn't for his benefit.

'Oh yes? Who's the lucky man?'

'Someone I work with at the office.'

'What's he like?'

'Why do you care?' She sent him an arch look. 'I hope you're not jealous, Tom?' she teased.

'I'm just looking out for my cousin, that's all.'

'You don't have to worry about me. I'm not your cousin any more, am I?'

'You'll always be my family, Val.'

Their eyes met for a moment, then Val said brightly,

'What am I like? I was going to cut the cake and I ain't even lit the candles yet.'

'Here, let me.' Tom took a box of matches from his pocket and lit the candles carefully.

'Right,' Val said. 'Now blow them out and make a wish.'

Tom closed his eyes and blew. But he didn't make a wish. He couldn't think of anything more he could wish for.

If you loved *A Nurse's Secret* don't miss the rest of the Nightingale Girls series by

Donna DOUGLAS

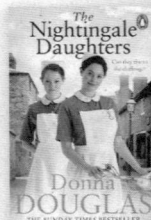

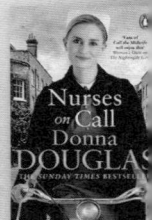

Dive into the lives of trainee nurses at the Nightingale Hospital today.

On a station platform, with nothing to read,
and a four-hour train journey stretching ahead of him...

That's where the story began for Penguin founder Allen Lane.
With only 'shabby reprints of shoddy novels' on offer,
he resolved to make better books for readers everywhere.

By the time his train pulled into London, the idea was formed.
He would bring the best writing, in stylish and affordable
formats, to everyone. His books would be sold in bookstores,
stationers and tobacconists, for no more than the price
of a ten-pack of cigarettes.

And on every book would be a Penguin, a bird with a certain
'dignified flippancy', and a friendly invitation to anyone who
wished to spend their time reading.

In 1935, the first ten Penguin paperbacks were published.
Just a year later, three million Penguins had made their
way onto our shelves.

Reading was changed forever.

—

A lot has changed since 1935, including Penguin, but in the
most important ways we're still the same. We still believe that
books and reading are for everyone. And we still believe that
whether you're seeking an afternoon's escape, a vigorous debate
or a soothing bedtime story, all possibilities open with a book.

Whoever you are, whatever you're looking for,
you can find it with Penguin.